BOOK SIX

THE FAE REALM SERIES

OATH

CATHLIN SHAHRIARY

Oath by Cathlin Shahriary
Cover design by Indie Solutions by Murphy Rae
Editing by Amanda Bonilla
Formatting by Alyssa Garcia

To anyone who has ever felt burdened by living up to someone else's expectations, I see you.

And to my readers, thank you for joining me on this journey. I hope you love Lachlan and Branan's story as much as I do!

OATH

Part One:
Before

CHAPTER 1

HEAVY IS THE head that wears the crown.

Even though Lachlan had heard that phrase from a human, it seemed to apply to Fae as well. He certainly never wanted to wear the crown. The fact that he was the first-born male in his family didn't indicate that he was meant to serve. His older sister came into the world with the correct colored eyes. She was more fit to bear that burden than him, but it seemed to weigh heavily upon her more recently.

"Alfie, you know I can't." His sister's voice stopped him in his tracks before he rounded the corner to her study.

"You can, Orla," her lover pleaded. "You are queen. You make the rules."

Lachlan didn't understand why his sister kept denying both of them the happy ending they deserved. She'd tried to explain it to him before when he asked her about it, and he supposed there was some logic to her reasoning. She feared that marrying Alfie, the palace scholar, would make her appear weak to the Unseelie and would encourage King Ragnall to attack their people and attempt to seize their land for his own.

Ragnall's reputation as the Wicked King preceded him, and tensions between their two courts had been high since Lachlan's father passed and Orla inherited the throne. The Unseelie king's backward thinking on women as the weaker sex and his disdain for dealing with Orla showed in his latest letters and refusal to send an emissary to meet with her. It was clear he thought her to be beneath him, regardless that the magic of their land had chosen her. As a result, Orla's council had persuaded her that she needed to marry someone whose power was capable of rivaling her own, someone who had the capacity to aid her in intimidating the Unseelie King from pursuing war.

Lachlan disagreed with the council there. If King Ragnall had firmly decided on war and violating the treaty he had established a century ago with their father, there would be no stopping him. It wouldn't matter who she married. Besides, his mother had always preached that love could unite enemies and move kingdoms, that there was nothing more powerful than love. His chest ached with the reminder of how fiercely his mother had loved his father, so much so that when he died, she followed shortly after.

Lachlan chose that moment to make his presence known, ensuring his footsteps sounded a little louder than necessary so they would hear his approach. As he rounded the corner, Alfie knelt on one knee in front of his sister, gripping both of her hands. Orla quickly tugged her hands from his grip when her eyes flashed toward Lachlan.

"Dear brother, how nice to see you today." She cleared her throat and tucked a stray strand of dirty blonde hair behind her braid, a nervous tell she had developed in her younger years.

Lachlan smiled widely. "Did you suspect you would not?"

"It's hard to tell these days whether you're here or indulging in a tavern somewhere," she teased.

Lachlan pressed a hand to his chest in mock indignation. "Why dear sister, I was merely trying to be a man amongst our people." He wore the same rumpled shirt she had seen on him yesterday, so it wasn't hard for her to make that assumption.

Over the years he'd carefully constructed his appearance as a selfish prince who couldn't be bothered, but he was growing wary of pretending to be someone he wasn't. It started when he was younger. He found it easier to lean into other's expectations of him as the carefree spare, and it had grown worse from there.

Once he reached an age where he could drink at the tavern, he was known to overindulge and disappear for days at a time. And while that may have been true initially, lately he took advantage of the reputation he had built and used it as a way to travel around Seelie lands. No one questioned his disappearances any longer, assuming he was off partying somewhere, but recently he felt the need to keep one ear to the ground, to hear any complaints directly from their people in order to help Orla best serve their kingdom. Lord knows some of the council members weren't doing that. There were a few who were only interested in fulfilling their own interests, not truly the needs of their people.

Besides, the taverns were where people drank enough to speak their grievances freely. It was better he let everyone think he was a foolish prince wasting his life away.

Orla arched an eyebrow at his shirt and snorted a laugh, walking away from Alfie and pulling her brother into an embrace.

Alfie rose to his feet, his brows and lips drawn down. "This conversation is not over, Orla. Lachlan." He gave a curt nod of greeting before storming out of the room.

Orla sighed loudly, her lavender eyes following Alfie's retreating figure.

"Trouble in paradise?" Lachlan raised an eyebrow.

She smoothed her hands down her skirt and attempted a smile, bringing her gaze back onto her brother. "Nothing for you to worry about. I have it all under control."

Lachlan fought to roll his eyes. If there was one thing his sister cherished above all else, it was control.

"I'm sure you do." He fought to keep the sarcasm out of his voice, but judging by her sharp glance, he didn't fight hard enough.

"Now, what are your plans for today?" Her tone turned saccharine.

"I'd rather discuss when you're going to stop letting the crown dictate your life." Lachlan casually walked over to her chair and sat, swinging his feet onto her desk to annoy her.

"And I would rather discuss what you plan on doing with your life," she countered with narrowed eyes, the saccharine tone completely abandoned.

He returned her scowl, waiting in silence for her to answer his question first.

"I have to keep the needs of our people above my own." She repeated as if she had memorized the line over the last few years. He wasn't sure if she was trying to convince him or herself.

His scowl softened. "Orla, you know our land thrives when you do."

"It's not so simple, Lachlan. You don't understand."

"Then explain it to me."

"I have, but until you are in my position, you won't get it. You won't understand the sacrifices I must make to keep our people safe."

He could see that arguing with her would get him nowhere when she was worked up, so he pulled back. "I'm sorry, Orla. I only want to see you happy."

"I know." The corners of her mouth tugged up.

A knock at the doorway interrupted them. Her second in command waited in the doorway of her study. Lachlan briefly regretted not closing the door after Alfie stormed out. "I apologize, your majesty, but you are due in the throne room to hear your people today."

"Of course," she replied to him before turning back to Lachlan with an arched brow. "I trust you'll keep yourself out of trouble unless you'd like to join me."

Lachlan scoffed. "And listen to people's minor squabbles and complaints for hours on end? No, thank you."

She paused at the door. "Shall I see you at dinner?"

He could read the hope and hesitation in her voice. "I'll be there," he replied, swinging his feet off her desk as a familiar itch worked its way down his spine. It was time for a run in the woods.

His hooves dug into the soft dirt as he ran. He loved being in the forest. The smells, the way the wind brushed his fur, the exhilaration of being alive. He had inherited his mother's shifting ability, and when he was young his parents loved to debate what kind of animal he would be. Shifters were a bit of a gamble that way, the magic itself tended to choose which animal form fitted the person best, unless they happened to be a wolf. Wolf shifters were bound by the ancient magic of the land, and as such wolves were always born to other wolves. There were plenty of stories and mythology tied to the how and why, but much like many other stories passed down through generations, some of the finer details tended to be lost.

When the day of his first shift had finally arrived, Lachlan's father didn't hide his disappointment, while his mother was nothing but loving and supportive. He supposed he couldn't blame his father; a stag wasn't the most threatening animal in the woods, but the Seelie king had been rather vocal that his son should have been something fiercer, a predator, an animal that could protect its people instead of a deer who only frolicked through the woods.

His father's disdain for his animal form was only outweighed by the time he spent in the woods with his mother. Over the years, he'd honed his swiftness by running through the forest with her in her fox form. She'd taught him how to use his senses in the woods, how to make his steps light and quiet when needed, how to escape dangerous situations and use his animal to his advantage. It was the only time he truly felt free of the weight of his obligations as a prince.

He traveled the paths he knew well in the woods behind the palace until the sun was setting overhead and he was due home for dinner. Making sure he was alone, he shifted back and plucked a few leaves and a twig from his hair. He smoothed out his clothes which always tended to get a bit wrinkled with a shift and strutted out of the woods, grabbing his bow and quiver of arrows where he left them leaning against a tree. The guards always joked with him, returning empty-handed from his "hunt." His people were aware of his ability to shift, but only a select few were acquainted with his animal form. Despite his mother's objection, his father began circulating rumors that quickly spread across the land regarding the formidable creature his son had the ability to transform into. He was insistent that keeping Lachlan's animal a secret would protect the kingdom and Lachlan from enemies to the throne.

Apparently, the rumors worked as his father intended, Lachlan thought as he remembered the time a girl had approached him in the tavern asking if it was true that he could shift into a dragon and only refrained from doing so to prevent frightening any maidens nearby. Oh, how Torin had howled at that one, slapping him on the back and spilling his pint of ambrosia.

Shaking off the memory, he went inside and freshened up for dinner. Orla and other members of the court had already taken their seats by the time he arrived. "Nice of you to join us," she quipped, but he discerned from the twitch of her lips she was teasing him.

"And how did the hunt go today? Catch any game?"

Her mouth quirked further.

"Only the rabbits made an appearance today, and I decided to give them a break," he replied smoothly.

"So generous of you," she sipped her ambrosia, a Fae wine, this time failing to hide her grin, as a few of the others around the table chuckled. One of these days he would have to come back with sizable game just to shut them all up. It's not like he lacked skill with his bow and arrow. On the contrary, just as he'd discovered the importance of concealing his animal, he also discovered the significance of concealing his true skills and advantages until the right moment.

"How are things at the border, your majesty? I've heard rumors," one of the older men noted. Lachlan closed his eyes to keep from rolling them. He hated court politics. He hated how people skirted around what they truly wished to say, not knowing who rooted for his family or who plotted against them.

Sometimes he wondered if his people doubted the magic of the land and how the next ruler was selected, but they had all grown up hearing the same stories he had. Surely some of them were old enough to have witnessed how the Unseelie king once had been murdered by his power-hungry cousin before he sired an heir. The cousin seized the throne and threw the people into turmoil. The land seemed to reject him, throwing their court into the harshest winter in history. Their crops died, animals froze, and many starved. During those two decades, the Unseelie court earned the nickname of winter court. Many of their people had fled for the borderlands or human realm rather than stay and suffer.

Only when the murdered king's sister birthed a son with violet eyes, the now present Unseelie king, did the land warm up, returning to their normal passing of the seasons, although some say the air never truly lost its chill as if to warn others of what could happen. Only when passing between the border of the two courts could you feel the difference in the temperature, but it was there, and it had given Lachlan a chill down his spine every time he'd snuck across the border when he was younger to see if the rumors were true. Naturally, some Fae remained who held doubts about the magic of the land, considering the freeze to be only a freak weather occurrence that happened during the imposter king's reign.

His sister's smile flattened. "King Ragnall grows greedier as he ages," she replied vaguely, "but it is nothing we are not prepared to stop if necessary."

Alfie cleared his throat. "I'll be taking my leave tomorrow."

Orla's fork halted on the way to her mouth, and her brows drew together slightly. Lachlan paused, sensing that this conversation may need redirecting.

"It's those books I told you that I located. The seller wants to meet when he is passing through."

"Of course," she smiled politely, a mask of indifference sliding into place so easily others may not see it, but she was his sister and best friend, so he knew better.

Thankfully, conversation picked up around them, the rest of the court uninterested in hearing about books and the woes of the palace scholar, but Lachlan could tell Alfie caught Orla by surprise. Was Alfie's trip a result of the conversation he overheard this morning? His sister must be wondering the same thing.

Alfie frowned now, obviously not the reaction he was hoping for. Lachlan shook his head. If Alfie wanted a genuine reaction from Orla, he should have waited until they were alone and not brought it up in front of the court. The rest of dinner went as boring as normal. The daughter of some noble present sent him flirty glances across the table, but he wasn't interested.

As dinner concluded, he made a quick exit, hoping to deter the noble's daughter from getting any ideas. He hated rejecting women, the hurt in their eyes. It wasn't them; it was him. They just weren't what he wanted.

His favorite guard and drinking buddy, Torin, approached him as he exited the dining hall and walked beside him, matching his strides. While Torin was thirty years his senior, it never bothered Lachlan, not when you lived as long as the Fae did. Besides, Torin was still in the prime of his youth, quickly climbing the ranks within the palace guards, only now he had started thinking about settling down.

"Torin, how are you? Still recovering from the other night?"

Torin laughed. "The next time I think I can drink you under the table, do us both a favor and remind me that I can't."

"I do, but you never seem to believe me." Lachlan laughed. "And what of the girl you were moaning over?"

Torin's amber eyes lit up. "She has agreed to meet me tomorrow for a stroll in the market."

"A stroll in the market?" Lachlan guffawed. "I never thought I'd see the day. Are you going to hold her basket for her and everything, following her around like a puppy?"

Torin elbowed him in the side. "For her, I just might. Someday you'll meet someone you would happily follow around the market too."

"I'm happy for you. I hope it goes well, just don't mention that you can't hold your ambrosia." Lachlan ribbed, playfully returning an elbow to Torin's side.

Torin laughed. "True, true."

"I was thinking about going on a trip to the borderlands soon. Would you like to join me?" Lachlan asked. He had been growing restless lately, bored with the monotony of palace life.

"Do you think that's wise?"

"Probably not, but for my mental sanity it may be best. I need time to be free," he admitted. Torin was the only one he confided such things to. He couldn't tell his sister, as her burdens were heavier than his, and she would only remind him of his obligations. Torin on the other hand, had already joined him on a run in the forest more than once. With Torin's rapid speed, they loved to race through the woods together when they could.

Torin's eyes softened as they reached the door to Lachlan's room. "I understand. I'll see if the guard can manage without me."

"Thanks, Torin. Oh, and good luck with your girl tomorrow," Lachlan said before stepping into his room. He closed the door behind him with a soft click and then wandered out onto his balcony. The moon shone brightly overhead, not quite full. The stars gleamed like a curtain of diamonds nestled in the deepest of blue. He often wondered how different his life would be if he had more of his father's magic, or if he had been born to a common family instead of royalty. If he, like Torin, would be working his way into the guard or courting some girl. He chortled on the last thought. He could never see himself following a girl around the market. Now a handsome boy, that was an entirely different story, but he had yet to meet one that truly sparked his interest.

CHAPTER 2

THE NEXT MORNING, Lachlan caught Orla staring out the window watching as Alfie saddled a horse. Her mood was sour and judging by her body language she wasn't in the mood to talk. Perhaps he could catch Alfie before he left.

He raced out of the hall and headed for Alfie in the courtyard. Luckily, he caught him before he mounted. "Alfie, you can't leave like this."

"Leave like what?" he replied with a frown, his words clipped and short.

"Regardless of the words exchanged, I'm sure Orla didn't mean it. Please don't leave her right now. I'm aware that she can be a bit prickly, but she truly does care."

"And how long should I give her to show me she does care, Lachlan? How long? I grow tired of being the only one wanting to move our relationship forward."

Lachlan's mouth felt dry. "I know you don't want me

butting in…"

"Yet, here you are, once again," Alfie replied with a huff. "Why don't you worry about yourself. Perhaps if you would step up to your duties, if Orla had more support from you, she wouldn't feel as if she's carrying the entire weight of the crown."

Alfie's words delivered a blow, causing Lachlan's bruised ego to retaliate. "Perhaps what she needs is someone who's not going to pressure her into doing something she isn't ready for. Have you ever considered that? No, you only think about what you want," Lachlan retorted.

Alfie looked stricken. "I'm glad to see how little you really think of me," he replied before mounting his horse and trotting off.

Lachlan regretted the words. He had only reacted in anger, but it was too late. They were already out there, and there was nothing he could do now that Alfie had left. He wasn't about to get on a horse and chase after him. Still agitated by the truth behind Alfie's argument, he decided to once again escape to the forest. He could make amends when Alfie returned.

He shifted once he was clear from any peering eyes and darted through the trees, getting lost in the feeling of freedom and the joy of running. He stopped to drink at a stream and nibble on some sweet clover. A footstep crunching leaves had him swinging his head around, his legs preparing to flee. The male was several yards away, edging through the trees. He held his hands out in front of him, the only thing keeping Lachlan from bounding away instantly. That didn't mean the male didn't have a blade hidden in his boot.

"Please don't go. I'm not here to hurt you," the stranger soothed in a warm baritone. He stepped into the beam of sunlight filtering through the canopy, and Lachlan's heart stuttered. The boy appeared only slightly younger than himself and was incredibly handsome. His skin was a rich tawny brown, like the golden oak fox Lachlan had once whittled after his mother passed, and his hair fell in thick black waves to his shoulders with several small braids woven through.

Lachlan's body tensed further, preparing to flee. Despite how handsome the stranger was, he could be a hunter. Lachlan leaned into his father's magic, which had only recently manifested, to get a sense of the boy's character. It proved even harder to do while in his stag form.

"I promise, I will not harm you." The words zipped through the air, the magic warming Lachlan's body into relaxing. A promise from a Fae was not taken lightly. The stranger most likely thought him to be a regular stag and not a Fae, but he would still be bound by the words he spoke.

A sliver of tension faded from Lachlan's limbs, but he kept his senses alert. The young man could have others with him. He paused, using his hearing to sense the world around him, but only the sounds of the stranger's breathing, insects buzzing, and the rustling of the breeze through the trees greeted him. The young man was alone.

He approached slowly, keeping his hands outstretched with palms up in front of him, and crouching lower as he got closer as if to appear like less of a threat. He reached back into his bag, and Lachlan tensed again, preparing to run, but the young man only brought out a shiny red apple.

The lad's eyes met Lachlan's. They were a mesmerizing shade of light green with a ring of copper around the pupil.

"Would you like an apple? I have plenty to share," the lad asked, approaching with the apple resting in his out-stretched hand. Lachlan studied him more closely as he approached. He was lithe, but not without well-defined muscles that spoke of the same runs through the woods that Lachlan took to stay fit, although Lachlan's muscles were also toned through sparring and weapons training.

Lachlan sniffed the air, leaning into his stag senses. The young man smelled of crisp earth, but also something else…wet dog? Lachlan chuckled which came out as a sort of snort in his stag form and the lad smiled as if he could read his mind. Lachlan leaned into his secondary magic. He had only inherited a sliver of his father's magic. While his father was able to read people's intentions and even glimpses of their future actions, Lachlan could only get a read on their auras. The boy's magic met his own with a golden flare, such a pure heart it was almost too bright to look at. He carefully plucked the apple from the boy's hand with his teeth and chewed it, the juice dribbling down his fur. The lad laughed, a musical lilting sound. He reached his hand up slowly and stroked Lachlan's stag form on the side of his neck. Electricity buzzed underneath his skin in the wake of the young man's touch as if he could feel joy radiating from the lad which was odd. He stayed there, soaking in the lad's warmth for what could have been a few minutes or ten.

"Bran?" A voice boomed through the woods causing Lachlan to tense once again. He was so lost in the lad's touch he hadn't sensed anyone else approaching.

"I have to go, but it was lovely to meet you. Maybe I'll see you again." The young man smiled before darting back in the direction from where he came. Lachlan too bounded away, not wanting to be discovered by the owner of the voice. When he neared the edge of the woods, he shifted back to sit on the fallen tree trunk. He hadn't let anyone other than his mother or sister touch him in his animal form, so why had he made such an allowance with a stranger? He smiled, running a hand down the side of his neck where the lad had petted him. Would the young man have dared to approach him if he was not in his animal form? He shuddered as a sense of longing stirred deep within him. It had been so long since he'd been able to let his guard down around someone, to just exist without playing the part of the carefree prince to which he had become accustomed. Would the young man still want to touch him if he knew what or who he truly was?

The questions plagued him, fogging his mind as he went through his routines in the days following the encounter. He snuck away each day at the same time, hoping to see the boy once more, but couldn't find him. It wasn't until a week later when his wish had been answered. He left the palace that morning hoping to avoid his sister who had become anxious. Alfie was late returning from his trip, and Orla didn't want to admit it set her on edge, even though he could read the worry on her face plain as day when she let her mask falter at breakfast. He tried to reassure her. Perhaps Alfie had found a lead on some more books, gotten drunk in the tavern, or was even staying away to make his point that they should be together. She of course dismissed him and slipped back into her mask of indifference, using her duties and responsibilities as a reason to escape the conversation and set her worries aside.

Lachlan paused to graze on some clover when he heard sniffling in the distance. Wild hope beat through his chest and instead of tensing to flee, he leaned into his senses, sniffing the air for the familiar earthy scent mixed with wet dog. He had spent many hours wondering if the wet dog scent had something to do with the stranger's magic. Perhaps he was also a shifter, one of the canine varieties. He sighed when the familiar scent reached his nose, and trotted off in the direction of his scent and sound. He found the young man sitting on the forest floor cradling his head in his hands.

"I didn't mean to do it," he sobbed.

It was only when he got closer that the overwhelming coppery smell of blood overwhelmed Lachlan's senses, causing him to pause. The young man continued to sob, oblivious that he now had an audience. Not too far away lay the bloody remains of a rabbit by a sour puddle of vomit. Lachlan's heart sank and broke for this poor young man. He obviously had killed the rabbit in his animal form and had then been repulsed by the action. It was odd to think that taking the life of an animal like a rabbit would upset the young man so much. It wasn't like Fae didn't eat meat, and to not hunt would go against the young man's natural instincts as a predatory shifter.

Lachlan bled into his aura magic, still sensing the golden purity of light within the young man. His heart broke for him, and part of him wished to offer him words of comfort, but the thought of shifting now felt like an invasion of privacy. Instead, he crept closer to the lad. When the sound of his steps reached the lad's ears, he looked up, growling, his eyes glowing copper instead of mint green. Almost immediately the growl dropped, and his eyes went back to normal, his eyes wide and brimming with tears. "Go! I don't want to hurt you too," he waved his arm, attempting to dismiss the stag.

Lachlan ignored his pleas. He knew the lad wouldn't hurt him, even if the lad didn't trust himself. He stepped closer until he could rest his head on the boy's shoulder. Immediately, the young man wrapped his arms around the stag, sobbing into his fur. "I'm sorry, I'm sorry," he repeated. Lachlan was certain he wasn't just apologizing at growling at him, but more for what he did to the rabbit.

"You probably shouldn't be around me. I'm a monster. I didn't want to kill that poor bunny, but my wolf," the young man trailed off with a new rush of tears.

Scenes of a wolf hunting a rabbit through the woods flashed through his mind, unbidden. Lachlan hadn't stopped to consider what it meant to truly be a predatory animal, no matter how many times he'd wished it when he was younger. He took no great joy from killing animals in the hunt with his bow and arrow, but they were also necessary to his survival. He just assumed that hunting in animal form would be the same way. His mother certainly had no qualms about killing prey when they'd ran together, and she caught the trail of something. He wanted to tell the young man that it was okay. What he did wasn't wrong. That he didn't need to feel shame in it, but in his current form he was without a voice. Instead, he pressed his muzzle against the lad's neck and inhaled, letting his warm breath wash over the boy. The boy relaxed, absorbing the comfort he offered.

He wasn't sure how long they stayed like that, but eventually the young man's tears dried. Lachlan couldn't help but lick a few of the salty remains away, and the laugh that greeted him lit him up from the inside. He wanted to hear it again and again. There was a slight dimple in his left cheek when he grinned, and Lachlan's breath caught. The young man stood up and hugged him again. "Thank you," he breathed against Lachlan's fur.

"Branan!" The same voice from before called through the woods.

"That's me. I have to go." Pink stained the lad's cheeks, and his eyes darted toward the woods, where the voice originated, intentionally skating around the remains of the rabbit. "I'll bring you another apple next time." Branan's smile faded, making Lachlan want to pull him into his arms and hug him tightly. He watched the lad look back once more before disappearing into the thicker part of the woods.

He shifted suddenly, unaware of his actions until his hand was pressed against his chest, his heart thrumming so loudly he thought it might escape. "Branan," he whispered the name onto the breeze. He ignored the need burning through him to follow the lad, bewildered by his own desires. What in the world was happening to him?

CHAPTER 3

BRANAN SPRINTED THROUGH the woods, only pausing when he came across a small stream. He blanched, seeing his own bloodied reflection staring back at him and quickly scrubbed away the remnants of the rabbit from his mouth and hands.

"Bran!" His father called again, more insistently this time.

Branan shifted then, letting his wolf guide him back to his pack. Wolves were meant to stay together, but he always hesitated to shift in front of the rest of the pack. He was the runt. It didn't matter if his father was their alpha, some of the pack viewed him as lesser. Of course, they never let it show in front of his father, but he felt the way Shaw, his father's beta, was a little hesitant with him. Shaw and his boys found his behaviors odd, the magic he inherited from his mother as something unnatural. He understood some of their fear. There were Dyr whose powers were similar to his in nature, but a Dyr could control animals, some of the strongest rumored to have been able to control shifted Fae. He had tried explaining that he could only communicate with animals, not control them, but it made no difference to Shaw's three boys. They still feared he may be able to do more. It didn't help that he was a late bloomer, and his wolf didn't make itself known until a few years after most other wolves. He frowned, remembering how for so long he yearned to fit in with the rest of the pack but even now that he could shift, he still felt like an outsider.

He struggled to accept his wolf, now that he had one. Being able to communicate with animals from such a young age built such compassion within him. He hated the idea of harming animals, even going as far as to avoid eating meat, which his pack also thought of as unnatural.

His father loved his mother dearly, but when she died giving birth to Branan, it left him with a child he barely understood. It wasn't his dad fault. He tried his best to understand him, but Branan always felt like an outsider within the pack, like he didn't quite belong, no matter how much his father or Kyna, Shaw's mate and Branan's only maternal figure, tried to convince him otherwise.

The only place he felt at home was in the woods. It was there he honed his skills and made friends, like the stag who had licked his tears away and sent him feelings of comfort. His stomach turned once more thinking about the poor rabbit while his wolf howled in delight over the kill he had made.

He came across his father who smiled widely to see him in his wolf form. "Glad to see you're getting acquainted. Although, I'd prefer it if you ran with the pack. It's safer together. We aren't always the biggest threat in these woods." His father ran his hand through his fur, and Branan licked his father's fingers, playfully nipping at them. "Besides, the pack needs to get used to having you around. You aren't going anywhere, and they need to know you're one of us regardless of when you shifted for the first time."

Their pack wasn't big, only one other family besides Branan and his dad. Most shifters preferred to stay in small groups, so others wouldn't perceive them as a threat. Branan's pack lived outside of the woods toward the edge of the land surrounding the Seelie palace. Not quite in town, but not too far away from it. His father served in the guard with Shaw, and Shaw's family made up the rest of their pack. Shaw had three boys, an exceptionally large family considering how difficult childbearing could be for Fae, and their mother, Kyna, who was not a wolf. Since Branan's mother had died giving birth to him, Kyna had taken him in as one of her own, mothering him the same way she did her own boys which caused some animosity amongst her sons toward Branan. All Branan ever wanted was a family, a place where he felt like he belonged, instead of feeling like an outsider. He wasn't even sure he considered them his own pack, often referring to them in his mind as his father's pack.

He shifted back after a few minutes, still adjusting to the change, a reminder he was still less than. He hoped one day to be able to shift in an instant like the rest of the pack. "I know, but…" he hesitated. He knew if he told his father how the other boys treated him it would only cause them to become more hostile and secretive about it. At least, that's what had happened when he was younger.

A few years ago, Branan told his dad about something particularly ugly that Whelan, Shaw's oldest, had said to him. His father had growled which startled Branan, but then his features had softened, and he pulled Branan close. "Don't ever let anyone make you feel like less than. I have never and will never regret having you as my son."

His father had then called a pack meeting where he was quick to reprimand the boy in front of the pack so as to make an example of him for the other boys. Shaw's face promised some sort of additional punishment or scolding when Whelan got home. Branan had foolishly thought that would be the end of it, that the reprimand from the alpha would have been enough to make Whelan stop, but the anger only burned brighter in Whelan's eyes. It started as tripping him when no one could see and then "helping" him up and joking about Branan's clumsiness when the others saw him on the ground. The snide comments became threats if he told his father, reminders that his father wouldn't always be there. It only became worse as Whelan got his brother Malcom to join. He shuddered at the memories.

Branan was no longer a boy. He was nineteen. Although by Fae standards, he still hadn't reached adulthood. Shame colored his cheeks, remembering his crying fit in the woods. He certainly hadn't acted like a man there.

His father clapped a hand on his shoulder. "They'll come around now. Don't you worry. We also need to work on upping your sword training if you're going to take after your old man and join the guard." He winked, the copper color in his eyes flashing brightly.

Branan kept his eyes focused on the ground and nodded. He hadn't had the courage yet to tell his father he had no intention of joining the guard. If taking the life of a rabbit affected him so, he couldn't imagine how it would feel to take another Fae's life. Bile rose in the back of his throat at the thought. With animals, he could get impressions of their thoughts as images or words, send his own back to them, and feel their emotions, sometimes experience those emotions as if they were his own. His stomach rolled, remembering the fear in the rabbit, the terror it felt, and its final thoughts. He shook his head and plastered a smile on his face, unable to confess everything to his father for fear of disappointing him.

"You'll have to catch me first," he teased, taking off in a sprint. If there was one thing he was good at, it was running. He'd always been the fastest, something he used to his benefit when he knew he wouldn't be able to out-muscle others. He could hear his dad chase behind him, his laughter ringing through the air.

They ate dinner, just the two of them in companionable silence. Branan pushed the meat around on his plate, not able to stomach it. "Oh, before I forget," his father said after clearing the table. He reached into his bag by the door and pulled out a small parcel.

"For me?" Branan's eyes widened.

"Just a little something I found at the market."

Branan peeled open the brown paper, a small bound book inside. The cover bore no title nor the pages any words. He glanced at his father with questions in his eyes.

"Well, I figured since you loved to read so much, maybe you'd also like to write. Make your own stories for once. Maybe about some of your animal friends." His father smiled sheepishly.

"I love it!" Branan exclaimed, throwing his arms around his father. "Thank you, Da." His father swept a hand down the back of his head, then cleared his throat. "Alright, enough of that. Morning will be here before we know it. Time to turn in."

Branan went to his room and gingerly placed the empty book on his desk, his fingers trailing across the cover, already dreaming of what he might write. He changed out of his shirt, pausing when the scent of the deer overwhelmed his nose. Surely, his dad must have scented the deer too, but chose not to say anything. It was warm and comforting, like slipping under the blankets in front of the fire. He smiled, remembering the stag's soft fur under his hands and how it had granted him those moments to release his guilt. He'd make sure to bring several apples with him the next time he ventured into the woods.

CHAPTER 4

"YOUR MAJESTY," A guard burst through the door to the dining hall the next morning. Orla stood immediately.

"What is it?" There was a slight tremble to her voice that had Lachlan sitting up straight. His heart leapt to his mouth.

The guard paused to catch his breath, and kneeled in front of Orla, thrusting a piece of parchment out in front of him. Orla's fingers trembled as she reached for the parchment and Lachlan stood. He was next to her the instant her knees faltered, and caught her. Tears swam in her eyes.

"No, no, no." She repeated over and over again.

"Clear the room except for you!" he boomed pointing at the messenger, unwilling to let others bear witness to whatever was happening. The room cleared instantly with the exception of the guard who remained kneeling. He plucked the paper from his sister's fingers.

Dearest Orla,

I believe I have something that belongs to you. You can have him back...

for a price.

—Ragnall

"Son of a bitch," Lachlan growled. There was no mistaking who the Unseelie King now had in his possession. Orla wept openly now against his shoulder.

"How?" He asked the guard as if he would have an answer.

"I do not know, sire. An Unseelie soldier approached the border when I was on duty and said he had a letter of utmost importance that must be delivered straight to the queen," the soldier reported.

The letter wasn't sealed. The Unseelie King obviously wanted everyone to know he meant business. Lachlan looked at it again. "Why is the ink that color?" He wondered aloud staring at the rusty brown words before he brought the parchment to his nose. His hands released the note, wrenching away with horror. "That bastard wrote it in blood." Orla sobbed louder, and he regretted his words. He only hoped that the blood didn't belong to Alfie. "Fetch Torin immediately, and the queen's advisors. We must decide what is to be done." The guard nodded and took off, shutting the door to the dining hall behind him.

"Orla, look at me. We must decide what to do. I know you're worried about Alfie right now, but we have to decide how to proceed. For now, Alfie is safe. The Unseelie king would not send this note if he were not."

Orla sniffed and nodded, picking up a napkin and using it to wipe her tears.

"Your advisors will be here when you are ready to see them. I won't let them in until you are ready, so take the time you need and know that I will support you no matter what you decide." Lachlan said the words even though part of him longed to mount his horse and rush into the Unseelie palace armed to the teeth, ready to fight to get Alfie back. If he were king, he would not stand for this, but it was not his decision to make. His sister was queen. She needed to decide if Alfie was worth fighting for. If he was worth starting a war.

A knock sounded at the door, and he strode to open it. Torin stood, grim-faced, fists clenched at his side. He allowed Torin to enter and saw the advisors approaching. "Do not let anyone else enter," he told the guard by the door. "They will wait until the queen is ready to see them."

The guard nodded.

"Is it true?" Torin asked, his eyes wide but fierce.

Lachlan nodded, a million questions running through his mind. Orla's relationship with Alfie wasn't a secret, everyone at court knew that they were in love, but how had word traveled to the Unseelie King? Ragnall wouldn't have kidnapped the palace scholar hoping Orla would pay to get him back. He knew exactly who he was taking when he did it, so how did he know? Did they have a traitor in their midst?

"Where was he? How was he taken?" Torin asked.

Lachlan opened his mouth, but Orla beat him to it. "I'm afraid we don't know the answers to those questions. We only know that he is now in the possession of the Unseelie king who wrote me a note in blood saying he could be returned for a price."

Torin slammed a fist against the table. "Tell me what to do, my lady, and it shall be done. If you want the Unseelie king's head on a spike. I shall see to it."

"I'm afraid it's not that easy."

"You aren't suggesting we don't do anything…." Lachlan gaped at her. His heart dropped. He couldn't imagine what Alfie was going through.

"I am not," she replied coolly, "but we need more information before we proceed." The weeping woman who was on the verge of collapse a few minutes ago was nowhere to be found. In her stead stood a calculating queen. "Send in the council."

"Are you sure?" he asked.

A brief flash of pain, and she wiped around her eyes, removing any traces of her previous tears before smoothing down her hair and dress. She took a deep breath, masking all previous signs of distress as she shoved her emotions to the side.

"I am."

"We must consider all possibilities, Your Majesty."

Orla pinched her lips together. "I have, and I refuse to let this act stand."

Lachlan ground his teeth, the frustration building in his chest only slightly lessened upon hearing his sister was willing to fight for Alfie.

"The Unseelie king acted first. I take this as a violation of the treaty. There is no other way. I refuse to concede any of our land to that monster, nor to let this act against our people stand."

"Well, it wasn't really an act against our people, but one person," one of the advisors murmured. Eyes around the table widened, while Orla's narrowed.

"You're right, Eamon it was an act against one person, and that person is your queen. As my brother pointed out earlier, Ragnall knew he was taking my consort and not just the palace scholar. If you can't see that, then this court no longer requires your counsel. You're dismissed, Eamon," Orla all but growled.

"I...Your majesty...come now, certainly...." he stammered.

"OUT!" Orla yelled, her voice leaving no room for argument. Torin stepped forward to remove the advisor from his seat if needed. "He is no longer welcome in the palace," she told Torin who nodded, escorting the man from the room.

Lachlan grinned, as he sat back and crossed his arms against his puffed chest. His sister was finally standing up for what she wanted, even if she was a little late. Eamon had been one of the key advisors pushing her to marry someone powerful. What some of the Fae didn't realize was that his sister was powerful within her own right and needed no man to increase her own. She needed someone who could balance her, who could stand by her side and support her or tell her when she was crossing that line, as Alfie was known to do.

"Now, are there any other objections?" Orla smiled at the remaining advisors. It was Lachlan's favorite smile, the one that spoke of the ocean brewing beneath her skin, the one that she had given him many times growing up before she unleashed some rather heinous revenge for one of his pranks. Orla was no wilting flower, no matter how hard she had been trying to appease the court, and it was best they all remembered when push came to shove, she was most likely to bide her time for the perfect moment to strike like a krait snake.

There were shakes of heads and murmurs of, "No, your majesty." Before they left the room, effectively dismissed.

Lachlan smiled encouragingly at his sister. "You handled that well. It did them good to remember who is in charge."

Her earlier smile faded as she sank down onto the chair. "How did we get here, Lach?" she whispered, her head hung low. She bent forward and pushed her temple into her palms. "Never mind, I know how. It was me. I pushed him away and look where that got me." She glanced up, tears brimming in her eyes. "I could lose him. He's my everything, and I could lose him because I was too stupid to tell the world how much I love him."

Lachlan stood and pulled a chair next to her. He rubbed his hand in soft circles against her back. "Then you'll have to make sure and shout it from the rooftops when we get him back. And we will get him back. I'm not sure what you have in mind, or if you have a plan, but let me go."

"No, this is my fight, Lach." She sniffed, wiping furiously beneath her eyes. "I can't let you…."

"You can." He cut her off before she could finish. "And you will. The people need you here, Orla. They need you safe. You're meant to lead them. You always were. We can't risk you. Me, on the other hand, we know my powers may not be as strong as yours, but I make up for that with my skills with a bow and sword. It'll take a few days to get the troops organized and come up with a strategic plan, but it would be my honor to do this for you and for Alfie."

Orla sighed. He could tell by the drawing of her brow and lips she wasn't exactly pleased with his idea, but he wasn't sure which part she didn't like until she spoke.

"Only if you promise to return to me safely. Alfie may be my love, but you are my blood, and I need you to return to me even if it is empty handed."

He smiled and took her hand. "I promise to do everything within my power to return to you safely." The magic sizzled between them, zinging up his arm and swirling around his heart to bind his words.

The next few days were packed with training and strategy meetings. They had a plan, a solid one at that. It took some convincing to his sister that he was serious about leading the guard with Torin. Ultimately, he knew Orla would only trust him to bring back her beloved in her place. He didn't like the idea of leaving her behind, but the people needed her more. She was their queen.

It took more energy trying to convince the members of the guard that he could be a serious leader and not just a spoiled prince playing as a soldier. He had trained with them from time to time, but most of his training came from Torin or private instructors his father had trusted. Perhaps he had done a little too good of a job cultivating his carefree prince façade. It didn't help that they had such a large unit of soldiers, he didn't know them all, especially the older ones. Once or twice, he caught sight of a soldier who bore resemblance to the young man in the woods, and remembered Torin mentioning the elite guard had wolves. Could one of them be related to Branan?

He needed to learn more about the guard, the types of Fae they had at their disposal if he wanted to truly lead them. He silently vowed to learn more about each member and their strengths as they traveled so he wouldn't have to rely so heavily on Torin to help him with battle strategies. He would become the leader of the guard and the prince that his people deserved.

A familiar itch started at the back of his neck. If he went too long without shifting, his body had a way of reminding him. He recalled the first time it had happened. He hadn't wanted to shift again and see the disappointment in his father's eyes, so he kept fighting it until it felt like a thousand ants crawling under his skin, driving him mad. Eventually the stag burst forth, unbidden, and startled a maid who had entered his room to clean it, thinking it to be empty. Luckily, she was one of his mother's faithful servants and knew enough not to speak of the event. Instead, she ran and fetched his mother, who coaxed him into shifting back until they could reach the woods and run safely.

He knew the itch was only a start and he would need to visit the woods before he left so he could focus on the battle ahead. Immediately, memories of Branan, the lad he had met in the woods, swirled through his mind. He wouldn't lie to himself and say that part of him didn't yearn to see the young man once more before he had to go. Perhaps after the battle, he would meet Branan in person, and see if his attraction wasn't merely one sided and finally feel if his black, shaggy hair was just as soft as it looked. The thought brought a smile to his face and new determination to his task. He stripped off his practice armor, leaving it in a heap on the floor for one of the maids to clean. He strode out of his room at a brisk pace, practically bumping into his sister as he rounded the corner by the top of the stairs.

"Lachlan!" she gasped, drawing back a step, clearly startled to see him as much as he was to see her.

He grabbed her shoulders gently to steady her. "Sorry sis, I didn't see you there."

"No, I suppose you didn't." A brief smile flickered across her face. "Where are you off to in such a hurry?"

"The forest. I need…." A rather large shudder worked its way down his spine. He dropped his hands from her shoulders, scratched at his back, and shrugged.

"No need, brother. I understand. It will do you some good to spend some time there. Did everything with training go well?"

He nodded. "We leave on the morrow."

Orla bit her lip. "Don't stay too late. I'd like to have dinner with you."

Lachlan tugged her into his side for a quick squeeze

before releasing her. "I would enjoy that as well. Don't let the troops leave without me." He winked at her playfully before striding down the steps.

"As long as you don't sneak off a tavern tonight!" she called.

He grabbed his bow and arrow, nodding at the guards as he strode through the doors and neared the edge of the woods. He should probably tell Torin where he was headed, but another large shudder racked his form and pressed him to enter the woods instead.

He walked far enough to ensure he was alone before shifting into his stag form. His ears and tail flicked back and forth. He pranced upon the ground as the wild smells of the woods filled his senses and the freedom from his overwhelming responsibilities as a prince rushed through his veins. Then he took off, bounding through the woods, his second home.

He paused at the bank of a stream to get a drink, his mind still whirling with the tasks ahead. He heard a rustling in the bushes to his left and froze. His heart pounded in his chest as hope burbled up. He sniffed the air and the familiar scent of wet dog hit his nostrils, but this was different somehow. His heart plummeted. *Lachlan, you're an idiot,* he scolded himself. He should have run when he had the chance, but instead he hesitated, hoping it was Branan.

A low growl echoed through the woods. *Wolf.* Lachlan didn't hesitate this time, he sprinted away from the stream as a flash of brown fur streaked toward him. He debated shifting back to his Fae form, he would still have the knives he strapped to his belt earlier, but that would take precious seconds and leave him vulnerable. Right now, he didn't have those seconds. If he could just get ahead of the wolf.

He'd been so wrapped in his mind and how to escape, he missed the second growl and thunder of paws. Another wolf slammed into him. This one's fur was lighter than the first wolf. Although he was slightly smaller, his teeth were just as sharp as they ripped into Lachlan's side. He felt his flesh tear, but his adrenaline held the pain at bay. He kicked frantically and angled his head to use his antlers to his advantage as best as he could from his position on the ground. Thankfully, one of his hooves connected with the fleshy underbelly of the wolf and he heard it whimper as he kicked it away, but the pain in his side seared, leading him to believe a chunk of his flesh must have gone with the wolf. Lachlan scrambled to his hooves as best as he could despite his side aching, the warm, wet liquid seeping down his fur, and the metallic smell of blood filling the air. It was then he noticed he was surrounded by three wolves. He tried to shift then, deciding the use of his knives was much more necessary than the moments of vulnerability it would provide, but his magic balked. A sharp pain in his side reminded him of the wound that had been inflicted. *Shit.* His mother had warned him that minor injuries could be healed by shifting, but major injuries may prevent him from changing from one form to the other. Apparently, this was a major injury.

The wolves circled, clearly enjoying having successfully captured their prey. They communicated silently. He could see the other two almost nod their heads, then the larger, dark brown wolf growled and lunged. Lachlan angled his antlers toward the large wolf and braced for an impact that never came.

A smaller, black wolf rammed into the side of the large brown wolf and knocked him off course. The other wolves growled, unhappy with the new development, but the black wolf, backed in front of Lachlan, growling at the other wolves. He snapped his jaws when one of them dared to get closer. The large brown wolf regained his composure and snarled at the black wolf, but the black wolf didn't back off from guarding Lachlan.

The black wolf swung his head toward Lachlan and lowered it slightly, his bright copper eyes held a hint of mint green. *I'm sorry I wasn't here sooner, friend.* The words echoed in his head but didn't belong to him. The familiarity in the baritone's voice struck him, but the loss of blood from his wound suddenly made him dizzy. The snarls and growls grew to a frenzy as his vision darkened around the edges. He knew it was too late for him, but he hoped the black wolf, the familiar voice that shouted at him to fight as he lost consciousness and caused his heart to ache, survived.

CHAPTER 5

"WHEN DO YOU leave?" Branan asked his father.

"Tonight. Shaw and I have to report to the barracks so we can depart with the troops in the morning," his father replied as he shoved necessary supplies into his pack.

"And how long will you be gone?"

His father ran a hand through his hair. "You know you could be going with me if you had joined the guard already."

It was a familiar fight, one that Branan wasn't ready to concede. After the rabbit incident, he knew without a doubt that joining the guard was not the path for him. He chose to let his silence speak for him.

"I get it. You'll decide what you want to do when you're ready, but you are running out of time, son. You aren't a boy anymore. Now that we know you can shift, there are so many other opportunities open to you."

"I'll think about it," Branan grumbled only to appease his father and move the conversation along. "Do you know how long?"

His father shrugged. "I wish I had an answer for you, but this won't be an easy task. The queen's scholar was captured by the Unseelie king and ransomed. Our queen refuses to concede to him since the Unseelie violated the treaty, and we all know if you give King Ragnall an inch he won't stop there until he has everything. He wants to rule all of Fae, and we can't allow that to happen. We will fight because it is the right thing to do. We must protect the ones we love."

"How can you protect me if you leave?"

"I'm protecting your future, son. The future of all of our people."

He knew it was unreasonable to want his father to stay, but he didn't want to lose him. He was the only family he had left. Branan didn't think the Unseelie king would easily give into demands even when those demands were backed by force, which meant losing some of their soldiers in the battle was likely.

"We've got a pretty good stock of food if you don't want to scavenge or hunt. And I'm sure Kyna will check in on you while I'm gone, probably with food in hand."

Branan snorted. "I don't need a babysitter."

"True, but you try telling her that." His father winked. "Maybe you go on a run with the boys while we're gone. It would do the pack good to see you boys getting along. Speaking of...." His father nudged him toward the door where he could hear the boys' voices approaching.

A knock sounded not a minute later, and Branan's dad swung the door open. "Evening boys, how can I help you?"

Whelan, the oldest, smiled widely, always eager to please the pack alpha. "We wanted to know if Branan wanted to go on a hunt with us."

The word hunt turned Branan's stomach, but the hope in his father's eyes when he looked back at him had Branan shoving his queasiness to the side. He could go and run with them. Maybe he could pretend to be slower, so if they caught anything he wouldn't have to participate in the kill.

"Sure." Branan forced a smile. It wasn't that Shaw's boys hadn't ever made him feel unwelcome per se. They were just so rough and tumble, so aggressive and competitive, a nature that didn't quite fit with Branan's own which they quickly discovered and left him alone for the most part, only interacting on a surface level of politeness. It wasn't until Branan finally shifted that he noticed Whelan's competitive gaze more focused on him. It unnerved him. He knew his father probably expected Branan to become alpha of their pack, but he didn't think Whelan would be willing to settle as beta.

The thought of running away and leaving it all behind swirled through his mind. Perhaps when his dad returned, they could have a heart to heart, and Branan would finally tell him the truth, even if it was hard for his father to hear. It would be the only way for their relationship to flourish in the future. He couldn't keep going through the motions. His thoughts drifted to his stag friend in the woods, how he had seemed so understanding and compassionate. People who didn't know, may not be able to tell, but there was an aspect of empathy that crossed boundaries. Not all animals acted on a strictly instinctual level. They had the capacity for emotional intelligence as much as, if not more than, humans and Fae—especially knowing how cruel and predatory Unseelie Fae could be.

"Alright. You boys, have fun. Take care of each other while Shaw and I are gone," his dad said, addressing all the boys at once.

"You too, Da. Come back safe." Branan clasped his father's forearm, and his father gripped his in return. The more formal greeting and farewell for their pack. He ached to hug him one last time but didn't want to appear weak in front of the other boys.

His father smiled softly at him, love shining through his eyes. "I will, son. I will."

"Be safe, alpha," Shaw's sons called as they turned toward the woods.

"You ready, Branan?" Whelan asked, smirking at the other boys in a way that made Branan's stomach flutter.

"I suppose." Branan shrugged.

"You haven't really run with us yet. Think you can keep up?"

"I'll try my best."

Malcom, the middle child, scoffed and received an elbow in the side from the youngest, Shane.

"See that you do," Whelan replied, turning toward the woods and shedding his Fae skin for his wolf. The other boys followed suit, not even pausing to wait for Branan to join them before scampering off into the woods.

Branan huffed before shifting into his wolf form. His wolf was happy to be let out, soaking up all the scents the forest had to offer, and chasing after the other wolves.

He didn't realize how much he had longed for this, to feel like one with the pack, to finally feel like he belonged. He raced behind the boys, forgetting they were intent on hunting, instead enjoying the pace at which they ran. He kept up easily, but fell behind when Whelan turned his head and snapped at him, a warning Branan was tempted not to heed. Whelan ran faster, with the boys following behind, until he caught the scent of something. He sniffed the ground intently for a few minutes before letting out a short yip and racing off further into the woods. Branan wasn't sure how far they'd already run, or what they were chasing after. It wasn't until he was on the trail behind the rest of the boys that he caught the familiar scent of his stag.

No! The word screamed through his mind and echoed down the pack link.

Don't be such a baby, Branan. We're wolves. This is what we're meant to do. Whelan spoke back through their link.

Branan shivered, he hadn't meant for the others to hear him. He shielded his thoughts as he raced to catch them. Had he hesitated too long? Bile tickled the back of his throat, and he swallowed it down, pushing himself to run faster. He couldn't let them kill his friend. It didn't matter if it was only a stag, and he was a wolf. That stag had comforted him and shown him more compassion than the wolves running with him. It understood him in a way they never had. New determination increased his pace. When he found them, they were circling for the kill. The coppery scent of blood overwhelmed his senses. He couldn't be too late. He couldn't.

STOP! He yelled down the pack link. The boys hesitated.

Relax. This one's mine. Whelan snarled and his brothers nodded their heads in acknowledgement.

Whelan lunged, but Branan was faster, he plowed into Whelan's side, knocking him off track. He shook his head, not pausing to check if Whelan was okay before backing up toward the injured snag. He snarled and growled, flashing his teeth to his pack. *I'm sorry I wasn't here sooner, friend.* He sent the thought to the stag with his magic before trying to reason with the pack.

You can't kill him.

Watch me. Whelan said, getting to his feet.

Don't make me do this. Branan threatened.

You just attacked one of your own packmates. For what, a stupid stag? Here we thought you'd finally be one of us, but you don't have the heart of a wolf. You'll never be alpha. Whelan growled.

You'll have to go through me to get to him, and what would your alpha say then? Branan asked. Throwing out the only trick he knew that might get the boys to reconsider. If they injured him, they would have to face his father.

It's not worth it, Whelan, Malcom said.

Ooo a rabbit, Shane added, having caught a new scent trail.

Whelan huffed a laugh. *It'll die anyway. Such a waste. At least we know where you stand. You'll never lead this pack, Branan. No matter what your father thinks. Mark my words.* With that final threat, Whelan turned, and his brothers followed leaving Branan alone with the bleeding stag.

Branan shifted just as the stag went down. Its left side was covered with blood, a large chunk of flesh missing. He whipped off his shirt, pressing it into the wound to stanch some of the bleeding. *Shit.* There wasn't much he could do here to help, and he wasn't sure how much time the stag had left. It wouldn't survive the trek to his house in this state, and he wasn't strong enough to carry it that far. He scouted the area, gathering some fibrous vines from the undergrowth. It would be better if he could race home and gather supplies, but there was no telling if Whelan would circle back to finish off the stag, or another predator might catch the blood trail. He kicked dirt over the blood hoping to bury the scent of fresh kill, and refused to accept the stag was dead. He studied the rise and fall of its chest, assured it was still alive before he gathered some moss and leaves. His dad had given him basic aid training since he was young. *"Basic aid using the resources around you could save your life one day, son, best pay attention,"* his father's voice whispered in his mind. And he had paid attention, so now in his moment of need, or at least the stag's moment of need, he knew which moss would be best to stanch the blood, which leaves could act as a bandage, and which ones could be chewed and applied to a wound with some antiseptic properties.

He pulled his blood drenched shirt away from the stag's side and quickly patched the wound with chewed leaves and moss before placing the larger leaves on top and binding them to the stag with the freshly plucked vines. When he shifted the stag to work the vines underneath his midsection, he made a sound of distress so pitiful it made Branan's heart break. If his friend died, he would carry that guilt for the rest of his life. "You have to fight. Do you hear me?" He spoke directly to the animal's mind. *Fight!* The stag snorted in reply, its eyes still closed.

With that done, Branan shifted back to his wolf and quickly dug a deep hole. He dropped his bloodied shirt inside and buried it. He checked the perimeter of their area, and the overwhelming scent of blood had now faded, making it seem old. He hoped it was enough to not attract any new predators. Now, the only threat was the return of his pack. He briefly wondered how he was going to deal with that situation, but shoved the thought into a box in his mind marked, problems for another day.

The sunlight was fading now. His stomach rumbled, and he wandered to the stream nearby to get a drink, keeping his senses alert for anything approaching him or the stag. Still in his wolf form, he took a mouthful of water over the stag. He pressed his snout against the stag's letting the water trickle down. *Drink*, he said, using his magic. He knew he couldn't command the stag, like a Dyr could, but perhaps his request would be enough. The stag's nose twitched, and its tongue came out, seeking some of the refreshment he provided. When he finished, the stag still hadn't opened its eyes, but seemed to be resting more peacefully. He remained in his wolf form and curled up next to the stag, determined to be his guardian throughout the night.

Sunlight peeked through the branches to the east of the forest. The chirping of birds roused Branan from his sleep. He'd had a nightmare that his stag had been killed. He tried to sit up, but instead found himself standing in his wolf form. It was the first time he'd slept overnight as a wolf. A small sound behind him reminded him that his nightmare was real. He whipped his head toward the stag. The stag's chest rose and fell steadily, and Branan huffed a sigh of relief. He sniffed the air. He couldn't smell any fresh blood. Hope sparked in his chest. He gently nudged the stag trying to rouse him. They couldn't stay in this spot forever. It wasn't safe. The stag was still vulnerable being out in the open.

He shifted back into his Fae form, just as the stag's eyes fluttered open. Branan sucked in a breath, remembering how beautiful they were, like a rich chocolate brown. It was only now that he noticed the ring of copper around the iris. *Interesting.* The stag blinked at him. *Can you get up?* He asked, running his hand down the stag's neck in a comforting gesture.

Maybe, the stag replied. Branan backed up and the stag dragged his legs beneath him, staggering to a stand.

Shit. That hurts like a motherfucker. Branan's eyes widened. He'd never heard an animal use such language before, except for the birds which were sometimes known to repeat whatever they heard on the wind.

Are you okay? He asked the stag.

I think so, the stag paused with a look of concentration on its face. *Hold on.*

The air warmed around them, and the stag shifted into the most handsome Fae Branan had ever seen. His skin was the same sun kissed tan as the stag's fur had been, but his hair was black. The sides of his head were recently shaved with his black hair on top pulled back into a short ponytail that led Branan to believe when loose it would barely reach his chin. The haircut made the sharpness of the man's jaw and cheekbones stand out in a way that made Branan's throat dry. His eyes were the same rich chocolate as the stag's with a ring of copper "Too much," the man whispered with his full lips, and then collapsed. Branan lunged forward, catching him in his arms before he hit the ground.

"Well, that was… unexpected." He gathered the young man into his arms feeling a twinge of guilt at ogling the man before he passed out. The bandage had fallen away, the vine ropes not able to hold during the change. A few of the leaves clung to the man's skin where his shirt was shredded. He gave one a gentle tug, but when it didn't come away easily, he thought the blood might have dried to it and peeling it off could open the wound anew. Something he didn't want to do in the middle of the woods.

"At least you're easier to carry this way," he said. Clutching the man as gently as he could, he shifted the upper part of his body over his shoulder, careful not to disturb the wound on his left side. The man groaned but didn't show any other hint of regaining consciousness. Branan figured the effort the man took to shift must have wiped him out completely. He knew from experience that shifting could heal minor wounds like when he had cut his own paw on a particularly sharp rock during a run, but it also cost a great deal of energy. He had barely managed to stumble home before he passed out. He wasn't sure about large wounds and made a mental note to ask his dad about it when he returned home.

He used the strength of his wolf to carry the man

through the woods and back to his house. It took longer than he expected, because he moved at a slower pace, not willing to jostle his friend too much. His stomach flipped. The stag he'd come to think of as his friend was another shifter. The stag he had cried to and had snotted all over, was a handsome man. His cheeks burned and he was glad the man wasn't awake to notice.

The sun was midway through the sky when he reached his house. "Da?" He called, opening the door before remembering his dad had left for battle the night before. *Perhaps it's better this way*, he thought, unsure how he'd explain the man's presence to his father. His heart sank. He wondered if Whelan had told his dad what happened in the woods before he left. He didn't think so, but the only way to be sure was to talk to Whelan, something he wasn't willing to do. *Of course, if the pack finds out the stag I was protecting was also a shifter, they would forgive me.* He shoved the thoughts of his pack back into the box labeled problems for another day, and laid the man gently on his bed.

"This is probably going to hurt a bit, and for that, I'm sorry," he said before he cut the man's shredded shirt away and tugged the leaves off of his wound.

The man cursed loudly with the first one, a loud groan with the second, and his hands came up to stop Branan's with the third. "Please, no more," he begged.

Branan wasn't aware he had regained consciousness. He glanced into the man's vulnerable gaze. He looked young, only a year or so older than Branan. "I'm sorry. I have to get them all off and clean out the wound. There may be some infection. I didn't have the proper supplies last night and had to use only what was available from our surroundings."

The man closed his eyes, but nodded, drawing his lips tight.

"Two more," Branan whispered. He gripped them both at the same time, yanking them free with as much speed and efficiency as was possible. The man flinched and bit back another curse.

"I wish I could say this next part will be easier, but I need to clean everything out and flush the wound. I'm afraid some of the moss and herbs I used to treat your wound dried to your skin with the blood."

The man nodded with a clenched jaw.

"Hold on," Branan paused, gathering all of his supplies to clean and flush the wound. He was happy to see it didn't look nearly as deadly as the night before. It was still sizeable, but either the herbs and bandaging from the night before or the man's shift had helped somewhat. While rummaging through the cabinets for supplies, he stumbled across his father's homemade brew and grabbed a bottle. It probably had the highest alcohol content of anything else in the house. His father's moonshine wasn't exactly known for being the tastiest, but it would do the trick.

"You'll probably want to drink some of this first because it's going to burn when I pour it on your wound."

The man struck out a hand and inched up enough to swing the bottle to his mouth and take several long pulls. Branan shifted the man's body, so his injured side hung slightly over the edge of the bed. He put a basin of water next to him with a cloth. Underneath the man he placed another basin to hopefully aid with cleanup. This was going to be messy either way. He brushed and plucked as much of the loose moss and leaves as he could away from the wound.

"Ready?" he asked the man.

The man took another swig from the bottle before handing it back to Branan. He nodded and gritted his teeth.

"Here goes nothing." Branan set down the moonshine and picked up a pitcher of water, pouring it over the wound before using the cloth to scrub away the moss and leaves the best he could. The man moaned, clenching and unclenching his fists. When the wound was mostly clean, Branan then tipped the bottle of moonshine over it. The man yelped in pain, causing his own heart to lurch. Thankfully, exhaustion pulled his patient under shortly after. The wound was not pretty. Whelan had taken a good chunk out of him. It was smaller in his Fae form, but not any less deep. It bled anew with the alcohol. Branan cleaned the wound as best as he could before gathering his father's sewing supplies. He stitched the wound together as best as he could, frowning when he realized that even with tugging, he couldn't pull the skin close enough to close all the way. He stared at the sloppy stitches, knowing his father would have done a better job, but it would still help the man heal faster. In his earlier search of the cabinets, he discovered his father must have packed their salve. He'd have to visit Kyna to see if she had any on hand. If not, he'd have to make a trip to the market in town. It would be hard to leave the man unattended, but he didn't see any other way. They would need some of the salve to make sure infection didn't set in, plus it would aid the healing of the wound.

He wrapped the man's torso with a bandage to cover the stitches, trying his best to ignore how beautifully sculpted the man's upper body was. He had been impressive in his stag form, larger than any other stag Branan had seen in the woods, which in hindsight should have tipped Branan off that his stag was a shifter. Heat licked its way up Branan's neck. He covered the man with a blanket before he could be caught ogling him.

The man's hand grasped Branan's as he finished setting the blanket over him. "Thank you for saving my life. I owe you."

The familiar tingle of magic wrapped around their joined hands and Branan cursed lightly, dropping the man's hands. "You shouldn't have done that." His eyebrows drew down and he shook his hand out. The man may regret the carelessness of his words when he woke, but it was too late. The life debt was sealed.

Branan observed his patient throughout the day. The man slept fitfully, plagued by dreams that would cause him to cry out. "I have to go. They need me!" the man shouted in his sleep. Other times he shouted the name, Orla. A deep fever set in, making his skin so hot to the touch Branan debated as he changed the cold compress on the man's forehead if he should risk a trip to town or to Kyna's house. If he left for a healer, it would leave the man with no one to tend to him for several hours, and that was if he could get a healer to travel this far out of town, or if he had enough coin to afford one. The more he thought about the healer option, he dismissed it. As much as he didn't like Whelan, he didn't want to get his pack in trouble for attacking the man, besides he was more likely to encounter an apprentice who may not know what to do since most of the experienced healers would have traveled with the troops to battle.

Kyna's house was about a twenty-minute walk from his place, but only a few minutes run in wolf form through the thick woods. However, if he went to Kyna and Shaw's house, Kyna would surely help, but if Whelan found out.... He shuddered. He wasn't sure what Whelan would do, but something told him it wouldn't be good.

The man woke occasionally but was only conscious long enough for Branan to coax him into drinking some water or broth, and it was clear by his senseless ramblings, he didn't understand where he was. He would shortly drift back into another restless sleep.

Branan wondered if the man was a member of the guard like his father. Was he supposed to leave with them? Did he fancy himself in love with the queen, or was there another Orla out there who was his lover? The questions plagued Branan as he made himself something to eat.

That night, the man had calmed somewhat and slept a bit more peacefully. Branan decided to risk some time away and go to Kyna's house for the salve. He glanced out the window at the moon, knowing Whelan liked to go for a run at night before bed. If he wanted to get the salve without Whelan knowing, now was the time to do it. It wasn't that far of a hike and wouldn't take him long, even faster in wolf form. His chest ached when he considered what toll a night of fevering would take on the man. "Keep fighting, friend," he whispered before placing a cool rag on the man's forehead.

He shifted outside of the cabin listening to the howls

of Shaw's boys somewhere in the woods. Branan felt some of the tension leave his body. He hadn't spoken to them since he interfered with their hunt and didn't know what they would do when they saw him again.

He reached Kyna and Shaw's house in no time and exchanged his wolf pelt for his Fae skin. Knowing he needed a reason for Kyna to loan him the salve helped him calm his nerves for what he had to do next. He grabbed a knife from his holster, slicing his arm as deep as he could. He hissed in pain and then wiped the blade on the side of his shirt as if his arm grazed there before returning it to the holster. He raised a fist to knock briefly at the door then lowered his hand to cradle his injured arm.

Kyna opened the door with a kind smile. "Branan!" Her smile fell the instant her eyes zoomed in on his bleeding arm. "Oh dear, come in. Come in. Let me see." She ushered him over to the sink and snapped her fingers illuminating a light above.

"Sorry Kyna. Something struck my front leg while I was out running. I tried to fix it at home, but I think my dad took our salve with him when he left." Branan stared sheepishly at the floor and hoped she would buy his lack of eye contact as embarrassment while his stomach rolled at the lie.

"Of course, he did. I keep telling him he should have more than one on hand, but you know how stubborn grown men can be. She washed his wound gently and then applied the salve before wrapping it in a bandage.

"All better, now. Have you eaten yet? The boys are out hunting, but I'm sure they'll bring something good back for me to cook up."

The memory of the wound on the stag flashed through his mind. He swallowed it down. "I'm good. Thanks, Kyna. And thank you for your help with the wound. Do you think...?" He pointed to the salve and peered at her through his lashes. He hated lying to a woman who only showed him kindness, but he didn't want to involve her in his problems.

"Of course, dear." She smiled pressing the tin into his palm. "Unlike your father, I keep several of these around the house." She winked and he smiled.

"There should be enough in there to set you straight. Come by later this week for dinner," she called as he turned to leave.

"When do you think they'll be back?" he asked, chewing on his lower lip, his stomach clenched at the thought of his father engaged in battle, the possibility of injury or.... He shook his head, unwilling to let himself finish the thought.

As if Kyna could read his mind, she placed a hand on his shoulder and squeezed. "Not too long. It will take some time to get there and back, maybe a week or two if all goes well, and until then I intend to make sure you're fed. So, dinner later this week, yeah?"

"Okay," he lied after a moment of hesitation. He had no desire to see Whelan and his brothers anytime soon. They probably wouldn't say anything to their mom, but the glares across the table would grow uncomfortable and he didn't want to put Kyna in that situation. "Thanks again!" He waved before closing the door behind himself and sliding the salve into his pocket. Worries about his father and Shaw swirled in his chest and he thrust them aside. Now was not the time, not when he had an injured friend at his house, one who was depending on him.

CHAPTER 6

LACHLAN'S LEFT SIDE was on fire. He blinked his eyes open. The sheet that covered him was soaked with sweat. He moaned, trying to recall how he got wherever here was at the moment. It definitely wasn't the palace. The beams overhead were rough, speaking of some of the smaller cabins on the outskirts of town. He turned his head, the room he was in was small, but cozy. He inhaled deeply, from the way his head was turned the most prominent scents came from the pillow, a familiar earthy musk with a hint of wet dog. *Branan*. A warm, damp rag sat on his forehead, which he removed. He turned his head the other way and saw a glass of water on the table next to the bed. Gingerly, he pulled himself up as much as he could without causing himself too much pain.

He placed the rag on the table and sipped the water. Each tiny movement sent a shot of pain down his side. After his thirst was quenched, he pulled the blanket down and studied the bandage around his wound, recalling the wolves in the woods and the events that led him here. He hissed as he probed the wound gently, fingers tracing the rough rise of stitches through the bandage. The boy definitely wasn't a tailor. Lachlan had never needed stitches before but had seen them on some of the other men while sparring. Usually, the palace healer was able to fix whatever wound he had sustained throughout his childhood. The wound must have been deep, most likely even fatal, if Branan had not been there. While shifter Fae healed faster than most other Fae due to their ability to shift forms, wounds that affected muscle tissue and organs could take considerably longer.

"Branan," he called out, his voice rough, but was met only with silence. His nurse must be out of the cabin or asleep. He wondered how long he had slept. Was Orla worried about him?

Shit. Orla! Had she waited or sent the troops without him? And just how long has it been? He attempted to swing his legs over to pull himself out of bed and released a frustrated growl, the pain searing down his side. He would be in no position to ride, let alone fight for at least a few more days, especially without the aid of a healer. He felt for his shifter magic, but it was only a faint trickle, his stag sleeping in his mind. This was worse than he'd thought. He only hoped Orla would wait or leave the troops in Torin's capable hands and not do something stupid like lead them herself.

The closing of a door yanked him from his thoughts. He tensed, but the only scent his senses picked up was Branan's which caused him to relax. He wasn't sure if Branan knew the wolves who'd attacked him, but he trusted the boy who had risked his life to save his own. Branan's footsteps grew closer before he stood in the doorway. His long, black hair was pulled up this time in some sort of messy gathering. It was dangerously good looking on him, making the sharpness of his cheekbones and jaw standout even farther. The bronze undertones in his rich golden oak colored skin glowed in the moonlight, but most striking of all were his eyes. Such a pale shade of green with that ring of copper.

"Oh, you're awake." The eyes Lachlan had just been staring at widened slightly.

Lachlan attempted to smile in return, and Branan stammered. "Um, I went to get you some salve. I thought it might help." Branan's eyes slid slowly down Lachlan's bare chest where they paused for a moment before continuing on to his bandaged side, leaving a trail of heat in their wake. A blush stole across his face when he realized Lachlan was watching him. He thrust the tin out in front of him as if in explanation.

Lachlan licked his lips, his mouth dry again, but this time for an entirely different reason. Branan's eyes followed the movement, the copper overtaking the green in his gaze before he tore it away and coughed. "Can you sit up?" His voice was low and thick. He coughed again to clear it, which Lachlan found adorable.

"I can try again, but I warn you, it didn't go well last time," Lachlan teased.

"I'm sorry," Branan replied. His eyes were back to a minty green, brimming with unspoken sorrow and regret.

"You weren't the one who attacked me. I should thank you for saving my life back there. If you weren't there, I don't think I would...." He stopped and swallowed, unwilling to think of how close to death's door he had gotten.

"If I had known you weren't just a stag, it might have helped." Branan arched a delicious eyebrow in accusation, and this time it was Lachlan's cheeks that reddened.

"Yeah. Um, I," he paused unsure of how to explain. "I don't really let many people know what I am."

The teasing accusation faded from Branan's gaze as his brow drew down. "Why not?"

The question was so innocent and curious that Lachlan had no choice but to tell him the truth. "It's not exactly a powerful animal, like your wolf."

"Stags are powerful in their own ways. They're fast. They're born leaders. If you've studied the stars associated with a stag, you'd know that they are visionaries and hard workers. Your antlers can be wielded just as well as any weapon. The force of a stag's kick isn't something to laugh at either. They are noble creatures, the kings of the forest." Branan's voice rose as he spoke, becoming more solid and assured through his little speech.

Lachlan had never seen such an impassioned display over his animal form. His heart thumped loudly in his chest. "I've never thought about it like that. I was always told to hide what I was."

Branan's sharp intake of air drew Lachlan back from diving into his memory of his father. Branan placed his hand over Lachlan's. "I'm sorry you weren't told that more often. You are magnificent...." He paused, clearly waiting for Lachlan to fill in the blank on his name.

"Oh, um...." Lachlan hesitated for only a second. It was obvious Branan didn't know he was talking to the

Seelie prince, and if he told him his true name, he might figure it out. He'd seen the way children had played with him at court, out of masked obligation, or the way the ladies had tried to spark his interest, clearly hungry for only his title. "Torin," he replied, hoping the lie was believable.

"Nice to officially meet you, Torin. I'm Branan." Branan stuck out his hand which Lachlan shook. With Lachlan's hand still clasped in his own, Branan gently helped him into a seated position.

Lachlan grunted as each tiny shift of his muscles caused a needle-like pain to stab his side.

"Alright, let's get some salve on that." Branan smiled warmly at him, and Lachlan nodded.

Branan leaned forward to unwrap the bandage, his scent overwhelming Lachlan. The hint of wet dog he had sensed earlier, no longer held the same meaning. It was Branan's wolf, and the smell offered Lachlan an extreme amount of comfort and security. Warmth spread throughout his chest as Branan unwound the bandage, letting it fall to the bed. "Looks like you may have pulled a few stitches, but they're mostly intact." He probed the area gently causing Lachlan to hiss in response. Quickly, he snatched his hand back. "Sorry." He stared down at his hands while he worked to open the tin of salve. Lachlan used the opportunity to distract himself from his pain by studying the boy who made his heart pound.

"How old are you?"

Branan's eyes flicked toward his. A slight hesitation. "Um, nineteen," he replied.

Lachlan couldn't help but grin. He was right. Branan was only slightly younger than himself. He acted younger than nineteen. Perhaps he was sheltered. Lachlan hasn't seen the rest of his home, but he would bet he still lived with his parents. Although if that were true, where were they?

Branan frowned now that he had the tin of salve open. "It's not as full as I would like, but I guess Kyna thought it was enough to treat my injury." He tipped the tin toward Lachlan who frowned. *His injury?* It was then he noticed the bandage wrapped around Branan's forearm.

"Did you get this during the fight?" His stag reared back in his mind, both of them not liking that Branan may have been injured because of him.

Branan's face flushed. "No, I um… I had to have a reason for needing the salve, and I couldn't exactly explain… this." He waved his hand back and forth above Lachlan.

This sweet boy had taken a blade to his own arm to get the medicine Lachlan needed. A low growl rumbled from his chest.

"Don't worry. It's superficial. I'll be good as new in no time." Branan smiled at him before steering the conversation away from himself, and the rumbling stopped.

"It should still help, at least clear up any possibility of infection. I can go to the market and get some more if we need it. I should clean this first, though." He reached for a bowl of warm, soapy water and a rag he had placed on the desk in the room earlier. Gently, he dabbed around the stitches, erasing any trace of blood from where Lachlan had strained them.

Lachlan shook his head. "It's fine." Again, his mind wandered to Branan's family. If he was a wolf shifter, wolves tended to live in packs, and Branan wasn't giving off any alpha energy. "Do you live alone?"

"No," Branan replied, his focus still on cleaning Lachlan's wounds while causing him the least amount of pain as possible.

Lachlan let the silence hang in the air until Branan was ready to share more.

"I live with my dad, but he left the same night you were injured. He's in the Seelie guard."

Lachlan swallowed hard, his earlier fears resurfacing. "And how long ago was that? How long have I been here?"

"Let's see, we spent the night in the forest after you were attacked. Then you spent all of today fevering, in and out of consciousness." Branan returned the rag to the bowl, the water and rag now a shade of pink.

His breaths came unevenly, his heart galloping. If Branan's father wasn't back and had been sent with the troops, then they went without him. *Oh, Orla, what have you done?*

His stomach plummeted. He prayed with every fiber of his being that Torin was the one leading them in his stead, and his sister hadn't done anything foolish. What did the men think of him? Was Orla worried when he didn't return? Did they think he had found his way to the tavern and overindulged as they had so many times before? Of course, that was different, they weren't preparing for battle, only training.

"This is the most lucid you've been, so I would say we're on the road to recovery," Branan noted. "Can you lean slightly to the right?"

Lachlan did as he asked. Branan smoothed the salve across the stitched skin in a soft caress. Lachlan sighed, the stinging immediately ceased. In its place, a pleasant warm tingle of magic spread from the site of the wound, relaxing his muscles.

"Well, thank you, for taking care of me while I was not able to," Lachlan said.

Branan's eyes fixated where he rubbed the salve into Lachlan's side. He swallowed hard, his Adam's apple bobbing in a way that made Lachlan want to lick the side of his neck. Shivers raced down his spine from their proximity.

Branan mistook his slight shudder for something else and drew back, taking his delicious warmth with him. "Um, about that." He swallowed hard again and chewed on his bottom lip before his eyes finally met Lachlan's. "Earlier you were a little delirious after your injury and you made a life debt oath. I know you probably didn't mean it, but you know how magic is. It makes its own rules."

"Are you sure?" The news should have shocked Lachlan, but instead he knew that Branan did something most would not have in his position, and he truly did save his life.

Branan nodded. "I felt it." He opened his mouth, perhaps to apologize again, but Lachlan held up a hand to stop him.

"Were the wolves who attacked me part of your pack?"

Branan nodded, and Lachlan's pulse skittered. To go against your pack the way Branan had could be cause for expulsion. A life debt would be the least of what he owed him, if Branan were to be kicked out of his pack for saving him. "Then I did the right thing, and I will honor it." He wanted to take the words back as soon as they left his mouth. It was stupid to state he would honor it when he had no choice. The magic would demand it regardless. "I hope saving me won't cause too much of a rift between you and your pack."

Branan smiled sadly. "Nah, I'm sure it only reinforced their opinion of me. I was a late bloomer, only started shifting this year, so they didn't think much of me before."

That was late for a shifter to start changing their form. While most Fae didn't come into their full magic until they were in their teens, shifters' magic tended to manifest around between six and eight years old. It must have made things really difficult for him growing up.

Branan continued, oblivious to the inner workings of Lachlan's mind. "The reason they tolerate me is because my dad is alpha. I'll tell my dad what happened when he returns, that the stag was a shifter. He'll understand."

"Will your dad wonder how you knew I was a shifter when you defended me? Did you know?"

Branan's cheeks flushed pink again, and he shook his head. "I didn't, I just knew I had to protect my friend. You see, shifter is my secondary magic, which probably explains why I had my first shift so late. For a while, we weren't even sure I'd have enough of Da's magic to shift at all. I'm a Milyn, so I can communicate with animals. My dad will assume it's part of my magic, and I just won't correct him." The corners of Branan's mouth twitched mischievously at the last part, and Lachlan found it adorable.

"So, when you talk to animals like you did with me...."

"They can understand me, and I can read their emotions and some of their thoughts. Occasionally they can answer with words. It depends on how much they've been around Fae or humans, but it's mostly a lot of visual impressions mixed with emotions. I knew you were different somehow. Your impressions were usually harder to decipher, more complex."

Well, that made sense why he always spoke to Lachlan as if Lachlan could understand him. Lachlan had just thought Branan was a little sensitive and quirky. A stone dropped into his stomach, when he remembered how distraught Branan had been over killing the rabbit. No wonder the poor boy had lost it. It was one thing to kill something you couldn't communicate with or understand its thinking, it was another to take a life knowing exactly what you were extinguishing. His stomach churned. He supposed killing someone in battle may be similar, but even then, you're usually fighting to defend or with a purpose, not killing something innocent and defenseless where you can feel it dying. It would be hard to be a predatory shifter with magic like Branan's. Lachlan wanted to comfort him, but also not remind him of the event, so he reached over and placed his hand on top of Branan's where it rested against the sheets.

"That must be hard," were the only words he could settle upon as he squeezed Branan's hand.

"Sometimes," Branan replied, squeezing Lachlan's hand in return. "I should get you a clean bandage to cover that up." He picked up the soiled bandage from the bed, and the bowl of dirty water and left the room. He returned shortly with a clean bandage he wound around Lachlan's torso.

"Thank you." Lachlan yawned.

"Rest now," Branan replied. "Anything else can wait until morning. Hopefully then we can get you up and moving around. I'm sure your family might be worried about you. Your significant other perhaps."

Lachlan suppressed a chuckle. Besides not being a great seamstress, this boy was not smooth in asking if Lachlan was single. "No significant other, just my sister."

Branan smiled softly. "Sweet dreams."

CHAPTER 7

BRANAN STARED AT the pink water as he scrubbed the soiled bandage. How many times had he done this for his dad over the years? Too many. What if something happened to him? His throat tightened, the familiar anxiety building up in his chest. "Deep breaths, in and out," he whispered. He'd always been like this. Another reason Shaw's boys saw him as the weakest member of the pack. He didn't know why his thoughts could spiral and overwhelm him at times. How did others not experience this same thing? His dad always chucked it up to him being more empathetic than the average Fae with his ability to communicate with animals and sometimes tapping into Fae. But he often wondered if maybe his mom felt the same way sometimes. Was this something he inherited or was he just broken in some way? He focused on the breath rising and falling from his chest, shoving all concerns about his dad from his mind. *Da will be fine. He's*

a fierce and loyal protector, an excellent fighter. Da will be fine. He'll return home and things will be as they have always been. His breathing slowed and he returned his focus to the bandage in his hands.

As much as he hoped Torin healed, a selfish part of him hoped it wasn't quickly. He wasn't looking forward to being left alone again with only the silence and his thoughts to keep him company. A soft scratching at the door made him jump. He slid open a drawer and drew out a knife. Keeping the knife raised in front of him, he slowly crept toward the door. He paused, his wolf listening for any signs beyond the door, but sensed nothing. Cautiously, he opened the door. No one was there. He was about to close it when he noticed the blood trail from the yard leading to the front door. There on the porch set on top of blood-spattered earth rested the stump of a fox's paw. The rising panic Branan had battled earlier swarmed around him, causing his head to swim, and his vision to blur. His breaths came out in short pants and his stomach rolled so hard, he stepped outside and vomited on the grass. His hand trembled when he reached it up to wipe away the remains of the vomit. He flicked his eyes toward the darkness of the woods, spying a pair of yellow eyes before the wolf darted away. *Whelan,* his wolf growled. Of course, he would stay to see how Branan reacted to his warning. Branan fought the urge to heave again. There was something wrong with that boy, and maybe once Da found out about the attack on the stag shifter, he would see the same maliciousness in Whelan that Branan had always known was there.

"You poor, poor thing," he whispered to the night air and hoped the fox's spirit could hear him, know that someone mourned its death. Gently he reached for the paw to move it, when a rush of fear knocked him back on the ground. The poor animal had known it was going to die and had been absolutely terrified. Fear still clung to its fur, fear that now threatened to overwhelm Branan. Tears poured down his cheeks. He was glad Whelan had left already, couldn't bear the thought of Whelan witnessing his grief, but the message was clear as day. This was a threat, plain and simple. He wanted Branan to feel as afraid as the fox felt in his last moments of life, and it worked. Branan was terrified, but not for himself, for Torin. Torin would never again be safe in those woods as a stag. Whelan was relentless, and the fox's paw was meant to tell Branan that he couldn't save every animal in the woods, a promise that the next time Whelan caught scent of that stag, he wouldn't stop until he caught his prey, and would no doubt return with another sick "gift" for Branan. To gloat about his conquest.

When his tears subsided and his breathing slowed, he got a towel from the kitchen. Gently, he gently wrapped the fox's paw in it, and grabbed a shovel from the stable. He picked a nice tree and started digging at the base until there was a hole deep enough to bury what was left of the poor creature. If he knew where they had killed the fox, he may have been tempted to locate the rest of its remains, but this would have to do. He said a quick prayer to the gods to guide the fox on its journey to the spirit realm. When he finished, he returned the shovel and grabbed a rake, removing the blood-stained earth from the walkway at the door as best as he could.

Back inside he stripped out of his clothes, took the now

dirty bandage from his arm, and ran a bath for himself. His hands were stained with fox blood and dirt. They still trembled slightly when he reached for the faucet. The water from the well came out fast and icy cold. Branan's dad was much better than him at heating the water, but it was a simple enough spell that he managed to get it to a tolerable temperature before sliding in. He scrubbed his entire body, hoping to remove the smell of death and fear. He paid extra special attention to his hands and fingers, scrubbing until his skin was almost raw. Thankfully, the wound on his arm was now nothing but a red line and would need just a touch more salve to ensure it didn't scar.

He rinsed himself off and stepped out of the tub to dry himself off. He remembered Lachlan's used bandage still in the kitchen sink and slung the towel around his waist, wanting to hang dry the bandage before he forgot.

He finished draping bandage, close enough to the fire to use the warmth to help it dry, but far enough away it wouldn't be a fire hazard. From the next room, Torin groaned, followed by a thump and a not so soft curse.

"Everything okay in here?" he asked, opening the door to where Torin sat on the floor. "Obviously not," he observed.

Torin stared at the floor. "I thought I could make it to the restroom to relive myself on my own, but alas, it was not in the cards."

Branan chuckled, reaching down to help him up.

Lachlan's eyes widened as he took in Branan. He must be fresh from the bath. There was still moisture visible on his skin, skin that was very much on display, and good gracious did it make his heart speed up. Lachlan swallowed, his mouth suddenly dry. Of course, Branan seemed undisturbed by his lack of manners.

"I, um…." Great, now he was speechless as well. His eyes took in every muscled plane of Branan's chest as he helped him rise.

"Are you hurt, Torin? Did you pull your stitches when you fell?" His brow furrowed in concern, but what brought Lachlan back to the present was the fake name on his lips.

How would it feel to hear Branan mutter his true name? To say it breathlessly? A shiver raced down his spine in reply, warmth spreading throughout his body and waking up a rather inopportune part. It was only then he realized both of his hands were splayed across the chest he had just been admiring, seeming to move on their own. He snatched one away and coughed into his fist. "I'm fine." He coughed again, clearing his throat and mind. "I don't think I hurt anything other than my pride. I didn't realize how weak I still was."

"Would you like some help to the bathroom?" Branan asked.

Lachlan's face burned, but he nodded his reply as Branan draped his arm across Lachlan's back, shoving his shoulder under Lachlan's armpit to provide him with support as he walked. Even through the bandage he could feel the heat of Branan's hand. It didn't help that his other hand itched to trace Branan's chest again. He shook out his fingers.

"Thank you," Lachlan replied when they made it to the door. The scent of whatever soap Branan had worn in the shower clung in the air. "Nice to see you all cleaned up," he joked, drawing his body away from Branan's side to show he could take it from there.

"Oh, yeah, um." Now it was Branan's turn to blush as he glanced down at the towel covering his waist, his eyes widening as if he had just realized all he was wearing was that one piece of fabric clinging for dear life to his hip. "I'll get changed and come back to help you." He nodded quickly, one hand grabbing the towel to hold it up as he dashed from the room. Lachlan chuckled lightly until the pain in his side reminded him he shouldn't. He gingerly made his way to the toilet and took care of business. When he finished, he plucked the bar of soap from the edge of the tub and brought it to his nose, inhaling the pleasant scent before using it to wash his hands. He liked the idea of part of him smelling like Branan. Perhaps it was one of those primal things the shifter side of him enjoyed.

When he finished and opened the door, the movement threw him off balance, but Branan was there to catch him. This time, he was dressed in simple clothes, his wet hair left drips on the shoulder of his grey shirt, but he didn't seem to care. He helped Lachlan back to his room, the closeness of his body enough to distract Lachlan from the pain spreading from the wound. It looked like he wouldn't be going anywhere tomorrow. The muscle seemed to take its time to knit itself back together. He wondered if shifting would help speed up the process, but his magic still felt depleted. How long it would take until he could shift again? This time, his stag stirred at his question and snorted before returning to his slumber. He sighed. His wound must have been grave for his body to have forced a shift that left his magic so drained. He'd never felt like this before. Best not to mess with it and wait until he healed, or his stag felt stronger, whichever came first.

He had been foolish to wander so far from the castle when he knew he had to leave to lead the troops. He knew it was the boy next to him that drove him to make such a reckless decision. He only hoped his recklessness didn't cost him or his people too much. Hopefully Torin would do what needed to be done and lead the Seelie troops to demand Alfie's safe return. He knew the Unseelie king wouldn't immediately cave to their demand, but the display of their army should be rather convincing.

Branan helped him settle onto the bed. "Are you in a lot of pain?"

"I've had worse," he attempted to joke, but he didn't like the way Branan frowned at his reply. "I'm only joking. I'm okay. Healing, and alive thanks to you."

Branan shook his head, not wanting to get into that conversation again. "Well, it's getting late. We should both rest and see how you're doing in the morning."

Lachlan nodded.

"Thank you for your help," he said softly. He didn't like not being able to do things independently, especially something as simple as using the bathroom. "Goodnight, again. Hopefully for the rest of the evening this time," he joked, liking how the corners of Branan's mouth turned up.

When Branan shut the door, Lachlan took a minute to remember what had drawn him from his sleep. He peered out the small window next to his bed to the fresh grave at the base of the tree. He wondered what it was that Branan had grieved over and buried. As long as he lived, he would never forget Branan's small whimpers and sobs, the soft wolf-like howl that invaded his dreams. The scent of absolute terror drifted in from the window. If he had been able bodied, he would have been outside with Branan in an instant. When he watched Branan's hunched over frame stumble back toward the cabin, he had wanted to comfort him. It was that need that drove him to attempt to leave the bed and walk out of the bedroom on his own after gathering his strength. Now, his side ached.

For not the first time in his life, he wished he had been a Mara like his father. If he was, he could comfort Branan in his dreams, find out what it was by the door that left a haunted look in his eyes. He could prevent it from happening again. He huffed a sigh, knowing it did no good wishing he had been born a Mara, it never had before and that wouldn't change now. "*Wishes are only granted in fairytales,*" his mother's words floated through his mind as she had reminded him countless times as a child. "*Unless of course, you have a Djinn that I don't know about. Even then, Djinn can't change who we are, and a stag is who you are my son. You are a noble leader with a gentle heart. One who will chase adventure if you scent it on the wind but will always return to protect those you love and our land. Would you really want to change that if you could?*"

He remembered the way she stroked a hand down his hair. She understood how hard it was for him to feel like a disappointment to his father. She was the one who truly understood him. His heart ached, the pain of missing her always there in some small part. "You're right, Mama, you always were. Perhaps if you're listening you can help Orla be patient, return her love safely, and comfort Branan in his dreams." Saying the words out loud felt better than sending a prayer to the gods, a habit he'd formed after he lost both of his parents. If there was a way the gods were listening, they would have answered him a long time ago. At least speaking to his mother brought his heart some sense of comfort.

CHAPTER 8

THE SUNLIGHT AND a soft humming sound woke Lachlan this time. His dreams had been restful. He took stock of his body, noting that while improved, he still had a way to go before he could make the journey back to the castle. In fact, he should probably ask Branan how far they were from town. He could send him to fetch a healer from the palace which would speed up his healing, but did he want anyone knowing he was here?

Orla would be pissed, and rightly so, but it's not like it was intentional. He didn't blame her or Torin for not looking for him or sending out a search party. They probably assumed he went to a tavern to take the edge off of his nerves before battle and drank too much or passed out somewhere, not ready to bear the responsibility laid out in front of him. More and more he was coming to regret the façade he had built, and he silently vowed to work to repair his reputation when he returned.

Since Branan's dad hadn't returned, Orla must have sent the troops ahead with Torin leading them when he didn't show up. What good would it do for him to get a healer and be dragged back to the palace now? It would still take some time for him to fully heal, and the troops would be days ahead in travel, already crossing the border. That would make catching up even more dangerous, crossing the border by himself would be a dumb way to die. He shook his head while the guilt plagued him, there wasn't much he could do about it now. Returning home today wouldn't change anything, but it could put him at risk of reinjury, especially since he wasn't sure how far from the palace they were or if Branan even owned a horse, he could use. His side stung at the thought of attempting to mount and ride a horse in his current condition. If only moving caused discomfort, riding would be asking for the stitches to be torn open if he didn't pass out from pain first, and walking would be out of the question. He sighed more loudly than he thought as the humming stopped and a Branan's familiar face appeared in the doorway.

"Good morning, or should I say good afternoon?" he teased.

"I'd like to say that I don't normally sleep this late, but...."

Branan chuckled. "Truly? You're normally this lazy?"

"Nah, only when I overindulge at the tavern, which I've been known to a do a time or two." It was so easy to slip back into his selfish, carefree prince façade. His stomach turned, normally he didn't care what others thought of him, but for some reason he didn't want Branan to see him that way. His stomach twisted further, knowing when he didn't show up to lead the troops into battle, some of the men most likely thought the worst of him.

I'll do better, he promised himself. He was ready now to bear some of the burden Orla carried, to shoulder some of the responsibility of the crown. Maybe then she would feel comfortable enough to choose her own happiness and marry Alfie. She had done her best to provide him with as much of a normal childhood as she had been provided before having the crown thrust upon her, and he was thankful. When he got back to the palace, he would begin to repay her kindness.

"You look troubled. I've been told I'm a great listener if you're willing to share," Branan offered.

Lachlan sighed. "Just realizing how much of a mess I've been lately. I suppose surviving a near fatal attack will make anyone contemplate their life choices and how they can use their second chance to contribute toward the greater good." He meant to sound philosophical, but the way Branan's face paled made him wonder if he had made a mistake.

Branan wrung his hands together, rubbing them as if he were scrubbing them clean, but his eyes were stuck on the window, staring off into the distance over Lachlan's shoulder. Lachlan turned and looked to see what caught Branan's attention. He only saw the trees, but when his eyes caught on the base of a tree, there was a small mound of freshly tilled earth and a stone in the center.

"Did something happen?" he asked, keeping his voice soft.

Branan's gaze swung toward him, his eyes slightly widening. "Nope. Nothing for you to worry about." He attempted a smile, but it didn't reach his eyes.

Lachlan didn't appreciate being lied to by someone he cared about, but he also didn't want to force Branan to tell him what was wrong.

"Anyway. How are you feeling? We should probably change your bandages. Or perhaps if you feel up to it, a bath," Branan suggested.

"Trying to tell me I smell?"

Branan snorted. "I was trying to be polite when you were nearly dying, but now that it's clear you're going to live, you do smell a little ripe," he teased.

Lachlan moved toward the edge of the bed, and Branan took a step closer to show him he was there if he needed any help. He wrinkled his nose. Branan wasn't lying when he said he smelled a little ripe, pungent was more fitting. "You're right," he laughed. "A bath it is."

"Stay there and I'll go get the water started," Branan replied, rushing from the room. Lachlan pressed his hand against the bandage, happy to see no blood leaking through, but noticing its tenderness to his touch. Taking a bath would be a good test of his injury and his strength. It would be a step in the right direction to getting him back home.

Branan tried to calm his racing heart. The reminder of the fox from last night still hung heavy in the air. He knew that Torin meant what he'd said as joke, but he wasn't the one who witnessed just how close he'd come to death. His stomach turned and he pressed a hand against it to still its rolling. Unbidden, the image of him burying Torin like he had the fox paw entered his mind, and the edges of his vision began to blur. His lungs contracted, drawing in short pants, and his chest tightened as if a boulder pressed against it. He closed his eyes and tried to focus on inhaling slowly and deeply, but it was a struggle. Eventually he pulled his thoughts away from the dead fox and Torin's attack and centered them on the here and now. He quickly turned the faucet on, and stuck his hand under the water, focusing on the sensation of the water flowing over his fingers until his breaths slowed and his heart no longer galloped in his chest. Over the years, he had learned that focusing on the moment and on something as simple as a sensation not related to whatever triggered the attack, could calm him. As his heartrate decreased and clarity returned, Branan knew it wasn't the incident with the fox, but the thought of Torin's death that caused the initial panic. It was too fast for him to feel this way, right? He didn't truly know this man, only the affection he had held for his friend the stag, but he couldn't deny their connection had grown deeper over the last few days.

With his panic mostly subsided, he ran his fingers through the water, whispering the words his father had taught him to focus his magic and heat the water to a good temperature. He wanted it hot enough to help ease the aches in Torin's muscles, but not hot enough to scald him. He returned to his room and helped Torin rise from the bed.

"I think I can walk on my own," Torin grunted.

"Okay, I'm here if you need me," Branan replied. He

stayed close, slightly behind him in case he faltered. And although he did walk slowly, he was able to do so on his own. Meanwhile, Branan tried to ignore the deliciously defined muscles on Torin's back and did his best to keep his gaze above the waist.

When they reached the bathroom, Torin turned back to look at Branan over his shoulder. "I think I can take it from here." He winked.

"Of course." His face burned as he met Torin's eyes which sparkled with amusement. "Well, almost."

He reached toward Torin's bandage which would need to be undone before he stepped into the bath. The burn in his cheeks turned into flames shooting down his whole body as he gingerly unwrapped the bandage from Torin's midsection, revealing more well-defined muscles underneath. *Think about how he smells, you dummy. Think about birds in the forest. Think about Da.* He told himself anything he could to keep from thinking about how badly he wanted to see how Torin's skin tasted or how soft his lips might feel when pressed against his own.

When the last of the bandage fell between them, he stepped back. The earlier amusement was missing from Torin's gaze. Instead, a fire that echoed Branan's own lingered in their depths. They stared into each other's eyes for a moment, a rapid exchange of unsaid words passing between them until Branan stepped back.

"There's soap there. If you need anything, just shout."

Torin nodded and his lips parted, but he didn't say anything.

Branan closed the door, resting his forehead against it. He knew he should step away, but he couldn't find the strength, and when he heard the gentle thud of Torin's pants hitting the ground, he bit back a groan and pushed himself away, unable to endure a moment more of the self-inflicted torture. He lingered outside the door until he heard the slosh of water and Torin's gentle sigh to assure himself he had no trouble getting in the tub and then busied himself in the kitchen, preparing them some lunch.

Lachlan sighed as he sank into the hot water. His side did not appreciate the movement but with some clenching of his jaw and gritting of his teeth, he was able to get into the tub without assistance. Of course, now it was clear he was still in no position to travel. He wondered if he might have cracked a rib along with the other injuries he sustained. Perhaps that's why the look in Branan's eyes stole his breath, but he knew better. This sounded too much like how Torin had once described the way he felt when he met his current girl, the one he was willing to follow around the market like a puppy. If he closed his eyes, he could see himself doing the same just to make Branan smile. To see his eyes sparkle with happiness, to see that dimple appear like it did when he truly smiled. His tawny brown skin with that dark hair and light green eyes were a deadly combination, one that made Lachlan weak in the knees.

He exhaled, pushing all the air out of his lungs in order to focus on the task at hand. He lowered into the water far enough he could get his hair wet and began to bathe himself. He would never admit it out loud, but the thought of using the same soap Branan did, of smelling just like him, sent a spark of pleasure shooting down his spine.

He washed as much of his sides, back, and other important bits as he could reach without angering his injury too badly. He took especially good care to cleanse that area as much as possible. The skin was no longer red and angry. It seemed as if the wound had mostly knitted itself back together, forming a dark pink jagged line. Perhaps if all went well today, they could take the stitches out tomorrow. When he was sufficiently clean, he leaned back and just let his muscles soak in the warmth of the water. Branan had chosen the perfect temperature, hot enough his skin was sure to be flushed when he stepped out and his muscles would be soothed, but not hot enough he couldn't tolerate it. He wasn't sure how long he lay relaxing in the water, only that it was long enough for his fingers to turn pruney and his stomach to rumble.

He sighed, not wanting to leave the still warm water, but knowing it was time. He gathered his strength and tried to lift himself out of the tub, but it was too much, his side screamed at him, and he felt the stitches pull tight against his skin at the base of his ribs.

"Fuck." He slid back down. He took a moment to rest before gathering a deep breath and making a second attempt. This time one of his arms slipped on the lip of the tub and he landed with a thud and splashed back into the water. His side burned and he glanced down, grateful not to see any fresh blood. Looked like he wouldn't be getting out of the tub on his own. *Lovely*.

A soft knock at the door interrupted his moment of self-loathing. "Are you okay, Torin?"

"Yeah. I just… um… I don't think I can get out on my own," he admitted.

There was a moment of hesitation before Branan's soft, "Oh," reached his ears. "Okay." The doorknob turned, and Lachlan put his hands over his lap, doing his best to cover up, but also knowing the impossibility of retaining his modesty with what was to come next. Branan studied him and the room for a minute, working out the puzzle that would be getting him out.

Luckily the large copper basin was against a wall in the center of the room and not off in a corner. Branan stepped behind the tub at Lachlan's head. "Okay. When you're ready, let me know, and I'll support you under your armpits and hoist you up."

Lachlan glanced back to see Branan politely staring at the ceiling when he spoke. It was sweet to see him doing his best not to make the situation more awkward than it already was.

"All right." Lachlan took a deep breath and leaned forward, as Branan's arms came up under his armpits, hauling him from the water. A small amount sloshed over the edge of the tub from the movement. When Lachlan got his feet underneath him, he hissed at the stinging in his side, but was happy to see only a small amount of blood around his stitches. When he looked up, he caught Branan's gaze dart away from him and land on the floor.

"Here." He handed him a towel. "Let me get the floor before you step out and fall." He quickly pulled a hand towel down and used it to mop up the water that had landed on the floor before pulling the plug from the tub to drain it. Lachlan draped the towel around his waist.

Branan studied the floor for a moment. "Okay. I'm going to put my arm out in case you need to steady yourself when stepping out."

Lachlan got one leg out and had just put his other foot on the floor when it slipped on a wet spot. He latched onto Branan's forearm to steady himself, bobbing slightly instead of taking the full-on tumble he was sure he would have had Branan not been there.

"Thanks. I appreciate it." He swallowed hard, realizing how close they were. How he could feel Branan's breath blowing cool air across his wet skin. How Branan's forearm flexed with strength. He let go quickly and made sure the towel was still secured around his waist.

"I'll leave you to it then." Branan's voice was a low, harsh whisper before he strode from the room as if he were being chased.

Lachlan smiled. Apparently, the moment had flustered both of them. He dragged his fingers across his shoulder, tracing the path Branan's breath had spread over his skin for a moment before pulling himself back from the edge. *Pull it together, man. You haven't even told him your real name.* Sometimes his subconscious could be a real bitch, but he was right.

He dragged the towel across his skin, gently patting over the stitches and all the other parts he could reach before stepping from the bathroom. When he attempted to bend over to pick up his pants, he quickly realized that was a no go. With pink stained cheeks, he exited the bathroom.

"I... um... couldn't reach my pants on the ground," he called out, scanning for Branan who he found in the small kitchen area, his back turned toward him.

Branan stilled whatever he was doing at the sink before giving a quick nod. "I'll get them, and I'll get something of my Da's you can wear. You're about his size."

Lachlan ambled back toward his room and stopped before the bed, unsure of how he'd be able to get into it on his own. As it was, he wasn't sure he could bend all the way down to put on pants and briefs. He felt Branan before he heard him, goosebumps covering his exposed flesh.

Branan cleared his throat. "Here are the clothes. I made us some lunch. We can eat out at the table or if you want to climb back into bed, I understand. Lachlan took a measure of his body. He felt tired, sure, more tired than just taking a bath should make him, but it would be nice to sit somewhere other than the bed.

"I went ahead and changed the sheets while you were in the bath, so it should be better for you."

"Thanks."

"Okay, I'll leave you to it."

"Bran."

"Yeah?"

"I… um… I think I might need some help getting dressed." He swallowed again. Damn, this was embarrassing as hell.

"Oh." It was the soft way he said it with the same slight hesitation as earlier. The last thing Lachlan wanted to do was make Branan uncomfortable.

"Look I understand if you don't—" he started.

"It's fine. No problem, really," Branan replied quickly, interrupting him. He'd already bent down before him, taking the pants into his hands and tucked the underwear inside in a way that made it so Lachlan could step into both at the same time. He kept his head down. "Alright first foot," he ordered, and Lachlan dutifully lifted his right foot. Branan slid the garments over his foot and tapped the other. Lachlan complied again, and Branan repeated the motion with his left. He gathered the sides of the garments and pulled them up with him as he stood until he reached the edge of the towel.

Branan's Adam's apple bobbed as he swallowed. "Can you get it from there?" he rasped, but he still wouldn't meet Lachlan's eyes.

Lachlan decided that as embarrassing as the moment was, Branan's proximity was more intoxicating than any ambrosia he'd ever had. It left his skin flushed with heat, and his body begging for him to close the little distance between them. He needed to get Branan to leave before he really embarrassed himself. "Yep. I'm good," he managed to get out, but his throat felt thick, and his voice was low even to his own ears. Branan's eyes met Lachlan's before he coughed to clear his throat. The copper in Branan's eyes was shining like a brand-new pendant, almost overtaking the green. A wolfy whimper left his mouth before he snapped his jaw shut and spun on his feet to flee the room.

Lachlan felt their attraction like a match just waiting for the right kindling to spark a fire, and he wasn't so sure he wanted to stop it anymore. In fact, he felt like perhaps he was ready to burn.

CHAPTER 9

CLOSING THE DOOR behind him more forcefully than necessary, Branan leaned against it to catch his breath. His heart hammered against his chest. Helping a man that beautiful put on his pants was an extreme form of torture. He had to keep reminding himself that Torin was injured and that was the only reason he wanted or needed his help while he was in that state of undress. But he'd be a fool to deny the fire he saw behind his eyes, how low his voice had been, thick with desire. It was only a matter of time and healing before one of them broke and acted on their smoldering chemistry.

Lunch, go check on lunch, Bran. He walked away from the door softly so as to not notify Torin of his lingering presence. He stirred the bowl of vegetable stew on the stove and tasted it once more adding just a dash more salt until it was perfect. Then he ladled it into two bowls and put them on the table. He also grabbed some bread and butter, placing it at the center of the table by some flowers he had picked earlier this morning.

Thankfully, when he'd stepped outside this morning to grab some vegetables from the garden, there was no gift from Whelan to greet him. He didn't know if he could bear another one. He had waited so long to talk to his dad about Whelan and his brothers and how they treated him when his dad wasn't around, but no longer. When his dad came home, he was going to tell him everything and let him deal with it as their alpha. Whelan had crossed the line last night. He wasn't sure how safe he felt being out the woods now, wasn't sure how far Whelan would go.

A chill ran down his spine, his gut only confirming his fears. He would need to be on high alert and avoid them at all costs. He hoped Kyna would understand. The opening of the door pulled him from his thoughts. Torin looked good all cleaned up. His black hair was short in comparison to Branan's, curling softly under his ears, appearing just long enough he could pull the tops of it back if he wanted. He had developed a nice scruff along his jaw and above his lip. Branan wondered briefly how frequently he shaved. Was it daily? Was it bothering him now?

"I should have told you there was a razor in the cabinet if you wanted to shave," he mumbled.

"I'm good. Unless you think I need to?" Torin grazed his fingertips across his jaw, and Branan had the urge to replace them with his own.

"No," he swallowed. "It's fine."

The left side of Torin's mouth curled up, causing Branan to flush. "Lunch is ready. Do you think you can sit?"

"It'd like to try. Besides, it'll be a good test for me, and as much as I'm grateful to you for rescuing me and taking care of me, I'm a little tired of being stuck in that room. A change of scenery will do me some good."

Branan hovered behind Torin while he took his seat in case he needed assistance. He made it with only a few choice words under his breath during a sharp exhale. Once he was seated, Branan pushed in the chair gently and stepped around to take his own seat. "I made some vegetable stew, and there's bread and butter." Branan gestured toward the food spread out on the table.

"Smells delicious." Torin picked up his spoon and took his first bite. His eyes closed after the spoon touched his lips, a small sigh escaping him when he swallowed. "Delicious is right. I wish I could cook like that."

"What can you cook?"

Lachlan fought the urge to frown. Should he answer as himself or Torin? He knew how to bake almost anything thanks to his time with their cook when he was younger, but didn't quite feel ready to share that piece of himself. If he was pretending to be like most other Seelie guards, they wouldn't enjoy baking (that he knew of). "Mostly just roasting wild game over an open fire." There, that was a safe, reasonable answer.

"Would you prefer if there's meat?" Branan asked shyly.

"Not when it tastes this good without. Besides, you don't need to hunt for me. I remember...." He trailed off when Branan's eyebrows drew down, matching his mouth.

"Ah, the rabbit," he interrupted, and Lachlan nodded in reply.

Branan stared at his soup. "Yeah. That may have been the first and last bite of meat I've had since I could communicate with animals. And even then, it was only because my wolf couldn't resist."

The spoon paused on its way to Lachlan's mouth. "That must be hard on you. To be able to communicate with animals in that way when your animal is a wolf."

"It's worse when I can sometimes feel what they feel."

Lachlan watched a shudder work its way down Branan's body and his face pale before he forced whatever memory he was reliving away. "But with vegetables I don't have to worry about that." Branan smiled widely, and bit down on a large chunk of carrot from the stew as one might a steak.

Lachlan chucked, understanding this was Branan's way to change the subject and make light of his situation.

They ate in silence for a few moments before making small talk. Branan asked about his favorite foods, color, and animal, to which Lachlan replied, "A stag, of course," and then would volley the same questions back to Branan. And thus, they spent their meal learning about each other. Branan learned Lachlan had an older sister and his parents had been dead for quite some time, and Branan shared about his mom leaving and growing up with his dad and the pack.

"Does the rest of your pack know I'm here?" Lachlan asked.

Branan shook his head. "I don't want Whelan to find out." His eyes drifted to the window, staring at a spot in the yard.

Lachlan followed his gaze, his eyes narrowed, and his fingers tightened around his spoon for a moment. "So, I should keep out of sight for the time being?"

Branan nodded, but his eyes were stuck on the window for a few moments. When he turned back toward Lachlan and met his gaze, Lachlan fought the urge to hunt this Whelan down. He was sure it was the larger brown wolf who had led the others in his attack. He didn't want to risk upsetting Branan further, but it was clear something had happened last night, something to do with Whelan that had left Branan creating that small grave at the base of that tree. He could only imagine how much that must have hurt Branan, knowing how he had reacted to killing the rabbit. Perhaps when he returned home, he would have a trusted guard or two do some inquiries on this Whelan fellow, after rewarding Branan for his help. He took in the cozy home. It was clear they didn't have a lot of money to spare, especially if they were growing their own food. He should inquire about how much the guard makes and see if they were due a raise in pay. It wasn't that Branan's surroundings looked awful, you could just tell everything here was well used and well-loved. Plus, it would be good for morale to raise the guard's pay if possible. He'd make some inquiries to the treasury to see what could be done. Of course, if he were to reward Branan it would come from him as Torin, not from the crowned prince.

"So, will you eventually join the Seelie guard like your dad?" Lachlan asked after Branan told him how his dad had taught him to fight with a sword in case he never shifted.

Branan shook his head, his brows pulling together in

the center. "I know he wants me to."

"But...?"

"But I don't think it's for me. Don't get me wrong. I believe in what they do. It's an honorable profession. It's just not for me."

"So, what do you want to do?" Lachlan picked up the bowl and tipped the rest of the warm liquid into his mouth.

"I'm not sure yet. Probably something with animals, maybe like a healer for them."

Lachlan could picture that. How easily he wanted to help him as a stag. He smiled softly. "I can see that."

"What about you?" Branan fidgeted under the weight of Lachlan's eyes.

He paused, conflicted about what to tell him. The real Torin was in the guard. Lachlan on the other hand had built his reputation as a spoiled prince. He knew his parents expected him to eventually lead the guard, to be his sister's right hand, but if his sister wasn't the Seelie queen, he didn't think he would choose fighting or politics at all.

"I hadn't really thought about it. My family has kind of had my future mapped out for me. No one has really asked me what I want."

"Oh, that's kind of sad. I'm sorry."

Lachlan shrugged. "Don't be. I've grown to accept it. Sometimes we don't get a choice in this world. Sometimes we just have to do the best we can with what we've been handed and make of it what we will."

"It's still kind of sad."

"Lunch was delicious. Thank you," Lachlan said, changing the subject to safer territory.

"You're welcome." Branan cleared the table and began

to wash the dishes. Lachlan wanted to help, but the exertion of the bath earlier had left him mostly drained. Still, he offered. "I can help with that."

"Sure, you can help by staying exactly where you are. It'll only take me a few minutes. Besides it's only a few more dishes than if I had been cooking for myself."

"If you're sure."

Branan shot Lachlan a scowl over his shoulder. "Don't even think about it."

The serious expression on Branan's soft face had Lachlan chuckling which made his side ache. "Oh shit, don't make me laugh." He smiled, reaching for his side.

"So, do you want to go back to the bedroom or…."

Lachlan looked around the room for options. There was a cozy looking armchair by the fireplace and a small bed in the living area. This must have been where Branan had been sleeping. Whose room was he staying in? Was it Branan's or his dad's?

"Do you think I could stay out here with you? I don't know if I'm quite ready to go back yet."

"Of course."

Branan's heart ached for Torin when he spoke about his family. While the others in the pack hadn't made things easy, his dad was his number one supporter and he knew no matter what he chose to do, his father would still be his biggest champion. It sounded like poor Torin didn't have anyone like that.

Branan finished the rest of the dishes, dried them, and tucked them neatly back into their cabinets. He wasn't sure where would be the best spot for Torin to feel the most comfortable. Probably the bed. He quickly went over and tidied the sheets and comforter. "You're welcome to lie down here. It will probably be more comfortable than sitting in a chair."

Torin swallowed and nodded, so Branan walked back over to help him up. He pulled Torin's chair out, before stepping around to face him. This time when Torin stood with a soft grunt and wince, he was mere inches from Branan's face. Branan took in his chocolate eyes with the small ring of copper around the pupil, just like his own. The copper in them flared as they stared at each other, close enough to share each other's breath. A lock of his hair had fallen in front of his face, and Branan lifted his hand, his fingers gently tracing Torin's forehead before tucking the stray lock behind his ear. He should have dropped it there and stepped back, but he didn't. Instead, he ran his palm down the side of Torin's face, feeling the scratchy stubble his fingers had ached to touch earlier. Torin's eyes closed and he pressed his cheek into Branan's hand. Before he lost his nerve, Branan leaned forward and pressed a kiss to Torin's temple.

He thought he could stop there, but found his lips tracing down the side of Torin's face that wasn't pressed into his palm. He was about to pull back, when Torin's fists tightened around his shirt and dragged him forward, turning his head slightly and closing the last bit of distance between their lips.

The kiss was exquisite. Soft and gentle, quickly turning into something more, something greedier, before lips opened, and Torin's tongue swept into his mouth pressing against his own. From there he was lost, swept away in the moment until Torin hissed and he realized his hands had moved from Torin's face and were sliding down his ribs toward his hips, pressing lightly against Torin's injured side.

"Oh shit. I'm sorry," he replied breathlessly, dropping his hands and taking a step back. He licked his lips, savoring the taste of Torin on them.

Torin watched the movement with a shuddering breath. He tried to take a step forward to recapture Branan's mouth, but his body had other ideas, and he swayed slightly, stumbling into the table. Branan was there in an instant. His hands gently steadied him by the shoulders. "Let's get you over to the bed." He helped Torin over to the bed and then moved in front of him to help him sit.

Torin took advantage of Branan's position and once again stole a kiss. It was meant to be a quick peck, but it didn't stay that way, and when they both pulled back, they were breathless.

Lachlan wasn't sure if his legs suddenly felt weak because his body was still healing or if it was an after effect from the kiss. He smiled at Branan who blushed in the most adorable way. He moved to sit down and Branan helped guide him.

"What were you doing before I woke up?" he asked, his eyes searching the room until they landed on a book that was propped open, each side draped over the arm of the armchair.

"Well, I started with some work in the garden, but then I was reading." Branan tucked his hair behind an ear and fidgeted, which only made Lachlan want to kiss him again, but he had to admit defeat. His side was now aching something fierce and his energy was quickly waning.

"Would you read to me?"

"Sure. Is there something you want to hear?" Branan walked over to a bookshelf.

"Whatever you were reading will be fine." Lachlan lowered himself onto the bed and inhaled deeply, letting Branan's earthy scent surround him. He pressed his nose into the pillow.

"Are you smelling my sheets?" Branan's voice interrupted him.

"What?! No!" He argued, turning his head to him. The brightness of Branan's smile almost knocked the breath out of him.

"You totally were. You were smelling my pillow," he teased.

"I did no such thing," he denied again, but couldn't help that his smile betrayed him.

Branan chuckled lightly, a sound that sparked joy in Lachlan's chest. "Are you sure you want me to read whatever I was reading. I'm about halfway through already. I could start at the beginning," Branan suggested.

"Just give me a brief synopsis of what's happened so far."

So Branan told him about the maiden who had been captured and the sword fights that had already been fought, the beasts the main character had already battled just to rescue his one true love. And then he began to read. His voice was like smooth velvet, and after a while Lachlan found it hard to keep his eyes open. He closed them, allowing himself to get lost in the story, lost in Branan's scent on the sheets, and lost in Branan's voice.

When he woke, the sky was dark and Branan was nowhere to be seen. He took a few minutes to tune into his stag and listen. There he was. He could hear Branan's voice speaking with someone outside, someone female.

CHAPTER 10

A SOFT KNOCK had pulled Branan from where he had dozed off in the armchair. Luckily, he still held the book and the place where he left off. Torin had fallen asleep a few hours ago and continued to slumber deeply. He put his book back over the arm of the chair and stood up. He couldn't invite anyone in, not with Torin sleeping out here in the open. He peeked out the window, spotting Kyna before she could see him. Perhaps if he pretended he was just coming home from a run, she wouldn't expect to come inside. He opened a back window and slid out quietly, closing it behind him, then he shifted and darted off into the woods. He circled around quickly to an area a safe distance away, and began his staged approach to the house. When he reached the clearing, he spotted her and shifted back.

"Kyna!" he called, waving at her.

"Oh, Branan! I was hoping you would stop by for dinner, but when you didn't, I just wanted to check on you and make sure everything was okay."

"Oh yeah. Everything's fine. I guess I went out for a run and just lost track of time," he replied with a sheepish shrug.

"Oh, that's okay dear. I brought it to you since I made extra." She held out a basket.

"Wow. Thanks, Kyna."

"How's your arm?" she gestured toward the arm that reached for the basket.

"My arm?"

"Yeah, the one you injured."

"Oh, all fine now. Better than new thanks to you." Branan's stomach coiled. He wasn't made out for all this deception. He'd already forgotten how he had cut himself to get the salve for Torin.

"Oh good. Well, I'll just leave you to it," she said, but she didn't move to leave.

Branan stood there for a moment, studying her. He held the basket, while she wrung her hands.

"I just want you to know that you can come to me if you need anything."

"I know." And he did. She always made that clear, but he wasn't sure why she was saying it now. Did she know about Torin?

"I just. I overheard the boys talking and...."

He froze.

"I know they haven't always been the kindest to you no matter how hard I try, but I don't want you to think I'd take their side just because they're my sons. I'm not blind to their faults." She smiled softly, encouragingly.

"I appreciate that, Kyna." He nodded.

She paused for a moment longer as if she had more to say, but then changed her mind. "Well, have a good night, and don't be a stranger."

She waved before turning and walking back toward her cabin.

Branan set the basket on the ground. "Kyna, wait!" He ran toward her and gave her a hug, squeezing her tightly. "Thank you. For dinner. For everything."

When he released her. She nodded and wiped under her now watery eyes.

Then he jogged back toward home and plucked the basket off the ground before opening the door and returning inside.

"Friend of yours?" Torin's voice halted him the moment after he closed the door. His eyes were narrowed on Branan.

"Yes, that was Kyna. She's in my pack, sort of like a surrogate mother. She brought dinner."

The frown melted off of Torin's face, replaced with what appeared to be relief. "Oh."

"Hungry?"

Torin's stomach did the answering for him, and Branan chuckled. "I'll set the table and then help you over."

Torin watched him as he placed the plates on the table and unpacked the food from the basket. It looked like quite the feast and smelled tasty.

When Branan was finished he walked back over to Torin and helped him stand, but it didn't quite have the same fire as earlier and neither of them made a move to kiss the other regardless if they thought about it.

"She made you steak?"

"Well, obviously you can eat that." It was hard to explain to someone how he didn't like to correct others, how he didn't want to discount what they had done for him. In the past if she made meat, he had picked at it rather than create a scene and refuse to eat it. He knew the boys thinking he was a picky eater was better than a vegetarian wolf.

Branan set the steak on Torin's plate along with a large helping of mashed potatoes. "Salad?" he asked.

Torin shook his head. He arched an eyebrow accusatorily toward Branan. He wasn't going to let it drop.

Branan plated himself a large portion of salad and potatoes. "As much as I don't care for killing animals, I also don't like to upset those I love by criticizing the food they make me."

"But don't you think she'd want to know? I'm sure she'd feel awful and make sure in the future to always keep you in mind."

"But see, that's the point. I don't want her to feel awful. It's a choice I made for myself, and I don't expect others to make the same choice or accommodate me in that way. They don't experience things the same way I do."

Torin opened his mouth to argue, but Branan put up a hand. "It's fine. I appreciate your concern, but it's unwarranted. She was kind enough to make us a meal, so we will be kind enough to eat it in return."

Lachlan sighed. He knew if this Kyna person was the

surrogate mother Branan claimed her to be, she would want to make him happy and that would include preparing him a meal he could fully eat and enjoy, but he could also see there was no point in arguing this, so he changed the conversation, asking about the different dishes Branan knew how to make. And for someone who didn't care to eat meat, he knew a lot of ways to make it for his father. Something Lachlan found adorable. He showed the ones he cared about how much he loved them in the acts he performed for them, it especially showed how much he loved his father.

They chatted all through the meal about this and that, deepening their connection from earlier. Lachlan was sure when he had to leave Branan, which he would eventually, that he would be leaving a piece of himself behind. It was nice to just be able to be himself—well as much of himself as he could with only a fake name. Back at the palace there were so many expectations and rules regarding etiquette. There were the politics of court and statements steeped in pretense. It grew wearisome over time.

When they had both finished their meal, Lachlan insisted on helping Branan with the dishes. He was starting to feel better. The earlier bath had done wonders for his demeanor. Of course, Branan only let him do the rinsing and part of the drying, but it was something. It was nice to feel like he was contributing. It also gave him an excuse to stand shoulder to shoulder with Branan, sometimes playfully knocking into his side or just soaking up his warmth. Branan's responding chuckle sent warmth down his spine. His smile grew when Branan playfully returned a shove with his shoulder. When they finished, Lachlan playfully flicked his wet fingertips toward Branan, enjoying the way Branan's eyes and mouth widened in mock disbelief. In retaliation, Branan snatched the dishtowel off the counter and wound it up before whipping it out toward Lachlan. Lachlan blocked it with a laugh and tried to grab it, but Branan pulled it behind his back. He stepped closer to Branan and reached for the rag. He could feel Branan's sharp intake of air as he pressed his chest closer. This time when he caught the dishtowel, he easily tugged it from Branan's grasp. Branan's breath grew heavier in his ear as he pulled back.

"I win!" he said with a smirk.

Branan's expanded pupils darted toward Lachlan's lips as warmth blossomed in Lachlan's chest. They drank each other in as Lachlan reached the towel up toward Branan's face and gently wiped away any stray droplets of water. Branan closed his eyes when Lachlan's fingers lingered in the spot next to his mouth.

Lachlan could almost imagine them growing old together just like this. Both of them with gray hair doing something so domestic that then might lead to something else, something more. He stepped back, letting the towel and his hand drop from Branan's face and scolded himself. A future with Branan wasn't possible. He had too many obligations and responsibilities waiting for him back at the palace. He could only settle for enjoying what this was for as long as he stayed here.

Branan sensed the shift in the air before he opened his eyes. He had been waiting to see what Torin would do, and his heart shrank when Torin stepped back. Back on Torin's face was the contemplative frown from earlier, but Branan decided not to mess with it. Instead, he built a small fire in the fireplace and offered to read to him once again. This time he helped Torin into the armchair and when he went to get another chair from the kitchen, Torin grabbed his hand.

Torin didn't say anything, but his eyes spoke volumes, so without dropping his hand, Branan took a spot on the floor, leaning his back against the chair between Torin's legs. Torin sighed and gave his hand a quick squeeze before releasing it and handing Branan the book.

Branan picked up where they had left off, this time Torin stayed awake the whole time. Eventually Torin's hands drifted to Branan's head, running his fingers between the strands of his hair and scratching his scalp lightly. Branan stammered on a word, but Torin's fingers continued to play with his hair.

While Branan read, Lachlan's heart and mind battled. He knew he was playing with fire, but he grew tired of fighting what he felt for Branan, and finally settled on a decision. It didn't matter that Lachlan might be breaking his own heart when he left, he was willing to accept that consequence for a taste of what could be.

Branan's hair was soft as silk as he ran his fingers

through it. The way Branan stumbled on the word he was reading when Lachlan first touched his hair, brought a smile to Lachlan's face that hadn't left. He leaned forward slightly, causing himself a twinge of discomfort, but it was worth it when his fingers pressed into Branan's neck, and Branan sighed. He massaged the muscles there and down to his shoulders, savoring the feel of Branan's skin while Branan continued to read, his voice growing huskier by the word.

Branan chucked the book aside and turned toward him. He climbed up, pressing his hands on the tops of Lachlan's thighs before leaning forward and ensnaring his mouth with a heated kiss.

"How do you do it? How do you drive me so crazy?" Lachlan asked in between the kisses Branan showered down his neck and jaw before coming back to claim his mouth. The questions, of course, were rhetorical because he didn't give Lachlan the breath to answer them. He stole them with his kisses that turned Lachlan's insides into lava. He'd never felt such heat with anyone else before.

He wasn't sure how long the two of them spent kissing and exploring, but eventually Branan pulled away and rested his forehead against Lachlan's, both of their chests heaving to catch a breath, both of their eyes a bright copper. The fire had long since died away, only the smoldering embers remained. "We should probably get some rest. I can help you back to your bed," Branan offered.

Lachlan thought for a moment. He didn't really want to return to that bed. He didn't want to be alone. "Could I um, sleep out here with you?"

Branan's eyes widened slightly.

"Just sleep. I'd like to hold you." Lachlan felt like an idiot admitting it, but the blush that crept up Branan's neck was worth it.

"I'd like that," Branan whispered.

This time Lachlan was able to stand with minimal difficulty, and hand in hand they walked back to Branan's bed. Together they squished onto the bed with Lachlan on his good side curled up behind Branan, his arms wrapped around him. It was the best night of Lachlan's life.

A sharp pain in his back woke him in the middle of the night. It felt as if someone had stabbed him with a knife. He jolted up in bed, panting as if he had been running for hours. He clumsily ran his hand over where the pain originated in his back, fully expecting to feel a knife there, but there was nothing. He twisted his head back and forth, attempting to peer over his back, but nothing seemed out of sorts. Branan softly snored next to him. Grateful he hadn't woken Branan and confused why his back still ached from the phantom wound, he squeezed himself out of bed, managing to stand on his own with only some discomfort. He stumbled toward the bathroom but had to pause and grip a chair for support when he passed by. A wave of dizziness passed over him, leaving his body tingling from head to toe. He took a few deep breaths, unsure what was happening. There was a buzzing sensation under his skin that grew stronger for a few moments before fading away. Eventually he made it to the bathroom and relieved himself. He washed his hands, and when he glanced at his reflection in the mirror, he stumbled backward, ice running through his veins.

"No! No, no, no, no!" he whispered, shaking his head

as if his own denial would render it true. His heart took off, running away and leaving him behind. He stepped cautiously forward. He rubbed his eyes. He rubbed the mirror, but no, it was no trick of the light. His once chocolate brown eyes were now pale lavender. His heart plummeted to his feet, and he bent forward to brace himself against the sink.

"Orla," he whispered, as the tears began to flow. There was only one reason he would ever wake with royal-colored eyes. His sister was dead, and the magic had chosen him. He was now the Seelie king.

CHAPTER II

THE MINUTE BRANAN stirred he felt something was off. He'd never slept so hard in all his years, and he knew it was due to the comfort of the gorgeous Fae he was falling in love with. Already fallen in love with, if he were to be honest with himself. He knew it was fast, but there was something about someone seeing you when you were the most vulnerable as Torin had those times in his stag form, which built a strong connection. To be honest, he wasn't sure anyone knew him as well as Torin did. He missed having a connection with someone, and the fact that Torin felt more like pack than his own spoke volumes. In his heart he knew he could never be the alpha his father wanted him to be.

He ran his hand where it should have connected with Torin and his fingertips came up empty. That's what felt off. His eyes flew open, and he stared at the empty side of the bed. He shouldn't have left the bed. He still wasn't fully healed. "Maybe he's in the bathroom," he mumbled, even though a sharp tug in his gut told him his words were nothing but a comforting lie.

"Torin!" He called as he got out of bed and walked to the bathroom only to find it empty. His stomach dropped sharply. "Torin!" He called louder this time, frantically moving toward the kitchen. The emptiness of the house echoed in his heart. Foolish as he was, he still went outside and called Torin's name only to have the sounds of the forest answer him back.

Torin was gone.

His feet dragged as he made his way back into the house and dropped into a chair. His head rested in his hands and his eyes burned. His elbow scraped against something that shouldn't be there—a piece of paper.

Branan rubbed his eyes before he plucked the paper up, holding it with trembling fingers. He paused at the elegantly written script with a sense of dread, knowing the words held the potential to cut him further.

My dearest Branan,

I apologize for my sudden departure. If given the chance I would stay with you for as long as possible, but alas we are nothing but puppets at the whims of fate, and she has dealt me a cruel hand. I must return home, and I fear that we cannot see each other again for reasons I cannot say.

I will cherish our time together more than you'll know. They will give me strength during the darkest nights when I fear I'll need them the most. I have not been fully honest with you and for that I have dearly paid the price and will continue to do so. I wish for you to find the happiness and freedom to be yourself.

I truly owe you a life debt, one I intend to honor. Please know that if things were different...I would spend a thousand lifetimes with you, learning everything there was to know about you, and growing old with you...but they are not. And for that I'm truly sorry. I'll have your horse returned.

Yours always and forevermore

Great, so not only did Torin leave, but he also stole my horse like a thief in the night, Branan thought, also noting how Torin didn't sign his name. His heart lay on the floor in shreds. He knew that words were nothing but pretty empty vessels without actions to back them, and obviously Torin didn't intend to take any action with his words. A second thought struck his chest like a spear, ripping a fresh wave of pain. Not only was Torin gone, but so was his stag friend. He'd never felt so alone. He threw open the front door, letting the note flutter to the floor as he shifted. He howled out his pain, too lost to his emotions to care if the rest of the pack heard him, and ran to the woods as if he could escape his own heartbreak.

Lachlan raced the horse back to the palace, his jaw clenched against the pain from his side. It was nothing compared to the pain in his heart. He would survive it, and he needed to get back to the palace as fast as possible to find out what happened. He would have the horse returned to Branan by one of his men. It was still dark, and the only light he saw was from the baker's shop as he rode through town. When he approached the palace, the guard stepped forward.

"It is I, Lachlan," he announced. He didn't want the guard to see his eyes. He needed Torin. He needed some-one he could trust to help him decide the best way to let the people know the truth. He knew he was the only one right now with that piece of knowledge.

"Prince! It's good to see you. We weren't sure what to think when you disappeared," the guard said. Lachlan snorted. The censure in the guard's voice was enough to make him bite his tongue. He didn't owe anyone an expla-nation, but it was plain that they already thought the worst of him, that he had run off and shirked his duties, not that he had been mortally injured and on the brink of death.

The guard let him pass and he handed the horse off to the stable boy, keeping his head down so no one could see his eyes. He sprinted to his room and slammed the door be-hind him. He peeled away the bandages around his wound to find the long ride hadn't injured him further. His side was definitely sore from the hard ride back, but it only felt similar to when he had broken a rib during a sparring session last year. He debated seeing a palace healer, but he wasn't sure if anyone in the palace knew about his sister, and he didn't want to risk revealing his eyes to anyone in case news hadn't reached them yet.

More than anything, he wanted to grieve, but he also didn't have the facts. The council members she'd left in charge would have some of them, but he wasn't quite ready to face his new reality. They would look to him for answers, for what actions to take, and he didn't have the slightest clue. He dragged his hand across his face as he debated what should be his next steps.

He needed to know how it happened, how King Ragnall had ended her life. His heart lurched as he thought about waiting for his soldiers to return to get those answers. Would any of them return? He drew in a sharp breath; he didn't know what he would do if Torin had also been taken from him. He'd have no one here to trust. He needed some sort of plan on how to handle this the best. Alfie was gone, Torin was gone, his sister was gone, and he needed to take control of the situation, to show a strong front before some of the court elders tried to steamroll him as he'd seen them do to Orla.

Sweet Orla. His breath shuddered, his eyes releasing a few tears with her name. He would carry the guilt of her death for the rest of his life. If only he had been here to lead the troops, she wouldn't have done something so stupid as to jeopardize her own life. He shook off the grief for the time being, shoving it down and locking it inside a trunk inside himself. He flipped through his mental lists of the nobles, who may be the most loyal and valuable. Young Grady flickered in his thoughts. Grady and Lachlan had played together as children until his father had passed and his mother took him away from court, preferring the solitude of her hometown and the support of her family. He quickly worded a letter to Grady asking him to come to court as soon as possible. If he had grown up to be an ounce of the man his father was, he'd be the perfect fit and he was of age to accept his father's title if he wanted. He only hoped Grady would accept. Having a Skepseis, even if it was only Grady's lesser ability, would still be priceless at this time.

He rang for a servant and opened the door a crack, explaining he needed the letter delivered with the utmost haste. He added a few extra coins as incentive which the servant excitedly took and darted off. He knew he wouldn't sleep if he tried, so he kept thinking of who would be best to have on his side until the sun rose and with it, the palace stirred to life. Word had obviously spread of his return when a knock at the door asked him if he would like breakfast here or down in the dining hall. He requested a small tray be brought up, again speaking through a crack in the door. When the servant came to deliver his tray, he stepped into the bathroom as to not yet be seen. He knew if he waited too long one of the council members would find him. He was glad his sister had already dismissed Eamon, but he could see Eamon using his sister's death as a way to worm himself back in, and there were others who thought just like him that Lachlan would need to weed out.

He ate, bathed, and dressed himself as best as he could.

He'd decided to meet his problem when there was a sharp rap at his door. He opened it a crack. "Sire," a voice panted. It was the same servant he had sent to deliver the letter hours earlier. "I delivered the...."

"Oh, just let me through. If he sent the note, he obviously wants to see me." Grady elbowed his way through, shoving the door open. Lachlan thanked the servant with his head bowed and closed the door behind Grady.

"Now, what was so damn important to interrupt my sleep at some gods awful hour of the morning?" Grady asked.

Lachlan tilted his head up and looked Grady in the eyes.

"Shit," Grady gasped, leaning a hand onto the chair.

"Sounds about right." Lachlan smiled weekly at his old friend.

"I'm so, so—" he started to apologize, to give him his condolences, but Lachlan held up a hand.

"I know. I can't right now."

"Right, do you know...."

Lachlan shook his head sharply.

"All right so, do you have a plan?"

"I was kind of hoping you would help with that. I know you don't care to use your Skepseis ability, but I could really use it, and have someone I trust by my side right now."

"You have it, but I'm not sure how much help it'll do. And you have me for as long as you need, Lachlan."

Grady reached his hand out and Lachlan shook it, swallowing past the lump in his throat. "That's all I ask. Can you still sense if someone is lying?" Lachlan smiled knowing that since this was Grady's lesser ability, others would not know of it by his eye color. It was something they'd kept quiet when they were children, loving to test his ability with games of truths and lies. As far as Lachlan knew only his and Grady's family knew about it.

"You mean the sickening sweet taste in the back of my mouth whenever someone lies? It's a real bitch when I'm out at the market trying to get a good deal," Grady joked.

Lachlan smiled. "I'll take that as a yes. Do many know about your ability?"

Grady shook his head. "Same as when we were younger. Dad said it was best to keep it a secret."

"Your dad was a wise man. I could use his council now."

"He would know better than I what to do, but I'll do my best to fill his shoes until you no longer require me."

"Are you sure I'm not keeping you from anything?"

Grady's voice took on a note of concern. "Nothing that is more important than this."

It wasn't quite the answer Lachlan hoped for, but he'd take it.

"Good. First, we need to know what happened to Orla." He filled in Grady on his attack by the wolves and being helped by the son of a soldier. If Lachlan's omission of the importance of who helped him was felt by Grady, Grady didn't let on. Which reminded him, he needed someone to bring Branan's horse back, but he wasn't sure who he could trust with the task until he knew which of the soldiers had survived and would return. When it was time, he left his room, ready to face whatever may come with at least one true friend by his side.

Branan returned from his run, exhausted both physically and emotionally. He felt lost. His first love and only friend's departure had left a huge hole in his heart. He rubbed at the ache in his chest while he stepped in the bath, hoping the cold water would wash away everything. He had avoided the room Torin had stayed in, knowing his scent would be all over it, but he'd need to tidy up in case his father returned. It would probably be best for him to explain the situation to his dad before Whelan could twist it into something it was not.

He stood, finished with his bath when the breath was knocked out of him. He fell to his knees in the draining water. Pain coursed through every fiber of his being, along with emptiness, the absence of something he had felt his entire life. The alpha bond had been severed. He reeled back, dizziness causing his head to swim. "No, no, no, no," he muttered repeatedly as if his denial would make it true. Gooseflesh covered his skin and his wolf whimpered. "Da," he whispered as his frame shook with barely restrained sobs.

He gritted his teeth through the pain, managing to stand on shaking knees. He stepped out of the tub, taking a few deep breaths before getting his body to cooperate. His stomach lurched as he stepped forward, and his wet feet slipped against the floor causing him to crash to his knees. It should have hurt, but the loss of his dad overshadowed everything. A shudder worked its way down his spine as he knelt on all fours. His wolf wanted to take over, to take him away from the overwhelming emotions, but if he shifted inside, he'd be trapped. He panted as he used all his strength to crawl to the door and open it before his wolf took over.

The resounding howl he released into the air rattled the trees, sending a flock of birds into the sky. This time it echoed back to him by Shaw's boys along with a woman's wail forming a mournful chorus.

Torin was gone.

His dad was gone.

He was truly alone.

It was a day later when Lachlan learned the truth of what had happened to Orla. The day before he had faced the council with his head held high, a strength he didn't know he had steeled in his veins. Having Grady by his side had helped tremendously. They'd come up with a code for him to relay to Lachlan when one of the council members was lying. He gathered the council, all of the palace workers, and remaining soldiers in one place when he revealed the truth to them. He gave a grand speech, relaying to them how important it was to keep this information within the walls of the palace until they knew the truth of what happened and how. Only then should it be relayed to the people. He made them all swear a blood oath to not reveal the truth until he did. Then he went to work, planning what was to be done, how they would honor his sister and transition to his coronation. The council told him how Orla had led the troops when he didn't return from his hunt, and he told them a version of the truth, that he was attacked by a wolf during his hunt and gravely injured, unable to return until he had healed. He lifted the side of his shirt to show the jagged healed scar from where the wolf had torn into his side. He had decided not to go to a healer to finish the healing and instead let the physical pain take away from his emotional pain. As it was, his side only felt slightly sore now. He had to make sure to eliminate rumors that he had shirked his duties by drinking in a tavern somewhere or running away from his responsibilities. And judging by the grimaces and furrowed brows of the council, they believed him. Now more than ever, his people needed to be able to trust him and depend upon him.

The following morning one of the scouts he'd sent returned with word that some of the soldiers were returning, but their numbers were greatly diminished. "Did you see Torin amongst them?" he asked, but the scout shook his head.

"You told me to return to you once I laid my eyes on them, sire. They were still too far away for me to make out any individuals, but if you'd like I can return and see if I can spot him."

"No, I'm sure we'll find out soon enough."

And he was right. He waited out in the courtyard when he felt the stillness in the air, the sort of hush that followed the men through the city to his door. He knew everyone would know the truth without seeing him now. The small bit of hope he held in his chest for his dearest friend unfurled its wings and took flight.

Lachlan's relief came as a whooshing sigh upon seeing

a familiar mop of light brown hair and amber eyes, though they were the saddest he had ever seen. His armor was splattered with blood, but that didn't stop Lachlan from rushing toward his friend and pulling him into his arms the minute he dismounted. "I cannot say how glad I am to see you."

Torin pulled back, his red rimmed eyes spilling with tears. "It should've been me," he whispered. "It should've been me."

"Hush now," Lachlan wrapped his arm around his shoulder and pulled him inside. "Let's get you cleaned up, and then we can talk. I need a full report." Torin nodded. Lachlan turned to the closest servant. "Please escort Torin to my quarters. Bring him a fresh change of clothes and let no one disturb him."

She nodded in reply. "Come with me now, sir. I've got you." She took his arm and gently guided him inside.

Lachlan turned to the rest of the troops. His scout was correct. Their numbers were greatly diminished, close to a hundred deaths. The supply carts were now piled high with bodies. If King Ragnall were to attack him now, he honestly couldn't say if they would survive. He hoped his men took just as many Unseelie lives with them. He raked his gaze across the remaining warriors, meeting each one's eyes. "I know how bravely you fought for my sister. I know I was not there when you needed me, and for that I hope you can forgive me. For your bravery and loyalty, you will be rewarded handsomely. Now take some time and go home to your families. Be with your loved ones and let us pray to the gods for the families who will not see their loved ones returned this day. May we come together through our shared grief and use it to drive us forward."

The soldier all took a knee as two of the men stepped away from the crowd. Lachlan had been so busy looking at the living, actively avoiding the reminders of death to notice her. Between the two of them they held a roughly constructed stretcher, and on top lay Orla. She looked as if she were sleeping though her chest didn't rise and fall with breath. Someone had taken care to clean her body and she was surrounded by brightly colored flowers, a tribute to their Seelie queen. His eyes and throat burned, as he stumbled down the steps toward her. He knelt in front of her for a few minutes before rising. "Rest now, my sweet sister. Your fight is over. May your soul be at peace." He rubbed the backs of his fingers against her cheek.

When he was able to pull his gaze away, he took a steadying breath. "Thank you for bringing her home. Please take her to the healer's room for now."

"It was our honor," both men replied. One of them sniffled loudly.

Lachlan blinked rapidly, forcing the tears back, watching as the men carried the last of his family away. He couldn't fall apart now. There was too much to do, and he was the one in charge.

A hand clamped on his shoulder. "You, okay?" Grady asked, appearing at his side.

"I will be."

Grady winced slightly, and Lachlan was glad he didn't call him out on the lie. Instead, Grady shifted the conversation to matters at hand. Others might have mistaken it as coldness, but Lachlan saw it as a mercy, as if Grady knew he needed something to focus on.

"That was a good speech. I think you might just have it in you to lead them."

"I must if we are to weather this storm."

"You're a good man, Lachlan, and as such you will be a great king. The magic of our land chose you for a reason. I have faith in you, even if you don't have it in yourself."

"Thank you, friend. Now I must meet with Torin and learn what happened. When we finish, I'll send for you, and we'll plan our next move."

Grady dipped his head in acknowledgement.

Lachlan stalled outside the door to his quarters. His heart would never be ready to hear what happened to his sister, but he knew he must face it. He must know everything if he was to protect his people. When he finally entered, he found Torin sitting in the tub alone.

"Where is the maid I sent to help you?"

"I dismissed her. I could not bear for anyone else to witness my shame," he murmured, his head bowed and gaze focused on the water.

Lachlan walked over to his friend and thrust a bar of soap at him. "Wallowing in self-loathing will do neither of us any good."

"How can I not? When I failed you and our people so utterly?" Torin's gaze finally tore from the water and connected with Lachlan's.

Lachlan sighed. "If anyone is to be blamed for this failure, it is me. I was the one who wasn't there when Orla needed me. If I had been there, she wouldn't have gone in my stead." He picked up a bottle of shampoo and held it to Torin with a glare.

Torin begrudgingly accepted the bottle. "I would never

blame you," he growled as he began washing the mud and blood from his hair.

Lachlan's heart lifted a little. "Then you know that I feel the same about you. I have no doubt that you did the very best you could, Torin. None of this is your fault, but I need to know what happened, so we can plan what needs to happen next."

Torin nodded, sinking his head back into the water, giving it a rinse before rising again. "When you didn't return, I tried to convince Orla to stall. I knew you had a reason for not being there, that something must've happened to keep you from your duty, but she wouldn't hear any of it. She was determined to get Alfie. I think not knowing how he was being treated at the Unseelie palace was getting to her. We didn't know if he was merely being held hostage or if he was being tortured. She couldn't bear the thought of him being in pain because of her."

"Love made her act rashly."

"Yes, but she did what was right in her heart."

"Maybe for her, but not certainly what was right for our people," Lachlan growled, his fingers snagging on a tangle a little too roughly.

Torin hissed a breath. "I think I'll take it from here." He moved away from Lachlan's fingers and ducked under the water to rinse again. This time he took the bar of soap and started scrubbing the rest of his body.

Lachlan stared at the wall and took a deep breath. If Orla hadn't acted so foolishly, letting her heart lead instead of her head, she would still be here.

"Obviously, Ragnall was expecting us, but I don't think he was expecting Orla to be with us. He had Alfie dangling from one of his towers in a metal cage. Even from a distance we could see the bruising and dried blood on his chest." Torin swallowed, his hands stilling. "She fought hard, we all did, and we thought the tide was turning. Ragnall called a halt, offering to return Alfie in exchange for a parle with Orla. We were all shocked, but who was going to say no to an offer like that? We should've known. *I* should've known. It was too good to be true." The tears started to fall again, mingling with the water dripping from his bath.

Lachlan's stomach rolled, but he shoved down the emotion, knowing he needed to hear what happened. His sister was powerful. He had only a fraction of that power and if he was going to keep his people and land, he needed to know how she was taken down.

"He pulled the cage up and his soldiers retreated and regrouped in front of the castle. After some time, Alfie appeared to stumble out of the castle. He had a shirt on then, but we didn't pay it any mind. We kept on high alert until he made his way to Orla. When he was within our troops she ran to him, wrapping her arms around him. None of us saw the blade until it was buried in her back. She fell back, and I rushed forward to catch her. 'Stop him!' I yelled at the troops, but he smiled before shifting into the likeness of one of our own troops. The soldiers couldn't tell friend from foe, and they got away."

"A changeling?" Lachlan gasped. Torin nodded. Orla and the council had no clue that Ragnall had a changeling at his disposal. Changelings could shift into anything or anyone living. There hadn't been word of one in centuries, many thought the power must have ended with a family line, but they were wrong. How long had Ragnall kept that changeling secret?

Torin sniffled and stared at his hands. "I tried to stop the bleeding. I removed the knife and called for a healer, but the blade was laced with poison. I was too late." He sobbed silently for a few moments before continuing. "She held my eyes and made me swear to protect you. I think she knew the magic would choose you somehow."

This time Lachlan joined Torin in his sobs. His chest felt like someone had punched him. Of course, Orla's last thoughts were about him. He hadn't deserved her.

Once Torin got his sobs under control, he continued. "Ragnall's laughter filled the air after she left us, sharp and odious. He told us to run home and tell whoever would replace her to let this be a lesson to them and to not mess with what was his."

"I wanted to fight then, but I knew it would've been a massacre. We were outnumbered, having already lost so many, so we took time to gather our dead and I lead the troops back here."

"We will have a service tomorrow for the fallen soldiers, and the day after for our queen." Lachlan' smiled sadly, knowing he had to take charge. "We'll give the people time to heal before we decide what is to be done, unless Ragnall takes it upon himself to attack us."

"I'll have the most elite of the remaining soldiers ready to guard the palace just in case," Torin agreed.

"Thank you, friend, and thank you for doing what you could for her. You fought your very best and I will forever be grateful that at least one of you returned home to me. I'll let you finish and start making arrangements." Lachlan squeezed Torin's shoulder, Torin's hand coming up to rest on top of his and giving him a squeeze in return.

He stepped out of the room and snuck across the hall to his sister's quarters. It was only there, surrounded by all of her favorite things that he allowed himself to truly grieve for her. He cried until he didn't think there were tears left.

After he pulled himself back together, he summoned Grady and Torin to his study.

"Torin, this is Lord Grady," Lachlan offered as an introduction.

Torin bowed his head in greeting. "I remember your father well. He was a great man."

After a moment of scrutiny, Grady nodded. "Just Grady is fine. No need for this Lord business. Any friend of Lachlan's is a friend of mine, and thank you for your kind words about my father. I'm glad I can be here to serve Lachlan in his time of need."

"I remember the two of you were thick as thieves when your father was here. Didn't you help him leave frogs in the soldiers' barracks one night?"

The memory brought a smile to all three of their faces, a welcome reprieve from the grief that threatened to consume Lachlan. "I brought Grady here because he'll help us figure out which members of the council will be the best to keep and which I need to keep an eye out for."

"A smart choice," Torin said, most likely remembering exactly what ability Grady's father had.

Lachlan didn't feel that it was his place to disclose that information to Torin. Of course, he wouldn't keep it from him if he asked, but he didn't see Torin asking. Torin trusted him and that was enough. Now, if Grady wanted to disclose that information that was up to him.

"I'll need to notify the council of my intent to hold service for the fallen soldiers tomorrow. Torin, can you gather up a list of who we lost? We'll need to notify next of kin and spread word about the service across the land. Grady, if you will send for all available messengers, I'll start penning the missives. I'd also like to offer the families of the fallen soldiers a penance to make up for their loss of income, and the soldiers who fought and survived deserve a bonus."

Grady nodded in agreement, and Torin smiled softly at his thoughtfulness. "I'm sure they will appreciate that."

"Good. I will meet with the exchequer to see what we have available."

With the tasks assigned, the men set to work. After meeting with the exchequer, the council caught wind of what Lachlan intended to do and made their opinions known both positive and negative, but Lachlan didn't budge. He made it clear that to keep the troops and to send respect to the fallen this is what must be done, and if they needed to tighten some belts around the palace to make it happen, so be it.

Eventually, Torin returned with a list of the fallen soldiers. His mind had been too busy with tasks and grief, but now that he was staring at a list of names, he remembered what Branan had said about his dad being a member of his guard. Again, guilt churned within him. He should have been with them. He should've known each of these men personally. He made a silent vow to do better in the future.

"Torin, can you tell me if any of these men were wolf shifters?" Lachlan coughed, his voice catching, and his hand ran to where his healed wound still ached on his side. He had yet to tell Torin what kept him from his responsibilities, but he would.

Torin lifted one of his eyebrows. "We had several wolf shifters. Two lone wolves and two who were packmates." He scanned the list and swore softly, pointing to two names on the list. "These two were our best of the shifters—the packmates. They lived in the woods less than a day's travel from here. I saw one of them go down early on in the battle, the other was one of the last to fall before the armistice. Took out quite a few Unseelie soldiers before he went down. Both were gravely injured, and passed before we were able to treat their injuries. Two of our healers didn't make it, and the other was spent from doing what he could to try and save as many as he could. We just didn't think…." Torin trailed off, lost in memory. Lachlan sucked in a sharp breath. He didn't think it was possible for his heart to break anymore that it already had the last few days, but it proved him wrong. He knew with a sinking feeling in his gut that one of those two names was Branan's dad. He ached to return to Branan, to help him through what he must be feeling. He knew how much his dad had meant to him.

"Fuck," he swore softly. He took a deep breath. "What I am about to tell you will not leave this room, do you understand?"

"I promise to never reveal any of your secrets, your majesty," Torin stated. The magic his promised carried swirled around them. Lachlan was taken aback for a moment, it was such a heavy promise to make, but it was also a relief to finally tell someone everything. He told Torin about his meetings in the woods as a stag with the wolf shifter, how he had saved him after he had been attacked, how he had brought him to his house and nursed him back to health until the morning he awoke with his eye color changed, how he left with only a note and "borrowed" horse to return home. He only didn't divulge that he had used his friend's name, unsure how Torin would feel about that. Lachlan finished with, "I owe him a life debt, if he ever calls it in."

Torin listened, his face showing his every emotion, anger that he had been attacked, concern for his friend, and ending with an incredulous stare as he swore softly.

Lachlan lifted a hand. "I don't need a lecture about the life debt. What's done is done. But I do need you to be the one to deliver the news for me, not a messenger. His horse needs to be returned, as well as payment for helping to save my life. I know it won't cover the life debt, but maybe it will make a difference."

"You don't...." Torin started, but Lachlan cut him off.

"I do." Lachlan eyes turned hard, and his words held a sharp edge.

"It's okay to let someone else in, Lachlan. It's okay to have someone you can trust by your side."

"I do, I have you and Grady."

"You know that's not what I mean."

"And you should also know that if love is what got Orla killed, I want nothing to do with it. Love has brought me only misery by ripping away those I cared about. I refuse to lead with my heart as Orla did. I'll lead with my head."

Torin shook his head sadly, and Lachlan knew he disagreed with him, but was kind enough not to argue about it. "Very well, I'll do as you ask."

"The horse is in my stables. The boy there will know which one. I'll get you the coin." Lachlan walked away, effectively dismissing Torin.

There was too much for him to do to think about the broken-hearted boy in the forest. The one who was surely grieving. He could do nothing for him. He had lied to him, and he was sure he would find out soon enough just how badly he had betrayed Branan's trust. It probably should have scared him that Branan knew his secret about what he was, but he knew no matter how hurt Branan was by Lachlan's actions, he wouldn't reveal it. Their time together may have been short, but Lachlan knew Branan wouldn't do anything to endanger the kingdom. He was too good, which was why Lachlan couldn't have anything to do with him. He would ruin him, just like he did everything else in the end.

CHAPTER 12

BRANAN RAN THROUGH the forest until he passed out. Initially, Shaw's boys had met up with him, each of them attempting to outrun their own pain. Eventually Kyna called the boys back to their home, and urged Branan to follow, but he darted away. He didn't want to be around them. The pack bond had dissolved with his father's death, though he'd been too lost in his own grief to notice it then. Now, without it he felt untethered. At least Kyna and the boys had their family bond to hold them together. He was a tiny vessel floating amongst the vast ocean without a sail or even an oar.

Eventually, he found his way back home. Kyna had left him some bread and stew in a basket on the porch. Even though he couldn't feel the boys through the bond, their howls held more pain than just losing their alpha. The pack had lost Shaw, too. Kyna would want to take care of Bran-an now, to honor his father's memory, but the thought of being forced to be around Whelan was enough to turn his stomach. He shoved the thoughts away, problems for another day. He carried the food inside and picked at it even though he wasn't hungry. Part of him knew he should eat something. His father wouldn't want him to waste away. He stumbled to his father's trunk and pulled out his clothes to create a nest of his scent on the floor where he curled up and fell asleep.

He wasn't sure how much time had passed when he heard a knock at the door. Figuring it was Kyna leaving food for him again, he ignored it. She usually gave up after pleading at the door for him to open it. The knocks grew louder this time, and instead of a soft feminine voice, he heard a low gruff one shout his name. His heart lifted for a moment, hope fluttering in his chest. *Perhaps Torin had returned.* He swung the door open only to be greeted by an unfamiliar Fae. The hope crumbled to dust. His mouth filled with ash when he noticed a familiar horse tied to a tree.

"Branan?" The man asked.

He nodded in reply.

"I believe this horse belongs to you." He gestured toward the mare, and Branan nodded again, swallowing past a lump in his throat. He wanted to ask how the man knew Torin, but the words wouldn't come. Instead, his wolf gave a small whimper.

"I also have this. I'm sorry for your loss, son. Your father was a great man and fought bravely until the very end. There'll be a service tomorrow recognizing all of the fallen soldiers at the cemetery by the palace," the man replied, holding out to Branan a letter resting on top of an intricately carved wooden box.

The lump in his throat grew larger, and Branan coughed, staring at the paper and the box. He gave another small nod to the stranger and took them from him. He wanted to ask how the stranger knew his dad, how he knew Torin, but the words wouldn't come. His tongue was too thick and heavy to form them. The man stood there for another moment, studying him before Branan clutched the letter and the box to his chest and nodded again, closing the door. He placed both items on the table, not brave enough to open either of them yet. Instead, he took care of the mare outside, noting she looked well-groomed and cared for. He led her back to the stable and got her settled, gathering food and water for her. He didn't realize how much he had missed her until he leaned into her, taking in her comfort. His dad had given her to him as a gift as soon as he was old enough to ride, and holding onto her felt like he was somehow still holding onto a piece of him. The tears came again, and he buried his nose into her mane. She leaned into him, sensing his grief. "He won't be coming back, girl," he whispered, knowing she would understand and then he felt her own grief. A picture from her perspective, of him as a young boy and his father laughing sent a fresh wave of tears down his face as he buried it into her fur. An equal mix of warmth and sadness radiated from the image. "Thank you. I know you loved him too."

The envelope and box taunted him that evening. He once again picked at the food Kyna left. This time she made threats to knock the door down if he didn't answer. "You will go to the service with us tomorrow," she shouted before she left. He admired her dedication, but he didn't want her pity or to share in her grief. As it was, his own was threatening to drown him.

When he ate as much as he could stomach, he placed the rest in the icebox for later. He picked up the envelope, tracing his finger across his name, his heart aching until he simmered with anger over the way Torin left. He cast the letter to the side, not wanting anything to do with it and shifted into wolf form to avoid the sharpness of his sorrow. Animals felt things differently. In his wolf form, his grief was more bearable, not as complex, slightly muted. Once again, he curled up in the nest he'd made of his dad's clothes and drifted off to sleep.

Pounding on the door awoke him the next morning.

"So help me, Branan, if you do not open up, I will let the boys break this door down. Don't think I won't," Kyna shouted.

He sighed, knowing he had avoided her long enough and pulled open the door. Her fist was raised mid knock, and she sighed at the sight of him. "Come here, my boy," she said before pulling him into her arms and squeezing him. He lightly returned her embrace, afraid that if he allowed himself to sink into it, he would once again become lost to his grief. When he pulled back, he noticed the boys at the edge of the woods. Whelan & Malcom stared at him, eyes narrowed, while Shane sniffed and stared and the forest floor, digging his toe back and forth into the dirt.

"You look too thin," Kyna clucked at him. "Have you been eating?"

He shrugged in reply.

She sighed again. "I suppose you've been eating the best you can like the rest of us. Come now, we're headed to the service at the palace. We need to honor them. Go get yourself cleaned up. We'll wait for you to be ready. We'll do this as a pack."

Branan nodded in acquiescence and headed for the bathroom. He bathed quickly and dressed in his nicest clothes. When he was ready, he joined Kyna and the boys outside. Kyna mounted a horse while the two older boys shifted and followed her lead, heading off into the woods. Only the youngest, Shane, stood there. "I'm sorry, Branan." He sniffled before turning and darting off after his siblings. Branan wasn't sure what he was apologizing for— the loss of his dad, their alpha or the dead animal left on his porch—but he knew neither of them were Shane's fault.

"Me too, Shane," he whispered before shifting and following after them.

When they reached town, it seemed everyone was making their way to the cemetery. He heard murmurs that the queen had also died in battle, and his heart sank. He knew his father would have given his life for her, and he did, but what difference did it make if she'd died too? Anger swirled in his belly, barbed and bitter. His father shouldn't have been off fighting some stupid royal's battle. What were they even fighting over? What was the cost of his father's life? He could never serve them the way his father did, not when they were the reason he was dead.

He drifted away from Kyna and the boys, stewing in his rage when they reached the cemetery. He saw the rows of freshly dug graves. Did one of these hold his father? Or did they just leave him where he fell in battle? His wolf ached to howl, but he pushed him away with a snarl. Shifting now would only reinforce the false belief that some

Fae thought of shifters as uncontrollable beasts.

A familiar figure caught his attention, and his heart leapt. "Torin!" he shouted, the words leaving his mouth unbidden, his hand waving in the air as if it had a mind of its own. Torin didn't turn, but the strange Fae who showed up at his door did. He was walking next to Torin. His eyes searched until they found the source of the voice, their eyes connecting across the crowd. Branan's hand fell. The man looked puzzled and then pressed his lips together into a tight line giving him a small nod before turning around.

Branan's heart plummeted. Torin behaved as though he couldn't hear him, but with his stag hearing, he should have been able to. The other Fae obviously had. And why didn't the other Fae say something to Torin when he clearly heard and saw Branan? Unless Torin didn't want to see him again. He once again felt like a ship cut loose and lost to the whims of the sea. His stomach churned as his eyes continued to track Torin's progress toward the raised platform. Why was he headed there?

He held his breath as Torin climbed the steps. His fingers itched to trace that jawline and profile he had become so familiar with over the last week. Torin kept his head bowed as the crowd around him quieted. Silence hung in the air as if the land itself was holding its breath. When Torin lifted his head, his eyes opened, and Branan was struck by the color. He staggered backward. The familiar warm brown shade was nowhere to be seen. His eyes were now a shocking shade of lavender, pale and ethereal.

"Thank you for joining me here today. I know there are no words that I could convey to make up for your loss, but I hope to offer you some comfort. Your loved ones died fighting for a worthy cause, for their queen.

"The Unseelie king thought because we had a queen and not a king that he could just take what he wanted, that he could violate the treaty he had established with my father and use our palace scholar to gain land that is rightfully ours. Land that some of your families have held for generations. Orla had debated what to do, but ultimately came to the decision that if we gave Ragnall anything, it would only make him greedier for more. Even though our loved ones lost the battle, they fought bravely for each and every one of you against the threat the Unseelie held. And while your hearts may cry for vengeance, we must also honor those we loved by living, by making peace, so we can live and carry on their legacy. I can only hope to live up to the standard that my sister and my parents set before her."

Branan staggered back into someone behind him. "Sorry," he mumbled.

His feet were moving before he could stop himself, melting back into the crowd. His breath came in short pants. He finally managed to escape the crowd and duck into an alley to catch his breath. Queen Orla's brother wasn't named Torin. He had sometimes heard his father talk about Prince Lachlan. Earlier he had felt like a ship who had its tether cut and drifted out to sea, now he felt as if a giant wave had crashed into the ship, decimating it and he was left clinging to the wreckage to keep from drowning. Was anything they had shared true or was it all a lie? He could still hear Torin's—no—*Lachlan's* voice drifting over the crowd. He could hear the vows he made to the people. He wanted to scream at them that their new king was a liar, he couldn't be trusted, but he couldn't find his voice. He swallowed against the burning sensation in his throat. He heard the applause of the crowd and knew if he didn't find Kyna, she would go looking for him.

He jostled his way against the crowd now leaving the cemetery until he found the fresh graves and searched for Kyna and the boys. If the world had any sense of justice, Shaw and his dad would be buried close together at least. A shaky sigh escaped his lips when he found his father's grave. It was near Shaw's. Kyna kneeled on the fresh dirt, one hand on the stone grave marker, talking softly while the boys bowed their heads behind her. Shane wiped furiously at his eyes, and Branan tore his gaze away from their grief. The other graves were filled with a similar sight, people openly weeping, one woman was wailing, collapsed into herself while a second woman rubbed her back. The air was heavy with grief.

Slowly, he sank to the ground in the dirt next to the grave marker. "Hey Da," he whispered, tracing the letters of his dad's name which had been engraved in the stone. Someone had been kind enough to decorate it with the head of a wolf and a small inscription—*soldier, alpha, husband, and proud father*. The guard must have kept some sort of record to know those things about him. He tore his gaze away from the words, "proud father." Would his dad be proud of him? His dad had always been careful to hide his disappointment over the years when Branan couldn't shift, but Branan still felt it whenever his dad shifted into wolf form thanks to Branan's Milyn magic. His dad's wolf unknowingly projected the disappointment, and his eyes always lingered on Branan with a bit of sadness before he darted off into the woods to run with the rest of the pack.

He struggled to find any words past "Hey, Da," to convey all that he wanted to say. His throat became thick and his tongue unwieldy in his mouth. He swallowed several times, but it didn't help. It seemed those were the only words he would get out as the tears overtook him.

"I… I…." He tried again only to find nothing he wanted to say would have felt sufficient in the moment. He let the grief sweep over him and pull him under again like the unruly waves of the ocean. When he finally came up for air, his throat was raw. "I'll miss you," he whispered. He wiped his eyes and stood.

Kyna and each of the boys came over to touch the headstone and whispered, "Alpha."

"If you need more time," Kyna suggested, but Branan shook his head and trudged behind Shaw's family as they left. At the edge of the cemetery, he stopped, his eyes scanning for something familiar, but they found nothing. Without his father and without his stag, who'd awakened his heart and soul, there was nothing left for him there. he

They walked the several hours long trek back to their land in silence. Kyna hugged Branan before he parted, making him swear he would eat something. She only released him after he met her eyes and nodded in acknowledgement. The house felt empty, and he wasn't looking forward to staying in it without his father, but what choice did he have? He sat at the table. How long before Whelan decided he wanted to be alpha? Branan had been too consumed by grief earlier, but now with only emptiness, he noticed the new sensation in his chest. There were bonds waiting if he wanted to cast them. The magic tugged at him. He was the next chosen alpha, which he knew would never sit well with Shaw's boys. They would never accept him. Whelan was probably power hungry enough to convince himself and the family that the magic had chosen him, when he knew that wasn't the case.

Branan knew from his father's teachings that a pack can form with a beta, but the bonds would never be as strong. And if Whelan knew the same stories Branan did, he knew he could also challenge Branan for the right to become alpha and steal the magic by winning. An alpha challenge was rare, as most wolves respected the magic choosing what was best for the pack, but every once in a while, someone got greedy, and it never ended well for them or for the pack. Sure, the challenger would win the magic, but usually their wolves weren't strong enough to harness it which is why they weren't initially chosen. Eventually the magic could drive them to madness which is how the humans got their tales of "werewolves." It was also said that the emptiness of an alpha losing his position could drive the alpha crazy or eat away at him until he felt he had nothing left to live for.

If Whelan challenged Branan for alpha now, surely Whelan would beat him. He was bigger and stronger. The thought of it caused bile to rise in the back of his throat.

He shook his head, vowing silently to himself that he would never allow Whelan to become his alpha. There was only one other option. He needed to leave and find a place to start over, but with what? Shaking his left hand out in frustration, it accidentally struck the intricately carved wooden box the soldier had left him. He plucked the letter up first. His fingers at the seal, searching to see if he could handle reading it, but all he felt was empty and numb.

Branan looked a little more closely at the wax seal, which held a partial mark of the royal crest. Of course, he hadn't noticed that the other day. He tucked a lock of his hair behind his ear and then pried the letter open, breaking the seal.

My dearest Branan,

I'm sorry doesn't seem sufficient, but I truly am. I'm sorry I lied to you. I'm sorry I left you the way I did, but most of all, I'm sorry about your dad. I know this won't be enough to make up for the loss of your father or for the pain you are feeling, but I hope it's a start. Perhaps even a start on the debt I owe you. Thank you. You have no idea how much I'll cherish our time together in the days to come. Please let this gift help you with the next chapter of your life, whatever that may be. I wish you the best.

Sincerely,
Lachlan

He could already feel the distance Lachlan had placed between them with the wording of this letter compared to the last. Setting the paper down, he pulled the box in front of him. He lifted it to his nose, inhaling the rich cedar scent. Then he studied the carvings on it. The top held an intricate swirling design with leaves perhaps made to look like branches from a tree with a stag's head at its center. It was quite a bit heavier than he had noticed before. He placed it down in front of him and undid the latch, holding it closed. Lifting the lid, he sucked in a sharp breath. The interior was filled with gold coins and gems nestled on top of red velvet lining.

Here he had just been lamenting that he wouldn't be able to start over, and now... now he could go anywhere. A small chuckle worked its way out of his throat but turned to a sob. While he was grateful to have the coin, he would gladly pay it and a crate more to have his father back. No, it definitely wouldn't make up for losing his father or for being abandoned by Tor—Lachlan. He closed the box and shoved it to the side, deciding he should fulfill his promise to Kyna and eat. While he ate leftovers from what she had left him last night, he came up with a plan. There was nothing to keep him here. He could use Lachlan's money to travel. He'd always wanted to see the Human Realm. It'd be a fresh start. He wouldn't have to worry about Whelan challenging him for alpha. He wouldn't have to live in this empty house without his father.

After finishing his meal, he cleaned the house and picked up his father's clothes off the floor. He packed what he wanted to take with him, including his father's favorite knife, a couple of his dad's shirts, his own clothes, and his favorite books. Next, he scripted a letter to Kyna explaining that he was leaving, but may return some day. He knew she would keep the house in working order if she thought he might return to rejoin them. He explained how staying right now was too painful, and he was sure she would understand.

When he woke the next morning, he gathered all the things he wanted to take and saddled them to his horse. He laid the letter to Kyna on the table and swept his eyes across the house one more time. With a curt nod, he closed the door on his old life.

PART TWO:
NOW

CHAPTER 13

THUNDER ROLLED OUTSIDE the palace and Lachlan frowned. There had been clear, blue skies the last time he had looked out the window, and he was certain the weather wouldn't fluctuate that quickly. Unless… unless they had another Aimsir close by. His heart skipped a beat, an Aimsir would be handy to have on hand to help the farmers with their crops. The last one had been Torin's son, Reid, who was taken from them much too early. His blood still boiled when he thought about his best friend's son's senseless death at the hands of Casimir. He shuddered. The only relief to his anger was knowing that Casimir was not who would inherit the throne, not when the magic of the land had already selected another.

"Sire."

He jerked his gaze toward the voice, not realizing he had almost walked completely into one of his guards.

"Pardon me, Angus, I must've been lost in thought."

Angus fidgeted nervously, and Lachlan narrowed his eyes. "Is there something I should be aware of?"

A heated flush stole up Angus's neck. "Um... that is to say... um...."

"Spit it out now."

Angus rubbed the back of his neck and opened his mouth to speak, but closed it quickly.

"Does this have anything to do with the sudden change in weather?"

Angus nodded.

"Very well, please bring the one responsible to the throne room along with whoever else is with them."

Sometimes it seemed as if work never ended. There was always some problem for him to take care of, some petty squabble between his people that needed settling, someone who broke a law that needed punishment. It grew rather repetitive after a while.

Angus nodded and then continued down the hallway, while Lachlan changed course and headed to the throne room. A shudder ran down his spine when he reclined on the throne. He needed to go for a run soon, but even that secret was becoming harder and harder to maintain. Tired of keeping it, he also knew it was something the Unseelie King could exploit to his advantage if he so wished. He wondered if perhaps this new guest was the Fae taking Conall's place as the Unseelie emissary, since he had left for the human realm.

The doors opened and in walked Torin with his best tracker, Maddock, and a stranger with wild auburn hair and hazel eyes. He leaned forward, taking them in. He could tell his best friend and Maddock were nervous, but this stranger almost seemed a curious mix of rebellious and scared. She was a brave little thing to walk in with her head held high in the face of the king.

He relaxed back into his throne as if he were bored, an action he had perfected over the decades. "You can imagine how surprised I was to bump into Angus in the hallway and hear we have a guest." He stared at them coolly, but almost broke the façade when he caught Torin's eye roll.

"I was just assessing the situation myself when we were told to come see you, my liege." Torin explained.

"And what did you discover, Torin?" Lachlan's lavender gaze drifted down to his spotless doublet, which he scratched at with his fingernail, once again masking his genuine emotions.

"It seems my son has been quite busy."

"Wasn't our last unexpected visitor also due to *your* son?" He tore his gaze from his doublet and cut it back toward Torin. He let a bit of his annoyance break through, adding a sharpness to his tone. The Fae princess pretending to be human. He was even more curious to learn more about her. It had been quite amusing the last time she was here, how she thought her foolish human tricks wouldn't allow the royal color of her eyes to bleed through when she became overwhelmed with her emotions, not to mention that her aura gave away her magic. He'd known from the start their little prisoner had not been entirely human.

"Yes, she was, and while you may feel differently knowing my part in all this, please consider that I always have your best interests at heart."

Lachlan nodded, knowing Torin was being completely honest. He had been nothing but honest and loyal to him from the beginning.

"This is Callie." Torin waved a hand at the wide-eyed female.

Lachlan quirked an eyebrow. *Now we're getting somewhere.*

"This is the human girl that my son, Evin, had taken from the human realm. The girl you met before was her best friend who came to save her. Evin, thankfully, saw the error of his ways and returned the human girl to her home, and once her friend had also returned, we thought all had been settled."

Finally, someone was willing to let him in on what they'd been hiding. He probably should be angry. If he were another king, he'd be livid, and he'd be remiss to say that Torin keeping something like this from him, did not settle well. When had he let their friendship fall so that he saw him more as his king than his best friend?

Torin continued, "And all was well until the quanlier made its way into the human realm, where Callie was bitten."

He studied the girl again as she absently rubbed at her leg. *Well, doesn't this get more interesting by the second?*

"Evin took Callie with him back to the Fae realm to avoid the quanlier hunting her while he figured out its origins and how it came to be in the human realm. During the investigation, they rescued a Djinn girl kidnapped by goblins and they returned her to her mother after getting the information that might help the investigation as well as wolfsbane laced weapons, which is when they ran into Maddock. Maddock took over tracking down Bronwyn, which you well know."

Lachlan nodded. He still wasn't exactly sure if he'd handled the situation well. Especially when the poor girl started ranting and raving about a changeling. His anger had overtaken him, recalling the last time a changeling had been mentioned in his presence was in regard to the one who killed his sister.

"Evin returned to the human realm to slay the quanlier. And while they had some help from Conall, what they didn't account for was the quanlier's determination to reach its prey. It attacked Callie, causing her grave injuries."

This time, the girl visibly shuddered.

"Thankfully for Callie, Evin had a Djinn's wish at his disposal, from the mother of the girl they rescued, and he used it to save her."

Lachlan's eyebrows shot up. A Djinn's wish was scarce and could grant you almost anything. Evin must have cared about this girl greatly to use it on her.

"The only way the Djinn could save her was to bind her life to Evin's." Torin's mouth tugged down. Lachlan could only guess how his friend had mixed emotions about that. It was a careless decision. There were so many things that could've gone wrong, which is why it wasn't something Fae did anymore.

When it was clear Torin had finished his explanation, Lachlan rose from his throne and approached the girl. She swallowed roughly as he neared, and the sky darkened almost as if to mirror her uncertainty. His eyes widened slightly. *So, this is Aimsir, what an interesting twist.*

He reached forward, tipping her chin up to see the dark gray swirls in her eyes. "Her magic is potent... stronger than I would have thought knowing how she was made." Lachlan turned toward Angus, who was standing guard by the door. "Angus, you may leave us now. Thank you for bringing this matter to my attention."

Angus straightened with the words of praise and left them alone. Lachlan didn't want anyone else to be here for the next part when he finally got the full truth out of them instead of what he had pieced together himself.

"Now, about the other visitor...." He dropped his hand from the girl's chin and crossed his arms over his chest.

Callie's breath shortened, chest heaving, and a crack of lightning flashed outside. Maddock moved toward her, but Lachlan beat him to it. "Take a deep breath, Callie. No one here is going to hurt you." When that didn't seem to have the effect he wanted, he added, "Or the girl you're trying to protect. I won't hurt her. I'm not mad at anyone here, not even Evin. In fact, I understand more than you think. She may have had those bloody contacts in the entire time, but heightened emotion tends to bring out our color more than we realize. When I last spoke to her, there was little she could do to hide the violet shining through."

"So... you already know the truth about Ianthe?" Callie asked, her breaths evening out.

"Is that her name?" he asked, and Callie nodded in reply. "Then, yes, I already knew the truth about Ianthe, and contrary to what some may think of me, I have no desire for war. I remember what the last one cost." A sharp pain stabbed him in his chest, and he shoved the emotion away like an unwelcome visitor.

"I quite enjoyed her while she was here. Tell me, is she still with Conall? Is that why he left his post?" Callie nodded. Her mouth dropped open and closed several times, but no words left her lips.

"I wasn't sure after what she witnessed in the garden, but it confirms parts of Bronwen's confession." He glanced back at Maddock. "Was she telling the truth about the Changeling, then? I mean, it still doesn't justify her behavior, but now I'm curious."

Maddock bowed slightly, eyes cast down to the ground as he responded. "Yes, sire. I apologize for not saying anything sooner. I felt it was—"

"The best way for us to avoid a war—yes, yes, I understand that. However, I wish you'd give me more credit." Lachlan waved his hand dismissively, this time not bothering to shove away his annoyance. "I assure you all I'm quite content with things as they are, and if anything, I look forward to making the future Unseelie queen an ally."

"But she's not their future queen. She will never be," Callie stammered.

Lachlan smiled at her sadly, knowingly. "Some fates cannot be avoided, no matter how hard we try."

A commotion outside the door interrupted their conversation, and Evin burst through a moment later, a flash of movement before he pulled Callie behind him. He kneeled before the king. "I humbly accept whatever punishment you see fit to give me, Your Majesty. Just please spare the girl. She didn't have a choice in the matter. I did it against her will."

He almost chuckled at the poor fool. It was obvious Evin was smitten with the girl.

"Rise, Evin. While I wish you had disclosed this information sooner, the situation is not as dire as you make it seem." Lachlan suppressed an eye roll, wondering when everyone had started to think of him as so callous and savage.

Evin stood as Callie piped up from behind him. "I'd also like to note that it wasn't done against my will."

He swung toward her, grasping her hands. "What?"

Her gaze met his. "It wasn't against my will, Evin. That's what I stupidly ran into Fae to tell you. You have to stop blaming yourself. If I had been conscious, I would have told you to do it. I wouldn't have wanted to die and leave you. Sure, right now it's a lot of change to take in and I'm going to need your patience, especially with the whole Aimsir thing—"

Evin cut her off with a fierce press of his lips against hers. She wrapped her arms around him and the two were lost to the world until Torin cleared his throat loudly. Callie pulled back and blushed where Evin smiled widely, almost proudly.

"So, we're okay?" he whispered to her, and she nodded before Lachlan also answered his question.

"Everything will be fine. Now, if you'll excuse me, I have something else to attend to," he declared, effectively dismissing them all as he walked out of the room. He paused at the doorway and turned back. "Oh, and Callie, you're a Seelie now, so you're welcome at my court any time. In fact, Evin, the sooner you can bring her here and teach her some control, the better. I'm not sure if our villagers would appreciate another Aimsir ruining crops, let alone what the humans will make of the unpredictable weather."

"Aimsir?" Lachlan heard Evin's voice echo behind

him. While he may have kept a cool demeanor in front of them, he needed time to process everything that had been revealed.

It wasn't long before Torin trailed after him into the hallway.

"Your Majesty, there's something else you should know."

He sighed and turned back toward Torin.

"Something else you've been keeping from me?" This time, he wasn't able to hide the bite in his voice, and Torin's eyebrows furrowed as he nodded in affirmation.

"The Changeling... It's Casimir."

The breath left Lachlan's lungs in a whoosh. This was something he should have been notified of sooner. "You and I will have words soon," Lachlan warned, before striding away.

When he reached his room, he closed the door and locked it before slumping against it, his heart racing. Lachlan hadn't heard of a Changeling in decades except for the recent rantings of a madwoman. Or had it been a century by now? Time was a funny thing when you were practically immortal, and the Fae often lost track of it. It didn't matter how long it had been, the word still elicited the same visceral reaction. With years of training in how to keep his emotions suppressed and the façade of a king in place, he hadn't reacted with more than curiosity at the confession from Maddock, Evin, and Callie that there was a Changeling, but now that he was behind closed doors in his chambers, he shuddered.

His chest ached knowing his oldest friend had been hiding something so huge from him, but then his friend hadn't always seen him at his best, especially in his early days on the throne when Grady and Torin helped him sort through the court and sniff out any possible traitors. He hadn't had as great control over his emotions then. He didn't like to be reminded of his failures—of Orla's death. That was usually when his control slipped. Although, he also thought that while most of his people liked to think of him as the happily aloof king, it was sometimes nice to remind them he could be a powerful adversary when necessary.

It was a Changeling who had murdered his sister for the previous Unseelie king, curse his name. A Changeling that was most likely related to Casimir. While Lachlan's relationship with Corydon, the current Unseelie king, was contentious at best, it was better than any future with Casimir. If Casimir ever got his greedy fingers on the Unseelie throne, it wouldn't be good for any Fae. Not only was he not the true heir, which would cause an imbalance with the magic of the land, but he lacked any sort of empathy. Instead, he reveled in chaos and terror. It was no way to lead people, especially the Unseelie, who needed a steady hand to stay in line.

He walked over to his bedside table and picked up the intricately carved cedar box he kept there. His fingers first traced over the wolf. He smiled sadly, knowing in the days after he had inherited the throne, he had carved it as a way to process his grief. It was a reminder of the time he felt most himself and a reminder of what he couldn't have, how his time with Branan had cost him everything. He opened the lid and carefully lifted out a letter. The parchment had yellowed over time, some of the ink smoothed away with the folding and unfolding, other spots bled where his past teardrops had landed. He read it once again as if to remind himself he'd made the right choice then and continued to make the right choices today.

Dear Lachlan,

By now you know what has happened to our darling Orla. My words will never be enough to express the depth of my guilt and sorrow for her death. I know we both said some things we regret the last time we spoke, but I need you to heed me now. Do not come for me. Forget I was ever part of your court. It's for the best. I deserve whatever the Unseelie King has in store for me as penance.

I tried to talk your sister out of starting a war for me, but she always was a stubborn one. I couldn't bear it if any more lives were lost in my name, especially when there is nothing for me to return to. I know you will be a great king, even if you don't believe so right now. You've always had it in you. Orla believed in you, and I know she wouldn't trust anyone else to take her place. I see why the magic chose you. You are worthy. Keep her close to your heart in your decisions and hold true knowing they were the right ones. Do not expect any further contact from me, but don't believe for a second that it won't mean I won't be praying to the gods to keep you safe. I know you'll do what's best for our people. Take care of yourself.

Alfie

Even though he knew Alfie was right, it didn't hurt any less to leave him in the hands of the Unseelie king. He was glad when he heard of Ragnall's poisoning by his own daughter-in-law, however misguided it was. Corydon was a better option than Ragnall, even with his fluctuating moods. He didn't have the thirst for conquering that Ragnall did.

It would do him well to reach out to Conall and Ianthe to clear the air and establish some sort of alliance. He heaved a sigh. He hated court politics, but they were a necessary evil. At least in this case, he liked the girl. He wasn't sure she would have what it takes to lead the Unseelie, but the magic of the land had chosen her to be Corydon's successor for a reason, regardless of whether Corydon had exiled her or not.

You could never avoid the destiny fate had drafted for you.

He knew this all too well.

CHAPTER 14

BRANAN WHISTLED WHILE he tended to the animals in his care at his home in the borderlands. When he finished, he looked around for the first time in a long while, assessing his life. The pain of losing Reid had grown to only a dull ache. He knew losing Reid was a risk when Reid first started pursuing him. He hadn't dallied with any of the knights in either court because of that, but Reid had been so persistent that he eventually wore him down. And despite his loss, he was grateful for their time together, for the love they'd shared. His father's death had taught him many things, and one of them was never to take life for granted.

He thought back to those first few years after he had left his childhood home and severed ties with the pack. He'd spent quite a bit of time in the human world, something he still continued to do today. There was something so fascinating about humans and their imaginations. He loved collecting their stories, first as books, and then as movies as their technology advanced. Anything featuring werewolves or magic amused him especially. There were so many things they got wrong, but often things that were so spot on. He wondered if the author had stumbled into the Fae realm or perhaps had glimpsed someone like him running through the woods.

He mostly stayed in smaller, more rural areas that offered a safe place to run when he needed. One time, he even enrolled in a human university and stayed long enough to receive a degree in literature. Of course, it took some careful manipulation to fake the documents required to enroll, but it wasn't anything he didn't have access to. He'd made quite the network of Fae in the human realm that could offer him what he needed, at a price of course, although he supposed that's where some of Lachlan's gold had come in handy.

Eventually, he returned to Fae, but he still couldn't bear to return to his home. He did contact Kyna by letter and had sent her some money for the upkeep of the house. She assured him she had been taking care of it in case he wanted to return. That he would always have a place on their land. Through her, he'd learned that Whelan had taken over as the pack alpha. He doubted the bond was strong with him in charge. A beta could hold the pack together, when necessary, but it usually wasn't meant to be a permanent fix. It didn't matter to him, though. He would not return, not to serve as their alpha. He wondered how the boys had grown over the decades, or was it over a century now? It was hard to tell sometimes, and it's not like Fae kept track of time the same way the humans did. That was another thing that amused him while he'd lived in the human realm: how dependent they were on their clocks and watches, although he was fairly certain their limited lifespan might have had something to do with it.

Eventually he'd made his home in the borderlands, and while his human degree in literature didn't do him much good there, the business and finance classes he took out of curiosity certainly did. His business started with rescuing a few injured creatures and using his powers to communicate with them and nurse them back to health. Once he found them homes, an idea formed. He could do this for a living, make a business out of trading rare and common creatures. Of course, he wouldn't sell an animal to someone they didn't want, but other Fae didn't need to know that. It had started with asking around at the goblin market and finding a few influential people who had special requests. After that, word of mouth spread quickly and he could set up a tent, gauging interest in what animals people would like as pets. Now he was known as the best animal trader in the borderlands.

He'd built a pleasant home on a large parcel of land backing into the woods. It was everything he could hope for, but he'd still felt like something was missing. He once read that you could still feel lonely in a crowded room, and he knew the author was right. Despite having everything he could dream of, a home and a purpose, something was still missing. As much as he'd loved Reid, he even still felt that hollowness when he was with him (although it was muted). He wondered if it was his wolf longing for a pack, the absence of a pack bond.

He didn't like where his thoughts were going, so he

shrugged them off. Maybe he was just due for another trip to the human realm. He would need to find someone to take care of his animals and his shop if he did. Smiling, he knew he had the perfect solution. He could ask Amani, sure she would say yes, knowing how much her daughter Eshna would love the opportunity to take care of the animals. They could stay at his place if they wanted, even bring her pet owl griffin she had lovingly named Little Bran. He felt lighter, resolved to ask Amani if she'd be willing to take over for him while he went on a brief vacation.

He bathed and got dressed, made himself lunch, and grabbed a roll slathered with peanut butter for breakfast. That was another thing he would need to stock up on with a trip to the human realm. Fae who had never experienced peanut butter, didn't know what they were missing. He packed the saddle bag and prepped his horse before leading her out of the stables and setting out for the goblin market.

As someone who worked in the goblin market, it never ceased to amaze him how different it could be from day to night, how some of the more salacious products were hidden away until the light of day dimmed, as if the dark gave some creatures more freedom, and perhaps it did. He didn't care for all the stalls. Some turned his stomach, some he even avoided going near on purpose, but who was he to judge others? Just because he couldn't stomach the thought of purchasing a necklace of human teeth, didn't mean that he should judge anyone else... although with that one he supposed the manner in which the teeth were collected would hold weight. He didn't like others being forced to do things they didn't want to do, and he still wasn't a fan of any form of violence, so he avoided Niall and his tent at all costs. He growled just thinking about that tent, his wolf shimmering through for a moment. That was the thing people forgot when they went to events like those. It was one thing for Fae or humans to fight each other if they were both consenting, but no one bothered to give the animals an opportunity to consent and had they, most would not be there. It was a disgusting and outdated practice. He had only dealt with Niall once professionally and it was enough. Once he'd realized what the animal Niall had purchased was used for, he paid him a visit and let enough of his wolf shine through that Niall knew what the punishment would be in the future for using his animals. He'd collected the kelpie and rehabilitated it, but the poor thing was never quite the same. Thankfully, he'd had a client who owned land with a lake in a rural area of the realm, and she'd taken the kelpie. His wolf growled now, just thinking about it.

He took a few deep breaths to reset himself. It wouldn't do any good to get wound up about it, not when he was powerless to stop it. At least with him here, Niall knew there would be someone to hold him responsible if he heard any murmurs of cruel treatment of the animals involved in the games (other than the cruelty of the game itself). He learned fairly quickly that being in the borderlands was like the wild west to the humans. The only laws and regulations were the ones other citizens would enforce around them, and for the most part borderland Fae kept their noses out of other people's business. None of them wanted to attract any intervention from a court or king. There was a small group who made it their business to ensure the safety of those visiting the market to ensure continued business, but otherwise it was more of an anything goes place. Most days Branan made his peace with where he lived, focusing on the animals in his care and providing a supply of animal care products, basically burying his head in the sand, or rather, in his own tent.

When he arrived, he hitched his horse out back, in the shaded space he had for her, and stepped inside his tent, checking on all the animals. They chattered happily, filling him in on what noises and curious things they heard throughout the night. The merry chatter turned into excitement when he fed and watered each of them. He cleaned out a few cages that were looking worse for wear and re-stocked some products on his shelves. Once he was done, he flipped over his sign to open and tied one flap back, allowing in a refreshing breeze.

The afternoon sun was dipping down to the west when a familiar golden-haired Fae with burnt orange eyes stepped through. "Maddock! It's good to see you!" he called, peering around his shoulder, expecting his green-haired companion to be with him. When she didn't step through, he arched an eyebrow.

"Enora doesn't know I'm here." Maddock blushed and glanced at the ground.

Branan smiled, finding Maddock's embarrassment amusing. "Well, let's hope she doesn't make either of us talk, shall we? I wouldn't care to anger a woman who knows over fifty-three plants that can kill me and how to make eight of them undiscernible in food or drink."

Maddock chuckled. "Her threats are pretty amazing."

"Now, how can I help you today?"

"I was hoping to get her a gift. The last time we were here together, she was admiring the…." Maddock trailed off, unsure of which animal it was, but luckily Branan knew exactly what he was talking about.

"Guinea pigs?" Branan finished for him. Enora hadn't been shy about her love of the guinea pigs the last time she visited, and while they might be common pet store animals in the human realm, he was pretty sure he was the only animal trader who carried them in Fae.

"Yes. Thank the gods, you knew which one, because I couldn't remember their name only that their little squeaks matched her squeals when she spotted them." Maddock smiled fondly, and it warmed Branan's heart.

"I still have the same pair of girls. I have to warn you they must go together. Guinea pigs don't do well on their own. They need a companion."

"Don't we all," Maddock joked.

Branan smiled tightly in reply and saw the minute Maddock's face fell.

"Sorry, Bran…." he started, but Branan put his hand up to stop him.

"No need to apologize. And you're right," Branan replied. He hated how guilty his new friend looked.

"Are you seeing anyone yet? It's been some time now, so it's perfectly normal either way."

Even though he knew Maddock meant well, it still felt a little strange to talk about his new love life with his dead lover's best friend.

"Not yet. Unless you're suddenly single?" He joked to lighten the mood.

Maddock chuckled, a slight pink tinging his cheeks.

"I'm flattered, but I'm afraid my heart only belongs to my silver-eyed beauty." He paused before adding, "You'll find someone when the time is right."

Branan swallowed but nodded. He knew it was true. While he had been unlucky with love, it would come again.

"So, what kind of care do the guinea pigs require?" Maddock asked, redirecting the conversation to safer waters, and Branan explained their habitat, diet, and other care needs while gathering any necessary supplies for Maddock.

It was quite the pile when he was done. "Uh, I only have my horse today, and I'm not sure the girls would like that ride, or if I could manage them and the rest of the items. Is there any way you'd be willing to make a delivery?"

"Of course. I can get someone," he started, but Maddock shook his head.

"I should have been more tactful with my words. What I meant to say was I'd love it if you would honor Enora and I by delivering them yourself. We'd like to host you at our home. I know she could do with a friendly face at the palace."

Branan swallowed, his chest tightening. "The palace?"

"Well, we have a place on the palace grounds where one of the old court healers used to live with his wife. It has great garden access, so for now Enora will be content there, and it's better than the soldiers' barracks," Maddock chuckled.

The tightness in his chest eased. Surely, he could manage the delivery/visit without running into the king. It's not like they were staying in the palace itself. As it was, he had mostly avoided delivering to the town surrounding the palace, choosing instead to send a trustworthy delivery boy. "Yeah," he croaked before clearing his throat. Maddock studied him carefully. "Yeah, sure. I can do that. It'll take me some time to get someone to take care of the animals in my stead, but I can probably make arrangements and be there in about four days?"

"That'd be perfect!" Maddock beamed. "Four days it is. Now, can you point me in the direction of a trustworthy herb shop? Enora's running low on a few of her stock and I'd like to see if they have them here, so she won't suspect where I ran off to, or at least it will distract her enough not to ask any more questions." Maddock smiled, and Branan totaled his purchases. Maddock insisted on leaving extra coins to cover the delivery fee before he took off.

Branan looked at the guinea pigs, their little bright eyes staring at him. "Well, girls, looks like you have a new home," he said. Using his magic, he showed them an image of Enora and they squealed with delight at the prospect of their new home.

Branan wished he could be as excited. It'd been ages since he'd last seen Lachlan, when he'd known him as Torin. He smiled softly, remembering the first time he'd heard from Reid that Torin was his dad, and he had practically done a spit take with his coffee. He coughed, telling Reid his coffee had gone down the wrong pipe, but what was the coincidence? Of course, it didn't take long for him to figure out that Torin was the man who had delivered the gold to him after his dad had died. Made sense that Lachlan would use the name of the closest guard instead of his own, although it still hurt. Why didn't Lachlan trust him with that piece of himself back then? It wouldn't have made a difference to Branan what Lachlan's name was or who his family was.

It would be fine. He'd visit with Enora, deliver her gift, and that would be that. There'd be no need to see the king, and he'd avoid the palace at all costs. Now, he needed to get word to Amani and see if she could watch the shop. He figured if he was going to travel to Seelie land, he should probably make a stop at his old home and make sure it hadn't crumbled into ruin. He owed his dad that. It also made logical sense, as it was on Seelie land, not too far from the palace and a good place to rest for the night during his journey. It looked like it was finally time to face the ghosts of his past—well those not named Lachlan at least.

CHAPTER 15

AMANI WAS QUICK to agree to help him out. He wasn't sure why it should surprise him. It didn't matter how many times he told her to stop thanking him for his role in returning Eshna to her after her kidnapping. He'd tried telling her that Callie and Evin had done all the rescuing, only fate or pure coincidence landed them in his shop with Eshna in tow, and he merely provided them with who she was and how to get her home.

At times like this, he wished the Fae were more into technology, what he wouldn't give for the people he need-ed to contact to have a cell phone instead of sending letters through a messenger. They had magic to light their homes, how much would it take to get better communication devic-es? Sure, you could purchase magically enchanted objects for communication, like mirrors, but those only worked between two people. You'd need multiple objects to chat with multiple Fae that way. Perhaps he should look into investing some coin with one of the more tech savvy Fae. Knowing Callie would fully support it, he smiled. He was truly blessed to have her adopt him as her, "big brother," as she liked to say, and he wasn't about to argue with her. He'd blushed the first time she explained to him he had no say in the matter, when it was quite the opposite. She made him feel like he had family again, and he was happy to claim her as his new sister. He had yet to hear if she had developed any powers, but it wouldn't surprise him in the least. If anyone would survive being nearly killed by a quanlier, bonded to a Fae for life, and still come out swinging, it was Callie. She was a fierce thing to be reckoned with. He was pretty sure she was the main reason Evin had been back to check on him so often. Maddock would probably know where Evin lived if he wanted to stop by, but he may be in the human realm visiting Callie while she finished her classes for the semester.

The guinea pigs squeaked from the corner of his living room where he had them out in a pen. "Yes, yes. I know you're hungry. I'll get you some food. You need to make sure you eat well today because we'll be leaving soon, and I won't be able to feed you much until we arrive at our stop for the night." The guinea pigs sent him images of carrots, fresh hay, lettuce, and plums. Branan smiled. "Alright. You're lucky I happen to have all of those on hand."

He gathered what they requested, and they rewarded him by wheeking excitedly. His heart warmed, knowing they would go to someone who would love and appreciate them the way they deserved. His favorite part of being an animal trader was finding the perfect match between people and their animal companion. Most people thought him peculiar, the way he could talk to animals as if they understood him. If only they knew that he also understood the animals, that's why he could find the perfect match for people.

After feeding the girls, he made his rounds to the rest of the animals in his care at home and in the stables. He explained to each of them he would be gone for a few days, but Eshna and her mom would be around to take care of them. That made most of them excited, as Eshna had made it her mission to befriend all of his animals when she stayed over with Callie and Evin. He was grateful that the situation had ended as happily as it did. Shuddering, a shiver ran down his spine. He hated to think what could have happened if Callie hadn't been captured by the same goblins as Eshna and taken it upon herself to rescue the half Djinn.

"I guess I must pack." He sighed and went about gathering all the supplies he needed and loading them into the wagon. It was the easiest way to transport the guinea pigs and larger loads. He also sat down to make himself a list of items he may need from town. If he was going to venture all the way into Seelie territory, he may as well make the most of it. The truth was his nerves were setting in and keeping busy was the best way he knew to keep them at bay.

As he lay in bed that night attempting to sleep, his mind wandered back to a time he hadn't thought of in decades, a time he didn't allow himself to think about. The time before his dad's death when he was young and carefree, simply trying to figure out who he was, with a stag in the woods he confessed his deepest secrets to who then turned about to be the first boy he ever fell in love with. He knew they'd both been young, but those moments were many of his firsts, which made them impossible to forget. He slept soundly that night, lost in memories.

When he woke in the morning, he fed the guinea pigs breakfast before gathering up the last-minute items and loading them into the cart and hitched it to his horse. Finally, he loaded his two furry companions and headed out.

He made fairly good time, despite how often his horse wanted to stop to graze at the wild clover along the road, and how many times he gave into her wishes. It wasn't like they were in a rush, and if he were completely honest with himself, he was stalling. He was nervous about seeing Kyna again after so long, about how his wolf would feel being so close to his old pack, about how he would feel being in his old home. He'd made such a hasty departure. Were his father's things still there? When the horse neared familiar territory, Branan's heart skittered toward the cabin in the distance.

It looked the same. It was an odd sensation, coming home after being gone so long, knowing how young he was when he left and how much he'd changed. He dismounted and picked up the cage for the guinea pigs from the wagon before heading toward the door. He placed his hand on the handle and paused, hoping it would recognize his magic signature. Fae didn't need locks with magic at their disposable.

He sucked in a sharp breath. There was a staleness to the air. His and his father's scents had long since faded from the home. He set the girls down in the living room and opened some windows, hoping that would help the stifling heaviness, but he feared it had nothing to do with the air and more to do with his emotions.

Everything was tidy, not a cobweb in sight which surprised him. How often did Kyna come over and check on things? He unloaded the supplies he needed from the wagon and parked it by the stable. Noting certain spots on the roof that looked as if they had been replaced, as well as the siding on the stable, he wondered just how much she had done to the place to keep it like this for him. After unhitching the horse, he led her to the stable, got her fresh water and some fresh hay from the wagon before covering the rest of his supplies with a tarp he had purchased from the human realm. Human ingenuity never ceased to surprise him. He loved how they found other solutions to problems Fae so easily solved with magic. It was as if they made up for what they lacked in magic with their creativity and problem-solving abilities. Sure, he could purchase a waterproof cloth at the goblin market, but it would be terribly expensive where his tarp had been cheap and done the trick just as well. Many Fae wanted nothing to do with the human realm. They found it too odd or beneath them, which was why so many of them viewed exile to the human realm as something worse than a death sentence, but not Branan. The human realm endlessly fascinated him.

His wolf grew restless, a familiar itching beneath his skin until it grew to be almost unbearable. He glanced at the yard and house before shifting. His wolf practically whined with delight, pawing at the familiar grass and scents. He took off, racing through the woods over trails he had run countless times until his nose caught a well-known scent and followed it. He let his lesser instincts take over to avoid his complex human emotions until they lead him right to Kyna's door. After he shifted back, he rocked back on his heels. How would she react to seeing him? Were the boys around? He breathed in the air deeply, but her scent was the most prominent. There were a few others, but they were faded, so it was hard to know exactly who they belonged to or how old they were.

A light was on in the window, making him wonder when the sun had dipped beyond the horizon. He took a deep breath and knocked on her door. It took what felt like ten minutes, but in reality, could've only been thirty seconds where his mind raced over a million and one doubts and hesitations before she opened the door.

She gasped. "Branan," she whispered before pulling him into her arms. He'd grown a few more inches since he'd left, but she didn't care. She held him just as she had when she came over after his dad died. She sobbed quietly, and he returned her warm embrace. It was so motherly, it made him ache.

"No need for tears, Kyna. I can assure you I'm not worth them," he joked darkly.

She pulled back and smacked his shoulder slightly. "You're worth every one of them, you silly boy. I... I thought...." She sniffed. "I didn't know if I would ever see you again."

He nodded, his lips pulled into a tight line. "I wasn't sure if I'd ever have the courage to return." That was the thing about running away from your past. It didn't matter how far you ran or how long you ran from it, it was still there waiting. It was something you needed to face head on and work through in order to put it truly behind you.

Avoidance was only a deferral, not a solution. A truth he was only now coming to terms with.

She hugged him close once more before releasing him. "Come in, come in. I was just about to make myself dinner, but I have enough for two if you would be kind enough to join me."

Branan's throat grew thick at her simple acceptance of him, treating him as if he had never left. "I'd love nothing more. I've missed your cooking." He smiled at her, and she beamed in return.

She busied herself in the kitchen and he offered to help, but she shooed him away. "Sit, relax. Did you just arrive? If so, you must be tired from your journey."

"Yes. I can't thank you enough for taking such good care of Da's place."

"Hush. It was nothing. And it's not his place, it's yours. It's always been yours." She shot him a pointed look before turning back to chopping vegetables, which she placed on a pan with some fresh rabbit meat.

He wasn't sure what to say, so he shifted the conversation. "How are the boys?"

Taking quickly to the topic, she filled him on the many exploits of her three sons while she seasoned the vegetables and meat before placing it in the oven. She told him how Whelan and Malcom joined the guard like their dad, how Whelan was hoping to get promoted to elite guard sometime soon, how Shane was working at the palace treasury as an apprentice for the exchequer, how Malcom had settled down and found himself a wife, but Kyna was still waiting for her first grandchild. She was so animated that he could feel the love and pride flowing off her for her boys. The emptiness inside of him ached. He wondered if anyone had ever spoken about him in such a way since his dad had died. Probably not.

Kyna kept talking, oblivious to his inner turmoil. Apparently, the boys all lived in quarters on the palace grounds, but they came to visit her often.

"Why didn't you go with them? Move there?" Branan asked. It would have made sense for her to go with them. There was nothing all the way out here for her.

She smiled, "Oh, you know, they wouldn't want their mother around. They left to go start their own lives, so it would do me no good to chase after them. Besides...." Her smile faded and her eyes moved to a framed photo on the wall. "Someone needed to take care of the pack lands, of our homes." An arrow of guilt struck Branan in the chest. He couldn't bear the thought that his request for her to take care of the house kept her from being happy.

She quickly dispelled the notion as if she could read his mind. "I know what you're thinking, but that's not it. It's not because you asked me, Branan. It's because this was our home. We were all happy here. This is where all you boys grew up, where Shaw and I made our first home, and if I leave, I'm leaving every bit of Shaw behind." Her eyes watered. "That's just not something I'm willing to do."

He'd left because he couldn't bear to be around the memories, and she couldn't stand to leave them behind. He thought about Reid's jacket that he had only recently moved into his closet, his father's clothes he took with him when he left just to have a piece of him nearby, and the knife he still kept on him, even now.

"I understand." He swallowed hard, his throat suddenly thick. He noticed Kyna blinking rapidly, and his own eyes burned.

She coughed as a timer went off in the kitchen. She pulled the food from the oven and plated it as they both moved to the table. He glanced down at his plate, remembering a time long ago when someone had encouraged him to be more truthful with those he loved. "There's something I have to tell you."

Kyna swallowed her bite of rabbit and looked him in the eyes.

"I'm vegetarian." He blushed.

"Oh no. I'm so sorry. Here." She reached for his plate and pulled it to hers, scraping all of the rabbit from it onto her own and filling his with more vegetables. "Is that better?"

He smiled and nodded, endeared by her actions. "Yes, thank you."

"How long?"

He paused, this time finding he couldn't meet her eyes. "Since my first hunt as a wolf."

"But that would mean... oh, oh no." The lines around the corners of her mouth deepened with her frown. He met her eyes then and reached a hand over to squeeze hers.

"It's not your fault. I should have said something. I just didn't want you to think any less of me back then."

"I would never." She squeezed his hand. "Thank you for telling me now. Is it okay if I eat meat in front of you?" Her face flushed.

"Of course. I have no problem with anyone else eating meat, it's just not for me. Not with what I know and can do." He withdrew his hand from hers and tapped his temple. "I lost my thirst for it pretty quickly after that first time." He stabbed a chunk of sweet potato with his fork and put it in his mouth. "But like I said, I have missed your cooking."

She grinned, clearly pleased by his compliment, and changed the subject. "So, tell me, what about you? What have you been up to?"

Over the next half hour, they ate while Branan filled her in on all the things he had done since he'd left, about his time in the human realm, about opening his shop in the borderlands, even about his affair with a Seelie soldier. She laughed at the funny parts and put her hand over his when he got to the part about losing Reid.

"Your father would be so proud of the man you've become," she said when he had concluded. He didn't realize how much he needed those words until she said them with as much warmth and pride as she had when she was talking about her own boys.

"Even though I ran away from my responsibilities here?" He swallowed against the burning in the back of his throat.

She smiled sadly and squeezed his hand. "You were young when we lost him, and I know you didn't feel you fit in with the other boys. Your father often worried about you finding your place in the pack, especially with you having been such a late bloomer with shifting."

Branan opened his mouth, but she gave him a look and he closed it quickly as she continued. "The thing with not fitting in that some people don't realize is that we need people who stand out. Those are the ones who are going to shake things up, to challenge us and our beliefs in a way that will make the world a better place. He would be proud to see how you are using your gifts for good, how you have found your own piece of happiness, even if it wasn't what he had imagined for you."

"Being a parent is a funny thing. We only want the best for our kids, even if it doesn't fit what we had imagined for them. Do you think Shaw would be disappointed to know his youngest son is keeping accounts for the king instead of training for battle?"

Branan hadn't thought about that, but he knew Shaw would've loved and bragged about Shane either way. Perhaps there was some truth to what Kyna was saying.

She continued. "Yes, your da was a soldier, and a damn good one, but Branan, he knew how you felt about hurting creatures as small as spiders. He knew with your gifts that you would have a difficult time, that violence and hunting weren't in your nature as much as they were in his. Trust me, he'd be proud of how you are using them today, how you turned an idea into a business, and a successful one from the sounds of it. It would have to be if you're making deliveries all across the land."

Branan thought about how much he had struggled against his wolf's instincts. Sometimes it was hard, like his magics were contradictory. His animal instincts would catch the scent of prey and take off until he cornered the other animal, its fear filling the air and images assaulting his mind causing him to halt, and his stomach to churn with guilt. He never had the chance to talk to his dad about it, but thinking back, his dad had never made a fuss when he'd only pick at the meat on his plate, preferring to eat the other offerings. In fact, the few nights before his dad left for battle, he'd stopped serving him meat altogether. His dad hadn't said anything, but in his own way, he'd let him know that he saw him. Warmth blossomed in his chest. It'd been a while since he'd remembered the little things. He made a silent vow to do a better job of remembering his dad and honoring his memory instead of running from it to avoid the grief of missing him.

"Thank you, Kyna. For the meal and for your words. I didn't know how much I needed them."

She smiled widely. "Of course, my dear. You may not have been born to me, but I still consider you one of my boys. Are you staying or just passing through?"

"Just passing through."

Her smile fell.

"But I'll stop back by on my way out of town, and I'll make an effort to visit more often." He half expected her to say it's about time, but her smile only grew.

"I'd like that."

He helped her clean the dishes before he hugged her goodbye and ran through the woods back to his home. *Home.* It had been a while since he had thought of it as home, but the rightness echoed through his chest.

After taking care of the horse and guinea pigs, he climbed into his bed. The emptiness he had felt in his chest for quite some time didn't seem so empty now.

CHAPTER 16

LACHLAN GRABBED HIS bow and arrow, strolling off into the woods. He had notified Torin that he was going "hunting" today. The familiar restlessness had filled him since the revelations of the day before.

Some could accuse him of running away from his problems, but sometimes he did his best thinking when he was in stag form. It was almost as if his animal could sense the simplest and easiest solution instinctually. And right now, there was a lot of information to work through. There was only a slight doubt that Ianthe would be opposed to setting up an alliance with him. He knew her to be the Unseelie heir due to her violet eye color that snuck through those silly contacts when she was overcome with emotions. She certainly wasn't his daughter, so he drew the logical conclusion. It was still hard to imagine her as an Unseelie because she seemed far too soft hearted. Of course, he knew better than to characterize Fae based on their court. There were always variations and anomalies. It's what made life interesting, after all.

He wondered how much Conall had told her about her unique situation. That her position wasn't one she could just hand over to someone else, that eventually she would need to become a queen, especially if the other option was Casimir. He sneered at the imp's name before he hung his bow and quiver of arrows up in a tree, looking around cautiously before he shifted into his stag form. Then he was off, running on instinct through the woods. As he ran, he realized all the problems he thought were so complex were really simple when it came down to it, and he was on the right track. He would enlist Callie and Evin to set up a meeting.

He darted throughout the woods, occasionally stopping to graze or drink at a stream. It wasn't until a familiar scent caught his nose that he stopped instantly. His blood pounded through his veins and into his ears. It couldn't be. He hadn't smelled that scent since his stay in the cabin near the borderlands. Pausing, he looked around. He didn't realize how far he had traveled. He inhaled deeply, but it was there—mossy earth mixed with a dash of wet dog, and it was recent.

How long had it been since he had last seen him? It felt like forever. Lachlan rarely allowed himself to stray so far from the palace. The last time he had ventured out this far, decades ago, Branan's scent had been so faint Lachlan had known Branan must have left his home for good.

There were several times after he was first coronated that he made the journey, his heart needing to smell the familiar scent to remind himself that it had been real and not just a dream. Of course, afterward he would berate himself for hours for how foolish it was to wish for things that could never be. That their love was another life, and not the one he was allowed to have. The guilt of knowing if he had only forced himself to leave sooner, he could have been there, he could have stopped his sister during her journey. He could have saved her. Then his logic would take over and remind him it was impossible. He'd had to heal. He wouldn't have caught Orla even if he'd tried. And the other part of him would argue that he would never know because he didn't try. It was a vicious cycle. One he hadn't put himself through in quite some time. Eventually he had come to terms with the life he was now supposed to lead. He accepted his responsibilities and pushed away silly notions like love because they only lead to pain.

He turned away from the scent. It didn't matter how much his stag longed to follow it, how much his heart ached when he shoved it aside. He took off before his baser instincts could take over and made his way back to the palace. Even if it was *his* scent, surely Branan wouldn't want to see him. Not after how he'd left things.

Lachlan shook himself as if he could slough off the feelings that threatened to trickle back in. He was the one in control. He couldn't afford those feelings, not when they had brought him nothing but pain and loss the last time.

He raced back toward the palace and the responsibilities that waited for him there. When he emerged from the woods empty handed, no one bothered to comment, not since he had taken the crown. He had proved himself repeatedly when required in those early days after his coronation, so no one doubted his deadly hunting skills despite how much it made his stomach sour and reminded him of the boy sobbing over a dead rabbit in the middle of the woods. It didn't matter if he hated it, he had to be the king they all expected him to be.

After his coronation, Lachlan had worked closely with Torin and Grady to eliminate the two council members who wanted to manipulate him for their own gain, and one who was even plotting of a way to get rid of him. Lachlan and his trusted duo were the only ones present in the interrogation room when they questioned each of the council members, and while he may not be proud of the monster he became in the dark, in some ways, it was necessary. You couldn't hold such a position without a balance. Over time, he found he was most deadly when he played the role of an indifferent king, one others thought they could bend to their will. People let some of their true intentions slip through, and then he would strike like a serpent. He never needed to make an example out of anyone, not when the members of his court who openly contradicted him or plotted against him were dealt with quickly and quietly, never to be seen again.

He swallowed hard. It had been a tough transition, and a healthy dose of fear was the only way he had found to ease it. He couldn't please everyone, and he'd learned quickly that it wasn't his job. His job was to protect his people and their land. Some of the council had grown greedy. They'd wanted retaliation against the Unseelie king for taking Alfie and killing Orla, and as much as he'd craved the revenge, he'd known it wasn't right. Alfie had made his wishes known, and Lachlan had respected him enough to keep them. He'd also learned that if he was going to play the games of the court, he would have to do it behind the scenes, in a way that no one knew. The deadly viper hiding in stag's clothing.

When Ragnall had sent his eldest son as his emissary for a visit to establish terms with the new Seelie king six months after his coronation, he'd discovered the perfect opportunity. At first, Lachlan had been confused why the king would send his own son as his emissary, but it had been plain to see that Ragnall cared little for his eldest, as he did not have the right colored eyes. Even more interesting was that the prince had brought his wife. Apparently, she had insisted on accompanying him, and Lachlan had sensed that she was the one who craved the power and authority that her husband didn't care for.

Grady had read the lies on the prince's wife's tongue when she'd spewed false flattery, but it was when she'd spoken about her own king, her own father-in-law, that she'd unknowingly revealed her true desires. It had only taken a few books placed on the shelves in her room on their second visit, books he'd thought might interest her about local floral and fauna. Did he know at the time that she would use that knowledge to poison the king? Not for certain, but he'd hoped, and she hadn't disappointed.

The way Lachlan had seen it, he had merely watered the seed of malcontent planted by her king. It had ultimately been her decision, what to do with the knowledge he'd left within reach of her fingers. Did he feel slightly guilty when he'd discovered it cost her life? No, it had ultimately been her decision. He hadn't influenced her. He'd been certain she would have found another way to attempt to seize the power for herself. What he did feel was a twinge of guilt about her husband. The poor sap had been so blinded by her beauty and his love for her that he hadn't seen the monster lurking underneath her skin, the one that sought to thrust him onto the throne by murdering his father and brother. He often wondered what happened to Rodric. His sources only told him that Rodric had wandered into the human realm one day and never came back. Just vanished. He wondered if finding out the one he loved the most had betrayed him so deeply had driven Rodric insane. Was he another victim of love?

"Your majesty," one guard greeted him as he stepped back into the palace, pulling him from his thoughts. He nodded and headed toward the small room where he kept his personal weapons and hunting gear.

"You know you have servants who can put those things away for you?" Torin spoke from the doorway as Lachlan hung his bow.

"Just because I can, doesn't mean I should, or that I'm not perfectly capable of doing the task myself." He knew Torin was only teasing him. He never liked people waiting on him hand and foot.

"Of course. We wouldn't want a repeat of the manservant episode," Torin joked.

Before coronation, the council had tried to thrust a manservant upon him to help him get dressed. As if he needed help pulling up his own damn pants. He understood why his sister had maidservants after seeing all those damn laces on that corset contraption she wore, but he needed no such assistance. Torin had walked in on him mid tirade and told the poor boy it wasn't his fault and to go help in the stables. That's when Lachlan started putting his foot down with the council. If he was going to be king, he was going to make his own decisions, and he certainly didn't need anyone to help him dress.

During that meeting, Grady had pressed a hand over his mouth, but not before some of his sputtering laugh leaked through. Later Grady and Torin told him they were proud of him for standing up for himself, but he probably should have waited to rage until he was in front of the council and not taking it out on the poor lad who had been sent to help. What they didn't know was that Lachlan had found the boy later and apologized and slipped the boy some coin, guaranteeing him a job elsewhere in the palace.

"I thought that poor lad was about to shit himself if I hadn't come and rescued him." Torin smiled as Lachlan turned to face him. It was easy to slide back into their friendship, to forget the secrets his eldest friend had kept from him.

The smile on his face withered as did Torin's in return.

"I'm sorry," he said, and Lachlan felt the truth in his words. "I shouldn't have kept things from you."

"You promised me you wouldn't."

Torin shook his head. "I promised I would protect you at all costs. I thought by keeping those things from you, I was protecting you, but now I can see how wrong I was. You deserve to know everything."

"What hurts the most is that you thought so poorly of me."

"I didn't," Torin interrupted, but Lachlan held up his hand to silence him.

"I understand why you kept the things about Evin.

He's your son. It's the reason I went so easy on him when he kidnapped a human, and yet you feared I would use some poor girl to start a war with Corydon. Don't deny it. That's the only reason to have kept the Unseelie princess's identity from me."

Torin closed his mouth, his lips pressed into a thin line. "I'm sorry. I should have trusted you with that knowledge." His voice was thick with emotion, easing some of the sting in Lachlan's chest.

"You are my dearest and oldest friend, Torin. The one I trust the most in this world, but I cannot have you keeping things from me. I need to be able to depend upon you for honesty."

Torin nodded, his eyes brimming. "I promise to always be honest with you, Lachlan. I won't keep things from you again." The words swirled around them, heavy with the magic of his vow.

"That's all I ask." Lachlan nodded. There was an awkwardness between them now. He wondered if it would fade over time, if they could find their way back to their easy friendship now that the secrets were spilled.

"Is there anything else?" Torin asked.

"Yes, I will need to set up a meeting with Conall and Ianthe."

Torin's brow furrowed. "I'm not sure if that's possible. I don't think he'll let her come here, and I'm not sure how safe it would be for you to go to the human realm. You haven't been there since you were crowned, and things have changed."

He sighed. "What would you suggest?"

Torin thought for a bit. "It would be best to build a

relationship with Callie. She's one of your citizens now, and the best link to Ianthe. If Callie trusts you, I'm sure it would go a long way to earning the Unseelie princess's trust."

This seemed like the best route, even if it would take some time.

"You may also want to speak to Maddock. He established some trust with the girl when she was staying here and may have more insight."

"Very well. See if you can locate him."

One thing was evident: just because he found the simplest solution, didn't mean it was going to be easy. Perhaps he would visit the one other place besides the forest where he did his best thinking.

Torin nodded and turned, stopping just short of the hallway before throwing parting words over his shoulder. "Also, since I'm now bound to be completely honest with you, you stink. Go bathe before you offend anyone else with your foul odor."

Lachlan's jaw dropped. Torin hadn't spoken to him like that since before he took up the crown, and Lachlan didn't realize how much he missed it. He turned his head and inhaled near his shoulder. Yep, he should definitely shower first.

.

CHAPTER 17

WHEN BRANAN WOKE the next morning, the familiarity of the room struck his heart. He almost expected to hear his da's voice booming for him to get up and get started on his chores. Running a hand through his hair, he sighed before he got out of bed. He bathed and fed the girls a little breakfast.

When he opened the door to check on his horse, he found a plate with a few warm muffins and a note that read, "I made your favorite. Hope to see you again soon. Love, Kyna." He picked up a muffin, inhaling deeply. *Mmmm pumpkin and pecan.* He smiled before taking a bite and moaned, catching any crumbs with his tongue. They tasted just as he remembered. He took time to eat them, savoring the sweet taste and memories that came with them. Sitting at the table while he ate, he let his mind take in everything, all the furniture in its place. He could practically see a ghost version of his dad moving throughout the space.

Memories of his childhood played out before him. When he finished the muffins, he sighed and shook off the ghost images. It wouldn't do well to spend the day getting lost in the past, and no amount of remembering was going to bring his da back.

After washing and drying the plate, he tended to his horse and packed the cart. He should be able to come back the same day, but he tossed in his bag of clothes just in case he needed to find a place to stay in town. Finally, he loaded the girls and took one last look at the place before closing the door, this time knowing he'd be back.

The town around the palace had grown in his absence. He didn't recognize any familiar markers, except for the palace looming in the distance. He had a feeling he would need directions to find the shops he wanted to check out or visit for supplies. Maddock would surely have some recommendations for him. His heart picked up pace as he approached the palace. He still didn't know how he'd react if he ran into the king, but hopefully that wasn't in the cards for him. He had left before his coronation, certain that he couldn't witness him a second time, and even though it had been decades, his heart acted like he had just learned the truth about his lover's identity.

Cautiously, Branan pulled his cart to a stop in the courtyard outside the palace. "Greetings. I have a delivery for Maddock," he told a guard at the door.

The guard nodded. "Wait here." He stepped inside for a moment and returned so quickly Branan guessed he must have intercepted a servant he could send to fetch Maddock if he was on duty. Both guards studied him curiously as he waited for what felt like hours, when in fact had only been minutes before Maddock appeared.

"Branan! You made it!" Maddock exclaimed, pulling him into a half hug. "And you have the package?" Maddock smiled mischievously, obviously not wanting the other guards to know exactly what he had purchased.

"Yes, of course." Branan smiled.

"Excellent. Let me show you where to go. Mind if I?" He motioned to the bench on the cart. It would be a tight fit for the two of them, but Branan didn't mind.

"Of course not." They both climbed up on to the bench and Branan used the reins to urge the mare forward, following Maddock's directions and taking a small dirt path down around toward the back of the palace. From there they crested a hill, and he spotted a small cottage with a large garden on the edge of the woods. He saw Enora's familiar head of brown and green hair which grew greener with each visit amidst the tall plants, ducking and bobbing, obviously tending to the garden. She poked her head between two large bunches of flowers when she heard the wagon approach. She emerged with a furrowed brow until they got closer, and her frown turned into a wide smile.

"I have a surprise for you, darling," Maddock called, his dark orange eyes sparking with mischief.

"Branan!" she called, clapping her hands and bouncing on the heels of her feet.

When they got close enough, he pulled the horse to a stop and climbed down from the cart. Branan's feet had barely touched the ground when she launched at him, wrapping her small arms around him.

"Hey!" Maddock called. "I think you're hugging the wrong guy here."

She turned her head toward her partner. "Nope. I'm hugging the one I haven't seen in ages. I just saw you this morning."

Branan laughed and smiled. His arms wrapped around her in return. He had missed this.

She pulled back, her smile almost blinding. "To what do I owe the pleasure of your visit?"

He released her. "I suppose you'll have to ask the man you just hugged this morning for that answer," he teased.

Enora laughed, walking over to Maddock and pressing a firm kiss to his cheek. He growled before pulling her into a tight embrace. She giggled. "Hello to you too." He kissed her fiercely in reply, causing Branan to cough when they got a little lost in each other.

"Sorry." Enora pulled back, blushing furiously, but Maddock only grinned widely, obviously pleased with himself. "So, what brings you to our humble abode, Branan?"

He looked at Maddock. Maddock took a deep breath before facing Enora. He took both her hands in his. "I know some people might say we haven't known each other long, but I would beg to differ. I know you inside and out, all the beauty and goodness inside your heart. I've seen you at your worst, and I still was drawn to you. Finding you, Enora, was like finding a piece of myself I didn't know I was missing. I only knew because once I found you, I finally felt whole. Would you do me the honor of becoming my wife?"

Enora gasped, gentle tears cascading down her cheeks as Maddock moved to cup her face in his hands. He wiped the tears away with his thumbs while he waited for her reply. "Yes!" she finally said before collapsing into him. "Yes, of course, you silly fool."

He kissed her then and Branan turned away, surprised to feel a dampness on his own cheeks. Well, this was unexpected.

It was tradition for Fae to provide their partner with a meaningful gift when they proposed, a promise of what life could be like together, but he didn't think that's what the guinea pigs were for. Although now that he thought about it, the girls were certainly a fitting engagement gift for Enora. He pulled their carrier from the cart and communicated what had just happened to them. The guinea pigs squealed with delight, drawing Enora's attention and lips from Maddock. She stepped around him and turned toward Branan with wide eyes.

"Are they for me?" she whispered, as if she was afraid voicing her wish would keep it from coming true.

Maddock smiled. "I thought they'd be the perfect way to start our new family."

Enora sniffled, a fresh wave of tears flowing as she hugged Maddock again. She approached the cage, sticking her fingers through the holes where the girls nudged her and wheeked. "I love them so much!" She plucked the cage from Branan's fingers before lifting it and carrying it into the house, talking to the little creatures as she did and told them all about their new home.

Branan smiled wistfully. His happiness for the couple dimmed only slightly with his own yearning for a family. "Congratulations, man," he said, hugging Maddock. "If I had known that's what you intended, I could've put some ribbon on the girls."

"I didn't want to spoil the surprise, and I wasn't sure if you'd want to be here for it." He looked down, studying his boots.

Branan put a hand on his shoulder, squeezing gently. "I'm honored to be here. Reid would be happy for you, too."

Maddock heaved a sigh of relief, as if he needed someone else to assure him that his dead best friend would have approved. "I know it won't be an easy road, but I will gladly travel it every day if it means having her by my side."

"I'm happy for both of you," Branan replied. "And you chose the perfect gift for her. I brought a pen I had at home, so the girls can spend time in the garden with her. They can happily much away at the grass in the yard and play while she works."

"Thanks, Branan, that means a lot." The meaningful way he said it left no doubt that Maddock was thanking him more for his earlier words than for the pen.

"Now, let's get the rest of your supplies out of the cart and help your newly betrothed set up a space for them."

Maddock grinned. "Newly betrothed. I like it, although I know I'll like wife even better."

"No need to jump ahead to the wedding. You've got plenty of time." Branan's heart dropped, catching him mid-step, and he froze. Maddock didn't seem too aware and continued on in front of him. There was a time that Branan thought he had plenty of time before Reid was killed, so while he said the words, he knew they could be false. He sensed that may have been part of the reason why Maddock proposed. They both knew time wasn't something that was guaranteed even to beings who lived as long as they did.

CHAPTER 18

LACHLAN WANDERED THROUGH the grave-yard. He stopped at a familiar marker, plucking some weeds from the base and running his finger down the back of a small, wooden wolf before taking a single flower from the bouquet he brought for his sister and laying it on top of the headstone as had become his habit when venturing through the cemetery. Then he continued toward his sister's grave. "Hey sis," he whispered, running his fingers across the top and placing the bouquet down. He picked up the wooden stag figurine he had carved some time ago and traced his fingers along the wood, feeling the smoothness he had sanded for a while to achieve. The wood was darker than it should be, having been stained by his tears before he'd sealed it with magic. He placed it back on the ledge by her name.

"Things have taken an interesting turn." Even though no one was around, he enchanted the air so no one would hear him speak. A king could never be too careful. He told her everything, having found ages ago that spilling things to her helped him think. He liked to imagine that it was because her spirit was there to listen and guide him, but he wasn't sure if he truly believed that. Nonetheless, it had become a habit of his. It seemed his sister agreed with his plan. He could almost hear her urging him to make sure everything was right with Torin. *You can never be sure you would have the time to make it right if you put it off*, her voice whispered inside his head. He thought of how they had both left things with Alfie, sure they would see him again to set it right. He'd need to make sure everything was smoothed over, and he'd need to speak with Maddock to see what he knew about the Unseelie princess.

Perhaps it was time to lose the aloof façade he wore so well and to let more people in than just Grady and Torin. Grady had been absent from court for quite some time, having fallen in love and moved away to be with his wife and her family. Grady had been reluctant to go. He was worried about abandoning Lachlan if Lachlan still needed him, but at that time it had been over a decade since he'd first became king, and the kingdom was stable, so he'd relieved Grady of his duty and sent him off to find his own happiness. He still visited from time to time, and he was happy that his friend had found everything he'd wanted in life. Besides, he knew Grady hadn't really wanted to take over his father's position permanently. He had only stepped up because his friend needed him, and for that Lachlan was forever grateful.

Start with friendship, his subconscious masquerading as his sister's voice urged inside his head. He supposed it could work. Certainly, bonds of friendship were stronger than loyalty to a king. *Because they're built on love, brother. Quit denying yourself the love you deserve.* He could almost see her standing before him saying the words, her eyes filled with determination.

Lachlan shook his head. "I don't deserve it. Besides, love is a curse."

Love is the key. It's why I fought so hard, this time her words were tinged with a bit of desperation, and Lachlan growled. Love wasn't the key to anything.

"It's why you are dead!" he shouted, his breathing now labored. He stormed away from her grave. Frustrated with himself for arguing with his memory of her. What must he look like arguing with the voice inside his head?

"She's gone," he whispered. Pushing the internal argument away, he focused on a place he could start. He needed to find Maddock.

Branan could only take so much of the newly engaged couple's happiness before he needed a break. He helped get the guinea pigs settled before making an excuse that he had errands to run. He asked Maddock about the best shops to visit, and Enora insisted he stay for dinner, so he assured her he would return. He left the horse, choosing to walk instead, his legs taking him to the place he hadn't visited since the day his dad was buried.

He wasn't sure if he would recall exactly where the grave was, but his feet remembered the way, or perhaps it was some echo of the pack bond. "Hey da, long time no see," he whispered, sitting down facing the headstone. "Looks like Kyna's been taking good care of your grave in my absence," he said, noting the lack of weeds and a flower resting on top. "I'm sorry I stayed away for so long." His eyes traced the familiar words, then caught on a small wolf figurine. He picked it up, wondering how long it had been there. It was meticulously carved and smoothed, beautiful really. He could almost feel all the attention to detail and the love that went into it. Did one of the boys leave it? Setting the wolf back down, he stared in silence at the gravestone, and his wolf whined. He placed a hand on top of the grass, wondering if it would allow his wolf to feel some comfort. He didn't quite understand why some people visited the graves of their loved ones so frequently, because he didn't feel his father's presence any more here than he had at the house. It was in his heart where he felt him the most. It always had been, as if his dad had left a piece of his own heart beating inside his chest. He rubbed the heel of his hand into his chest above where he felt him. "I'll do better to honor you," he whispered, his throat suddenly thick.

He sniffled back a tear, and a familiar scent caught his attention. He picked up the flower, a simple sunflower, and sniffed the center. That wasn't it, but the scent was stronger. He dragged his nose down the stem, inhaling when he caught it and staggered back. He put the flower down on top of the gravestone where it had been placed and glanced to where he knew Shaw rested. There were no flowers on his grave, no little wolf carving.

His breathing became shallow. His heart kicked up its

pace. He smelled the air, now that he had the scent, and followed its trail as it weaved through the graveyard until finally it stopped. He raised his eyes, taking in the intricately detailed headstone on a raised dais fit for a queen. There on top lay a bouquet of sunflowers and at the base rested a small wooden stag. He picked up the stag, studying it. The wood was a match to the one on his father's grave, the artistic carving strokes too similar to leave any doubt they were created by the same craftsperson. And while his mind immediately started making excuses, not knowing how long both items had been there, there was no denying the flowers were fresh, as was his scent. His heart fluttered, a small sprig of hope blooming from the ashes, and goosebumps ran down his flesh. "Why?" he whispered, his finger caressing the stag's antlers.

It'd been so long; he was certain the king would've forgotten about him. It's not like Lachlan had made any effort to contact him after sending his soldier with the note and box filled with coins and jewels. Branan shuddered. He still had conflicting emotions about the compensation for his father's death. Shaw's family had received something, but it was nothing like he had. When he'd made that discovery, what he'd thought was a thoughtful gift turned his stomach sour, like he was being paid off for his silence or like the king thought coin could cover a life debt. So why would Lachlan leave a flower at his father's grave? Did he know Branan was here?

Branan looked around, scanning the area even though his nose told him that Lachlan's scent was at least an hour old. The cemetery was silent except for the chirping of birds and the hum of cicadas.

He frowned. His emotions were scattered like fallen leaves. Gently, he placed the stag back where it rested, and took a deep breath. He rarely felt the need to shift again so quickly, but something tugged at him, stirring his beast. He took deep breaths, attempting to stifle the itching under his skin, but felt his teeth sharpening. The need to shift was almost overwhelming. He hadn't felt like this since shortly after he'd learned about Reid's death, and before that, when his da had died, but he couldn't deny the hair sprouting along his arms. Looked like he was going to go for a run, regardless of whether or not he wanted to. He took off for the woods, sparing a glance back toward the sunflowers on the queen's grave and the one that rested on his father's tombstone in the distance before dropping onto all fours and racing into the trees.

His wolf raced through the woods, searching for something. While most of the time, they felt as in sync as one, sometimes he felt it was easier to retreat and let the animal take the reins. He loped around the woods at the back of the palace grounds until he caught the familiar scent of sunshine and earth after a rainstorm. His wolf whined, following the trail until it intersected to a well-traveled path. He turned, pressing his nose to the ground and following the scent to where it was the most potent. He lifted his head. There was a tree with a short stub of a branch that had been shorn and stripped bare, as if someone had created a place to hang something. His wolf's eyes studied the bark of the tree where it had been scraped, appearing as if his initial assessment was correct and someone had been hanging something from the tree. He turned back to the trail then and followed it until it reached the clearing at the back of the palace. His wolf whined again, but this time Branan pulled him back. *We can't.* He pulled his head away and took control, running back along the edge of the woods until he spotted the familiar cottage from earlier. Only after he shifted did it occur to him, he had nothing with him to show for his errands.

Crap. He shifted back and darted away, not wanting Enora to spot him. Guess he needed to head into town.

This time, when he reemerged from the woods in his human form, he headed straight toward the shops. He wandered a bit and found some of the items he required. He talked to the farrier about fitting his mare for new shoes. They were much better crafted here than what he had seen in the goblin market.

The blacksmith's work was incredible. Branan hadn't seen such intricate designs done in metal before. He studied one design in particular, a small lantern, picking it up to marvel at the metal vines and detailed blooms twisting up the sides.

"See something that caught your eye?" The blacksmith asked, clad in his heavy leather apron.

"I've never seen work as intricate as this." Admiration laced his words.

"You should see her jewelry."

"Her?" Branan had been sure the gentleman in front of him was the blacksmith.

"My daughter. She has a gift for metal."

"Oh, is she around? I'd like to speak with her."

The blacksmith crossed his arms and shot him an assessing look with a sharp eye.

Branan put his hands up. "I have a business proposal,

nothing more."

The man studied him for another moment before he nodded and ducked into a back room. He returned moments later with a small girl following behind him.

Branan tried to hide the surprise on his face. She was young, probably only recently come into her magic. If she was already doing such incredible work, he couldn't wait to see what she could do in the future.

"Hello, my name is Branan. I'm an animal trader in the borderlands, and I'd love to commission a few pieces."

The girl remained grim-faced and serious, studying him. He had a feeling if they were playing cards, she'd fleece him for all he's worth.

He cleared his throat. "Cages of varying sizes to accommodate some of the animals I sell."

"What do you sell them for?" she asked, sharp and accusatory. Her mouth pressed into a thin line.

"Companions. Pets. Both from the human realm and from here depending on which I think would be the best match for the purchaser."

She studied him again, but this time, her brows eased, leaving her face more open, but her pale blue eyes still narrowed. "Are you purchasing them outright?"

"I'd like to draft a contract. I would pay you for the cost of the materials...."

She scoffed and opened her mouth to speak.

"Of course, then we would mark them up and decide on a commission percentage that both of us are comfortable with."

This seemed to appease her. She nodded. "I won't take less than fifty percent."

Branan couldn't help but smile at her tenacity. He stuck out his hand. "Done." He wasn't worried about how much profit he would make from the items. He knew she would put the care and design into them that would make them so beautiful the animals would be pleased.

"I'll draft up a contract and bring it by tomorrow. What's your name?"

"Maille. I look forward to doing business with you, Branan." She struck her hand out, and he shook it before she turned on her heel and strode out of the room.

Her father chuckled. "She's a force to be reckoned with. It would be best to keep your word with her."

"I have every intention of doing so. To show my worth, I'll even send her a client. I just dropped off some animals with the palace healer, Enora. I'm sure she'd love her help to design a travel cage or a permanent residence."

"That should help."

"Thank you. I'll see you tomorrow." Branan shook the man's hand and headed to his next stop.

He felt accomplished, having already found some ways to expand his business opportunities with the prospect of custom cages. He headed into a general store next to see if there was anything he might use.

"Hello!" a soft, feminine voice greeted him.

"Good day," he replied.

"Anything I can help you with?" She was willowy and tall with a kind smile, honey blonde hair, and yellow eyes that reminded him of the sunflower on his father's grave.

He shook the image away. "Just browsing."

"Let me know if you need anything," she replied before turning back to a notebook she was writing in, most likely taking inventory or balancing the books. He found a few items here and there, as well as some fresh baked cheesy biscuits that smelled delicious. He would bring them to dinner to celebrate Enora and Maddock's engagement. After he placed all the items on the counter, the woman totaled them up. When he handed over the coins to pay, his fingers grazed hers and she stumbled back. The coins clattered to the floor, but it was her swaying that drew his attention. Quickly, he leaped over the counter and caught her just as she fell.

Her eyes flicked back and forth behind her eyelids. "Miss, are you okay?" he asked.

They shot open, glowing brightly, but she didn't respond to his question. Instead, she gasped, sucking in a deep breath of air. She turned her wild gaze toward him. "You can't do everything on your own. Your wolf will guide you. Trust him." Her voice now had a strange, airy pitch to it. When she finished speaking, she collapsed, dead weight in his arms as a man came in from the back.

The man took in Branan, and the woman passed out in his arms. "Alyss!" He dropped the basket he had been carrying and lunged toward the woman, gently picking her up from Branan's arms.

"I swear I didn't do anything. I only handed her the change, and then she swayed before she collapsed. I made it around just in time to catch her and then she said... she said...." He trailed off, unable to push the words out. How did this woman know his animal was a wolf? What was she talking about?

"Oh, love. What have you done?" the man whispered, his concern shifting to the woman in his arms. He turned his eyes back to Branan. "Please wait here a moment, while I put her in bed."

Branan nodded. He stood there, unsure what had just transpired, when he spotted a rogue coin on the floor and decided to make himself useful. Fastidiously, he picked up all the spilled coins and the basket with clothes the man had dropped. He set the basket on the floor next to the counter and the coins on top of the woman's open note-book. At first glance, it was a book of accounts just as he had assumed, but there at the bottom of the page instead of amounts, he saw a detailed drawing of a wolf that looked exactly like his. He sucked in a sharp breath just as the man appeared.

"Sorry about that," he apologized. "Are you okay? Do you need to sit for a minute?" The man looked at him warily.

Branan felt the color drain from his face. "Is she okay?"

"Yes, she'll be fine. It just takes all the energy right out of her."

"What was that?" Branan asked. He swallowed hard.

The man glanced at Branan again, as if unsure he want-ed to impart the next piece of information. He sighed. "Did her eyes glow? Did she say something she shouldn't have known?"

Branan nodded, his throat dry.

"She's a mouthpiece of the fates, so I would heed whatever information she gave you. If it makes little sense now, it will in time."

"A Seer?"

"Aye," the man replied. "Although, know that her vi-sions aren't set in stone. The littlest things can change them, which is why her words may have been vague, but you should heed them. She tries to guide as best as she can to the most desirable outcome, or to warn away from danger."

Branan replayed the words. *You can't do everything on your own. Your wolf will guide you. Trust him.* They echoed in his head as he gathered his items and headed back toward Enora and Maddock's place.

CHAPTER 19

ENORA'S AND MADDOCK'S cottage was only a slight detour on Lachlan's way back to the palace. He thought it best to check there before having Torin track Maddock down. He wasn't sure what his schedule was. Plus, it would do him some good to check on Enora and see how his Unseelie resident was fairing.

There was an unfamiliar cart parked outside, and a horse grazing in the distance. Hopefully, it wasn't a bad time. If they had company, he'd just tell Maddock he needed to speak to him at his earliest convenience. Raising his hand to knock, he took a deep breath and a familiar scent slammed into him. *Branan.* He looked around, but didn't see anyone. He could hear voices inside. Could he be here? His heart jumped at the thought as he knocked.

"Your majesty," Maddock sputtered, clearly flummoxed why the king was knocking on his door. "What can we do for you?"

He waved his hand dismissively, ignoring the urge to peer around Maddock and see if there was another male inside. "I need to speak with you about some of the information I received yesterday, but I also wanted to check how our healer was settling in."

"Please, come in." Maddock stepped aside, and Lachlan hid his disappointment to only see Enora inside with a small furry creature in her arms.

"Sire." Enora half curtsied before the creature attempted to wiggle out of her arms. "Now then Lily, that is no way to greet our king," she admonished teasingly.

Maddock chuckled, and Lachlan couldn't suppress the upward tick of his mouth.

"What is she?" he asked, stepping closer to Enora and the furry, brown, wiggling potato.

Enora held the creature up in front of him. "She's a guinea pig from the human realm. Maddock had her and her sister delivered today as a proposal gift."

Was that what the cart outside was about?

"A proposal gift?" Lachlan glanced back at his guard, whose cheeks stained pink. "Well then, congratulations are in order." He smiled at the two of them. While he may not believe he was destined for love, it was nice to see that sometimes she wasn't so cruel to others. Of course, there was no guarantee this would end well for them. Torin had the love of his life only to lose her in childbirth. But he shoved away the intrusive thoughts and focused on the couple in front of him.

"Do you want to hold her?" She didn't give him time to answer, instead thrusting the fuzzy potato into his arms. The creature squeaked up at him, her nose wiggling wildly. Stroking her soft fur, the corners of his mouth pulled up. She was a cute little thing with her large eyes. He had never seen anything like her. He looked up to see Enora smiling at him, holding another guinea pig, this one with white and orangey-brown fur.

Quickly he schooled his features, unwilling to show a weakness for the tiny creature in his arms.

"This one is Calla." She tickled its chin.

"Why two and not just one?" he asked.

"Just like us, they are social creatures. They thrive best when they have a partner."

She smiled over at Maddock, but Lachlan felt the weight of her words, and his mind drifted back to Branan's scent at her door. Almost immediately, he shoved the thoughts away like a stray fly. He handed the guinea pig back to Enora, and she placed them both down in a pen, where the girls started squeaking and running around.

"What did you want to talk about?" Maddock asked.

"It can wait. I'd like to host a dinner tonight for you both to celebrate your engagement. Please invite whomever you wish to join us. Torin will be there, of course, perhaps Evin and Callie?" Lachlan wasn't sure how close Evin and Maddock were, but they seemed friendly enough and it would do for the two newest members of his court to get to know each other better.

"Callie? Ianthe's Callie?" Enora's eyes widened as if she wanted to swallow the words back down. She shot a questioning look at Maddock.

"With my nerves and anticipation over your proposal gift, I forgot to fill you in on a few things." Maddock admitted sheepishly.

"It would appear so." Enora crossed her arms and drew her eyebrows down, sending a glare Maddock's way.

Lachlan winced slightly. It was clear she was not happy with this new piece of information. "And with that, I'll take my leave. I'll go ahead and send word to Evin." He opened the door, glancing at the cart again. "Again, please invite anyone else you wish." The words were spoken without consideration for the repercussions. He was fairly certain even if it was Branan's cart, and they invited him, he wouldn't attend. *And why would he after how I'd left things?* Lachlan's thoughts turned morose as he walked back to the palace. He'd need to inform Torin and the kitchen staff of this evening's celebratory dinner. He sighed. A king's job was never done.

Branan was still trying to make sense of Alyss's words as he wandered back to Enora and Maddock's cottage. He put his purchases into the cart, taking out the small, intricately crafted metal lantern as an engagement gift for Enora and Maddock. When he knocked at the door, Enora answered, and he held the gift out for her. "For you both. Congratulations!" Briefly he thought he caught the familiar sunshine and grass after rain scent, but shoved it away.

"Branan! You didn't have to get us anything. You've done enough by being here, by being a part of it, and bringing me my precious babies."

He smiled as she took it despite her protests and ran an appreciative finger over the detailed curling vine design.

"This is beautiful."

"It's the work of the blacksmith's daughter, Maille. I'm going to commission her to create some custom cages for my shop." He glanced down at his toes and hoped she wouldn't mind the next piece. "I may have told her I'd send you over for something for the girls as a sign of good faith."

Enora smiled widely. "Of course! I can't wait to see what designs she can come up with for Calla and Lily."

"Calla and Lily, huh?" He walked over to the pen, looking at the girls. He repeated their names and each of them responded by showing him sunshine. He showed them a picture of the flower Enora had named them after, and they squeaked delightedly. "They approve." He smiled back at Enora.

"Oh, good!" Enora gushed. "I just love them so. I wanted to name them after my favorite flower."

He reached down and picked up Lily. He could have sworn she smelled of Lachlan. She cuddled into his arm.

"You're staying for dinner, right?"

"I wouldn't dream of missing the chance to celebrate your engagement."

"Oh wonderful. Well, there's been a slight change of plans. We'll be dining at the palace tonight. The king insisted on hosting a dinner for us to celebrate when he discovered the news."

He was glad to have Lily in his arms to bring him some calming comfort. He looked up at Enora, and she studied him carefully. "The king is a good man. He won't bat an eyelash at you being from the borderlands, but if it's too hard to be where Reid once was, we understand."

She put a hand on his arm. Maddock must have told her about Reid because he hadn't mentioned it. Her kindness touched Branan, and he was grateful that while she could sense his hesitation, she didn't know the root. This place would never remind him of Reid, as they hadn't been there together. His bedroom was the place he felt most haunted by Reid's memory, but it had become easier with time.

Could he sit through a dinner with Lachlan? It had been so long ago. They were both different people now, no longer the boys of their youth. He gathered his courage.

"It would be an honor to celebrate with you." He forced the words past his lips and pasted a smile on his face.

He knew this trip was about facing some ghosts of his past, but Lachlan was the one he was hoping to avoid.

Later that evening, he frowned at his clothes, attempting to smooth out the wrinkles. He hadn't brought anything he'd consider nice enough to wear for dinner at the palace. Enora stood in her new gown Maddock had purchased as another surprise. It was a stunning beige with a corseted top and a flowy, gauzy skirt. Embroidered leafed vines crawled up from the bottom between a riot of colorful flowers. They looked so lifelike that he was almost certain they must be real enchanted flowers sewn into the fabric. As the flowers climbed up the dress, they were smaller in size and placed strategically, as if to appear they were growing naturally from her form. Topping it off were simple straps that appeared to be more vines. It was the perfect dress for someone who loved plants as much as Enora did.

Her brow furrowed as she took in his outfit. "I hadn't thought you might feel out of place with a last-minute celebration, but now that it's at the palace, I should have sent

Maddock to get you something to wear. I'm sorry, Branan. You don't have to go if it will make you uncomfortable."

"You know the king doesn't care as much about those things, Enora. How many times have we dined at court in our normal attire?" Maddock asked. It was clear he didn't understand the issue.

To be honest, Branan hadn't even considered his outfit until he saw them dressed up. All he had was his travel clothes, but it wasn't like he had something that fancy at home. His life was simple, and he hadn't minded that until now, when his clothes made him feel slightly less than. There was also a tiny part of him that wanted to look so handsome that Lachlan would regret the way he'd left things, regret leaving him so long ago. He smiled at Enora softly, touched by her consideration of his feelings. "I wouldn't miss it for the world."

Her frown deepened. "Maybe Maddock has something that would help. Come on." She gestured with a finger for him to follow behind her, but he looked at Maddock.

Maddock rolled his eyes. "Best to just go along with it. What's the saying in the human realm? Happy wife, happy life."

Branan walked through the door into the room Enora had just entered. She stood in front of a large armoire, sifting through some shirts.

"Perhaps you just need a change of shirt. You definitely are rocking those black leather pants, and they will do just fine with the right top. Besides, you're quite taller than Maddock, so his pants would look ridiculous on you."

Branan blushed. He mostly preferred black. He used to joke that it was to match his dark soul, but he supposed it was one way he'd used to express how he'd felt after his dad died. Besides, he found when he'd worn all black during his time in the human realm, most people left him alone. But a t-shirt to an engagement dinner at the palace seemed a little out of place.

"Oooo! Try this." She thrust a black button-up shirt in front of him. When he took it, she turned back around to the wardrobe. He took off his t-shirt and slipped the shirt on. While Maddock may have been more muscular than him, Branan's shoulders were slightly wider so it the shirt fit, only slightly looser than he thought the style demanded. It would work, but it seemed Enora wasn't done.

She spun back to face him and squinted. "Better, but…." She turned back to the wardrobe, rifling through the hangers. "Ah! Here it is." She plucked out a double-breasted vest and held it out to him. It was a blue so deep it almost looked black. The fabric was soft like crushed velvet, and occasionally the light would catch on a sparkle. If the night sky were to be captured in a vest, it would be this.

"Are you sure?" he asked. It was too fine a garment for him, even just to borrow.

"Let's see it on first."

He tugged it on. The obviously Fae made material adjusted, shrinking slightly until it molded onto his shoulders. He rolled his shoulders to make sure it wasn't too tight, and the material moved with him, adjusting perfectly.

Enora smiled, and buttoned up the front, the material once again adjusting to his frame. She studied him for a moment before unbuttoning the top two buttons of his shirt. "Perfect! Maddock hasn't worn this since I've known him. You look handsome. Hang on!" She ran into the bathroom and came back with her brush. Then she pulled his hair down from the bun he had it in, and it fell down past his shoulders in waves. She got on the bed and motioned him over, having him turn while she brushed his hair. He sighed. It had been ages since someone else had done that for him. Finally, she set the brush down on the nightstand and stood in front of him, grinning from ear to ear. She tugged his hand, pulling him across the room until he stopped in front of a full-length mirror. She was right. He looked perfect.

"Thanks, Enora." He smiled. He hadn't seen himself look that good in… ever. The vest hugged him in all the right places and looked incredible, paired with the dark shirt underneath. His hair fell down in black, shiny waves.

When they stepped out of the room, Maddock inhaled sharply, his face a little pale.

"What?" Enora asked. "He looks great, and I've never even seen you wear that vest. It's just been sitting in the closet collecting dust."

"You're right, love. It looks great on him." His voice was scratchy, and he coughed to clear his throat.

"Then what's the matter?" Enora's voice was now a comforting lull as she reached for his hands, sensing something was still off.

"It was a gift from Reid," he whispered, and a hush fell over the room.

"Oh," she said at the same time Branan said, "Shit."

They both stared at each other. "I can take it off," Branan offered. He liked the idea that Reid had picked out the vest, and now the way the material flexed as if someone might need to move in a fight made sense.

Maddock shook his head. "No, no. It just took me by surprise, is all. Enora's right, you look great." He smiled and color returned to his cheeks. "It definitely looks better on you than it did on me."

"Reid always had good taste. But I'm serious. I can take it off." The last thing Branan wanted was for Maddock to feel uncomfortable.

"No, this is perfect. It's almost like he's here with us." Maddock's eyes misted and Enora wrapped her arms around him. Branan turned away, allowing them a moment. He knew what it was like for grief to sneak up on you and remind you of what you were missing in an unexpected moment. He rubbed his hands down the soft material on his chest. Instead of feeling sad, he felt as if Reid had given him a hug, offering him comfort and confidence while he walked into the situation ahead.

Maddock coughed to clear his throat, having pulled himself back together. "Alright, you two, let's go."

"Goodbye my darlings, Mommy and Daddy will be back soon!" Enora cooed, waving at the guinea pigs. Branan laughed as Maddock held the door, staring after his fiancé like he was one giant heart eyed emoji. He could do this. It didn't matter if the first boy he'd given his heart to was hosting the party. He was there to celebrate two people he now considered good friends, to celebrate the happiness and love they had found. A rare gem in a cruel, careless world.

CHAPTER 20

AS SOON AS he returned to the palace, Lachlan informed the kitchen staff of the dinner, requesting several vegetarian dishes to be served, along with their usual selection as well. Torin found him just as he had finished and he filled him in on this evening's plans, assigning him to extend the invitation to Evin and Callie. Only after those tasks were accomplished, he shed his clothes and soaked in the bath for as long as time would allow. He had convinced himself that although this was a spur of a moment decision, it was a good one.

Now, as he soaked in the tub, his doubts surfaced. His intentions weren't as pure as he may have others fooled to believe. While he loved to celebrate those close to him, this was about more than that. He rubbed his hand across the faint scar on his side. The anticipation of seeing Branan again had him feeling like a teenager when he'd first started sneaking off to meet the boy in the woods. Only now it was tinged with remorse for how he had left things. He tried to shake off the nerves as he dressed in his usual royal refinery for a court dinner, but his stomach had other ideas and continued doing somersaults. He hadn't felt this nervous since he'd first taken the crown, which now rested in his hands. Contrary to popular belief, and the human saying, his crown wasn't heavy. It was made of an incredibly rare, lightweight golden metal from deep within the mines at the northern border of Seelie land. It wasn't the crown, but the responsibilities that he wore daily that often left him feeling its true weight.

For a moment, he allowed himself to consider how different his life would've been if Orla were still alive. It was a special form of self-inflicted torture, to allow himself to long for something he knew was impossible, for a life he could never have. Not for the first time, his thoughts turned to how peaceful Branan had looked in bed the morning things came crashing down, before the world crushed their blossoming love beneath its feet. But a moment was all he allowed himself before he shoved away the thoughts and feelings that came with them.

Lachlan would use tonight to solidify his relationships with the two newest members of his court. He hoped it would buy him enough favor for them to help set up a meeting between him and the exiled Unseelie princess. He refocused his mind on his objective, determined to ignore his stupid fluttering heart. "Stop it," he whispered, as if it would obey him, and pressed his hand against his chest.

He took a deep breath, determined to ignore the foolish organ in his chest, and walked toward the dining room. Torin intercepted him in the hallway.

"You know I don't require an escort around my home." He rolled his eyes at his oldest friend.

"It makes me feel better." Torin sighed.

Lachlan ignored the admission, even though it warmed him inside. "Have all our guests arrived?"

"Not quite. We're still missing the couple of the hour. Callie and Evin have already been seated, and so has Ronan, another guard who is friends with Maddock, but I'm afraid it will be a small gathering."

Lachlan pressed his tongue against the roof of his mouth and scrunched his forehead. "Has Maddock or Enora said anything about anyone treating our new healer poorly?"

Torin shook his head. "Not to me directly, but I know she notices when others choose to avoid her, how some maids will go out of their way to walk on the opposite side of the hall from her. She's too kind-hearted to say anything. I worry if it continues, it may wear on her."

"I had hoped she'd have some connections to this place other than Maddock by now. The old prejudices are hard to break, but we must encourage our people to give her a chance. She pledged her loyalty, and we all know when you have friends and family to fight for, it can make all the difference."

"Perhaps having Callie around will help. She has a way about her that draws people in despite her sarcastic nature. If others see Enora about town with another Seelie besides Maddock, I'm sure it will help."

"Let's hope so."

They reached the dining hall, and a guard stepped forward to open the door for them. Torin stepped back, allowing Lachlan to walk in first. Lachlan smiled at the waiting guests. "Thank you for joining us tonight. Our guests of honor should be here shortly." He smiled tightly and sat down at the head of the table, Torin taking the seat on his right.

"I can't believe they're engaged!" Callie squealed in what he was sure was meant to be a whisper to Evin, but was loud enough they all heard it. Her joy for the couple was palpable.

The servers had just come around to offer drinks when the doors opened, and Enora and Maddock stepped through.

"Congratulations!" Callie and Evin cheered.

The couple beamed in their finery, but it was the man behind them that drew Lachlan's gaze. His mouth opened slightly as Branan followed them toward the table. His features had sharpened over the years, his jaw more chiseled and his cheekbones slightly more pronounced. Lachlan had never seen a more handsome man in his entire life. His fingers twitched, aching to run through the luscious waves that fell down past Branan's shoulders.

He felt Torin's eyes on him, studying him, but he couldn't find it in him to care. The man who looked like sin itself completely captivated him, especially the way his pants and vest looked like they were molded to his body. Lachlan swallowed hard, finally dragging his eyes away from the feast in front of him and back to the other guests.

Torin leaned over. "You've got a little drool, right there." Lachlan's eyes cut toward him sharply, as Torin tapped the corner of his smile.

Lachlan scowled, remembering who he was and how a

king should respond. He glared at his best friend while he shoved down the lust that threatened to consume him and replaced it with his practiced mask of indifference.

Torin's smile faded, his brows drawing together.

"Branan!" Callie squealed, jumping from her seat and running to throw her arms around him. He pulled her to him, throwing his head back in a laugh as she squeezed him tightly.

The sound was a familiar tune, transporting Lachlan to a happier time in the past until he firmly grounded his feet in the present. *Now is not the time to reminisce. Remember your objective.*

Branan released Callie, who then repeated the same gesture with Enora, and the two women chatted like long-lost friends. He heard Ianthe's name, which helped him re-focus his attention and keep his eyes off the one place they drifted toward. Branan took a seat on the other side of Evin while Maddock finally got the two women to separate, and they took their seats across from Evin and Callie, where Ronan had left a spot for them.

"Welcome all! We are here to celebrate the engage-ment of Enora and Maddock. These two continue to show the world that what matters most is who you are on the in-side. Despite the odds, they came together to show us that love can cross boundaries and forge new alliances. Their love is something I wish for all of my people, to find some-one worth fighting for." He had been doing so well, intent on staring at the couple of the hour, until the last sentence, when his eyes caught the familiar green eyes with a ring of copper which were centered on him. The traitorous or-gan in his chest sped up, and he pulled his gaze away. He forced a smile to his face and held up his glass. "To the happy couple!" The toast echoed back to him, and glasses clinked as he downed the contents of his own drink. The pounding in his chest only increased when he looked up to find Branan still studying him with a frown on his face. It was going to be a long night.

Branan frowned deeply. He knew he should be clinking glasses and smiling with those around him, but how could he with this stranger at the head of the table? His wolf whined inside his head. Something about Lachlan made them both uneasy.

As much as he would like to say that the handsome king didn't steal his breath when he laid eyes on him, he couldn't. He still looked like the same Lachlan he remembered, whose sharp jaw he had once held, whose full lips he had once tasted, but there were some big differences. His hair was short on top and shorn at the sides, making his cheekbones ever more pronounced. The warm chocolate brown eyes rimmed with copper were now a startling shade of lavender, and held a sort of coldness that Branan hadn't anticipated. Where Lachlan's expression had once been open and easy to read, Branan now struggled to see any genuine emotion. Sure, the Seelie king's words were genuine and rang with truth, but there was something behind his eyes that didn't echo the sentiments that poured from his mouth.

He thought he had prepared himself well for this encounter, but knowing it was coming and being face-to-face now were two entirely different things. He could tell his heart to stop pounding in his chest, but it was near impossible to get it to listen.

"Branan!" Callie's voice dripped with annoyance, cluing him in that this wasn't the first time she had tried to talk to him. He jerked his gaze away from the king and toward his friend. "Yes?"

"Where were you just now?" she asked, quirking her head. She glanced at the head of the table. "I'm sorry. I was so excited to see you I forgot this must be difficult."

Branan drew in a sharp breath. Had his residual feelings for the king been that obvious? Callie reached across Evin and patted Branan's hand, her voice dropping to a whisper. "Did you ever meet Evin and Reid's dad?"

Oh. Branan glanced quickly back at the head of the table, this time his eyes studying the familiar man next to the king. Well, that just made things a little more awkward. Reid had talked little about his father, only that he was a palace guard as well. Of course, he would have downplayed that his father was the right hand to the king, one Branan had met before under entirely different circumstances. Did Reid's dad know about him? He shook his head to answer Callie and stared at the food in front of him.

"Oh. Well, maybe you should." She reached her hand back and whispered something to Evin while Branan pushed the food around on his plate with his fork and hoped no one noted his lack of appetite.

As if sensing his mood change, Callie shifted in her seat before blurted out to the rest of the table, "I'm an Aimsir!"

Branan looked up at her wide eyes and Evin's slight wince as his breath left him in a giant whoosh. Enora was the first to react. "Oh, my goodness! Really?! That's amazing, Callie. I wasn't sure if you would manifest any type of magic."

"Us too! It came as a total surprise!" Callie giggled as her face flushed and she glanced at Branan from the corner of her eyes. He hadn't meant to make her feel uncomfortable, but it was obvious she knew Reid had been an Aimsir, and while she had been trying to change the conversation, she just reminded him even more about his dead lover. Surely, somewhere in the human realm, there was a romantic comedy novel written that described an awkward dinner party at your secret ex-lover's house surrounded by your dead lover's family, right?

He forced a smile on his face and reached out his hand toward her. "That's wonderful, Callie. It really is." He squeezed her hand, and she blinked her eyes rapidly betraying just how important his reaction to her news was to her. "He would have loved that." The truth of his words pierced both of them, bringing him peace. He was right, Reid would love that his brother's love now carried his powers. Callie released his hand with a watery smile in order to fan her eyes and stave off her tears.

Evin leaned over and kissed her forehead. "See, sweetheart, I told you, he wouldn't mind." Branan's heart warmed from her concern. She obviously cared about him deeply, even though they hadn't known each other that long. It struck him that for so long he had thought himself completely alone in this world, but meeting with Kyna, Enora and Maddock's desire for him to be here with them, and now Callie's reaction told him there were more people in this world that cared about him than he realized. He wasn't alone. Feeling Lachlan's gaze on him like a caress, he flicked his eyes toward the head of the table. Lachlan quickly turned away. Perhaps he had never been as alone as he had felt, even after his dad's death.

The dinner carried on with joyous conversation after the initial awkwardness, although he realized the king preferred to sit and watch as an outside observer, rather than truly take part. Sure, he answered when he was asked something, but he didn't really contribute, and that stupid stoney smile of his remained in place the entire time. What had happened to him since becoming king? Branan's wolf growled in discontent, and Evin turned toward him before Branan coughed, covering up the sound.

"Wrong pipe," he squeaked out, and Evin helped by pounding on his back, but Callie wasn't as easily convinced as she chewed on her bottom lip. Her eyes narrowed on his plate and then glanced around at the rest of the table before the corners of her mouth turned up.

"Isn't it interesting how many vegetarian dishes there are tonight, Evin?"

Evin's puzzled expression was almost comical. "Huh? Oh yeah, it does seem there's less meat than usual in the dishes." Branan's eyes darted around the table. Sure enough, there were quite a few vegetarian dishes available. He hadn't even noticed as he had barely tasted most of the meal, although he was sure it was as delicious as it looked.

"Enora, are you a vegetarian?" Evin asked.

Enora coughed, almost choking on the large piece of venison she had just shoved into her mouth, while Maddock laughed and patted her back. "Obviously not. She must have mentioned it to the king earlier that Branan here was visiting and didn't eat meat."

Enora only nodded, choosing to chew her food slowly instead of speaking, but the look in her eyes told Branan all he needed to know. He couldn't help his gaze traveling the length of the table to see a flush steal its way up Lachlan's neck, cracking that stupid stoney smile he had worn for most of the dinner. Branan wanted to crawl across the table and rip the entire mask off, to see if the man underneath was still the same one he remembered. The king's façade may have fooled the others, but now that Lachlan had slipped, Branan was desperate to see how much of him was left underneath.

He turned back to Enora, who raised an eyebrow.

"Ronan, has Enora met your sister yet?" Lachlan asked.

Ronan startled, clearly not used to the king addressing him directly. He swallowed. "No, your majesty."

The king's face tightened. "Perhaps she should," he suggested.

"Of course," Ronan stammered, looking apologetically at Enora and Maddock. "I'm sorry I didn't think of it sooner. If you'd like Lady Enora, I'd be happy to arrange for the two of you to have lunch this week."

Enora smiled, but her eyes narrowed at the king before turning her attention toward the soldier. "That would be lovely, Ronan. Thank you."

The king's mask slid back into place as he leaned back in his chair with a smug smile, studying them all like they were simply pawns on his chessboard, and it rankled Branan's wolf. He narrowed his eyes at the king as he felt the wolf rise to the surface in defense of Enora. He could tell his eyes were glowing by the shift in his vision before he took the reins from his wolf and pushed him back down. The king and Torin's gazes were locked on him when he resurfaced.

The king leaned forward, his stag flashing behind his eyes, answering Branan's challenge. "Branan, is it?" he asked, the conversation around them quieting. His wolf snarled. He knew damn well what his name was, but if this was how he was going to play, so be it.

"It is." Branan nodded. What he found most interesting was the way Torin eyed his king, as if he too were puzzling over what game he was playing.

"How do you know the lovely couple?" He reached for his goblet and took a sip before leaning back.

"Branan is an animal trader in the borderlands. He helped Maddock before he ventured into the Coille, and again when we returned," Enora interjected, as though determined not to let the king interrogate him.

He didn't want her to upset the Seelie king in her new position, but one glance at her steely expression told him she was used to playing court games. Her bright smile contrasted against the challenging glimmer in her eyes.

However, the king was not deterred. "And yet, you also know Callie and Evin?"

He took a deep breath, unsure how he wanted to proceed when Callie took over. "He helped us with the quanlier." The two women were clearly running defense for him, even though he was perfectly capable answering for himself.

"So, you're a borderland merchant who just so happens to enjoy helping others." No one could miss the sarcasm dripping from the king's tone.

Branan cut his gaze toward the king, wondering once again who this stranger was and what he had done with the Lachlan he once knew.

"If they're friends and family of Reid, then I do all that I can to honor his memory."

"Reid?" Torin's breathy question cut through the tense silence. The man looked as if he had seen a ghost and was now studying Branan with new eyes.

"Yes, he was…." Branan swallowed hard. The word lover seemed inadequate to what they had been, but they had never really applied labels to their relationship. At one time he may have convinced himself that Reid was the love of his life. But it was obvious now that he was once again face-to-face with Lachlan that those words didn't seem to fit either, unless it were possible to have more than one love of your life. And perhaps it was. Who was he to know when his experience with relationships could be counted on one hand.

Luckily, those words were enough. "You're the one he was seeing in the borderlands?" Torin asked. Apparently, Reid's dad had known about them.

Branan nodded. Torin stood and the rest of the table watched as he made his way over to Branan. Branan stood, unsure what would happen next. "It's nice to meet you, sir." He had only just managed to get the words out before he was pulled roughly against the other man's chest.

Torin embraced him tightly. "Thank you for making my boy happy," he whispered. His voice was rough with emotion as tears filled Branan's eyes.

The embrace felt so close to the ones his father had given him once upon a time, paired with the words Torin spoke were too much.

Torin stepped back, wiping his own eyes. "Let me get a good look at you, son." He studied him more closely and inhaled deeply. "You're Raymun's boy, aren't you?"

The last thing Branan expected to hear from Torin was his da's name. He nodded, and Torin smiled.

"Of course you are. I can see him in you. We fought together, your father and I. He was a true warrior who served his realm with honor." He squeezed Branan's shoulders before releasing him.

"Thank you." Only when he pulled back from Torin did he realize the rest of the table studied him curiously. He hadn't told them about his dad, and they hadn't ever asked. Reid knew once upon a time, but the rest of them had no clue that he was born a Seelie and left for the borderlands of his own accord, but based on their expressions, they would certainly ask questions now. Questions he wasn't sure he was ready to answer, but that's the thing about running. You can't run forever. Eventually, the past catches up to you.

CHAPTER 21

WHY COULDN'T HE just keep his mouth shut? All he had to do was focus on the objective, but no. When he saw Branna's wolf rise to the surface, something inside of him snapped, and before he knew it, his mouth had taken over. He sighed. He certainly couldn't have predicted where the conversation would have led.

"Yes, he was...." Just thinking about the implication of those words when Branan was speaking about Reid was a dagger to his heart. He didn't think he could be jealous of a dead man, yet the proof was there in front of him at the way his own beast rose in response, pawing at the ground, wanting to break free. It took every ounce of his determination to regain control of himself. Even then, he was lucky everyone else in the room was distracted by Torin and Branan's exchange. He wondered if Branan would have referred to him in the same way. They had never defined what they were in the short time they were given.

It was obvious after the exchange that the others in the room knew nothing about Branan's past and for that, he couldn't help but feel a little smug. There were still parts of Branan that he knew better than anyone else. Perhaps it was that smugness that drove the next words to leave his mouth.

"How long will you be staying?"

Torin looked back at the king, his eyes now dry of tears. His best friend missed nothing. While he now knew this man had once belonged to Reid, he also knew the life debt he owed.

"I'm due to head out tomorrow," Branan replied tightly.

"So soon?" It was Callie who asked, which Lachlan was grateful for.

"Yes, I have to get back to my shop," he replied.

Callie pursed her lips. "Who's watching it now?"

"Amani," Branan sighed, as if he knew what would come next.

"Then you can stay awhile!" she exclaimed, completely undeterred even as Evin muttered her name as a warning.

"If you have someone watching your shop for the time being, I insist you stay a few days and see all that we have to offer." The words were out before Lachlan could pull them back in. "In fact, we have plenty of room here."

Branan opened his mouth, and Lachlan knew if he let him speak, he would reject the offer. He also knew how foolish his offer was, how hard it would make it to keep the man who still held the other half of his heart at an arm's length, but it was as if someone else had taken over his brain and his body.

"Surely you wouldn't want to impose on the newly engaged couple for the evening." It was a low blow, but one he knew would make Branan take his offer.

"Don't be silly, we would be happy to have you." Enora tried to smooth things over.

"Oh, please say you'll stay a few days. I want to show you my new powers," Callie interjected.

"It would be nice to have you around in case we need anything, as we get used to being guinea pig parents," Maddock added.

Lachlan savored the defeated drooping of Branan's shoulders and the taste of victory on his lips.

"Fine. But only for a few days, and I have a home only a few hours outside of town where I can stay."

Well, that wouldn't do at all. "Nonsense. A room at the palace would be much closer to both Enora and Callie." Lachlan watched as his target opened his mouth to refute. "Truly, I insist," he added with a bite of command to his voice, making it clear to decline the hospitality of the king was not in anyone's best interest and basically backing Branan into a corner. He should've been ashamed of himself and his tactics, but at the moment, he only cared about making him stay.

Branan's sharp eyes glowed with a flash of copper, and his wolfy smile told Lachlan he knew exactly what the king had done. "Of course. I thank you for your hospitality, *your majesty.*"

The last two words cut him like a sharp blade. Branan only accepted his offer as to not offend the king. Not the man, the king. It was the reminder Lachlan needed to slip back into his role. It didn't matter how much he wanted Branan to stay, he was the king. He had people to worry about and a kingdom to consider. He couldn't afford to be selfish and follow his heart like his sister had.

"Glad that's settled." He motioned toward a servant and instructed them to make sure a guest room was prepared.

The dessert course was served, and the celebrations continued, but Lachlan's thoughts drifted.

His silence drew Torin's eyes more than usual. "You're not being as subtle as you think," his second whispered eventually.

"About what?" He took care to cut off a bite of his cake before lifting it to his mouth as if nothing weighed upon him at the moment.

"All of it. The suggestion for Ronan to introduce his sister to Enora, the invitation for Branan to stay. You may have the others fooled, but I know you."

"We talked about this, Torin." He sighed. "It would do well for Enora to build relationships. I'm just trying to help her find the right ones. You yourself vouched for Ronan's sister, saying that she's open minded."

"True, but your delivery could've used some work."

"Well, then I put you in charge of it. You and Evin both. He should have a vested interest, as Callie is also new to Seelie lands. We'll see if your delivery fairs any better than mine."

"And Branan's invitation?"

Lachlan sighed. He forgot how much of a mothering hen Torin could be. "That subject is not open for discussion at the moment."

"Lach," Torin started, but Lachlan wasn't having any of it.

The stormy glare must have been enough for now because Torin put his hands up. But his posture stiffened in a way that told Lachlan they would continue this conversation again later. He let his eyes drift back across the table to where they had wanted to stay for most of the evening. Branan's smile was pasted on, but there was a sadness in his eyes that tugged on Lachlan's heart. Had he always carried this sorrow, or was it merely because of his boyfriend's death? His stomach soured. He had liked Reid. Reid was an excellent strategist, a significant loss to their troops, and an even greater loss to Torin. Lachlan had thought he might lose Torin after they'd lost Reid. But just like when he'd lost his wife, Torin had thrown himself into something. That time, instead of immersing himself into being a good father, he had taken an interest in Lachlan's personal life. It was irksome, but Lachlan also knew Torin had done it because he cared, and Torin was the only thing close to family he had left.

Branan and Reid, though. He'd had no clue the two had been involved, but really, what right did he have to know? The part of him that cast Branan aside when he'd realized he was king was happy Branan had moved on, but jealousy also burned through his chest at the thought. How quickly before Branan moved on? How many others were there? Did what they'd had mean so little to him? As his mood grew darker, Branan turned toward him as if he could feel his heavy gaze upon him.

He expected the glare that met him, how Branan's eyes

flashed copper with retribution. What he didn't expect was how quickly Branan's gaze softened into something else. A foot nudged him from Torin's side. He tore his gaze away to look at his best friend, who had his head inclined toward Callie. When he turned toward her, it was apparent she had asked him something. "I'm sorry. What was that?"

Branan studied Lachlan as Callie repeated her question. The naked vulnerability that had met his gaze earlier when he felt the king's eyes on him was unexpected. It was as if for a moment, the king had forgotten to don his mask and he was once again the boy Branan had known. Of course, that was the moment Callie had asked her question, unaware that in doing so, the king would instantly replace the mask he wore so well. Branan wondered if any of the people present at this table had ever met the real Lachlan, or if they were all fooled by the man he pretended to be. His wolf bristled, and he felt a familiar itch at the base of his spine. He felt like he was nineteen again and newly shifted, with his wolf this close to the surface. Was it being back home that had caused it? Resurfacing memories? Something else?

For as much as he liked to think he knew about his kind, most of his knowledge had come from books. To lose your father when you are not yet an adult left him without certain knowledge that was passed down once a young wolf came of age. It wasn't like there was anyone around he could ask, not while he'd been trying to forget everything during his time in the human realm, and certainly not from anyone in the borderlands by the time he'd returned. They would have laughed at him. Besides the other wolves he'd encountered, there were lone wolves who bristled at his gaze, sensing a challenge which he had wholeheartedly avoided.

Or perhaps it was just the feeling of being on edge that brought his wolf to the surface. He wasn't sure what game Lachlan was playing by insisting he stay a few days, and it's not like he could publicly deny a request from the king without drawing censure and questions he wasn't ready to answer from his friends. *Friends*. Warmth bloomed through his chest as he studied the surrounding group. It was nice to have more people who cared about him. His mouth pulled up into a smile as he listened to Callie explain sushi to the Seelie king. Neither she nor Enora had given him much choice with their friendship, as if declaring it so made it true. Paired with their visits and letters, he'd never stood a chance of refusing them, nor did he want to. Callie had brought such joy into his life when he had needed it most, with her sarcasm and fiery sense of humor, often making Evin bring him some Hufflepuff related trinket or latest album she was listening to. Lately she had taken to including small portraits of her favorite K-pop singers. She called them photo cards and would tell him all about the man pictured in each. He often wondered if Evin knew about her obsession with these Korean men or if he ever got jealous of the men in the pictures. He chuckled under his breath at the animated way Callie described how to use chopsticks to dip sushi into soy sauce and eat fried dumplings. The king seemed interested, while Evin watched her with awe, and Torin watched his son with a smile that spoke of love and joy at his seeing his son with someone he loved.

As if sensing his gaze, Torin looked up at Branan and his smile grew. Heat stole across Branan's cheeks, and he looked down. "How long have you lived in the border-lands?" The unfamiliar soldier asked. *Ronan,* Branan remembered from introductions earlier.

"Ages it feels like."

"But you used to live here?"

"Yes, I grew up a few hours outside of town."

"So, what made you leave?" His head tilted to the side and the slight furrow of his brows let Branan know his intentions were genuine and understandable. Although it was a question he hadn't been asked before. Most of the people he met in the borderlands just assumed he grew up in the borderlands. He couldn't fault the man for his curiosity. Conversation around them quieted.

"A mixture of things. My father was the alpha of our pack when he was killed in battle."

"Oh, shit. I'm sorry." Ronan winced.

Branan picked up his cup and swirled the ambrosia around. "It's fine. It was a long time ago. It didn't help the situation that I had been seeing someone at the time. I even thought we could have had something great. He'd been staying with me while my dad was gone and then one morning, I woke up and he was gone. Disappeared like a thief in the night, leaving behind only a note saying he would have my horse returned and he was sorry." A coil of satisfaction sprang in his belly, traveling through his limbs. He was finally telling someone the truth, albeit leaving out the name of the guilty party. Perhaps now Lachlan would realize just how badly he had messed up.

"He stole your horse?! What the hell?!" Callie interjected. Only then did he look up from his cup to see the entire table was riveted by his story. Lachlan's mask had slipped again. This time, his jaw was clenched, and his cheeks were tinged pink.

"Well, to be fair, he sent someone to return the horse later with another note apologizing and wishing me the best."

"Yeah, that does not help. What a coward," Callie grumbled.

Only then did he realize he may have revealed their relationship to Torin as he had been the one to return the horse. He risked another glance toward the head of the table and Lachlan's knuckles were almost white where he gripped the arms of his chair. Torin studied the king like a puzzle he had finally solved.

"Was that the last time you saw him?" Enora asked.

Branan shook his head. "No, I saw him from a distance at the ceremony the king held for all the fallen soldiers, and I discovered I didn't know him. Not really. He had hidden parts of himself from me, even going as far as using a fake name."

The girls both gasped and one of the men released a disbelieving no.

"Maybe he had his reasons." Torin's words drew wide eyes from everyone, but Branan could see the compassion on his face.

"Perhaps, and perhaps those reasons were completely valid, or perhaps he played me for a fool, but I guess I'll never know, as he has never sought me out to share them with me." He tore his gaze from Torin and swept it over Lachlan. Lachlan's breaths were heavy, his knuckles still white on the arms of his chair, but his head was bowed, so Branan couldn't read his expression. Was he ashamed? Angry? Branan drew his attention back to the others around the table. He shrugged. "So, after that and with my dad being gone, my home just didn't feel like home anymore, you know?"

Ronan nodded. "Makes sense."

"I packed up what I wanted to take and headed for the human realm. I spent a while there, learning all I could, even attending university and getting a few degrees, moving around when necessary, before I decided what I wanted to do. Once I had a business plan, I headed back to our realm and set up my shop at the goblin market. I deal mainly with animals, matching them with Fae companions, and also with items that aid in animal care."

"Cool," Ronan replied.

"Oh, you should see his shop, Ronan," Enora gushed. "He has the cutest critters from both realms. In fact, you should bring your sister over to meet the newest members of our family, two small furry beauties that Branan brought us from the human realm. They're called guinea pigs, and they make the most adorable noises when they're happy!"

"Oh, she would love that," Ronan replied with a chuckle.

"You have guinea pigs?" Callie asked excitedly.

Enora then entertained the table with the story of how Maddock asked her to marry him. By the time she finished, the king's mask was firmly back in place. Sure, he smiled and laughed when appropriate, and to anyone else it would appear he was genuinely happy for the couple, but his smile never quite stretched as far as it was meant to, and his eyes lacked the familiar spark Branan had once known.

They toasted the happy couple again, and this time, Callie yawned. "You'll have to excuse us. Someone is on break from school, but still hasn't adjusted to the time difference," Evin chuckled as they stood.

"Sorry," Callie apologized sheepishly.

"Nonsense," Enora replied, waving off her concern. "I'm so glad you could join us."

"Please come back in the morning and join us for breakfast," the Seelie king offered. "I'm sure our guest would appreciate the familiar faces."

Branan opened his mouth to refute the offer, but saw it was pointless. Perhaps the king would have some pressing business instead and he could enjoy his breakfast with his friends.

"That offer stands for all of you. We're glad you could be here tonight to celebrate Enora and Maddock."

"Here, here," Evin, Torin, and Ronan echoed as Callie clapped in happiness for the couple.

And with that, the celebration came to a close. Branan stood to go with Enora and Maddock. Perhaps he could make an escape without the king noticing. However, a servant quickly approached them. "Please allow me to show you to your room, sir," she said meekly.

Branan frowned. "I must go fetch my things."

"Nonsense." Lachlan's voice caressed the back of his neck. When had he gotten so close? "I've arranged for someone to accompany the happy couple and gather your items while you get comfortable."

Of course he did. Branan sighed as he watched Lachlan shake Maddock's hand before Enora threw her arms around him. He jerked slightly and stood stiff as a board, unsure of what to do. It would've been comical had Branan not caught sight of the way his face instantly relaxed and melted into her embrace for a moment. His heart lurched, longing to gather Lachlan into his own arms. Just as quickly as Lachlan had melted, he stepped back and nodded to the happy couple before striding out of the room, leaving Branan to stare after him and wonder how long it had been since anyone had hugged that man. His heart cracked. Perhaps Branan wasn't the only one who felt broken.

CHAPTER 22

"**T**HIS ROOM? ARE you sure?" Branan asked after he stepped inside the most luxurious bedroom he'd ever seen. The wallpaper was a light gray with a faint design. The bed was massive, with the most ornately carved bedposts draped with thick black curtains. Not to mention the entire room was massive. It would have fit the entirety of his childhood home inside.

"Yes, sir. Do you require anything else this evening?" the girl asked him with a squeak.

"No, thank you."

She shot him one more curious glance before darting out of the room and closing the door behind her.

He sat on the bed, lost in thought, when a knock sounded on his door again. This time, a young man brought in his bag from his cart. He stood and retrieved the bag. "Is there anything else you require from your supplies? Lady Enora thought this was all you might need."

"That should be fine. Thank you."

"Just press this button to ring for someone should you require anything else." The boy also gave him a curious once over before nodding and closing the door with a smirk.

He studied the room more closely, dragging his fingers against the silk on the walls. *Is that?* It was. The design, which may have looked rather damask at first, was in fact a repeating pattern of stag's antlers. *Curious.*

Next, he wandered to a connecting door, which led him into an enormous bathroom with a copper claw-foot tub in the center. He turned the water to hot and let it fill the tub, sprinkling in some salts from a tray next to the tub. It would do him some good to unwind after that confusing and stressful event masquerading as dinner. He undressed and draped his clothes over a chair in the corner. Stepping into the tub, he released a sigh as he lowered himself down into its warmth. He closed his eyes and took several deep breaths, attempting to release any tension he felt. Being so close to Lachlan kept him feeling wound tightly, but eventually he could feel his beast stop pacing below the surface.

He picked up the bar of soap from the tray and brought it to his nose. He breathed in the scent of what could only be described as sunshine after rain. When he closed his eyes and inhaled deeply, a familiar stag took shape in front of him. He had often wondered why the deer carried such a scent mixed with its animal musk, but now he held the answer in his hands. He lathered up and washed, leaning back to relax when his nose and skin were full of the familiar fragrance. His wolf finally relaxed, curling up into a ball in his mind's eye with a soft sound of contentment, and Branan closed his eyes.

Lachlan stared at the ceiling above his bed. He couldn't explain to anyone why he had chosen that room for Branan. It hadn't ever been used as guest quarters. In fact, the guest quarters were in the opposite wing. To her credit, the head housekeeper managed to pull her eyebrows back down after he made the request and didn't verbalize whatever she was thinking. He just couldn't stand the thought of Branan being so far away in his own home. He wanted him nearby. Besides, it wasn't like he used the room anymore, not since he had taken over the king's quarters a few months after Orla's death at Grady's insistence that his people wouldn't want a king who feared ghosts or reminders of his dead family. The next morning, he'd had the staff move most of his things to his father's room, the one he had shared with his mother. It had taken longer to tackle Orla's things which were in the queen's quarters (because every woman should have a place to escape, as his mother used to say), so he'd packed up her clothes and jewelry to decide what to do with later. Except now, so much time had passed that he had forgotten about them.

He wasn't sure if he did it to torture himself or Branan, but knowing Branan would sleep in his old bed eased the hurt he'd felt earlier when Branan spoke at the table about his lover who had "disappeared." His cheeks had burned so badly he wondered if his face was on fire, and if anyone had noticed. Callie had called him a coward, and she was right. But the thing about the past is no matter how much you wished you could change it, you can't. He had acted like a coward, fleeing like a thief in the night, but at the time he had been grieving the loss of his sister and the additional responsibilities that were thrust onto his shoulders. The last thing he'd wanted to do was pull someone else down with him. He'd thought it was the for the best, but now he had his doubts.

Perhaps tomorrow he would have enough courage to get Branan to sit down with him somewhere in private and finally clear the air. His mind set, he closed his eyes and drifted off to sleep.

He stumbled through the woods on four hooves, diving through the thicket to outrun the beasts pursuing him. He drew up sharply against the bank of a river, realizing this was their intent the entire time—to corner him. His breath came in short pants, and he glanced around for a way to escape when he saw the shadows move, eyes glowing in the distance, low growls as they approached. There were three of them. Fuck. This would not end well. And blast it, if these were his final moments, he would go down fighting. He reared back on his back legs, kicking his front out at the closest assailant, but he dodged them. When he landed, he lowered his horns, ready to attack, but was too slow. One wolf lurched from the left, catching Lachlan's flank with massive jaws full of sharp teeth. Lachlan bellowed, kicking wildly, hoping to dislodge his attacker, when a flash of black slammed into his attacker's side and the teeth were ripped from his skin, taking a chunk of flesh with them.

The familiar scent slammed into him as he recognized

the wolf. Branan. Where did he come from? How had he known? His left knee wobbled as he felt the warm blood trickle down his side. The wolf Branan had slammed into got up, but this time he was much larger, and much meaner. "You dare to challenge me?" he hissed at Branan. "You're the one who tucked tail and ran away. You have no place here, and you never will." He flashed his teeth and a few more wolves joined the circle, closing in. The wolf lunged at Branan, striking with impossible speed. The other wolves growled with increasing volume, watching the fight and paying Lachlan no mind.

His heart pounded in his chest, increasing with speed until he feared he was going into cardiac arrest. Run, Branan! he wanted to scream, but he knew Branan wouldn't run away, not when Lachlan's life was at risk. The wolf struck again, tearing a chunk of flesh from Branan, his snout dripping with blood. "Stop!" Lachlan yelled, but it was as if no one could hear him. The larger wolf snarled, circling Branan and dodging all of his attacks. When he saw an opening, he struck, this time wrapping his jaw around Branan's throat.

"Noooo!" Lachlan screamed, but it was too late. Blood flowed freely from Branan's torn throat and he listed to the side before collapsing. "It is done!" The wolf yelled at the others before they all turned and bled back into the darkness of the woods.

Lachlan transformed in an instant, running toward Branan's wolf. He caressed his fuzzy face. The wolf whined, struggling to remain in the land of the living. Lachlan's chest shook with sobs. "You can't leave me. You can't. I need you!" he yelled, but it was no use. He watched help-

lessly as the copper left Branan's eyes as they glazed over, leaving him in ruins.

He awoke with a start. Tears still flowing freely down his face. It took him a moment to realize that he was in bed in the palace and not in the woods. His heart still pounded, and he stood with shaky legs. His old injury twinged as it sometime did when he moved too abruptly. "Branan," his voice cracked on the harsh whisper. The dream had felt too real. He swiped at his cheeks and stumbled from his room until he reached his old bedroom. He opened the door quietly, not wanting to wake Branan if he was asleep, but he needed to see him, needed to set eyes on him to know he was okay.

Quietly, he crept further into the room, but his heart plummeted when he discovered the bed was empty. "Branan?" he called out into the darkness. His breath came in short pants as he scoured the room until he saw a faint light under the door from the bathroom. He opened the door and saw Branan lying limp in the tub. He choked on another sob before reaching for him, shaking his shoulders. "Branan!"

Branan opened his eyes with a slow, dazed blink. "Lachlan?"

Lachlan's breath left him in a loud whoosh. "You're okay."

"Of course, I'm…." Branan's mint green eyes widened as he pulled away from Lachlan and glanced at the tub. He quickly moved his hands to cover anything that may be seen in the water.

"I just fell asleep in the tub. Now, if you could please leave, I'd like to dry off." He motioned toward the door with his head.

Lachlan's neck flamed as he realized Branan was naked in the tub. He had been so wrapped up in his panic before, but now there was no denying the spans of chiseled chest in front of him. "Oh... um... here." He quickly marched over to where the towel hung and pulled it off the rack, handing it to Branan and turning around to face the door. He heard the movement of water as Branan stood and risked a peek over his shoulder, where he saw Branan drying his arms with the towel before dragging it across his chest.

"Like what you see?" Branan's voice was rough, startling Lachlan, who whipped his head up to Branan's face. Branan's eyes flashed with copper as he stared back. Lachlan's entire body burned as he turned back toward the door.

"Now that I know you're okay, I'll be going."

"Yeah, about that—" Branan started, but Lachlan cut him off by leaving the bathroom.

He heard him stumbling to step from the tub and had his hand on the doorknob when Branan's voice stopped him.

"Are you sure everything's okay?"

Lachlan glanced back over his shoulder, but he should have kept staring straight ahead because now Branan was standing in front of him with only a towel wrapped around his waist.

Lachlan nodded sharply. "Fine. Everything's fine." He swallowed hard and opened the door. "See you in the morning." He strode out of there before anyone could stop him. When he reached his own quarters, he closed the door with a click and sagged against it, letting the weight of his body carry him down until he was sitting on the floor with his back against the door. His heart still pounded in his chest, but this time for entirely different reasons. Time had treated Branan well. He was everything Lachlan could ever want and completely off limits, so there was no use in wishing for what could be. He rubbed his temples. Hopefully, they would both forget about this in the morning.

This time when he closed his eyes to sleep, there were no wolves, only Branan and that blasted towel.

CHAPTER 23

THE SUN'S RAYS filtering in from the window to his left woke Branan the next morning. He stretched and took survey of the room that now appeared even more grand in the sunlight. He turned his head toward the window basking in its warmth as he sat up and stretched. From the bed he could only make out some of the tops of trees. He walked closer for a better view and saw a lush garden. There was a small copse of what looked like cherry trees just at the edge of his view and for some reason they made him sad. Perhaps it was the way the small buds of greens on the tips looked frozen in time, stunted in growth, as if the tree didn't have enough energy to burst into full bloom.

The word burst brought Branan's mind back to when Lachlan burst into the bathroom last night and the events replayed through his head. Lachlan's panic at finding him asleep in the tub. Lachlan, whose eyes were red and puffy as if he had been crying, who then stared at him hungrily as he dried himself off with a towel. At first, he'd been embarrassed to be found in such a state, but then he'd realized he could use the situation to have a little fun and tease Lachlan enough to embarrass him. Instead, he only lit a fire they both weren't ready to face, as evident by how quickly Lachlan had fled the room. And while he'd wanted to savor it, was clear Lachlan still wanted him, what bothered him even more was not knowing what made Lachlan so upset that he snuck into Branan's room that night. Now he had even more reasons to get him alone and finally have the conversation he thought they both needed. It had been long enough, and it was obvious from the company he kept that seeing him again in the future was becoming fairly unavoidable.

He sighed as he pulled clean clothes from his bag and dressed. The thought of teasing Lachlan by somehow sliding a reference to last night into conversation over breakfast had his feet quickly carrying him into the dining hall. He spotted Callie, Evin, Enora, and Maddock, but the chair at the head of the table was noticeably absent, as was Torin's seat from the night before.

"Good morning!" Enora called.

Callie mumbled something resembling a greeting, and Evin chuckled. "Don't mind her. I'm sure you remember she's not exactly a morning person."

Branan laughed in return when Callie mumbled something else and raised her middle finger at Evin before bringing a steaming mug back up to her lips.

"Join us! We only just arrived," Enora said.

He glanced at the empty chairs again, trying to hide his

disappointment. "Oh, Torin popped in for a moment and stated the king had business to attend and wouldn't be able to join us this morning before he headed off to steal some of the cook's famous fresh scones," she added, catching where his gaze traveled.

He took the seat next to Enora, Torin's chair from the night before to be exact, and it felt both odd and right at the same time.

"Did you sleep okay?" Her voice was low and soft as Callie grumbled something else to Evin about his...balls? This time Maddock laughed loudly.

"Yes, thank you Enora." He blushed thinking about the bath.

"Is everything else alright?" She laid a gentle hand on his arm, her bright silver eyes peering up at him. He nodded again as he took a cup of coffee offered by a servant. "I was worried. I know you hadn't planned to stay, but I'm glad you decided to. It'll be nice to have another friendly face around here." That pulled his attention toward her.

"Are they treating you well?" he whispered.

Enora shrugged in reply. "As well as expected for an Unseelie in Seelie lands."

Branan knew what she meant. When he first arrived at the goblin market, many people refused to speak to him because he was an outsider. He'd dealt with vandalism at his stall until one night, he'd guarded it in his wolf form. After that, no one seemed to mess with him, but it didn't make any of them friendlier to him. Old prejudices died hard for some people.

He put his hand over hers and squeezed. "You'll get there. Give them a chance to get to know you and they'll see what we all see, the amazing person and healer you are."

She smiled and squeezed his hand in return.

"Now, tell me when you guys are thinking of having a wedding?"

That did it. Instantly, her mood lifted, and her attention pulled away from her concern for him. She lit up from the inside with joy as she talked about all what she wanted for their wedding and begged him to arrange for someone to take care of his shop so he could attend when the time came. She only relented when he said he promised he would ask Amani when they had a date set.

While they ate, conversation flowed. The food was delicious now that his nerves settled, and he could actually taste it.

"Would anyone like a power demonstration today?" Callie asked after her second cup of coffee and her mood had picked up. They all agreed, and Branan went to his room to collect a few things before they headed out. He needed some coins and to find someone to send another letter to Amani arranging for her to stay at the shop for a few more days. He didn't think it would be a problem, but he didn't want her to worry or to cause her any inconvenience.

Branan opened the door and walked into the hallway. He had only taken a few steps when he bumped into someone. "Oh, pardon me," he said, glancing up from where he'd been situating a few things in his satchel.

Torin laughed. "Actually, you're just the person I was hoping to talk to." His smile was so reminiscent of Reid's it sent off a small pang in Branan's chest.

"I am?"

"Yes, can we?" Torin asked, motioning toward the door Branan just exited before plowing on. "And before you try to tell me the others are waiting on you, Callie said they would browse the market and meet you by the blacksmith's shop. Evin seemed to think you would know where it is, or at least be able to locate it," Torin arched an eyebrow as if daring Branan to come up with another excuse.

"Of course," Branan acquiesced. He opened the door and stepped inside, leading them both to a small table with two chairs.

"It's been a while since I've been in here," Torin mumbled quietly, looking around.

"Did you used to stay here?" Branan had been curious just whose extravagant room he'd been staying in.

"No. I'm actually surprised you haven't figured it out, but perhaps given more time you would."

Branan had to admit after falling asleep in the tub and waking with his plan to see if he could rile up Lachlan enough to get him to drop his façade, his curiosity about the room had faded into the background.

Torin wandered over and picked up a small rectangular jewelry box off of the bedside table and brought it over to where Branan sat. He handed the box to Branan. It was so familiar it made his heart ache. He had a box just like this at his home, the one Torin had brought to him filled with coins. This one was almost a duplicate except where his box had an intricate carving of a stag's head at its center surrounded by branches with leaves, this one had a wolf's head. His fingers traced over the design. It was then that the familiarity of the wallpaper design struck him. It was the same as the design on the cedar box he had received so long ago.

The pieces all clicked into place. "It's his, isn't it?" Branan whispered, placing the box on his lap and looking up at Torin.

Torin smiled tightly. "I knew you were smart. Had to be if Reid had taken a liking to you. He always needed someone who could challenge his mind."

"I'm sorry," Branan started, but Torin waved him off.

"I'm not here to talk about Reid, although I wouldn't be opposed to that conversation at another time, but now I feel there's a more pressing matter." Torin nodded to the box which Branan was absently tracing his fingers over. "He carved that himself, you know. Not long after he came back."

He didn't need to say from where. An uneven breath stuck in his chest as Torin continued.

"He wouldn't tell me what happened. Still won't, as a matter of fact, although it's not for my lack of trying. I think he guards your time together as something sacred, something he's scared to share with anyone else. Perhaps he fears judgement, or he thinks by keeping it compartmentalized in this tiny box shoved so deeply inside himself he won't have to wonder why or how things could have been. See, I've learned something throughout my years and losses that our king has yet to grasp. Life's too short not to take what you want. While some of us may be on this world for a few centuries, it's still just a tiny blip of time in the grand scheme of things.

"He used to be different. He used to be so full of life, one of those almost careless risk takers. At least he was when I first met him, but losing his sister changed him in ways I haven't been able to help fix. He's jaded. He sees what she did as an act of love that cost her life. Worst of all, he still blames himself for not having been there and having enjoyed his time with you instead."

Branan eyebrows squished together. His heart caught in his throat as Torin continued. "Now you and I both know that what happened was beyond his control. He was injured in a way that would have kept him out of the battle even if he had made it back sooner, and blaming himself is pointless. Perhaps initially he may have even blamed you, as unfair as that it is, and even though he hasn't spoken of it, I can tell what eats him the most is that he was so fucking happy when he was with you, while his sister was taking her last breath. Why else would he send your compensation in a box he'd carved himself, when everyone else received a small pouch? Why else would he spend time while he was grieving to carve your likeness into a box he kept by his own bed, getting frustrated when it just wasn't right? I didn't understand his obsession at the time and passed it off as some strange manifestation of his grief. I thought a wolf's a wolf, right? But now, I see.

"He may have done many things wrong where you're concerned, but know that he was a boy shoved into a role he never wanted, drowning in grief when he left. His sister's death only twisted things more. She had refused to marry the one she loved because she was scared the council wouldn't approve. When he was taken and she finally realized what she was going to lose, she fought, but it cost her life. So, he views love as something that can destroy, and he was too young when his parents were killed, but I wasn't. I remember how our lives thrived the most when the king or queen is truly happy, as if their joy and contentment breathes life into everything around them, including the land."

A tear fell from Branan's eye. He had no idea.

Torin leaned forward and wiped the tear away as a father would. "None of that now. That's not why I'm here. I know you loved my son, and I thank you for that, but you loved someone else before him, and I think a part of you never stopped loving him."

Branan shook his head and opened his mouth to refute or confirm his claim, he wasn't sure which. His insides twisted as Torin held up a hand. "I'm not done. Now I know Lachlan did some things that hurt you, but I wanted you to have the bigger picture, to have the pieces I had before you made any decision. Yes, he owes you an explanation. Yes, he can be difficult and stubborn, but at dinner last night I saw more pieces of the man I once knew than I had since his sister died, and I know that's because of you. So have faith, be strong, fight for what you want, and most of all, don't be afraid to love again."

Torin stood and squeezed Branan on the shoulder, leaving him speechless as he closed the door behind him.

There was so much to unpack from that conversation, if one could really call it a conversation, when all he'd done was listen. His heart ached. His wolf whined. It was all such a knotted jumble he'd have to untangle the only way he knew how. He only hoped his friends would still be waiting when he was done.

Lachlan walked restlessly through the castle. Earlier he had skipped breakfast, having it sent to his room instead. His cheeks burned when he thought about his actions the previous night. He had used palace business as an excuse. It's not like he actually managed to accomplish anything with every idle thought jumping back to last night. The truth was, he was afraid to see Branan after the incident last night. How could he look him in the eye after acting like such a fool?

He was passing by a window overlooking the woods at the back of the palace when movement caught his eye. As if summoned by his thoughts, Branan was striding toward the woods with purpose. He stopped right at the edge and took a quick look around before hanging his satchel on the branch.

"Enjoying the view? It is a nice day." Torin's teasing made him jump. He hadn't even heard him approach.

"Oh, um…." Lachlan started, before coughing to clear his throat.

Torin peered around his shoulder and caught the wolf darting into the woods. He smirked at Lachlan, who flushed.

"I see you're not busy, so now would be the perfect time for us to finish our conversation from last night."

Lachlan sighed. "I'm not in the mood, Torin."

"You're never in the mood, so now shouldn't be any different from later," Torin countered.

"You're certainly snarky this morning. Did someone's

favorite cook not have a fresh scone set aside for him?" Lachlan teased.

Torin frowned. "Now that you mention it."

Lachlan hoped the distraction might derail the conversation and refocus it on Torin, but alas, his hopes were dashed.

"It doesn't matter. We need to talk. Friend to friend, not king to second. *Friend to friend.* We were those before you ever became king."

Lachlan winced. "You're right, old friend. I've a feeling we'll need some privacy for this conversation."

Lachlan led the way to his study and closed the door, locking it behind Torin. He didn't want to be interrupted by any staff and have them possibly overhear anything. He sat at his desk, hoping the space between them might help.

"You told me once that you were attacked by wolves and Branan saved you, that he nursed you back to health and you owe him a life debt, but there's more to it than that, isn't there?"

Lachlan stared down at the papers on his desk and nodded his head.

"What's the story?"

Lachlan was weary of carrying the burdens of his past all on his own, so he told his best friend everything. He confessed how he used to sneak away for runs in his stag form just to find the boy in the woods, how he grew to care for him. How on that fateful day he'd gone to see the boy one more time before he left for battle just in case he didn't make it back, but he was attacked by a trio of wolves from Branan's pack. He told him how Branan had come to his rescue, had saved his life, and essentially turned on his pack members. At this, Torin vowed retribution, but Lachlan told him how they hadn't known who he was or even that he was a Fae. How he hadn't ever shown Branan his Fae form until he had no control over it. He confessed how he had used Torin's name instead of his own because he was afraid Branan would recognize it as the prince's name, and it would change things between them. How over those days he fell in love with him and had considered keeping him until he woke that dreaded morning with a new eye color and he knew the true consequences of his actions.

"Oh Lach, I wish you had told me sooner." Torin sighed.

"We were both grieving. You just didn't know I was not only grieving the loss of my family, but the loss of my first love."

"Your only love," Torin corrected, acting on a hunch, but Lachlan nodded in confirmation. "Why didn't you go after him? Try to fix things? You didn't have to lose him. He could have been by your side, helping you through your grief."

"Don't you see? Love got Orla killed." Lachlan exclaimed, trying to summon the familiar and sharp anger that usually accompanied his beliefs on love, but the words now felt empty and hollow like nothing more than a fearful excuse.

"Oh, Lach. Think about it. Love didn't get her killed. Denying love did. If she hadn't denied herself what she and Alfie both wanted, he never would've gone on that stupid trip. He never would've taken the risk. He would've been here by her side." Torin rose from his seat, smacking a hand down on Lachlan's desk. "Now you're repeating her mistakes, and I can't stand by and watch it anymore."

Lachlan opened his mouth to speak, but Torin kept going. "You haven't been yourself since she died, and it's been killing me. I know the responsibility of the crown weighs heavily upon you, but you don't have to burden it alone. That's what Grady and I tried to get you to understand in those first few months. You're not alone. You can still be the man you once were. The one who laughed often and smiled all the time. I know you created this cold and calculated façade when you first took the throne and have kept reinforcing it over the years, but you don't need it anymore. The council members who once sought to control you are gone. We made sure of that. You can still be the prince your people once loved. You deserve to be yourself, and most of all, you deserve to be happy.

"You may not remember, but when your mother and father were both here, our land thrived in a way that cannot be explained. The harvests were more bountiful, the flowers smelled sweeter. It was as if their happiness fed the land through the magic. Stop denying yourself what you're meant to have and embrace it. It's what your parents would have wanted. It's what Orla would've wanted for you, and it's what I want. You still care for Branan. It's clear in the way you remembered he was vegetarian and had the kitchen prepare plenty of dishes he could eat. In the way you practically cornered him into staying and then put him up in your old room. And absolutely do not use the same excuse your sister once did about what other people will think. Fuck what other people will think. Besides, they'll get over it as soon as they see how your true happiness influences the land."

Every excuse Lachlan had on the tip of his tongue fizzled out. What if Torin was right? He thought back to when he was young. He'd always thought he viewed the world with rose-colored glasses in his memories, but perhaps it was more than that. Perhaps the land was actually more vibrant, the flowers actually smelled sweeter.

Torin sighed. His voice was softer when he spoke. "You've been given a second chance. Don't waste it, friend. You deserve the happiness I shared with Indra. Now, I've said my piece and I'll take my leave."

"Only if you'll do one thing," Lachlan said, finally finding his voice. Torin paused at the door.

"What's that?"

"Take your own advice, Tor. Just because Indra's gone doesn't mean you don't deserve love. She'd want you to find it again. She would want you to be happy, too."

Torin grimaced and left without another word. Lachlan knew his friend could be just as stubborn as he was and would need some time to think on what he said, but he couldn't pretend to be ignorant of the way the way Torin would sneak away to chat with the cook in the kitchen, nor the way she always seemed to have a special treat set aside just for him. If he was going to take Torin's advice, he expected his friend to also give it the same consideration.

CHAPTER 24

BRANAN TOOK IN the surrounding sights. The market was busier than yesterday. His eye had just caught on a familiar fountain where he had made a wish with his dad once upon a time, and he stumbled slightly.

"Careful there," firm hands helped steady him. He looked up into a familiar face, although the last time he'd seen him, he'd been but a pup on the cusp of adulthood. Shane was much older now. He supposed they all were.

"Holy shit! It is you," he said on a breath, his copper eyes widening in surprise. But just as quickly, a wide grin stole across his face. "I thought... but it's been so long...." he trailed off and fidgeted the longer Branan went without responding.

He's not his brother, he scolded himself. Shane had always been nice. Sure, annoying like a little brother at times, but always kind to him. Shane had never once held it over Branan's head when he shifted sooner than Branan, despite the age difference. Instead, Shane had been the one who tried to help him shift, describing the ways he did it and offering suggestions away from the prying ears of his brothers.

Branan smiled. "Shane."

He put his hand out, but instead of grabbing his forearm in greeting, Shane pulled Branan into a fierce hug. His wolf whined softly as he returned Shane's embrace. He had missed this. Despite how much he'd tried to deny it, his wolf was happier around others.

When he finally pulled away, warmth radiated throughout his body. "How have you been? I heard a bit from your ma, but I'd love to hear it from you."

"You saw ma? I bet she gave you an earful for staying away as long as you did. I mean, we all understand...."

Branan chuckled. "She certainly did."

Shane joined in with his laughter, and it was as if the years of absence between them had never existed. "I've been good. I'm working at the palace now, in the treasury." He ran a hand through his dirty blonde hair, a nervous tick from when he was younger.

Branan smiled. "It fits you." The other man's shoulders visibly relaxed. "I take it your brothers don't feel the same."

Shane pursed his lips. "You know how Whelan is. When I decided to apprentice in the treasury, he told me Da would be disappointed in me, but Ma was quick to shut that down. I think he just wanted me close so he could keep an eye on me. After everything, he assumed leadership of the pack and I worried he might use that to force me into the guard, but Ma reminded him that a good alpha needed a balanced pack. Although, I'm not quite sure he could actually force me. It's strange. His orders don't seem to hold as much command as your dad's did, but perhaps that's because I was a kid at the time." Shane cocked his head to the side, a line drawn between his brows.

Branan fought the urge to fidget under his scrutiny. He knew exactly why the pack bond felt weak, but explaining so would only lead to trouble. He kept his face neutral as he guided the conversation back to safer waters. "And now? How does he feel about your choice?"

Shane shrugged. "He lets me handle the pack finances, but you know how he and Malcom can be when they're together."

Assholes is what Branan wanted to say, but he didn't know how Shane would take to it. He chose his words carefully. "Bossy and condescending."

Shane chuckled, "I suppose some things haven't changed." Shane chewed on his lower lip. "I'd advise you to avoid them if you can. I'm not sure they'd be as welcoming." He shifted from one foot to another and changed the topic before Branan could process his warning. "Are you staying or just passing through?"

"I'm only here for a few days for business." Branan then filled him in on his animal trading business at the goblin market in the borderlands.

"That's awesome, Bran. I know neither of us followed the paths our fathers would've wanted, but I'd still like to think they'd be proud of us for doing something different." Shane smiled. "Well, I have to run. I'm only on my break for lunch, but you have an open invitation to visit me at the treasury any time."

"Thank you, Shane." This time, Branan was the one to pull him into a hug. "I'd like that. And if you're ever in the goblin market, come find me." *Pack,* Branan's inner wolf growled. *Not anymore. He's someone else's pack now,* he answered, shoving his wolf back down.

Shane grinned as he released Branan, but the expression faded as though a thought crossed his mind. "Bran, I really do think you should avoid Whelan if you can. Some days it seems as if he's just itching for a fight, and I wouldn't put it past him to pick one with you."

Branan nodded in reply, and Shane strolled off, moving deeper into the market. Branan let his thoughts run as he wandered toward the blacksmith's forge. The thought of Whelan made his wolf growl so loudly he felt it push through and vibrate in his chest. He had every intention of avoiding Whelan at all costs. There was no predicting what might happen if they crossed paths.

"There you are!" Callie called, waving wildly at him as he approached the forge. When he got closer, she ran up to him and threw her arms around him. "Everything go okay?" she asked softly. Branan nodded against her shoulder. "Good." With one last squeeze, she pulled away.

"Alright, who's ready to see some magic?" she called over to the other three. She rubbed her hands together and grinned maniacally. "Let's do this!"

"Babe, we talked about this. You know I love you, but when you smile like that…." Evin shuddered. "No good things happen. You're just going to do a small demonstration, alright. Small. No hurricanes. No torrential downpours."

Callie stuck her tongue out at him. "We'll you're no fun. So where to?"

"There's a nice open field between our place and the palace that should work," Enora offered.

Callie bowed, waving an arm out in front of her. "Lead the way, milady." She looped her arm through Enora's and the two girls walked off, not even bothering to look back and see if the boys followed them.

"Perhaps getting those two together more isn't the best idea." Maddock sighed.

"Speak for yourself!" Evin chuckled. "Enora will be a great influence on Callie."

"It's not Enora's influence I'm worried about," Maddock grumbled.

Evin elbowed him in the side and Branan laughed.

He hadn't felt this light in ages.

"Callie! That's too much wind. You're going to ruin my garden!" Enora scolded, her hair whipping around her face. Branan was glad he had the sense to pull his hair up into a bun this morning, but even then, the wind was tugging strands loose.

Callie twirled with her arms spread wide, laughing at the sky. As soon as she stopped, dropping her arms to her side, the wind died. The familiar stormy gray glow in her eyes made his chest ache a little. He missed Reid, missed having someone to confide in and take comfort from. He'd spent so long shoving everyone away, but Reid hadn't been the least bit deterred. His stubbornness had eventually won Branan over. Only now Branan was coming to realize how wrong he had been to push everyone away after his dad died.

You could have family, a pack, his wolf urged, and for the first time since he'd felt the alpha magic, he wanted to agree. His smile fell as a bolt of lightning struck a nearby tree. He didn't know any wolf shifters to even consider asking to form a pack. *Who said anything about shifters?* his wolf asked.

A large bolt of lightning streaked across the sky. Evin glanced up at it and swallowed. "Alright Callie, that's enough, sweetheart. We don't need another forest fire."

Callie stuck out her bottom lip in a pout. "Last time wasn't my fault. Besides, I put out that fire with rain afterward. No one was harmed."

Evin shook his head while Maddock doubled over with laughter.

"Well, well. Who do we have here?" A deep, faintly familiar voice asked.

Branan's heart stuttered when he caught the scent of wolf. Whelan.

"Whelan, Malcom, I didn't expect you to be over here," Maddock replied stiffly.

"We were over on the training field sparring when we were first treated to a light sprinkling of rain, followed by some powerfully high winds which caused us to investigate," Whelan replied.

Branan didn't dare glance over his shoulder, but hurried toward the girls. Both of them stared curiously, but the second they read whatever emotion played out over his face, their eyes flashed. Callie moved to take a step forward, but Enora put a hand on her arm. Shaw's boys may not have been able to read the girls' expressions from there, but they were sizing up the perceived threat in front of them, and Branan would bet good money that Enora's siren was a sight to behold, one she kept on a tight leash for good reason.

Finally, Branan turned, placing himself between the girls and the new arrivals. Evin and Maddock stood side by side. Evin's posture was more relaxed than Maddock's, but Branan could still see the tension underneath and the casual way Evin rested his hand over the hilt of his blade. It was an interesting dynamic as all four of them belonged to the palace guard, but there was definitely something there. He wondered what other run-ins the other two may have had with Shaw's boys.

Malcom's eyes widened and inhaled deeply before elbowing his brother in the side. "I told you I smelled him earlier, but no, you said I was lying. Well, there you go. He's not a phantom."

He pointed directly at Branan and Whelan's eyes met his, turning full copper. His wolf's hackles raised, ready at a moment's notice to shift and attack. The girls stepped closer behind him, and one of them placed a comforting hand on the small of his back.

"As you can see, we're just fine out here. No one requires your assistance, and we're just wrapping up, so you can go back to the training grounds now," Maddock stated.

"What are you doing here?" Whelan growled, ignoring Maddock completely.

Maddock and Evin turned, questions in their eyes, but

he could see they were putting the pieces together. They had to know Whelan and Malcom were wolves, and while Branan may not have directly told them, he could feel his wolf so close to the surface it wouldn't be hard to take one look at his eyes and be able to tell.

"Do you know these two pricks?" Callie asked, stepping up next to him and staring the others down with a menacing glare. She pressed her knuckles against the palm of the other hand, cracking them loudly.

Branan would have laughed at her posturing if he hadn't seen firsthand how quickly Whelan could take down an animal while in wolf form, and that was before his decades of service in the guard. "Unfortunately."

"Whelan, Malcom," he nodded curtly, letting a bit of his wolf's growl leak into his voice, enough for them to know he wouldn't take any threats lightly.

"You're not supposed to be here," Whelan snarled, stalking forward.

Branan took a step forward to place himself once again in front of the threat and the girls as thunder rolled in the distance, the air stirring with electricity. Maddock moved, but not as quickly as Evin, who positioned himself in front of Whelan.

"Branan can be anywhere he wishes. Last time I checked, you weren't his mom," Evin spat.

Branan sighed. He knew Evin meant well, but that dig would only agitate Whelan's wolf. "I was invited here, and don't need your permission to visit my home." He stood a little straighter as he interjected, refusing to be cowed by Whelan. He wasn't the runt of the pack anymore. His wolf rumbled in his chest, eager to get out and show Whelan just how much had changed, but Branan tamped down and held him back. He couldn't risk a conflict between them spilling onto his friends. For now, he would let his past color Whelan's perception of him. He didn't want to mess with old pack dynamics when he had no intention of sticking around.

This time, it was Malcom who spoke. "Home. That's an interesting word. You turned your back on this place the minute you could. Broke Ma's heart, you did." His jaw clenched, and a pang of guilt struck Branan in his chest.

"I'm sorry about that. I never meant to hurt Kyna." His softened his expression so Malcom could see the genuine regret there.

Malcom's shoulders relaxed, his claws retracting back into normal nails. Whelan, on the other hand, looked a second away from shifting.

"I would remind you, Whelan, that an act of violence against a civilian will not be tolerated by your commander." Evin glanced down and flicked an imaginary speck of dirt off his left shoulder, feigning disinterest in the entire affair.

"Not to mention that you're severely outnumbered," Maddock added. At some point, he had retrieved a blade from his arsenal and now casually twirled it across his fingers. The sky above them darkened with storm clouds, a loud roll of thunder nearly shaking the ground.

Whelan's eyes moved across the group, even taking in the women who once again had stepped up next to Branan protectively. Whelan's canines elongated slightly. He'd always been one to let his wolf loose a little too freely, using it to intimidate others, something which obviously hadn't changed as he aged.

"This isn't finished," he growled low.

Branan stiffened, his wolf making his own claws sharpen in response to the threat. "It is," he commanded with alpha authority.

Malcom's eyes widened as he tugged on Whelan's arm. But Whelan shook him off, practically shoving him away. His eyes narrowed, and he snapped his teeth at Branan before turning and striding away.

"Well, that was interesting," Evin noted, turning back to their group. He walked over to Callie and pulled her into his arms, pressing a firm kiss against her lips. The skies above them cleared instantly, clouds fading from gray to white before dispersing. "Well done, love. Look at how much control you had!" he praised Callie as he pulled away from her. Callie blushed in return.

Maddock grabbed Enora's hand and pressed a kiss to her palm. She shivered, the silver bleeding from her eyes. "Thank you," she whispered, while Maddock smiled comfortingly.

Callie stepped out of Evin's embrace and made her way toward Branan, poking him in the chest. "You, sir, have some explaining to do."

"That is, if you want to tell us. If you don't, we understand that, too. Our pasts are not always something we wish to share with others," Enora added softly. He knew Enora was Unseelie, but he had never directly asked her about why she left because he knew too well what it was to wish to leave everything behind, and now it seemed Enora had sensed the same about him.

Branan looked at each of them, nodding at Enora's

words.

"Despite what Callie may say, please know you don't owe us an explanation. She gets a little overzealous when it comes to anyone threatening her friends," Evin added.

Callie blushed and nodded. "It's true."

Branan sighed and paused. *Tell them*, his wolf urged. "Whelan's family was part of my pack. The one my da was alpha of, so we grew up together. A family unit of sorts, and sometimes a dysfunctional one." He swallowed. He'd only told Reid about his past once, and even then, he was careful what he disclosed.

"I was a late bloomer with my shifter magic. For a while, my da and I weren't sure I could ever shift. As you can imagine, Whelan didn't make that any easier. He's only a year older than me, and when his younger brother could shift at an early age, it was even worse. For a while I felt like an outsider in my own pack.

"I'd been too caring, too sensitive, too gentle when I was younger. They saw the way I cared for animals as an oddity, a contradiction to the nature of a wolf. And while it's true, our wolves are predators, they are also fierce protectors. When I finally did shift, I still felt like an outsider. The first time I allowed my wolf to hunt and catch a rabbit, I cried. I wasn't much of a meat eater before that, but that made me go full vegetarian."

He shook off the memories of Lachlan's deer comforting him in the woods, how he sobbed into his fur, feeling the deer's concern and compassion. "When my da was off training with the guard, Whelan's mother watched over me, and I was expected to be with the boys. We were pack after all."

He bent his neck down, bracing himself for the next part of the story.

Callie's arm wrapped around his waist as she leaned into him. "I'm so sorry."

"Thank you. It wasn't all bad. My da was amazing. He never once made me feel less than, even when I couldn't shift. I made friends with some animals in the woods. One stag, in particular, was my closet friend. My ma's magic allows me to communicate with them. I can get images and feelings and convey those back to them. It's hard to kill something when you can sense its pleading, its panic, see pictures of its life."

"Oh, Bran." Callie squeezed him tighter.

"The others, they didn't understand. They saw what I could do as a weakness. Whelan would constantly call me a freak for talking to the animals. My da died with theirs in the great battle when Queen Orla fell. It was then that I lost my best friend too, and a part of me died, as well. I didn't have anyone to anchor me here and without an alpha, the pack was reeling. A few days later, I fled to the human realm and spent a long time trying to figure out who I wanted to be before eventually making my way back to Fae and to the borderlands. I wasn't ready to face everything I left behind."

"Until I insisted you deliver the guinea pigs," Maddock huffed.

Branan pulled away from Callie to reach over and place a hand on Maddock's arm.

He shook his head. "Nonsense. As Evin put it earlier, I'm allowed to be anywhere I wish. For far too long, I let the heartbreak that this place reminded me of dictate how I acted. I wouldn't come visit Reid and eventually he stopped asking. Something I regret now. You reminded me I still have people here who care about me. That I may not have a blood family, but I have a chosen family and sometimes that's better than the one you're born to."

"Damn straight," Enora added before she and Callie sandwiched him in a hug.

"Thank you all for standing with me," Branan said when the girls pulled away.

"Any time," Evin replied.

Branan's heart was full as they wandered back to his room in the palace. The two couples bid him good night after making plans to meet up again tomorrow for a tour of the gardens and Enora's apothecary, and for Callie to see the guinea pigs. It would be good for him to check one more time that the guinea pigs were adjusting well to their new home.

He thought about extending his stay. The thought of returning to his house in the borderlands didn't hold the same appeal it had before he made this trip. Perhaps he should look into expanding his business and opening a shop here. There was only one problem with that.

The clearing of a throat pulled him from his thoughts, and he looked up at the same problem he was just considering. Lachlan leaned against a pillar in the hallway dressed casually in brown leather pants and a white shirt covered with a deep purple vest that hugged his muscles in a way that left Branan's throat dry. "Did you have a nice day?" Lachlan asked, his lavender eyes sparking with interest, an eyebrow cocked as if to ask Branan if he liked what he saw. He closed the distance between them in a few strides.

Branan swallowed. "I did." He wasn't expecting to be caught with the Seelie king in the hallway alone. He glanced around, and sure enough, there wasn't a servant in sight.

"Good." Lachlan's smile was genuine, but it faded almost as quickly as it had appeared, and Branan's fingers itched as if the smile were an object he could snatch and give it back to the king. "Have you eaten?" Lachlan scowled almost as soon as the words left his mouth.

"I have eaten food today, yes." Branan couldn't resist teasing him.

"I meant dinner... I mean... ugh...." He huffed and ran a hand through his short black hair.

Branan's fingers twitched. Lachlan's hair was shorter than he remembered, and he wondered if it was still just as soft as when he had run his fingers through it, offering him comfort while he slept.

The king flushed before he finally blurted, "Will you have dinner with me tonight?"

"Huh, not insisting this time," he teased again, but when he saw the king flinch and look away, he stopped. "Yes, I would like that very much."

Lachlan's eyes met his, and his heart stuttered. He felt his wolf rumble with approval.

"Excellent." Lachlan grinned widely. "Meet me downstairs in an hour."

The king turned and hurried away, leaving Branan puzzled. He thought things had been going well. So why did Lachlan leave so soon? He scratched at the stubble growing across his jaw before continuing back to his room. He told himself it was just dinner, and he was a guest who needed to be fed, after all. It wasn't anything to get excited about.

A date, his wolf interjected.

No, just a friendly dinner, he countered.

Then why was he waiting for you in the hall to ask you to join him for a meal? And he left immediately after receiving the answer he wanted?

To be nice, he argued.

His wolf huffed with agitation, choosing to not respond, and even Branan could feel how flimsy his excuse was. He just didn't want to get his hopes up, only to have them come crashing down at his feet.

CHAPTER 25

LACHLAN'S HEART RACED as he rushed to the kitchen. As much as he wanted to stay in Branan's presence, he didn't want to give him the opportunity to change his mind. Not when it had taken so little convincing to get him to say yes. He hoped Torin wasn't wrong.

"Niamh!" he called as he approached.

"Yes, sire," the curvy cook with pale blue hair replied, wiping her hands on her apron.

"You have the evening off. You and the rest of the kitchen staff," he added, looking at the two other Fae in the kitchen.

"Sire?"

"I only ask that you stay for a few moments to help me prepare something, but the rest of your staff is dismissed for the evening."

"Are you sure?" she asked, her deep blue eyes wide.

He nodded, and she clapped her hands. "You heard the man! You have the evening off, quick before he changes his mind," she added jokingly. The other two Fae quickly finished their tasks and fled the scene before he could call them back.

"Now, what is it that you require my help with?"

He rubbed his jaw. "I'd like to prepare a picnic."

"A picnic?" her brow furrowed.

"Yes, for two."

The corner of her mouth lifted. "And does our guest require a meal this evening?"

"He'll be the one joining me."

She pulled her lips in tight, attempting to fight a smile, but he could see it reflected in the way her eyes sparkled.

"I'll be happy to help you, sire."

Lachlan selected a large variety of cheeses, breads, fruits, and vegetables, slicing them appropriately, while Niamh prepared a dip. When he had a nice collection going, he poured some ambrosia into a large flask. While Niamh left to fetch a basket for him, he put together a small platter with some items he had just sliced and some of the dip, tucking it below the counter for the time being.

When Niamh returned with the perfect basket, they loaded the items together and he added two goblets, but Niamh immediately pulled them out. "I think you'll find the experience of drinking straight from the flask to be much more enjoyable," she said with a conspiratorial wink.

He shook his head and pulled the hidden platter out from under the counter. "And I think you'll find sharing this with a certain someone to be much more enjoyable than eating it by yourself."

She blushed furiously and tried to refuse, but he insisted. He picked up the basket.

"Thank you for your help. Oh, and Niamh, Torin's heart may be guarded from loss and grief, but I assure you, it still can be won over."

Niamh smiled, tucking a strand of hair behind her ear. "I hope your guest knows how lucky he is."

"Trust me, I'm the lucky one," he added before heading for his room. He had just enough time to freshen up before they were due to meet downstairs.

As he took a few minutes to brush his teeth and freshen up, he tried to calm his nerves. He'd had all morning to consider Torin's words, to decide maybe his oldest friend was right, and he had been wrong to deny himself love all this time. When he saw Branan for the first time since his world had been altered, he knew he hadn't buried his heart; it had only been lying dormant, waiting for the only one who had ever made it beat. He also knew he had some work to do to even see if Branan would be receptive to a second chance, but he was ready to tackle any problem that came their way.

With the basket over his arm, Lachlan returned downstairs to wait for Branan. He glanced inside the basket, running a list in his head to make sure he hadn't forgotten anything when a voice interrupted him. "What is that for?"

Lachlan turned to see Branan walking toward him.

"There's somewhere I want to show you, and I thought it might be nice to dine there instead of here, if that's okay with you." He blinked up at Branan, his heart in his throat. Branan's answer would dictate Lachlan's next moves and tell him just how many mountains he may have to climb to overcome what was broken between them.

"That sounds nice," Branan replied.

Lachlan's stomach settled. "Perfect! If you'll follow me." He led the way toward the lower level of the palace. Branan frowned but followed behind in silence. When Lachlan opened the door to his study, Branan broke the silence. "Your study? Is this a working dinner or do you just not want us to be seen together?" Branan's voice dripped with hurt as he came to a dead stop.

Lachlan's steps faltered, bringing him to a halt. He reached out and grabbed Branan's hand. "It's not like that. Just trust me. Where I want to take you is not somewhere inside the palace, but this is the easiest way for me to get there."

Branan's sea green eyes searched Lachlan's gaze, looking for something. He must have found it because he nodded slightly, his furrowed brows smoothing out. "All right, lead the way."

Reluctantly, Lachlan released his hand. He didn't want to risk Branan deciding this wasn't worth it, but he couldn't hold his hand, carry the basket with their dinner, and open the hidden passageway all at the same time.

Once they were both in his study, he locked the door before moving across the room to push against the hidden panel, revealing a secret passageway.

"Oh," Branan said on a breath from behind him.

Lachlan hesitated, hoping he was making the right decision. He turned back toward Branan. "Torin is the only other person alive who knows about this."

Branan stared directly into his eyes, copper swirling with mint green. "Thank you for trusting me with this. I won't tell another soul."

Electricity shot through Lachlan's veins. When Branan looked at him like that he didn't need the magic of a promise to know Branan would keep his word. He nodded before turning back toward the passage. He still felt the spark, but did Branan?

With butterflies fluttering in his stomach, he took a lantern off of its hook on the wall and held it up to light their way. They walked for a little while before Branan broke the silence.

"Has this been here since the palace was built?"

Lachlan nodded. "That's what my father told me. The Seelie king, who originally built the castle, had the tunnels made as a way for the royal family to escape in the event of a siege. Supposedly, after it was constructed, he used his magic to wipe its existence from the minds of the builders."

"Makes sense. Do you come here often?"

Branan's breath against the back of his neck caused a bolt of heat to shoot down his spine. "Sometimes, when I want to get away without anyone bothering me." He swallowed. "I used to come down here a lot as a child to play hide and seek with Orla." He smiled, remembering how many times he and his sister got scolded for getting dusty while playing in the tunnels.

They came upon a fork in the tunnel, and he took the path to the right. "There are many offshoots of the passage, only a few leading to other hidden panels within the palace's walls. The others comprise dead ends or winding ways that get you so turned around when you join the main path, you doubt your original direction. They were meant to confuse and trap anyone who wasn't familiar with the route."

"In other words, if I want to get back, I need to stick with you?" Branan chuckled.

Lachlan shrugged. "I'm not the one who built them, but I wouldn't suggest wandering off."

"Has your family ever had to use them for their intended purpose?"

Lachlan shook his head. "Thankfully no. Though I made quite a habit as a young teen, using them to sneak out and go for a run in the woods and later meet up with a raven-haired boy I was infatuated with." He didn't need to turn to know a blush crept across Branan's face. Instead, he savored the slight hitch in Branan's breath.

"And what happened with the raven-haired boy?" Branan asked, his voice barely above a whisper.

The butterflies in his stomach turned into hummingbirds, rapidly beating their wings. It was time to give him some of the truth. He owed Branan that much, and based on the hesitation he heard in his voice, Branan needed answers. "I ruined it. First, I used a fake name with him. I'd grown accustomed to people judging me or wanting to get close to me simply because of who I was and the position I was born into. They never once stopped to consider if I even wanted to be prince, let alone king. I was scared that if the boy found out who I truly was, it would change things between us in a way we couldn't come back from. It would ruin this relationship that had become so precious to me." He heard Branan's steps falter behind him.

"Just a little further," he added knowing that it was his words, not the distance that caused Branan to stop. Lachlan pressed forward, not wanting to have this moment in the dank tunnel. He heard Branan's steps continue and close the gap between them.

"Seems like a somewhat justifiable reason to give a fake name, but did you consider he wouldn't care? That the boy may not have even put two and two together with your name and that of the Seelie prince, or that it wouldn't have made one drop of a difference to him."

Lachlan swallowed. "I didn't." Now it was time for him to stop. Branan stumbled into his back. His heart sped up when he felt the press of Branan's hands against his waist and the heat of Branan's breath across the back of his neck. Even though he knew Branan was only using him to steady himself, his skin tingled from the warmth until Branan stepped back, putting space between both of them. He swallowed. "We've reached the end. Hold this for a minute." He turned, handing the lantern to Branan, who stared at the rock wall in front of them with an arched brow.

Facing the rock once again, he plucked a knife from his belt and pricked his thumb and ran it down the wall, leaving a bloody streak behind. The rock glowed faintly, the blood fading from its face before the wall completely faded away. He turned back to get the lantern from Branan, savoring the wide set of his eyes and the way his jaw had dropped open. It was old blood magic. "Thanks." He grabbed the lantern from his hand and stepped through where the wall had once been.

"Okay, now that was pretty cool," Branan admitted after he stepped through the wall. Within a few moments, the wall reappeared. He pressed his hand against it, and Lachlan smiled, knowing he would only feel the rocky surface of the hill. The only indicator that something was different was a small symbol carved into one of the rocks near the bottom left, which someone could easily mistake as some sort of random hieroglyph for the sun, fairly common to be found on Seelie lands. When they wanted to return using the passage, all he'd have to do was once again prick his finger, but this time place it on the center of the sun. He decided against saying anything about that now so he would see that look of astonishment on Branna's face once more. He placed the lantern next to the rock. The light of the moon was so bright, they wouldn't need it to light their path until they returned to the tunnels.

"This way," he said, once again leading Branan through the dark, but this time it was through the canopy of the woods. Lachlan inhaled deeply, letting the scent of the woods mixed with Branan fill his lungs. Then he paused and reached his hand out. He held his breath, waiting to see if Branan would take his hand, and released it when he felt Branan's warm fingers close around his. It was a step in the right direction, and the hope of it gave him buoyed his steps as they walked through the woods.

They walked in silence for a few minutes until they came upon the clearing by the small lake. The surface of the lake was mostly still, with only the occasional ripple hinting at the life beneath. The moon was clearly reflected on its surface. "Here's a suitable spot." He found a place on the shore for their picnic, but was hesitant to drop Branan's hand now that he held it. Lachlan gave Branan's hand a firm squeeze before releasing it and then retrieved the blanket from the basket. He spread it across the ground for them to sit on, then kneeled on it and started unpacking the collection of bread, fruits, vegetables, and cheeses he had prepared earlier, along with the flask of ambrosia.

Branan smiled as he sat. "This is beautiful."

"It's one of my favorite spots. I used to come here a lot to escape, to dream about what I wanted to do with my life, or just to enjoy a swim. In all my times here, I haven't seen anyone else, so I assume I may be the only one who knows about it. Well, I guess you do too now." Branan's hand covered his own when he finished taking out the last dish. He looked up from his task to meet Branan's eyes.

"Thank you for sharing this with me." The look on Branan's face reminded him so much of the boy he once knew that those damn hummingbirds started flying once again, and his stomach flipped.

Branan picked up a slice of plum and placed it in his mouth. Lachlan tracked the movement and the way his lips closed around the piece of fruit. The way Branan used his thumb to wipe up the juice that escaped from the corner of his mouth before sticking it back into his mouth. Lachlan bit back a groan. Instead, he coughed slightly into his hand and focused on shoving a piece of bread into his mouth before he did something foolish like kiss Branan just to see if he tasted like plum.

"How was your day?" Lachlan asked, and between bites of food, Branan told him about wandering the market and Callie showing off her abilities. It sounded like a lovely time, but he noticed there were points where Branan hesitated. It made him wonder if he was leaving anything out. He pulled out the flask of ambrosia and offered it to Branan, who took a long swig. God bless Niamh and her foresight because the look on Branan's face when he wrapped his own lips against the mouth of the flask where Branan's had just been ignited the spark between them into a living flame. When they had both eaten their fill and were seated next to each other, legs outstretched toward the water, quietly gazing out at the lake, Branan spoke.

"So, you said the first thing you did to ruin things with the raven-haired boy was to lie about your name. What was the second?"

Damn. It looked like Lachlan really was going to put it all out there. "I never should have left you that morning the way I did. If I could go back, there are so many things I would have done differently. I woke up that night feeling like the wind had been knocked out of me. My heart was racing, and my chest ached something fierce. I stumbled into the bathroom as quietly as I could. I didn't want to wake you when you looked so peaceful. When I glanced in the mirror." He stopped and took a shuddering breath. "I knew my sister was gone, and the magic had chosen me to take her place. I panicked. Mostly, I blamed myself. I was supposed to be the one leading her army, but I had to see you one more time before I left."

"And that's when Whelan attacked you." Branan sighed.

Lachlan nodded. "I'd hoped she would wait for my return. I didn't realize how long it would take, and when I woke that morning, I knew I only had myself to blame for her death."

Branan clutched his hand. "You are not responsible for her death. Just like I'm not responsible for my father's. She could've waited for you to return. Your sister and my father went into battle knowing what it could cost, and unfortunately, they both paid that price, but you are not to blame."

Lachlan smiled sadly. "Torin keeps telling me that, but I think I've only recently come to terms with it. It was easier to blame myself. Easier to shoulder the responsibility I never wanted, out of duty and, as my penance for what happened to her."

Branan's heart broke for Lachlan. It was clear as day, despite what he said, there was still part of him that blamed himself for his sister's death, and it had tainted Lachlan's memory of the time they'd shared, just as his betrayal had tainted Branan's memory.

He sighed. They were both a mess, but perhaps it was a mess they could work together to untangle, and it would only start by being open and honest with each other. "I was there at the funeral you held for the soldiers."

Lachlan sucked in a sharp breath.

"I tried calling out to you, but when I shouted your name, Torin was the only one who turned and stared at me strangely. It was when I saw you take your place for your speech that I saw your eyes, and I knew why you had run that morning. The betrayal stung me hard. Here I was grieving the loss of my father, determined to find the only other person in the world who meant so much to me, only to see they'd lied about who they were."

Lachlan's eyes watered, a tear escaping down toward

his jaw. "Branan, I'm so sorry. I never meant to hurt you, but I know I did. The days we spent together are some of my most cherished memories. Knowing you were out there, and what we shared for a brief amount of time, kept me going those first few months."

Branan reached over and cupped Lachlan's face, using his thumbs to wipe away the tears that fell. "I understood. Once I had time to sit and process everything, I knew you'd made the choice you felt was right. You had the responsibility of the entire kingdom thrust upon you."

Lachlan sniffled, his tears slowing. "I went to your house after, a few times, but you were gone." It warmed Branan's heart to know Lachlan hadn't completely forgotten about them, that Lachlan valued their time together as much as he did.

"I couldn't stay. The house held too many memories and while they were happy ones, at the time they were painful reminders of what I had lost, so I ran. I went to the human realm and spent a long time there, went to their universities and lost myself in books. I pretended to be someone I wasn't and when that burden grew heavy, I returned and opened a shop in the goblin market. Trading animals and supplies, using my ability to match animals with their companions, until a request led me back here, and I realized that no matter how far we run, the ghosts of our past will always find us, because our past is part of us."

Lachlan turned his head and pressed a kiss into Branan's palm. "I'm glad you came back." The heat of Lachlan's breath sparked a fire burning inside of Branan.

Branan's heart beat wildly in his chest. "I'm glad too."

Using what courage he could gather, he pulled Lachlan's face toward his and pressed a kiss to his lips. There was a moment of hesitation before Lachlan kissed him back. His arms wrapped around Branan, pulling him closer until Branan tumbled on top of him. He laughed through the kiss, and Lachlan seized the opportunity to deepen it, their tongues tangling and tasting each other. Branan's wolf rumbled in delight. *Ours*, his wolf whispered against Branan's mind, but Branan was too lost in Lachlan to pay attention.

When they both came up for air, chests heaving, Branan felt energized. He was sure his eyes were full copper, and when he looked into Lachlan's he could see they were glowing, the lavender hue bright against the night sky.

"Let's go for a run," Lachlan whispered, his voice low and hoarse. Branan was fairly certain if they didn't do something else, being this close may lead to something they weren't quite ready for, not when they had only both found each other again. He nodded, licking the taste of Lachlan off his lips as Lachlan stood with a smirk and shifted into his stag form before darting off into the woods.

Branan's wolf growled. *If he wants a chase, he will get one.* He shifted and his wolf let out a happy howl before pursuing the stag. Lachlan was fast, but he was no match for Branan's wolf, and he quickly caught up. It'd been ages since Branan had felt this free in his wolf form, since he had someone to run and play with.

They ran for what felt like hours, simply enjoying each other and playing a version of hide and seek. Branan used his magic to send Lachlan images of his stag form paired with warmth and elation. He received similar images from Lachlan of him in his wolf form with an emotion attached—joy. Pure joy.

Finally, they both tired and looped back toward their picnic site. Branan was almost sad to see the evening end. They shifted back, and this time Lachlan kissed him before they put all of their dishes and leftovers back into the basket. Lachlan took a long swig from the flask of ambrosia before handing it to Branan, who this time took the pleasure of placing his mouth right where Lachlan's had just been. He smirked as he noted Lachlan studying him with fire behind his gaze as he licked his lips. They were both playing with something explosive that could consume them. He wondered if they gave into the fire, would only ashes remain, or would they be made into something new?

They packed the flask away with the blanket and Branan picked up the basket. Lachlan smiled and grabbed his hand, lacing their fingers together before he led them back to the seemingly normal side of the hill. This time Branan noted the small sun hieroglyph when Lachlan nicked his thumb and placed it in the center before the wall in front of them faded. He had to hand it to whoever had created that bit of blood magic ages ago; it was a handy trick guaranteed to keep out invaders unless they carried royal blood.

They both were quiet as they made their way back to Lachlan's study. Once there, he hung up the lantern and sealed the passageway. Branan had so many questions. Questions about what was happening between them and where they would go from there. It seemed impossible that they could make this work, but he didn't want to ruin the moment by asking them. Instead, they both seemed lost in their own heads until they reached the door to Branan's room. Only then was he able to find his voice.

"So, what now?" he said, breathy, his heart pounding as he waited for Lachlan's reply. Would he tell him that this was a one-off thing, a momentarily slip in his judgement?

Lachlan bit his lower lip. "What are you doing tomorrow?" he asked, looking more like the boy Branan once knew than the powerful Seelie king.

"Enora was going to show us her gardens and apothecary," Branan said with a twinge of disappointment. He wanted to say he had no plans and see how Lachlan replied.

Lachlan chewed on his lip. "Do you think I could join you?"

Branan's breath quickened. "I don't see why not."

"You won't mind?"

He looked so unsure it cracked a piece of Branan's heart. He leaned forward and dragged his nose against Lachlan's. "I'd be disappointed if you didn't, and I'm sure the others won't mind," he whispered before capturing his lips. When the kiss was finished, Lachlan smiled widely.

"I'll see you tomorrow at breakfast, then." He pressed a quick kiss to Branan's lips before darting away as if afraid at any moment Branan may change his mind.

Branan closed the door behind him and walked over to the bed. He rubbed his thumb across his bottom lip before picking up the box and tracing his fingertips over the wolf. Perhaps there was hope for them. Sure, there was plenty they needed to work out. He didn't live nearby, and Lachlan was king, but for now he was willing to put thoughts of the future aside and focus on the here and now. After all, if there was one thing he'd learned from his relationship with

Reid, it's that tomorrow was never promised. He changed and drifted off to sleep with a wide smile, knowing that he was sleeping in what was once Lachlan's bed.

CHAPTER 26

LACHLAN WANDERED THE halls that morning with a smile across his face that refused to go away. He replayed their night and had dreamed of Branan when he fell asleep. There were no nightmares, only blissful dreams.

When he stepped into the dining hall for breakfast, Torin was already seated and being served by Niamh. She leaned in to wipe something off Torin's face and blushed furiously when she caught Lachlan's eye before scampering back to the kitchen.

"Did you have to scare her off?" Torin asked.

"I did no such thing," Lachlan retorted.

Torin huffed before narrowing his eyes. "Is that a smile? Like a genuine smile I see?" He grinned. "I take it you enjoyed your night."

"Why? Did you miss me at dinner? Or perhaps you had someone else to dine with?" He shot back.

Torin's cheeks stained pink, and he pointed his fork at the king. "Touché."

A niggling thought wiggled its way to the front of his mind, and he frowned.

"Well, now I much prefer the smile to that." Torin waved his fork in a circle toward Lachlan's face.

"Do you think Evin and Callie would mind if I joined their excursion today with Maddock, Enora, and Branan?" He wasn't sure how they would take him practically inviting himself. Would they be on guard being around him, not able to enjoy themselves?

"That depends," Torin said between bites.

"On?"

"On if you're going to keep acting like the icy, aloof king, or if you're ready to let others see you. Besides Grady and I, that is."

Lachlan's brow furrowed. He opened his mouth to interject, but Torin kept going. "Listen, I get it. I get why you did it. Why you felt you needed it, and as a political move, it made total sense, but no one around here is doubting your leadership anymore. I think it's time to let that go. Let people see the real you. Sure, you can keep that icy prick façade when needed, like when dealing with our enemies or those you're uncertain of, but the people won't turn on you because you have emotions like the rest of us. In fact, I think you'll see your people will be more willing to fight for you, to respect you, when they know the real you. That's something Orla did really well. She was fierce when she needed to be, but she was also kind and soft with the staff. It endeared them to her; it made them want to fight for and protect her without ever being asked.

"And if this Branan is the reason for this sudden change, I'm all for it. Let everyone else see the Lach I know. They'll love you all the more."

Any argument drained out of Lachlan. He knew his friend was right. It was time to let others in, and if he wanted to win over Callie and Enora, that would be the way to do it. He saw how they interacted with one another.

"Thank you, friend." He smiled once again as a small cough alerted them to Branan's presence as he entered. Niamh also reappeared with two heaping platefuls of food.

"I was hoping our guest would join us this morning." She smiled widely before placing a plate in front of Lachlan and the other to his left, across from Torin. He thought she might've been just picking the most obvious place for Branan to sit until she turned her head and shot him a sly wink.

"You know Niamh, while I appreciate you hand delivering our meal, we have other staff who would be happy to do their job," Lachlan teased.

"Nonsense, your majesty. Besides, how else was I going to set eyes on our guest?" She smiled wickedly before turning to Branan.

"I hope you enjoyed the meal our king prepared for you last night."

Branan looked up at her with wide eyes after he sat.

"Such a fuss he made. Wouldn't really let me help him, you know."

"Niamh," Lachlan warned under his breath.

Torin, who had been taking a drink, must've inhaled it down the wrong pipe as he started coughing. Niamh moved smoothly over to pat his back forcefully before she smiled at all three men. "I'll let you enjoy your breakfast. If you need anything else, please send word."

Torin laughed loudly. "Oh, she's a little minx."

Branan smiled at Lachlan, his eyes practically dancing.

"Not another word," Lachlan warned, stabbing a piece of egg souffle and shoving it into his mouth.

The rest of breakfast went smoothly, with all three of them engaging in easy conversation. Torin seemed quite interested in Branan's business and how he'd started it. Lachlan couldn't help but wonder what that meant for their future. Would Branan be willing to leave behind the business he spent so much time building? It's not like Lachlan could move to the borderlands. He sighed. While it'd be so easy to indulge in the moment and not pay attention to the future, it was something they would need to discuss eventually. He just wasn't sure if he'd like the results.

When they had both finished eating and headed for Enora and Maddock's home, Lachlan's earlier doubts started creeping back in. "Are you sure your friends won't mind if I join you?"

"One, last time I checked, they were yours as well. You did just throw the pair of them an engagement party, and you can't just tell me that was part of your duties as king."

Lachlan's face heated. "Perhaps I had an ulterior motive for that one when I noticed a familiar scent while I was out for a run."

Branan scowled, but his eyes twinkled with amusement. "So, your insistence that I extend my stay at the palace was not entirely noble."

Lachlan laughed. "Oh, not noble in the least. While I'm happy to celebrate them, I definitely was using it as a reason to get you to see me again."

Branan smiled. "I should be mad."

Lachlan batted his eyelashes at him, going for his most puppy dog expression.

"But how can I after last night?" Branan grabbed his hand, squeezing it tight, and his reassurance loosened any remaining wariness in Lachlan's chest, and he smiled brightly.

His steps were lighter until they reached the door to Enora's and Maddock's home. His stomach rolled, unsure of how his presence would be taken. Though Enora and Maddock had never given him cause to believe they didn't like him, it was different when he was used to interacting with them as strictly as their king. The momentary panic caused him to loosen his grip on Branan's hand, but Branan, sensing what was going on, only held on tighter as he raised his hand to knock.

"Enora, Branan's here!" He heard Maddock's voice call out as he opened the door. Maddock's posture stiffened when he set his eyes on the king. "Your majesty, I wasn't expecting you."

"Just Lachlan today, please." Lachlan answered awkwardly. Maddock quirked an eyebrow and relaxed when his gaze traveled down to their joined hands.

"I hope you don't mind, I brought someone," Branan added as Enora approached behind Maddock.

"Nonsense. The more the merri—" she said, wiping her hands on an apron which stilled when they caught sight of the king. "Your majesty," she added, going to curtesy, but Maddock pulled her into his side.

"It's Lachlan today, love." He corrected her and pointed his gaze at their hands.

Lachlan's jaw clenched slightly and Branan squeezed his hand once more, pulling him from his inner turmoil.

"Oh. *Ooooh*." Enora's grin stretched from ear to ear. "Come in, both of you. I'm glad you could join us today. Although I'm sure his maj—I mean, Lachlan, has seen the gardens and apothecary before."

"I have to admit, I never paid them mind, so I'd be honored to see them from the perspective of a healer." Lachlan replied, which earned him a smile from Branan, one he would do whatever it took to see on his face every day.

Enora stole Branan over to check on the guinea pigs, who made such a raucous with their squeaks and squeals when they set eyes on him. Lachlan hadn't had the privilege of seeing Branan with animals like that before, and it was a sight to behold. He'd only occasionally been on the receiving end of Lachlan's gift when he was in stag form, but it was easy to see how much the guinea pigs loved him. Branan's smile grew with their joyful noises as he held each one. After a few minutes, he handed them back to Enora, who cooed and kissed each one on their heads. "They want you to know that they're both very happy in their new home and that you're an excellent mother."

Enora's grin was so wide now it made Lachlan's cheeks hurt. "Did you hear that, Maddock?"

Maddock came up behind her and wrapped his arms around her waist, placing a kiss atop her head. "I sure did, love. I told you there was nothing to worry about."

The moment was so sweet, making a pang of longing strike Lachlan's chest. Could he and Branan have that some day? The thought made him ache for things he didn't think were possible, things he hadn't given himself permission to want in his lifetime, until now.

Branan smiled at the happy couple. "They also said they love the apples you've been sneaking them, but I should probably remind you to moderate those, so they don't gain too much weight."

Maddock shook his head, trying to get Branan to stop talking while Lachlan chuckled. "You've been sneaking them treats?" Enora smacked his chest lightly before narrowing his eyes. "I knew you were a big ole cinnamon roll, and this only confirms it." She pressed a kiss to his cheek.

A knock at the door pulled Maddock's attention away from his fiancé and Branan rejoined Lachlan where he stood. This time, Lachlan reached for his hand and brought it to his mouth, where he pressed a kiss against his palm, acting purely on impulse. He'd almost forgotten the others when an excited squeal that could rival the guinea pigs came from the direction of the door where Callie was bouncing on her toes.

"Let it be known that I wholeheartedly approve of whatever this is." She moved her finger in a circular motion in their direction.

Lachlan felt a flush steal up his neck, but he wasn't entirely prepared for the way Evin studied them both with a wrinkled nose. He hadn't considered that Evin would have a problem with his and Branan's relationship since Torin had reacted so well to the news. Though Torin had known about their relationship before he ever knew Branan had once been Reid's boyfriend.

Callie turned toward Evin and elbowed him roughly in the side. He grunted, rubbing the spot where she jabbed him. "Serves you right. This is good." She lowered her voice to a whisper, although with his and Branan's shifter hearing, it didn't make a difference. "Reid would want Branan to find happiness again, so don't ruin this for him."

Evin pulled her into his arms and whispered against her neck. "You're right. I'm sorry. I just wasn't prepared." She squeezed him tightly before pulling herself away.

"Never doubt me. I'm always right," she teased before she went over to hug Enora and then Branan.

"Now, I expect all the details later. And I mean *all* the details." She winked before releasing him. The pink staining Branan's cheeks made Lachlan chuckle. Callie was an endless source of entertainment, he decided.

"And you…." She turned on him, her expression fierce, cutting off all of his laughter. "If you hurt him, I don't care if you're the Seelie king or even if you can shift into a giant dragon like people say. My retribution will be swift and painful."

"Callie!" Evin and Enora both gasped.

Even Branan stiffened slightly beside him, as if unsure how he would take her threat, but Lachlan grinned. It warmed his heart to know how protective Branan's friends were.

"Message received, but seeing as I have no intention of doing just that, I think you can hold off on plotting my demise." He winked at her, and the rest of the Fae in the room exhaled and relaxed. She nodded her approval and pranced back to Evin.

"Alright, lady and gents. Let's head to the garden," Enora called out, breaking any remaining awkwardness.

As they made their way out the door, Branan leaned

over. "Sorry about Callie. She can be a little much if you're not used to her."

Branan's breath against Lachlan's ear shot sparks off in his body, but he focused on the fact that they were in the presence of others and squeezed Branan's hand. "No need to apologize. I like that she's protective of you. You deserve to have people in your life who see how wonderful you are, who care about you."

"Hurry up, lovebirds!" Callie called. Lachlan hadn't noticed they'd stopped walking, but at Callie's words, Branan tipped his head back and groaned, causing Lachlan to laugh.

"You heard the lady." He tugged Branan's hand as he quickened his pace to catch up with the group.

The rest of the day was the most fun Lachlan could re-member having since he'd lost Orla. Callie proved to be a never-ending source of amusement with her unique humor and human mannerisms. Enora was insightful and he could see how much she loved what she did by how she practi-cally glowed when she described all the different plants and their medicinal properties, and showing off her apoth-ecary and attached patient room. While most of the time, she would go to those who needed her services, occasion-ally it was easier if they came to her. Since she had worked for him, she'd mainly seen and treated any soldiers who were a little too ambitious or overzealous in their sparring, and one of the stable boys who'd accidentally stepped on a rake. He hoped eventually the rest of his town would grow to appreciate her and see how great of a healer she was.

It was nice to see the more relaxed side of Evin and Maddock, and he thought they may have been equally pleased to see a different side of him. He knew Callie and Enora did by how they chatted with him, at one point Callie even came over to link her arm with his and steal him away from Branan, so she could entertain him with one of her tales of a university party after she was turned Fae and how she drank all the poor frat boys under the table. He wasn't sure what a frat boy was, but he laughed along as she described the scene and could imagine just how the party would have celebrated a female besting the males in a drinking competition.

They wound up back at the palace for lunch, which Torin joined them for. When he tried to ask about any palace business he may need to complete for the day, Torin shoved him off with, "Any issues today will still be there tomorrow. Enjoy your day off." Which was true. Plus he trusted Torin to keep things running the way they should in his stead.

The day was one of the best Branan had had in a while. Lachlan continued to surprise him. Gone was any trace of the icy, calculating king he had first encountered. He could see the others were also surprised to see the change in their king, though they tried to hide it.

It wasn't until Callie asked him for an update on Eshna that he remembered all the responsibilities waiting back for him in the borderlands. This time, his wolf bucked at the idea of going back to the solitude of his house and shop. It confused him. His wolf had always been so easy before, like communicating with your baser instincts. After the rabbit incident when he was younger, his wolf had no issue with not hunting to wound or kill. It was like they had formed a sort of truce between them where Branan was the one mostly in charge and his wolf more or less faded into the background, only rousing in the presence of other wolves in the borderlands, a perceived threat, or when he needed out to run. But lately his wolf had felt more present and more vocal.

After Branan reassured everyone he would stay for a couple more days, they made plans to meet up again the next day and left him and Lachlan to their own devices for the afternoon. Lachlan was showing him the library when Branan asked, "Does your stag ever talk to you?"

Lachlan paused. "No. I mean, I know when it's been too long, and I need to shift. I feel a familiar itch. A restlessness in my skin, but when I do shift, it's still just me. I operate on more of my baser instincts when I'm in my stag form, but it's only ever just been me. Why? Does your wolf talk to you?"

Branan's heart dropped, but he nodded. He couldn't remember his dad ever explaining he could have conversations with his wolf, but then again, they hadn't had much time together after Branan first shifted. Was something wrong with him?

"Maybe it's just a wolf thing," Lachlan offered. "I could ask the palace scholar to pull what he has on wolf shifters, or do you have anyone from your old pack you can ask?"

"No," Branan replied, immediately thinking of Whelan and Malcom. No way he would discuss this with them, and

Kyna might be pack, but she wasn't a wolf. But then he remembered Shane. "Wait, maybe. The youngest one of Shaw's boys works in your treasury."

"Why don't you go talk to him while I make arrangements for dinner?"

"Another picnic?"

"Perhaps." Lachlan smiled.

They left the library, and he gave Branan directions for the treasury before heading toward the kitchens.

Branan's palms grew slick with sweat, and he wiped them on his pants, pushing down the familiar hum building under his skin. Over the years he'd learn to better control his anxiety, but occasionally it got the better of him. Waves of hot and cold rushed through his body and his hands shook as he approached the door for the treasury. What if Shane wasn't there? What if Shane didn't have any answers either?

A wizened, older man in robes answered the door. "Can I help you?"

"I'm looking for Shane. King Lachlan said I might find him here."

The man grunted and turned. "Shane!" he called before walking away to a table heavy with books. Branan stood awkwardly at the door, unsure if he should enter, when Shane popped around a corner.

"Branan!"

"Hey, Shane. Can I, um, talk to you for a few minutes, in private?"

Shane's head tilted to the side. "Albert," Shane started.

"Go! I may be old, but I'm certainly not deaf, and I don't need you two interrupting my calculations," he grumbled.

Shane nodded and stepped into the hallway, closing the door behind him. "Sorry about that. Albert is a little rough around the edges, but once you get used to him, he's not so bad. There's a room up here we should be able to use."

He led him down the hall to a small sitting room that didn't look like it was used that frequently. While it was clean, the curtains were still drawn and drop cloths were draped over the furniture.

"This work?"

"Yes, thank you." Branan's throat was dry. "I have a pretty random question to ask, but I wasn't sure who else might understand."

Shane's blonde eyebrows drew close together. "I'm listening, and despite what you might think, there are many things I don't share with my brothers." He smiled reassuringly.

Branan took a deep breath. "I've been hearing from my wolf recently. Do you talk to yours?"

Shane shook his head, and Branan's heart plummeted. "I only get mostly emotions and images, but not exactly words." He thought for a few minutes before his eyes grew as wide as saucers. "Oh shit. *Oh, shit.*" His eyebrows shot up to his forehead. "After both of our dads died, I did some research. Even though Whelan told us he was alpha and felt the bond, it never felt the same. It wasn't as strong as with your dad. His commands could be bucked after some time. He couldn't communicate with us across as far of distances as your dad used to either. We thought maybe it was because he was so young, or maybe he just wasn't as strong as your dad, but that's not it, is it?

"While sources could be hard to track down, one I read talked about alphas and how some of the strongest alphas claimed they felt their wolf as if it were part of them, but also a separate entity. That they could have full-on conversations with their wolf. You know what this means, don't you?"

Branan's relief was swift. There wasn't something wrong with him. It also explained why his dad always encouraged him to try to talk to his wolf when he was younger. "I already I know I'm an alpha, Shane. I've known since we lost my da."

"You knew you were meant to be our alpha, and you still left?" The soft whine of a wolf in Shane's voice struck Branan.

"I'm sorry. I was so lost without my da, besides you know how the pack bond works. The connection only establishes if both parties want it, and Whelan would have never accepted it."

Shane paled. "I'm sorry I wasn't able to stand up to my brothers back then. The way they treated you wasn't right, but you're right Whelan wouldn't have accepted it. In fact, you can't stay here. If Whelan has even an inkling that you're the chosen alpha, I have no doubt he will challenge in order to steal your alpha magic through defeat or death. Branan, you have to leave. I don't think... I love my brother, but he's changed over the years. He's become even colder and even more cruel...I'm not sure if he'd just let you walk away even if he defeats you in a challenge."

Branan sucked in a sharp breath, Whelan's earlier threat echoed in his ears. He knew Shane was right, Whelan wouldn't see reason. He wouldn't care that Branan didn't want to be the alpha of his dad's old pack, not when he had finally started to form his own, but he also couldn't leave. Not when he and Lachlan were just figuring out where things might go. *We stay, we fight to protect those we love*, his wolf growled.

Shane's stricken expression clued him in that his wolf's growl hadn't just been in his mind. He put his hands up. "Easy there. I'm not the one issuing a challenge. I just don't want anything to happen to you."

Branan coughed. "I know, Shane, and I appreciate the warning. I'll do my best to stay away from your brother, but we had a run-in yesterday, so it may be too late for me to just leave town. Besides, I'm not leaving. I don't want to fight him, but I'm also done running. My home was once here, and perhaps it should be once again."

Shane sighed. "Just be careful."

Branan dipped his head in appreciation. "I will, and thanks for the chat, Shane. I've missed this. Maybe when things are settled, we could go for a run like old times?"

Shane smiled. "I'd love that."

He left then, trying to calm the racing heart and uneasiness he felt inside. Part of him knew the possibility of Whelan challenging him for alpha. It was part of the reason he'd left in the first place, after all. Back then, he would have rather been the one to leave than to have Whelan shove him out the door by attacking him when he was at his weakest. He would do what he could to avoid Whelan this time, but eventually he knew he would have to face him, especially if he planned on sticking around and seeing where things went with Lachlan.

It wasn't another picnic, but watching Lachlan work at the stove made his stomach flip. The small table in the kitchen where the staff usually ate had been cleaned and prepared with a tablecloth and candles. A small vase of flowers sat in the center, and he wondered if the cook, Niamh, had anything to do with that. He couldn't picture Lachlan wandering outside to pick them, but they were fresh enough he knew they had only recently been gathered. Lachlan refused his help no matter how many times he offered, insisting that he was the guest, which made Branan smile. It was something so simple, but having someone care enough to prepare a meal for you felt like something huge. He was usually the one who cooked for Reid, as their time had been limited when he would visit. Well, that and the only thing Reid knew how to cook was eggs.

Lachlan plated up the food and brought it over to the table. The pasta smelled delicious, and the noodles looked handmade, not like that boxed stuff he ate on his occasional trips to the human realm. The sauce looked rich and creamy with mushrooms and fresh herbs.

"Thank you," he said as Lachlan sat down in front of his own plate. He picked up his fork and twirled it around a bite of pasta while Lachlan watched him. He looked up to meet the king's lavender eyes. His adorable cheeks flushed a pale pink. Branan's lips parted before bringing the fork full of pasta to his mouth, loving the way the color on the king's face deepened. Lachlan chewed on his bottom lip, a nervous tell Branan had just noticed now that the king's mask was finally off.

Branan's mouth closed around the fork, savoring the explosion of flavors in his mouth. "Mmm," he moaned, closing his eyes. He chewed and swallowed before opening them. The king stared at him, his mouth slightly agape and eyes now a darker shade of violet.

"Are you going to eat as well?" Branan asked, batting his eyelashes at the king. Lachlan immediately dove into his own pasta, taking such a large bite it caused him to cough and Branan chuckled.

"You did an excellent job. When did you learn to cook?" Branan asked before taking his next bite.

"When I was younger, I was very active. Even while sitting still, I had to be moving. It used to drive my family batty. My mom thought the best way for me to channel my energy was to keep my hands busy, so one day she took me to the kitchen and asked the cook to let me help. He was a kind, elderly gentleman and a fantastic mentor, eager to have an extra pair of hands to peel and chop or to knead dough, and while we waited for the dough to rise or the bread to bake, he also showed me how to use a knife to turn a piece of wood into something beautiful."

"Did you carve the wolf figurine on my father's grave?"

Lachlan nodded while he chewed, the pink returning to his cheeks. He swallowed his bite. "Is that okay?"

Branan's throat suddenly felt thick, so he bobbed his head in reply before getting out one word. "Why?"

Lachlan looked down at his own plate, studying what was left of his pasta. "I missed you something fierce after I left, but I couldn't allow myself to dwell on it. I couldn't lose myself in grief. Grief for my sister, for losing you and the future I thought I would have, no matter how much it threatened to pull me under. I had to stay strong for the kingdom so no one could doubt my rule, so I found other ways to keep busy and when I picked up a knife, that's just what came out. And since you'd left, I thought it fitting for a symbol of you to keep watch over your father's grave." His eyes met Branan's and the naked honesty behind them knocked the breath from Branan's chest. He didn't know what to say.

Lachlan shrugged. "Of course, I've had to replace him and the stag on my sister's grave a few times over the years due to the wind or a child carrying them away."

Goosebumps ran up and down Branan's arms. Lachlan had not only carved that wolf after he left but also kept checking on his father's grave enough to know when it needed to be replaced. That dispelled any remaining doubts about Lachlan's feelings for him. All these years, he was still carving a wolf, just like the one on the box next to his bed.

Branan took Lachlan's hand and pressed a kiss to his knuckles. "Thank you."

They continued eating with more casual conversation. It seemed after Callie's stories earlier in the day, the king was eager to learn all about Branan's time studying at university in the human realm. When he asked Branan if he thought they should start a similar school here in the Fae realm, Branan was touched that he was seeking his advice.

Finally, when they finished dinner, Lachlan said, "Now, for part two!"

"Part two?" Branan asked.

Lachlan smiled at him wickedly, holding out his hand

for him to take. "What about the dishes?" Branan asked.

Lachlan laughed. "Niamh threatened to quit if I didn't leave something for her to do since I was 'refusing to let her feed me and my guest tonight.' Her words, of course, and I would hate to lose her."

Branan laughed as Lachlan tugged him through the hallways, but this time, instead of exiting through a secret tunnel, they exited through a door leading out to the back patio area by the garden. Unlike Enora's garden, this one was not for harvesting. It was grand and decorative with hedges shaped into various animals and bushes bursting with flowers.

"It's beautiful," Branan said.

"It is, but it's not why we're here. Come on!" This time Lachlan dropped his hand and ran off, disappearing around a corner of a hedge. Branan took off in a sprint, eager to catch up and not lose sight of him. His wolf yipped in the pleasure of the chase. Lachlan's laughter was wild as Branan chased closely behind him. Branan finally caught him when they emerged from the maze at the edge of the woods. Lachlan was casually leaning against a tree, but his panting breaths and heaving chest gave away how much exertion he used to stay ahead of Branan.

"I thought maybe we could go for a run… that is, if you'd like to," Lachlan suggested once his breathing had evened out.

Branan cocked an eyebrow. "Isn't that what we just did?" he joked.

"Well, yes, but I thought we'd both prefer letting our animals run."

Branan's wolf wagged his tail in agreement. He smiled

wildly. "I'd love nothing more."

"Nothing more? Really?" Lachlan asked before stalking over and crashing his lips over Branan's mouth in a hot, demanding kiss that made Branan's knees weak.

When Lachlan pulled back, he arched an eyebrow before whispering, "You're it." He tapped him lightly on the shoulder, then turned and shifted in the blink of an eye before taking off into the woods. Branan shifted a second later, his wolf releasing a happy howl before pursuing the stag through the forest.

They ran for quite some time, and while Lachlan's stag was faster than Branan's wolf, Lachlan paused at the small clearing where they used to meet. Branan's wolf smiled, slowing to a stop still in the thick of the woods before sneaking around the clearing. He leaped from the bushes, easily tackling Lachlan to the ground, and they both shifted, laughing as they rolled. When they came to a stop, Branan was pressed on top of Lachlan, and he realized just how close they were positioned. This time it was he who conquered Lachlan's mouth, demanding entrance until they were both panting. He pulled away quickly, leaving a dazed Lachlan staring up at him as he tapped his shoulder and took off running. "Now, you're it," he called before shifting.

"Oh, that's just evil," Lachlan murmured in the distance, and Branan's wolf barked out a laugh.

Branan was so lost in their game he didn't realize where he was leading them until he came upon the familiar cabin in the moonlight. He stopped just as Lachlan tackled him in his human form.

"Got you!" he exclaimed, practically bear hugging

Branan's wolf. It was then Lachlan realized where they were. He released Branan, giving him space to shift back. They both stood in the clearing, staring at his childhood home.

"Do you miss it?" Lachlan asked.

"I didn't. Or maybe it's that I didn't allow myself to think about it, but I stayed here the night before I made the delivery to Enora, and I think part of me does." They both sat in the grass, eyes still on the empty cabin.

"Do you think you'd want to move back?" Lachlan asked hesitantly.

Here it was, the main conversation they'd both been avoiding. He sat for a few moments, thinking before he stood and started wandering. Lachlan followed closely behind, but gave him space and silence to process and ponder on possibilities.

Hope blossomed in Branan's chest. What was really tying him to the borderlands besides his business? Once he let the possibility of what could be free, his imagination ran with it. "Maybe…." Branan started. Lachlan inhaled quickly, but Branan kept his eyes on the area. "It would need some work, of course." He wandered the perimeter of the clearing around the cabin. He'd have to clear a bit of the land to accommodate pens he would need and enlarge the stables for his animals. A small space for a sanctuary, maybe. He bet Enora would be thrilled to help him with any of the sick or injured creatures. He could set up a shop in town. See if Amani wanted to stay on full time and take over the place in the goblin market, or close it entirely and send word to his loyal customers where they could now find him. He knew they'd still come to him for what they needed with the reputation he had worked so hard to build. He knew of at least a few Seelie who would be pleased to have him closer to home. Sure, it may cost him his Unseelie customers, but he could make other arrangements with them, deliveries and special orders he could take himself to the borderlands to meet up with them. If this was something he truly wanted, he could make it work.

Lachlan's arms wrapped around him from behind. He felt his breath against his neck before he pressed his lips there in a soft kiss. "Just you considering it is enough for me right now. Thank you." He rested his head on Branan's shoulder, and Branan reached his arms across where Lachlan's were wrapped around him and squeezed. They stood there, both soaking in the other's presence while Branan stared at his childhood home, imagining the possibilities. When he was ready to go, he turned his head and pressed a kiss to Lachlan's cheek. Lachlan's eyes fluttered open, and he smiled, sighing in contentment.

"I suppose we should head back, shouldn't we?"

"We wouldn't want anyone to worry," Branan replied. He wasn't quite ready for them to go inside the cabin, even though it was easier now to focus on the happy memories inside the house than it had ever been before.

"I suppose Torin might be quite cross with me. I wouldn't be surprised if he came after us, to be honest. He's used to me going for a run, but we usually have an agreed upon time allotment before he comes searching, and I'm certain we exceeded that."

Branan made a tsking sound with his tongue. "Then we should definitely get back." He pulled himself from Lachlan's arms, then turned and pressed a kiss to his forehead.

"First one there wins a prize," he whispered before turning and running toward the woods.

"Wait! What's the prize?"

Branan paused. "Winner's choice!" he called before shifting and taking off on four paws.

"Oh, I can think of a few things," Lachlan teased before Branan heard hooves hitting the dirt behind him.

They stayed neck and neck until the palace came into sight. Then Lachlan surged forward, quickly outpacing Branan and letting him know he could have beaten him all along. Branan was laughing as he shifted back, and tried to stifle even more laughter when he saw Torin waiting for them with a scowl on his face. "Looks like you're in trouble," Branan whispered, nudging Lachlan in front of him to face Torin's ire.

"Do you have any idea how worried I was?" Torin exclaimed. "First, you usually tell me when you're going for a run, but this time I had to hear about it from Niamh, who saw you two dash out into the gardens. Second, you were gone for much longer than normal."

"I suppose that's my fault," Branan piped up. "But you don't need to be so worried. I wouldn't have let anything happen to him," he added.

"No offense, son, but you aren't a trained soldier."

Branan knew Torin meant well, but his wolf bristled. Pulling Lachlan behind him, he stood between the perceived threat. His voice was deeper, laced with an alpha growl, and he knew his eyes were bright copper as he replied. "I'm a wolf. I can protect him better than anyone." His fingers sharpened into claws as his wolf pushed through. *We would never let harm befall our stag*, his wolf snarled.

"Down boy," Lachlan teased, patting him on the head. "Torin didn't mean it as an insult, he's just used to playing the role of my overprotective older *brother*." He leaned closer, his breath caressing Branan's ear, "Your wolf has nothing to be jealous of." He pressed a kiss to Branan's cheek.

Instantly Branan's claws shrank back, and his wolf receded after murmuring, *ours*.

"Alright, point made. Let's get you both inside so I can go to sleep." Torin shook his head like he was dealing with two teenagers. "I swear, between you and Evin, I'm lucky I don't have a head full of gray hair," he muttered under his breath.

Lachlan released Branan and threw an arm over Torin's shoulder. "Like the pesky little brother you never had, I seem to remember you once telling me. Now, let's get this old man to bed before he gets even crankier," Lachlan taunted before Torin shoved him off and into Branan's side.

"He's your problem now," he huffed to Branan and stomped off toward the palace.

Lachlan laughed. "Love you too, Tor!"

Torin saluted them both with a middle finger, not even bothering to turn around.

The pair were still giggling when they arrived outside Lachlan's old room. "I know why you put me in this room, you know," Branan claimed, pressing a kiss to Lachlan's mouth.

"Figured it out, did you?" He narrowed his eyes. "Or did someone let you in on it?"

Branan smiled innocently in reply. "I may have had a little help."

Lachlan chuckled before pressing another fairly chaste kiss to Branan's lips. "So, if you're so certain you know why, tell me."

Branan pulled Lachlan closer, this time making sure his kiss wasn't so chaste. He let his hands wander over Lachlan's muscled back and bit back a groan. "I think you like the thought of me in your bed," he whispered, pulling back with a wide grin at Lachlan's slack face. "Goodnight, Lachlan," he said, closing the door behind him with Lachlan still frozen in place.

"Well, that's just not fair," he heard him grumble from behind the closed door before he walked away.

"Sweet dreams!" Branan chuckled.

CHAPTER 27

LACHLAN GRUMBLED AS he made his way back to his room. Branan was right. He did like the thought of him in his bed, not that he would do anything about that. *Well, maybe just to sleep,* he thought, remembering the night so long ago when he fell asleep with Branan in his arms.

After a night filled with the sweetest of dreams, Lachlan woke with a smile on his face. Could things between them actually work out? He knew what Branan would sacrifice by moving back here, and he vowed to make it worth his time and effort if he stayed. He bathed and dressed, preparing for the day, slightly disappointed that the tasks he'd put off to free up yesterday still needed to be dealt with today. There were several petitions from his citizens that he needed to hear and make decisions about and a few conflicts he needed to help settle. He hoped he could free up part of his afternoon if he attacked each issue with gusto. All was quiet now with the Unseelie, but that didn't mean the peace would hold.

Uneasiness bit at the back of his throat, feeling like he did the day before everything came crashing down, that things right now felt good, almost too good to be true. He shoved the wariness away, determined it must be his own attempt to self-sabotage his chance at happiness.

He had just sat down to eat in the dining hall when Branan stumbled in, rubbing the remnants of sleep from his eyes. "Good morning," he mumbled, his voice low and raspy.

The corners of Lachlan's mouth tugged up. "Morning. I trust you slept well."

Branan put up a hand to stifle a large yawn. "I did, but I guess I could use some more. I didn't want to miss breakfast with you, though."

Lachlan grinned. "I appreciate that. I was hoping to see you before I had to tend to the waiting tasks. What are your plans for today?"

Branan smiled in reply. "I need to gather my supplies and tend to my horse. I also agreed to tea with the girls later today at Enora's house."

"Ah yes, I remember them badgering you until you agreed yesterday." He laughed. "That should be a fun time." His smile fell as he remembered something else Branan had mentioned. "Why do you need to gather your supplies?"

Branan tugged at the collar of his shirt. "While I'd love to stay for much longer, it's probably best if I head back to make more permanent arrangements. It's different arranging for Amani to cover the shop ahead of time than imposing on her to extend my stay. I already fear I've asked too much of her."

Lachlan's heart dropped. He didn't want Branan leaving, not so soon after they just started seeing each other again. "Do you have to go?" He couldn't hide the disappointment dripping from the words.

"I'm afraid so, but I plan to be back within a week, two at most. If you'd have me."

Lachlan's heart lifted. "I'd be delighted."

"If that doesn't give me enough time to get things squared away and decide how to move forward, then I'll let you know."

"I'd appreciate that." He wasn't happy Branan was leaving so soon, but if it meant he was leaving so he could make plans to move closer, Lachlan couldn't fault that.

After they finished eating, Branan gave him a kiss goodbye and agreed to have dinner with him. Lachlan wished him good luck with his work, and he set off to find Torin and determine the order in which the tasks needed to be conquered. They could make this work, he told himself, but that uneasiness tugged at his gut once again.

Branan noted what remained in his cart and wandered the market, looking for what else he needed to bring back. His head was full of plans, and he needed to have a face to face with Amani to see whether she'd even want to run the shop in the borderlands. If she didn't, then he would definitely close it. Although, his house was larger than the cozy little place she and Eshna lived. He wouldn't be opposed to throwing that into the deal. It might give the pair a fresh start.

He wandered back to the blacksmith's shop to check in with Maille, but her father informed him she was out running an errand. As he turned to leave, a display of jewelry caught his eye. It had to have been hers, he could tell by the intricate details and flourishes. There was a locket wrapped in silver vines and a finely crafted ring, the top of which was the blossom of a rose, and the band made up the stem, wrapped around with thorns and leaves. He paused on the piece his eye caught initially; it was a large ring, appearing more masculine. Carved into the side were the woods surrounding the village with the palace in the distance perfectly captured in metal. He picked it up, studying it closely. It was the most phenomenal piece of jewelry he had ever seen, and he knew the perfect person for it. His wolf rumbled with pleasure at the idea.

"Told you her jewelry was a sight to behold," the blacksmith spoke from behind him.

"Well, you're not wrong there."

The blacksmith stepped closer and nodded toward the ring in Branan's hand. "That's her newest piece. She said it came to her in a dream," he chuckled. "Just like her mother, with her head in the clouds."

"Then you'll be pleased to know she drives a hard bargain," Branan smiled, and the blacksmith grinned.

"Aye, that's where she takes after me."

"I'll take the one, but tell her she needs to raise her prices when she returns. These are worth more than she's charging," he said, handing the blacksmith what he thought was the appropriate amount of coin for such a piece.

The blacksmith nodded. "I've tried, but perhaps now that she's doing business with you, she'll take someone else's opinion about her pricing. Would you like a pouch for that?"

"Not necessary. Thank you, and please tell Maille I'll be leaving town, but should return in a few weeks and I'll expect to see a cage or two then." Branan slipped the ring into his pocket and went on his way.

He stopped in the same general store, but the blonde woman and her husband were nowhere in sight, instead a younger version of the woman stood behind the counter and greeted him with a smile. He picked up a few items and paid with coins. The woman's words from a few days ago echoed in his ears. *"You can't do everything on your own. Your wolf will guide you. Trust him."* His wolf had definitely been more present since she'd said those things. Was she truly a gifted Seer, as her husband had claimed? He had no reason to doubt them, but the words were still a mystery. He always listened to his wolf, didn't he? The more he thought about it, he realized how quiet his wolf had been since his dad died, only making himself known when he needed to shift and go for a run or when there may have been some sort of danger present.

His mind turned over what she might have meant and before too long, he found himself in front of Enora's house for tea. He packed the items he had purchased in his cart.

"Need any help?" Callie asked from behind him. He should have heard her approaching, would have if he wasn't so lost in his thoughts about Lachlan.

He scolded himself for not being more aware of his

surroundings. "Just finished up, as a matter of fact. Ready to head in?"

Callie cocked her head to the side, and her brow wrinkled for a moment. "Something's different."

Branan tried to keep the rising heat away from his cheeks. Before he could reply, Callie scrunched her nose. "Fine, if you don't want to tell me. I'll just have to figure it out on my own." He groaned as she pulled his hand, leading him inside Enora's house.

"Enora! Your guests are here!" she called.

"We could have knocked," Branan scoffed.

"What's the fun in that?" Callie snorted as Enora popped her head around the corner with a plate full of tea cakes and cookies.

"Oooo sweets!" Callie dropped Branan's hand and took the plate from Enora and set it down on the table before popping a cookie into her mouth. She closed her eyes and moaned, while Enora and Branan stared at her, slightly wide eyed.

Enora laughed. "You remind me of Grace when she was much younger. Her antics always made me laugh."

Callie narrowed her eyes. "That's right. Man, I forget you guys are practically grandparent age or older. I wonder if I'll age just as slowly."

"I'd be surprised if you didn't," Enora said as she sat and gestured for Branan to do the same. A teapot and cups were already on the table, ready for them. She lifted the teapot and filled each of their cups before passing around cream and sugar.

Branan stifled a chuckle as he watched Callie add more sugar and cream than anyone he had seen. "Would you like some tea with that?" he teased.

"Oh hush," Callie responded. "Do you really think I'll age slowly? I mean, I've talked about it with Evin, and Ianthe and I have theorized, but it would be interesting to get a healer's take on it."

"I do. The magic that links you to Evin tied your lives together and balances each other out. I have a feeling both of you will age more like a half Fae, like Ianthe."

Callie frowned. "So Evin will age more quickly than he would've before."

"Yes, but I wouldn't worry about it. I don't think he'd see much point in living without you. He knew exactly what he was risking when he made that decision."

Callie sighed. "You're right. It's not like we can change it."

Enora paused, tilting her head slightly to the right as she lifted the steaming cup to her lips. "Would you if you could?"

Callie stared down into her cup for a few moments. "No. Obviously, I like the fact that I'm still alive. I just… it makes me worry, you know. I don't like that he gave up so much to be with me."

"You can't think about love like that," Enora stated plainly, setting down her cup. "It's not a who gave up the most for the other person competition. Evin didn't sacrifice his lifespan for you. I mean, while some may view it as that, he never will. He doesn't see it as a sacrifice, and neither should you. He didn't give up part of his life for you. The fact is, he couldn't imagine living without you, so there was really no sacrifice to be made."

Callie nibbled on a cookie pensively. "I hadn't thought

about it like that."

"Well, you should. There may be things we do to accommodate love, things we change. Those are risks we're willing to take when the reward can be so great. When someone thinks of something they changed as a sacrifice, it devalues what the other person changed. You also gave up your human mortality. You'll age slower while your family will age at the same rate as normal humans, and while you may not see it now, that will affect you later. Now you have powers you don't fully have control over or may not even fully understand yet. You've been thrown into a world you weren't even familiar with for most of your life. I don't say these things to hurt you." She placed a hand over Callie's where she had placed her half-eaten cookie on her plate.

"There are many things I've changed to accommodate love, but I'll never see it as a sacrifice, because I know that while Maddock hasn't had to move, he's had relationships with some of the guards change because of who and what I am. Considering what you or someone else has changed as a sacrifice builds resentment or guilt and neither of those emotions are good for any relationship. Eventually, they'll ruin it."

While Enora said the words to Callie, they rang true for Branan as well. He may be changing things to make his relationship with Lachlan work, and while they never felt like a sacrifice for him, he may want to check in with Lachlan to make sure he understands that they're not. They were both changing to accommodate their love, and would both face obstacles, but in the end, it would be worth it.

Callie sniffed, her eyes brimming with unshed tears.

She released a long, heavy breath. "Thank you, Enora. You're absolutely right. I'll have to have a talk with Evin later to make sure he understands that as well. He shouldn't shoulder any guilt for what happened, just as I shouldn't carry any for his decisions." She shoved the rest of the cookie into her mouth and Enora smiled.

"How much longer will we have you for, Branan?" Enora asked while Callie chewed, her cheeks full like a little squirrel.

"I'm actually heading out tomorrow morning." He noted the way both of the girls' faces fell with disappointment. "But… I'll be back in a couple weeks."

Both girls' smiles returned, but Callie's quickly turned sly. "This wouldn't have anything to do with a certain smoking hot Seelie king you were holding hands with and was sending you glances so hot I thought I might need a cold shower, would it?"

Branan choked on his sip of tea, and Enora patted him on the back. His face burned, but he couldn't help the tug at the corners of his mouth. "Maybe."

"I knew it!" Callie pumped a fist in the air and squealed while Enora grinned from ear to ear.

"You deserve to find your happiness, Branan." She said, resting her hand over his and giving it a squeeze before releasing it.

Branan picked up his mug and took another sip of tea to hide his smile.

"Wait! There are a couple things I've been dying to ask you since I found out you were a wolf shifter. First, what happens to your clothes when you shift? Do you have to get naked first like Jacob in Twilight? Because while all that nudity sounds hot in theory, like where would you even hide all those clothes so you could always make sure you had some to change into?"

He laughed and Enora held a hand in front of her mouth to cover her giggles. "You know I've never really thought about it. I suppose sometimes we just accept the way things are and don't question why. It's the magic that allows me to shift, so any clothes or small items I have with me must shift with me and become part of my wolf, and then shift back with me."

"Could you imagine all the clothes a growing shifter would need to go through as they learned to control their magic if they ripped apart every time they shifted?" Enora laughed.

"You've seen the Twilight movies?" Callie practically vibrated in her chair.

Enora laughed harder. "Grace has always loved to show me movies or shows featuring different types of Fae and we would laugh at what they got wrong. So yes, I've seen all of the Twilight movies, and I can also tell you that the vampires we have do not sparkle, but they do have red eyes."

"So, watch out for red eyed Fae, got it. We should definitely plan some movie nights too. I'd love to learn more, so Evin doesn't have to correct me every time I think I know something, but it's wrong."

"I'd love that," Enora replied.

"What was your other question?" Branan asked.

"Do you guys have a mate? Because I've read some fantastic romances with fated mates… and if that shit is real…." Callie sighed dreamily.

"Some do." Branan nodded, and took a minute to drink his tea, knowing her next question before she even asked it. One he hadn't even given himself permission to consider.

"So is the Seelie king yours?" she asked innocently.

His mind flashed back to a conversation he'd had with his dad when he was a young boy.

Branan sat across from his dad at the table, a plate of dinner in front of them. "Do we have mates, da? Because Whelan was bragging about how his mom and da were mates today."

His father set his fork down, chewing on his steak before he answered. "We do."

"Were you and ma mates then?" Branan asked, the question full of innocence.

"I loved your ma very much, son, until the last breath she took, but no. She wasn't my mate." His eyes held a sorrow so deep the both of them could drown in it if they allowed themselves to.

Branan's brow furrowed. "How do you know?"

"Mates are incredibly rare, but if you ever find yours, your wolf will tell you."

"What if I don't have a wolf?" he asked, his head tilting down, eyes returned to his plate, unable to see the look of disappointment in his father's eyes. He knew he should have shifted by now. Shane did last week, and he was two years younger than Branan.

His dad reached across the table and tipped his head up. "Look at me, son," he ordered when Branan wouldn't meet his eyes.

Branan feared what he might find in them, but he

couldn't resist his dad's command.

"My love for you will never change. It doesn't matter to me if you ever shift or not, but my wolf tells me there's a wolf inside of you, and I've learned over the years that my wolf is never wrong."

Is Lachlan my mate? he pondered. *Ours,* his wolf growled in response. *Fine. Is Lachlan our mate?* He felt his wolf roll his eyes in annoyance, but Enora's voice pulled him from his inner dialogue and whatever his wolf was about to say.

"You don't have to answer that, Branan. Callie, there are some things we don't ask other Fae."

"Wait, the nudity question was totally cool, but this one isn't? Seems simple enough of a question to answer. The Seelie king either is or isn't his mate. There's no shame in that."

"Mates are a sensitive topic."

Callie opened her mouth to retort, but Branan interrupted. "I don't know…." His stomach flipped. *Liar,* his wolf growled at him.

"Oh shit," Callie said, stealing the words from his thoughts, as if she could see what he was just now figuring out. "He is, isn't he?"

Ours, his wolf repeated, and Branan knew he was right. Lachlan was their mate. He felt the certainty like a bolt of lightning, sudden and strong. *Took you long enough,* his wolf sighed.

"I… um… I need to…." Branan stood abruptly, a sense of urgency filling him. He needed to see Lachlan.

"Of course. Callie, let's walk Branan back, shall we?" Enora suggested, rising from the table.

"Yeah, you couldn't pay me to miss this," Callie exclaimed, shoving back from the table and pushing in her chair. "It's like my favorite K-Drama just came to life in front of me, and I am so here for it." She rubbed her hands together excitedly.

"Callie," Enora grumbled.

"You're right. We're going because we love and support you, Branan, not because we also love other people's drama," Callie deadpanned.

Enora sighed, and Branan laughed. He knew she meant it when she said she loved and supported him, and that was all that mattered.

When they stepped out of the cabin, he offered each of the girls an arm and they took it, linking theirs around his.

They hadn't walked very far when his wolf shouted, *danger!* He immediately stopped, unlinking his arms from the girls and pulling them behind him. A lone figure crested the top of the small hill they were approaching. He inhaled deeply and his wolf growled in recognition. "Whelan," he hissed, and his heart thudded painfully against his chest.

The girls stiffened. They must be remembering the last time they encountered this particular Fae. His eyes scanned the area, but he didn't see anyone else.

"Ah Branan, just the person I wanted to see. I think we have some unfinished business, you and I." He stalked closer to them, and Branan's growl grew louder. An errant thought about Malcom tugged at the back of his mind, but his wolf was unwilling to take his eyes off of Whelan to search for him.

"Is it just you? Where's your brother?" The sky above them darkened ominously.

"Oh, you know Malcom. He likes to do his own thing these days. Sometimes his wife keeps him busy, but he's usually not too far behind." There was a mischievous glint to Whelan's eye that made bile rise in the back of his throat.

Callie gasped over his shoulder, and Whelan's low laugh made him turn. Malcom stood behind her with a knife pressed to her throat as he reeled her in closer to him.

Branan snapped his teeth, his wolf fighting to protect his pack. "I wouldn't do that if I were you, Branan. One false step and Malcom might just let that knife slip," Whelan called.

Branan swung his head back to his former packmate realizing Whelan's earlier words were a ploy to prevent Branan from hearing Malcom's approach.

"Evin won't take kindly to you threatening the one he loves. I suspect you may find yourselves without a job. Is it worth career suicide?" Enora tried to reason.

Malcom's glance flickered between her, and Callie and his brother, but Whelan laughed. "You think we care about being in the guard? We only joined to learn how to fight, and they've taught us everything we need to know."

"Wasn't your father in the guard? Would he be proud of you now?" Enora asked, squaring her shoulders. It looked like she'd done her homework after their last encounter.

Malcom winced, but Whelan's fingers sharpened into claws. "You don't know what you're talking about, you Unseelie bitch. My father followed someone else's commands his whole life and died because of it. He wasn't strong enough to be alpha. Not like me."

Branan's stomach rolled as Whelan took a threatening step toward Enora. He drew Whelan's attention back to him. "But you're not an alpha, are you?" he countered.

"What's he talking about, brother?" Malcom asked from behind him.

Whelan's wolf growled, his teeth sharpening and eyes glowing copper. Thunder rumbled overhead, a storm brewing.

Branan answered Malcom's question, but his eyes never left Whelan's. "The magic didn't choose your brother to be alpha, Malcom. It chose me. I didn't ask for it, Whelan. You know I didn't. I would have stayed if I wanted it."

Lightning whipped across the sky, its fingers crackling unnaturally. Surely that would at least draw Evin' attention and send him to ensure his girlfriend's safety. Unsure if Callie did it intentionally, Branan risked a quick glance back at her. Her eyes were as dark as the sky above them; her emotions were in control.

"Try to hit me and I guarantee the bolt will go into you through this blade," Malcom hissed, pressing the knife deeper into Callie's throat, drawing a drop of red that slid down to the collar of her faded t-shirt.

Enora's nostrils flared and her eyes swirled silver.

"Don't even think about it, Siren. I'll slit her throat before you can sing one tiny note," Malcom barked.

Enora sucked in a harsh breath as a loud clap of thunder made her jump. "Callie, shove it down, get control."

Callie gritted her teeth. "I'm trying," she hissed as another bolt of lightning struck, this time hitting a patch of grass about a half mile away.

A figure crested the hill then, but it was too slender to be Evin. His mop of blonde hair bobbed as he ran, "Don't do it Whelan!" he called.

Shane came to a stop, huffing between Branan and his brother. "You can't... I tried... even if you challenge him, there's no guarantee... it's the magic that determines...." he huffed. "Besides. You know it would break ma's heart... she loves Branan like he's her own."

The last statement seemed to have the opposite effect than what Shane hoped for. Whelan cackled. "You think I care? If you've always been her favorite, then he's been her second favorite. She felt so sorry for you, but she couldn't be bothered with us. Could she, Malcom?"

Malcom didn't respond, and Shane continued moving closer to his brother with upstretched hands. "She loves you. You know she does, and she wouldn't want this. She wouldn't want you to do this."

"I don't care what she wants. I deserve to be alpha. Not him. Not some stupid runt who shifted years later than the rest of us. The magic is supposed to choose the wolf meant to be strongest, the one who will keep the pack together and protect it. He ran. It should have never been you!" he roared, turning his attention back to Branan with the last sentence.

Shane tugged his brother's arm. "It isn't worth it, Whelan. Please don't." Branan knew Whelan's wolf was mostly in control, but either Shane didn't recognize the signs or thought his brother wouldn't hurt him. Whatever it was, he was wrong. Using the strength of his wolf, Whelan shoved Shane away so hard, he flew back past Branan and landed with a sickening crack a few yards away. The scent of blood filled the air and Branan's heart sank.

"Enora. Check on him. He's bleeding. Something's wrong," Branan pleaded.

She looked from the prone body not too far away to Callie, who still had a knife held to her throat, a small stain of red running down her neck. "I'm fine. Go," Callie whispered.

Malcom swallowed hard, the blade relaxing slightly away from Callie's neck as his hand trembled. "Help him," he pleaded, so Enora sprinted toward the boy.

When she reached Shane, one arm was pinned beneath his body, bent at an unnatural angle. Branan watched as she gently moved Shane's arm out from underneath him and then leaned down, pressing her fingers to his pulse point and her ear to his chest, listening for breath and a heartbeat. She looked up at Branan with relief and nodded. A heartbeat was good. Next, she gently lifted his head.

Branan's stomach rolled when she withdrew her hand, and it came back stained with red. His wolf thrashed beneath his skin. *No one threatens what is ours,* his wolf seethed.

Enora tore off some of the fabric of her skirt and wadded it up, using it to apply pressure to the back of the man's head as she searched her pockets for anything that could be of aid. Her magic would only help him so much and was always stronger with a combination of herbs.

Branan jerked his focus back to the threat in front of him when the sound of a thud behind him drew his attention. Malcom was on the ground, holding the side of his stomach. Within a second, Evin had Callie in his arms, staring darkly at the line of red trickling down her neck. "How?" Callie asked breathlessly and Evin's eyes flicked to the sky.

"I felt it, your pain and your fear. Remember, we're

linked. Also, the lightning show was kind of hard to miss." His eyes searched her body for any other signs of harm.

"Enora needs my help." Callie said, and Evin swept her up into his arms and deposited her next to Enora within seconds.

"Evin, listen to me. That deranged idiot about to issue an alpha challenge. You know what that means. Get your dad and Lachlan here now," Enora ordered.

"Do you really think...." Whatever else Evin was about to say died on his lips as Enora stared at him, her eyes swirling silver.

"Get them both now!" she ordered. He glanced back at Callie, clearly torn. Enora softened her tone. "She'll be safe with me. I won't let any more harm befall her," she assured him.

"I'm fine. Go! Hurry!" Callie added, kneeling next to Shane on the ground.

"Maddock should be here shortly," Evin yelled before he dashed away.

Branan pulled his gaze back on to the threat in front of them, as the girls worked to help Shane.

"Callie, hold this under his head and keep an eye on the other one while I work, please," Enora said.

Rain fell from the sky in large drops, quickly turning into a downpour. A bolt of lightning struck closer just as a loud crack of thunder echoed around them.

Whelan circled Branan, studying him. Branan shoved away his worries for the girls and Shane. Enora would save him. She had to, and Callie, well, he figured she was a force to be reckoned with when she was pissed, and holding a knife to her throat would've pissed her off quite a bit.

Malcom would be a fool to attack them now. Especially if he wanted Enora to save Shane. It was for Shane's sake he tried to reason with Whelan again.

"You don't have to do this. You can walk away from this right now. I don't want it, Whelan," Branan pleaded as he stepped away from the others toward the center of the field.

"That's not the way this works, and you know it. You're a threat to everything I've built. We. Don't. Need. You. No one does. We were better off with you gone," he hissed.

"I don't want to hurt you."

Whelan crowed, "You couldn't hurt me even on your best day. While you've been running away, I've been training and honing my skills, bringing honor to the pack."

"Some honor. You just attacked your own brother," Branan grumbled with a glance toward Shane as Enora did all she could to help him. When he glanced back at Whelan, he saw Maddock had crested the hill, sprinting toward them and a handful of unfamiliar figures approached from the direction of the training grounds. "Your dad would be ashamed of you. Contrary to what you think, he wasn't weak. He was strong enough to know that the only way a pack thrives is through the contribution of each member. He recognized he didn't have alpha magic and was happy to let my da carry that responsibility. Reconsider, please. He wouldn't want this, Whelan," he pleaded one last time.

"You don't know what he would want!" Whelan roared.

The unfamiliar figures approached closer and Branan noted the uniforms of the Seelie guard. They must have been around them, drawn by Whelan's shouting, the storm swirling in the sky above them, or the tension permeating the air.

"I challenge you for alpha," Whelan snarled.

Branan took a step back. The magic, like an army of ants running down his spine, raised his hackles. His wolf howled, eager to face the challenge head on. There was no way to back out now, no way to turn it down. There were regulations and rules for a challenge, but once it was announced, the magic demanded it be fulfilled.

CHAPTER 28

"NOT PLAYING HOOKY today?" Torin tcased as Lachlan sat at his desk looking over a petition by one of his citizens.

"As if the council would allow me to," he joked.

"Here's the thing you sometimes forget. You're king, Lachlan. If you want to take some time for yourself, you can. You make the rules. You don't need to ask the council for permission. They are there to assist you when you need their advice, not the other way around. I know your sister may have seen it differently, but this is your kingdom. It has been for a while."

"You're right." He set the paper down.

"Of course, I am. Now, with that being said, it might be time to replace some of the elder council members. They're too stubborn to tell you that or you've built enough healthy fear for them to worry you may not approve, but I've heard a couple of them mumble dreamily about when they can retire. Plus, you have a few new assets that could give a unique perspective if you would allow them."

"You think Enora and Callie should be on the council? You're right that they could offer some perspectives we haven't had before. Of course, I'll have to see if either or both of them would even be open to the suggestion and willing to serve in that capacity. I could understand why they wouldn't." Lachlan knew his people could be stubborn and set in their ways and that might make the girls uncomfortable, and while he wouldn't want that, he thought the kingdom could benefit from their perspectives and ideas. He also realized the current council members would have a larger objection to the Unseelie defector, but ultimately, it was his choice. One he would not make without the girls' approval.

"Now that you're thinking about that, I believe there's something else you should consider."

"Well, you're just full of suggestions this afternoon, aren't you?" He rolled his eyes playfully, but paused when Torin's gaze went to the window. The room grew darker, and he glanced at the gray clouds gathering not too far away as thunder shook the windows.

"Callie must be showing off for her friends again," Lachlan chuckled, thinking of the freak storm the other day.

"You're right, that's probably it," Torin replied, shaking his head.

"Either that or someone is working with her on her control, which we both know could still use some work," Lachlan chuckled, remembering how she had confessed to accidentally setting a small portion of the forest on fire during one of her practice sessions. "Now, the other thing you were about to suggest."

Torin snickered. "Yes, well. I know your father always told you not to tell others what animal you can shift into, but I've always thought that was stupid. It's not like you're a fluffy little bunny or a worm. Your stag is nothing to be ashamed of, and while the rumors of the Seelie king being able to suddenly shift into a giant dragon and roast any-one alive who went against him may have been helpful in the beginning, they haven't exactly helped to inspire any true devotion. Perhaps it isn't being in love that would al-low the land to thrive as it did with your parents. Perhaps it's about loving yourself and embracing exactly who you are."

"I've always embraced who I am," Lachlan retorted. He leaned back, crossing his arms over his chest.

"Not really. I mean, you know who you are and so do Grady and I, but it ends there. You haven't truly embraced your stag. If you had, there wouldn't be anything to be ashamed of. You're powerful just as you are. You just need to believe it."

Lachlan opened his mouth to reply when the door to his study crashed open. Torin's hand went to his belt in an instant, only relaxing when it was Evin they saw before them.

"You both have to come right away."

Lachlan shoved his chair back and stood. The panic on Evin's face made his heart kick up speed.

"What is it, son? Is Callie okay?" Torin asked.

Evin's head did a bobble that could be determined as a yes and a no. "It's Branan. Whelan is about to issue an alpha challenge."

The breath was stolen from Lachlan's lungs. His stag reared back inside him as he rounded his desk.

"Don't shift. Hold it together. Branan needs you, and we can get you there faster than your stag can," Torin said, grabbing onto Lachlan's arm. Evin grabbed his other arm. "Close your eyes and possibly hold your breath. The last thing we need is for you to puke once we're there," Torin warned before the two of them carried him at their speed.

He closed his eyes as the world blurred around him. Thankfully, he never had a problem with motion sickness.

They came to an abrupt stop and released his arms. Lachlan studied the scene for a moment. There were several other soldiers gathered on the periphery. Callie knelt by Enora, who was helping a prone man on the ground, while she stared down menacingly at one of his guards. Another one of his guards circled Branan, snarling. His heart plummeted.

"What's the meaning of this?" he boomed across the crowd. The guard stopped circling, but continued staring directly at Branan. Could this be one of Branan's previous pack members seeking revenge? The man looked like he was out for blood, and Lachlan's mouth grew dry.

Enora nodded, and Maddock took Callie's place next to the man as she ran over with tears in her eyes. She explained that the man in the middle and the other one she had been glaring at had caught them while they were walking back to the palace. He noted the dried blood on her neck and silently vowed to punish whoever put it there. Callie turned to Torin. "He just challenged Branan for alpha. What does that mean?" Her voice wavered as thunder rumbled in the distance.

Torin's face grew dark, but resigned. "He must accept."

Lachlan shook his head. There had to be another way. "No. I won't allow it. I'm king. If I decree, they can't proceed, then it must be so." Wasn't Torin just telling him how powerful he was?

Torin's gaze softened as he stared at Lachlan. "You know that's not how it works, no matter how much you wish it so."

Callie chewed on her lower lip as Torin finished answering her question.

"The magic demands the challenge be fulfilled. There's no stopping what the wolf just put into motion." Torin glared at his own soldier as if promising retribution for his foolishness.

Lachlan stared at Branan. How could he stand there and watch this unfold? What if Branan lost? He tried to remember what Branan had told him about his old pack, but the specifics slipped through his fingers. Then he remembered the fear in Branan's eyes and his soft sobs as he buried something beneath the tree. A stone sank in his gut as he realized exactly who the wolf was and what he was capable of.

Challenge be damned, Lachlan couldn't let Branan die.

The guard challenging Branan shifted confirming his suspicions, and Lachlan swayed slightly, his knees threatening to buckle. It was the same one who had almost ended his life.

His life.

The thought struck him, boosting him with hope. Magic, especially ancient magic like an alpha challenge, had its own rules and requirements that it followed, some of which they didn't fully understand, but he also had a life debt to repay, which was much stronger magic. If it came down to it, he would intervene. No one would be able to stop him.

Branan shot a desperate glance toward Lachlan. He didn't want him here to witness this. Lachlan's jaw hardened and his eyes narrowed, leaving Branan unsure what he was thinking. Before he could consider the possibilities, Torin's voice boomed across the field and drew Branan's attention away.

"If you were drawn here by the change in weather, rest assured it's just an Aimsir learning control." Torin motioned toward Callie with his hand, who took a deep breath, and the rain around them lightened to a drizzle. "That being said, an alpha challenge has been issued. As I am impartial to both parties, I will act as arbitrator of the challenge. If you are not a member of either pack, leave now." As Torin issued the command, most of the soldiers who had wandered over grumbled, but turned and left. On the outskirts, Malcom remained along with one other member of the Seelie guard.

"Should we leave?" Enora asked from behind him.

A low rumble left Branan's throat, all wolf, and Maddock chuckled. "Looks like we're staying. Branan must consider us pack if your suggestion of leaving garnered that response."

"Oh," Enora whispered softly with a mix of surprise and awe.

Branan's fingers shifted into claws, a neat trick that had taken decades to hone. Shifting was instinctual, partial shifting took an immense amount of control, something most wolves didn't have the patience for.

"I don't care if I'm pack or not, there's no way you're making me leave." Callie glared up at Torin in challenge, and Branan's wolf growled with a touch of humor at Callie's threat and a warning for Torin. Torin stepped back with his hands up and dipped his head in deference toward Branan. Callie grinned and turned back to Branan, clearly thinking she was the reason Torin gave in so quickly. His heart swelled for the friends he now considered family.

Enora sniffled behind Branan, and he heard her quickened footsteps approach him. Her small arms wrapped around his middle from behind as she pressed against his back for a few moments. *"I belong."* He heard the words as clearly as if she had spoken them aloud, but he didn't think Enora meant for him to hear them. They were carried across the pack bond through her touch. Just as quickly as she held him, she released him. "You got this," she said before retreating back to her patient.

Branan's wolf didn't need the words to encourage him. He felt her across the pack bond, and he realized he had something that Whelan didn't, perhaps something Whelan couldn't understand. While Whelan was fighting for power and status, Branan was fighting to protect those he loved, because if he lost... he shuddered. Losing wasn't an option. Now that he had finally found a pack for himself, as unconventional as it was, he wasn't willing to let it go.

We'll fight for them. We'll protect them, his wolf growled in agreement.

"Evin, I need supplies now!" Enora called in the distance and his heart hurt for Shane. *She'll fix him. It's what she's best at. Trust your pack*, his wolf soothed. He took a deep breath, steeling himself for the battle ahead.

His focus shifted to the wolf in front of him and he finished his shift. Now completely in his wolf skin, he leaned into his senses. Whelan's wolf was bigger than Branan's as they had been while they were kids, but size didn't mean everything. Speed was just as equally important, if not more in battle. *Please forgive me, Da. I didn't want to do this. I know you wouldn't want it.*

Sometimes part of what makes an alpha's position difficult is doing what needs to be done to protect the pack. They're not always easy decisions to make, but you'll understand when you're older. The words were his father's spoken when he was much younger, but the memory resurfaced now as if his father were there to offer the advice when he needed it the most.

He took a deep breath as Whelan lunged first. *Move*, his wolf demanded as Branan darted to the left, nearly avoiding the brown wolf's snapping jaw. His heart pounded like a war drum against his ribs, and he felt the rush of adrenaline fill his veins.

Rules of an alpha challenge dictated they continue until one of the two yields or dies, whichever came first. He wasn't aiming for death. He couldn't imagine hurting Kyna in that way despite what Whelan might do to him. *We will do what must be done*, his wolf urged, but he pushed back against the urge to draw blood.

We try my way first, he argued as he decided to use his speed to his advantage. Perhaps he could tire Whelan out first and gain the upper hand to force a yield. Branan ducked and rolled out of the way when Whelan approached next, but climbed to his feet a little too slowly. Whelan managed to snap at his tail, but not gain any purchase other than yanking out a bit of fur. *Not good enough*, his wolf barked. The next time Whelan lunged, he darted to the side, barely avoiding a claw swipe, and kept sprinting until he stood closer to where Enora was helping Shane. *Too close*, he thought as he dashed away from them. The last thing he needed was his pack getting hurt in the crossfire. This was between him and Whelan. He took a minute to study the way his opponent moved. It was clear he had been trained for battle in his wolf form, an advantage Branan clearly lacked. If he wanted to win, he needed to change tactics.

We tried your way, now it's time for mine, his wolf demanded, and Branan knew that he was right. It was time to go on the offensive. His chest squeezed as he leapt, this time aiming directly for the back of the larger wolf.

Lachlan watched as Branan darted this way and that, avoiding the other wolf's snarling maw. His heart was caught in his throat the entire time. He felt a hand slide into his own, small fingers threading between his with a squeeze.

"He's got this. We just have to believe in him," Callie said.

Lachlan looked down into her face as she stared at the

two wolves. He might have believed her if the wind hadn't picked up when the larger brown wolf jumped, landing on the smaller black wolf and knocking him to the side. Branan rolled and jumped up quickly, shaking off the attack and was on the move again.

Evin dropped off whatever Enora needed next to her and the prone man before quickly returning back to them. Lachlan would need to investigate what happened there when the challenge was over.

"Callie, you can't interfere. Fight for control, love," Evin said, pulling her to his side, but she still clutched Lachlan's hand as if it anchored her.

Callie nodded and this time Lachlan squeezed her hand, offering her some comfort. They stared as the two wolves continued battling, and while occasionally Branan lunged toward Whelan, mostly the larger wolf was the aggressor. Was that part of Branan's plan? Lachlan sighed. If it was, Branan would quickly find out that wouldn't work, not for one of his guards.

The larger wolf lunged again, but this time instead of dodging to the side, Branan's wolf jumped, landing on his opponent's back. "Come on, Bran," Lachlan whispered.

The larger wolf shook hard, but Branan clung on with his teeth embedded in the wolf's back below the neck. After a few tense moments, the wolf threw himself to the side as if to flip Branan off, and Branan's grip loosened as they both fell, rolling in a large mass of fur and tangled limbs until they came to a stop a few yards away. The larger wolf regained his balance and stood, assessing Branan's wolf. When Branan got to his feet, a sharp whimper cut through the air. He favored a paw that had been trapped underneath his body when they rolled. The other wolf grinned, his sharp teeth glinting against the darkening sky.

Lachlan's breath came in short pants. This wasn't good. It wasn't good at all.

"Yield, dammit," Evin snapped.

"I don't think it would matter to the other wolf. He's out for blood," Callie concluded gravely.

Branan huffed out the fresh dirt that filled his nostrils from the tumble. He spat out the fur from his mouth. The blood on his lips gave him some satisfaction. He had drawn first blood. He dug his claws into the earth and pushed himself to his feet. When his full weight hit his front right paw, he staggered. A sharp whimper left his throat at the pain radiating up his leg. It felt as if he'd stepped on a shard of glass, although he knew that couldn't be. He replayed the tumble in his mind, remembering how his paw had been caught underneath them when Whelan slammed both of them to the ground. He lifted it gingerly, assessing his injury. Something was most likely broken. If he shifted quickly enough, he might be able to heal it, but it would leave him completely vulnerable while he did so.

Branan glanced at Whelan who grinned at him smugly, snapping his teeth in satisfaction. Panic and concern from others swept down the pack bond, but Branan shut them out. He couldn't afford to let their feelings overwhelm him. Grimacing through the pain, he stood on all fours. His paw would have to hold for now. There was no other way.

Staring at his opponent, the blood dripping down Whelan's fur offered Branan little comfort. He could see in the other wolf's eyes that Shane was right. Whelan had no intention of yielding or honoring a yield from Branan. *We don't yield. We fight,* his wolf growled, frustrated that Branan was still holding back and not going for a lethal attack. *You're going too easy on him. We won't win this way. You must trust me to do what needs to be done,* his wolf said.

Alyss's prediction rang in his ears, and he knew, even if he might hate himself for it later, he had to completely let go and trust his wolf. *You have control,* Branan whispered as his wolf surged forward more present than Branan had felt him in ages. The last time was during the rabbit incident in his youth. After that Branan had decided he always needed to maintain some control. He'd forgotten what it felt like to let the wolf run completely free. The wild, unleashed magic and power filled his essence as he prepared to strike.

This time when he lunged toward the brown wolf, he went for his jugular.

At some point Lachlan had dropped Callie's hand and taken a step forward, only Torin's tight grip on his shoulder held him back. He watched Branan struggle for a few moments until something shifted. He wasn't sure exactly what it was, but this time, the black wolf was on the offensive. Branan's wolf surged forward, right for the brown wolf's neck. The other wolf dodged him at the last second, but not before Branan swiped a paw up, dragging his claws across the side of the other wolf's snout.

This time, it was the other wolf who released a yip of pain but recovered quickly. The wolf darted toward Branan, but Branan sidestepped him. Lachlan's brow furrowed. Was it just his imagination, or was Branan's wolf even faster now, despite the injury to his paw? He spared a glance at Maddock, who frowned at the two wolves. Branan's wolf struck the brown wolf again, this time landing a bite to his back haunch. The brown wolf jerked, pulling away from Branan, but Branan's jaw held tight. In response, the other wolf kicked out his back leg and caught the black wolf in the neck. Branan shook his head, regaining his footing in a position to leap again.

"Yield, you idiot!" Torin yelled as the brown wolf limped toward where the two men from Whelan's pack stood, and Lachlan narrowed his eyes. Uneasiness crept up along his spine. Something was off. A glint of silver caught his eye from the one guard's hand, but before he could utter a warning, Branan's wolf pounced. The other wolf ducked and rolled out of the way. Branan's body twisted as he attempted to turn, his front paws fighting for traction, but it was too late. The momentum carried him right into one of the two men and knocked him down. All eyes were glued toward the black wolf as he got back on his feet. Branan's copper eyes met Lachlan's with a million unspoken words before he swayed to the side. Painstakingly slow, the black wolf turned. Lachlan sucked in a sharp breath as his eye took in the silver glint from the handle of a blade protruding from Branan's flank.

Fuck, that stung, Branan thought. He turned his head, staring at the hilt of a blade protruding from his side. *Something's wrong*, his wolf growled as Branan's vision swam. *Yeah, we've been stabbed*, Branan agreed. He had been so focused on attacking Whelan that he missed the moment that Malcom drew his blade. When Whelan dodged to the side, Branan had tried to turn and continue pursuing him, but he'd slid directly into where Malcom had stood waiting with the blade, holding it in front of him as if bracing himself for the impact he already knew was coming.

Branan huffed as he shook his head. Of course they had planned it. Gods, he was dumb to think Whelan wouldn't play dirty.

No, it's something else, his wolf replied. He tried to step away from Malcom and the other shifter back into the area where he had been fighting, but his balance was off, and he lurched to the side. His wolf was right. A stab wound shouldn't cause that much damage unless… unless the blade was poisoned. His heart sank as a chill struck his core.

He looked across the field toward Lachlan. *I'm sorry* he whispered to him, hoping he might feel it or see the apology in his eyes. He didn't want them to end like this. A tremor ran through his body, and his limbs began to tingle.

He took another shaky step, and the ground titled up to meet him. Whelan's wolf snarled in delight, taking his time to limp over to where Branan now lay. The world continued spinning around Branan even though he knew he was laying still, and he bit back at the bile filling his mouth. Whatever was on that blade was strong.

A primal scream filled the air as he took a ragged breath, wishing he had more time, more time with each of them, but most of all, more time with Lachlan. It seemed just plain cruel for the king to lose someone else he loved. He hoped his death wouldn't break him. He opened the pack bonds once more and sank into them, sending his newfound family all the love he had felt from them until the numbness took over his entire body and he drifted into the void.

Lachlan's breath caught as Branan's copper eyes met his. He could see an apology there that he didn't want. Callie screamed beside him, and he was moving before he even realized what he was doing, a force pulling him forward. He shifted in an instant, not sparing a glance for anyone else. Lachlan's gaze was centered on the brown wolf approaching Branan to strike the killing blow now that he had fallen. He lowered his head and ran as fast as his legs could carry him.

The soldier who had stabbed Branan shouted as he got to his feet, and the brown wolf turned his head, but it was too late. Whelan wouldn't be able to move fast enough, certainly not with the injuries he had already sustained from Branan, but Lachlan would wager the larger wolf wouldn't have even been fast enough on a good day. Lachlan rammed the wolf with his antlers, piercing the wolf's hide and shoving him away from Branan. Evin was there in an instant, blade drawn, standing between where Branan lay in the grass, and the other two members of Whelan's pack as Enora helped the previously injured man sit up and ran over with her bag in hand.

Pinned between his antlers and the ground, the brown wolf went limp. Lachlan dislodged his antlers from the wolf's side and stared down at the prone form as it shifted back into the Seelie guard, whose lifeless eyes stared at the sky. He turned, determined to process that death later when Branan's life was no longer in danger. Within a second, he was at Branan's side, and suddenly found himself back in his Fae skin even though he hadn't made the conscious decision to shift. He was only confused for a second before the notes of Enora's song reached his ears. Her eyes were full silver as her Siren demanded that Branan shift back. She sang louder, her voice pleading for his wolf to retreat and let her save him. Finally, the wolf shrank in front of them, turning Fae in the blink of an eye. She sighed before thrusting a cloth toward Callie.

"Hold this to his side." Enora peeled his eyelids back. "The poison is spreading. We need blood to flush it out." Her words were clipped and short.

Lachlan's fingers trembled as he kneeled beside Branan. "Take mine," he said.

Enora shook her head. "Won't work. You're not the right animal. I need a wolf."

She glanced up at the two men from Whelan's pack, now on their knees on either side of Torin, hands bound behind their back.

"I'm not helping 'im. He just killed my brother," one

of them spat.

Lachlan narrowed his eyes. "Do they need to be conscious for it?"

Enora shook her head. Before Lachlan could march over and punch the guy who had spoken in the face, a voice piped up from behind him. "Take mine."

Enora shook her head at the blonde man. "I just patched you up. I'm not sure how much blood you can give."

He frowned. "Please. If it's not enough, I give you full permission to knock my brother Malcom unconscious and take his."

Enora sighed. She summoned Evin again with a quick request for supplies and where to find them. He returned a few heartbeats later with the supplies in hand. Lachlan picked up Branan's hand, squeezing it tight. "Don't give up, Bran. Keep fighting."

"He is," Callie affirmed from where she held the cloth to his side.

Lachlan stared at her, unsure where the confidence in her voice came from.

"I feel it. A tug. Right here." She placed her hand below her sternum. "I felt it the moment after I told Evin's dad that I wasn't going anywhere, like a rope pulled taught between the two of us snapped into place."

"It's the pack bond," the blonde clarified. "He's your alpha. He claimed you and you claimed him back. That's how it works. I feel him too."

Lachlan closed his own eyes and breathed in and out for a couple of seconds. *I claim you as mine. You hear that? You're mine!* He willed the thoughts toward Branan, and he felt it too. A thread that was already there hummed loudly in reply. *You aren't allowed to die on me. We have too much to do, you and me. You have too much to live for, so you better fight.*

Mate. The word echoed in through Lachlan's entire body, warming him from the inside out. In his mind, he saw Branan's wolf nuzzle his stag. *Ours.*

When he opened his eyes, he saw Branan's eyelids flutter. Enora had hooked up some sort of tubing with needles and a pump between the blonde man and Branan, allowing his blood to flow into Branan. Enora rubbed at the spot below her sternum, but her eyes were wet as she stared at Branan. When she proclaimed she had taken all the blood she could from the young man, she unhooked the tubes.

Branan still hadn't moved or shown signs of waking, which worried Lachlan, but he closed his eyes and the connection he felt earlier was stronger, no longer a thread, more like a steel cable. He breathed out, allowing him to feel that Branan was out of danger.

Enora worked methodically, cleaning and stitching the knife wound. She handed him a tin of salve to rub over the wound while she searched for any other injuries that might need healing and examined the hand that Branan had favored in battle. The knuckles were swollen, and one finger sat at an unnatural angle. "Brace him. Please. This will not be pleasant, and I would hate for him to open the stitches I just neatly sewed into his side."

She pushed the finger back into place, and sure enough, Branan shot to sit up, but was held down by Lachlan. Branan groaned and Enora smiled. "Signs of pain are good. I think we got to him just in time. He may still be out of it for a while due to whatever poison is still working its way out of his system, but he should recover."

Her words were what they all needed, and they released a collective sigh. Lachlan pressed his forehead to Branan's. "You can't go. Not just yet, but rest for now. I'll protect them while you do," he whispered before pressing a kiss to his forehead and leaning back on his heels.

Callie got up and marched over to where the other two guards were still kneeling on either side of Torin.

She narrowed her eyes, staring down at the one who had stabbed Branan. He had ratty long brown hair that had fallen into his face from where he had it bound back, but his facial features were similar enough to the dead man and Shane's that he must be their brother Malcom.

"What do you want, bitch?" Malcom spat at the ground again, this time right next to her feet, before staring up at her defiantly.

Torin and Evin opened their mouths to defend her, but she held up a hand and grinned menacingly at the man before kneeling in front of him. She held up a blade to his face, and he blanched. Lachlan glanced at the empty spot where the poisoned knife had rested after Enora pulled it out of Branan's side.

Malcom paled, his throat bobbing as she smiled.

"I think this belongs to you, so I just came to return it." She dragged the blade across his neck lightly enough to not break the skin. "What's the punishment for interrupting an alpha challenge?" she asked, looking up at Torin and blinking innocently.

"Depends on the interference. Usually, it's decided by the alpha or the pack on behalf of the alpha. However, I'd imagine in this case expulsion from pack territory," Torin replied.

Callie dragged the poisoned blade down Malcom's shirt to his pants, resting it right between his legs, where she applied some pressure.

"And what's the punishment here for attacking the king's mate?"

Malcom's eyes widened, glancing between Lachlan and Branan. He paled further, if it were possible. "I didn't know," he confessed.

Lachlan wondered if that knowledge may have prevented the challenge. Not from the dead wolf, but perhaps from the other culprit.

"I didn't know. I swear," he pleaded. "Please spare me. You already killed my brother."

And he'd do it again if it meant saving Branan. "I did."

"But that means you also interfered," he whimpered.

Callie huffed. "Man. You were off to such a great start. I actually had some hope for you, but then you let your stupid mouth run off again." She pressed the blade closer to his manhood, and he yelped.

Torin nodded. "He did, but I'd wager that repaying a life debt might outweigh that, seeing as your brother didn't take the yield. What would you say, Blayne?" Torin asked the other Seelie guard, who kneeled at his feet. Blayne had red hair and bore no features similar to the other wolves. He must have been another member of Whelan's pack.

"The king was justified in his interference. The magic of the life debt would have called him into action, and it was not a conscious choice. If the little miss is correct and they are mates, then you have another strong bond that would call him to act. He cannot be faulted. Malcom interfered first, and Whelan should have taken the yield when the other fell," the man stated calmly.

"Good answer. One more question. Where does your loyalty lie?" Torin asked.

Blayne stared into Lachlan's eyes. His gaze held strong and steady. "With my king, always. I tried to talk Whelan out of issuing the challenge. It was stupid to take some childhood animosity to such lengths, and frankly, an abuse of the alpha challenge. I had no clue that Malcom planned on playing dirty or I would've prevented it."

Lachlan nodded. He didn't need Grady to know the other man spoke the truth. He hadn't intervened during the fight and hadn't assisted Malcom. In fact, he looked rather disgusted by the other wolf. Lachlan gave Torin a nod.

"Looks like you're free to go," Torin said, cutting the binding on the man's wrists and hauling to him to his feet.

"As for you." Torin tilted his head and stared down at the other man.

"Ew!" Callie yelled, stumbling back with the blade. She dropped it and frantically wiped her hand on the grass. "He peed on me!" she wailed, staring at her right hand in abject horror.

Lachlan snickered softly and sure enough, the front of the man's pants was wet.

"You terrified him, didn't you love? Just scared the piss right out of him." Evin chuckled as he appeared at Callie's side with the bottle of disinfectant Enora had used on Branan. He uncapped the bottle and poured it over both sides of Callie's hand.

"Now, if we could get back to the matter at hand." Torin rolled his eyes and motioned toward the captive.

"Sir, if I may," the blonde man spoke from behind Lachlan before standing between him and Torin. Lachlan nodded.

"Malcom, what was the blade laced with?"

"I don't know, Shane," Malcom whined.

"And where did you get the blade?"

"I don't know!" he exclaimed.

Shane's brow furrowed. "What do you mean you don't know? You had to get it from somewhere. Did you buy it? Steal it?"

"No! Whelan gave it to me."

"When?"

"Today."

"And what did he tell you about it?"

Malcom sighed. "He told me if things took a turn, he would get Branan over by me and I was supposed to stick 'im with it. Just sticking him with it would be enough of an injury to slow 'im down so Whelan could finish 'im off. I didn't know it was poisoned."

Shane arched an eyebrow at him. Malcom cursed. "Fine, I knew it had something on it, but Whelan said it would only slow him down, not that it would kill him. I swear I wouldn't do that, Shane. You and I both know how much pain it would cause Ma. I didn't have any problem with Branan. It was always Whelan."

"So why did you go along with the plan, then? You had to know Whelan wouldn't let Branan yield."

Malcom swallowed and stared at his older brother's body. "He's... he was my brother."

"And yet you let him injure your other brother?" Callie interjected.

Malcom looked up at Shane. "I'm sorry Shane."

Shane sighed before turning back to Lachlan. "While I believe my brother deserves to be punished for his actions, I don't believe he knew the full extent of what he was doing. He was following the orders of his alpha, and I think that should be considered. My mother just lost one son, and I'm not sure she could handle losing another."

A finger twitched, locking onto Lachlan's finger, and he looked down to see Branan had hooked his pinky around his in his sleep. He looked back at Shane. "I'll take your words into consideration. And once Branan wakes, I'll take in his opinion. Anyone else who wishes to make their opinions known about this matter will have until then to tell me. For now, he's a prisoner. Take him to the dungeon, Evin, and then return with a stretcher so we can get Branan inside."

Evin nodded, grasping the man by the collar and shoving him in front of him, moving at a speed that made Lachlan think the piss wouldn't be the only thing staining his clothes when they stopped.

Lachlan turned to the other wolf. "Will you fetch a few soldiers from the barracks and see what the family wants to do with the body?"

The soldier nodded and shifted, running in wolf form.

It didn't take long for Evin to return with a stretcher in hand. Shane looked torn between helping them and his brother's body.

"Go, be his guide to the next realm." Enora grabbed his hand and squeezed. "Branan will be fine. You can visit him when he wakes. For now, your mother will need you. She would have felt when your brother passed through the bond."

Shane swallowed and sniffed. "Thank you. You're an amazing healer, and I'm sorry I ever misjudged you. We can't help the circumstances we're born into," he said to Enora, and Enora smiled softly in reply, nodding her acceptance of his apology.

Gently, Lachlan, Torin, Evin, and Maddock worked together to lift Branan and place him on the stretcher. Enora threatened them to move slowly to not disturb the stitches as they trudged back to the palace. When they got Branan inside, they waited for Lachlan to direct them.

"My room," he ordered, not bothering to wonder what anyone thought about it. He was ready to shout from the mountain tops that Branan was his, council and anyone else who disagreed be damned And he would too, as soon as Branan woke.

Cautiously, they transferred him to Lachlan's bed, and Enora once more inspected the wound to make sure nothing was disturbed. When she was pleased with what she saw, Lachlan offered all of them a room in the palace for the night, so they could stay close to Branan, and they all looked relieved. He called for several servants to help them get settled in the rooms closest to his in case they were needed during the night and ordered that food be sent to their rooms in case any of them were hungry.

When everyone had left, he curled up on the bed next to Branan and pressed a kiss to his cheek before resting his head on his shoulder. "Now, it's my turn to take care of you."

CHAPTER 29

BRANAN CAME TO slowly, loosening the remains of slumber. He felt the bed beneath him, soft and luxurious, felt he could move his fingers and toes, but not his arms and legs. A pain in his right side reminded him of the knife protruding from it. Not dead then, because surely he wouldn't feel pain if he were dead.

The next thing he noticed was warmth radiating from his left side, and the tickle of hair against his shoulder. He turned his head, glad to see that while his arms and legs wouldn't move yet, at least he could turn his neck. Lachlan was curled up against his side, resting his head on Branan's shoulder, eyes closed in sleep. Branan smiled, remembering how similar this was to the first time they'd shared a bed, except this time Lachlan was there when he woke, and if he had it his way, this wouldn't be a one-time event. He assessed the rest of his body, noting a distinct sensation in his chest.

We are alpha. They are pack bonds. His wolf snorted as if he should've already realized what had changed. It was a strange sensation to feel so many of them so strongly. He closed his eyes and focused on one string binding him to the others. Callie stirred in her sleep, sending rather steamy thoughts of Evin down the bond, and he instantly withdrew. Oh my. He did not need to see that side of Evin. He chuckled lightly as he tried again, selecting a different thread this time, leading to a worry about two familiar guinea pigs and who was going to feed them. So, Callie and Enora, he knew, but there were still four others. He closed his eyes, focusing on a different one, and realized he had now claimed Maddock and Evin. The second to last thread glowed a different color. It was familiar and warm, like slipping into his favorite pajamas. *Branan?* Shane's voice echoed in his head. *Oh, thank goddess, you're okay. Ma and I have been so worried.*

What happened to Whelan? Branan asked, almost hesitant to know the answer. Shane showed him images from the battle, how Whelan had been about to go for his jugular while he was unconscious until a powerful stag rammed him with his antlers at full force, and a final image of Whelan's still, lifeless form in the grass as everyone worked to save Branan.

I'm sorry, he said, and he meant it. While he didn't care for Whelan, he never wanted him to die or for Shane and Kyna to experience that pain. *How's your ma?*

She's dealing. I think she'll be better once she knows you're awake.

Good. Bring her to the palace later. We have much to discuss.

You got it, Shane replied happily.

The last thread was thicker than the others and felt stronger. *Mate*, his wolf growled, and Branan smiled. Figures. He tested the bond. *Wake up, love.*

Lachlan blinked his eyes open and looked up at Branan. "You're awake."

Branan nodded and concentrated. *Did you hear me wake you up?*

Lachlan's eyes shot wide open. *Did I just hear you, like in my head?*

Branan grinned. *It's the mate bond. I hope you don't mind.*

Lachlan's brows furrowed. *You won't hear everything, right? Only what I send you?*

Branan chuckled. "That's correct."

I love you, Lachlan confessed, staring into Branan's eyes. "I love you," he repeated aloud.

Branan twitched his arm, but couldn't pull Lachlan toward him the way he wanted. *I love you too*, he sent down the bond. "I love you too. Now kiss me, because I can't seem to work all of my limbs just yet, but I need those lips."

Lachlan laughed and then pressed a kiss to his lips, claiming his mouth just as he had already claimed his heart and soul. "Let me get Enora to look you over."

Branan smiled as he looked around the unfamiliar room. It had to be Lachlan's and the thought that Lachlan had brought him to his bed warmed him even more. He glanced out the window. Perhaps it was his mood coloring things differently, but his view out the window was striking. The trees seemed a brighter shade of green, the flowers in the garden appeared more vibrant. The small copse of cherry trees he had seen earlier from his room were now in full bloom, boughs full of bright pink blossoms.

Lachlan returned with Enora in tow pulling his attention away from the window. She was elated to see her patient awake and assured them both that it must be residual poison in his system, but it should work itself out within the next few hours. Already Branan could move his feet and hands, not just his fingers and toes. "Can you shift?" She asked, and he tried, but nothing happened. *Well, that's new.*

We're fine. We just need time, his wolf assured him, and he relayed the message to Enora and Lachlan. She threw her arms around him. "You aren't allowed to scare us like that ever again, and later, when you're completely healed, we will sit down to discuss what this pack business is all about." She pressed a kiss to his cheek. "Thank you for choosing me."

After she left, it struck Branan that he was supposed to be traveling back to his shop today. "Someone needs to send word to Amani that I'll be delayed a little longer. It's fine if she needs to take care of other things and just keep the shop closed."

Lachlan waved his hand. "I'm fairly certain Callie mumbled something about contacting Amani last night, so that may have been taken care of, but we can also send word. Would you like me to draft a quick note?"

"Yes please," Branan replied. Lachlan walked over to a desk and pulled out a piece of paper, recording a note as Branan dictated it to him.

"Now, I'll have this sent, but I want you to rest. I'll be

back shortly with some food. Hopefully, just a little more rest will flush the rest of the poison out of your system." Lachlan kissed him quickly before leaving the room.

Branan sighed. He didn't feel tired, but when he closed his eyes, he drifted off to sleep.

This time, when he woke, he could move the rest of his body. Gingerly, he sat up. There was a tray of food on the table beside the bed, but the call of nature had him cautiously pulling himself to the bathroom. When he had taken care of his needs, he stood in front of the mirror, washing his hands, and got a full assessment of the damage. He was shirtless and someone had changed him into a loose pair of brown linen pants. There was a bandage wrapped around his chest, so he couldn't see where the knife had struck him, but there were still a few bruises here and there. His fingers seemed to be back to normal, although one held a nasty bruise and smarted when hc bent it, so he figured he must have broken it during the fight. He took a second to admire how Enora must've reset it for it to look normal.

He stumbled back to the room and looked around for the clothes he had been wearing. His pants were draped over a high-backed plush chair by the fireplace. He stepped over to them and searched the pockets, letting out a sigh of relief when his fingers closed over the ring he had purchased. It wasn't lost. He slid it into his pocket and made his way back to the bed, wincing slightly as he sat where stitches tugged at skin. They also itched like no other, most likely because the skin they were holding together was already healed and he needed to have them removed. He nibbled on the bread and cheese and drank the bowl of soup by the bed. When he had enough, he placed them back on the table, reclining back to rest against the headboard of the bed while still sitting. Eating and moving around took more energy than he wanted to admit.

Lachlan entered and took stock of Branan sitting and the empty bowl of soup. "Oh good, you ate. Enora will be pleased. Much to Niamh's dismay, she insisted on adding a few ingredients to the broth that would aid in your recovery."

"I think my stitches might be ready to come out." Branan said, resisting the urge to scratch.

"I can get her unless you want to try using your alpha mojo." Lachlan waggled his eyebrows.

"I forgot I can do that, though I'm not sure how well it works with non-shifters." He closed his eyes and focused on her thread. *Enora, when you get a minute, can you take these stitches out?* He felt her surprise and then a quiet *I'll be right there.*

"I don't know if I'll get used to you being able to talk to others like that." Lachlan shook his head.

"Not everyone. Just our pack."

"And who's in your... I mean, our pack?"

"It started with just Callie and Enora, but when I woke up, I could feel you, Evin, Maddock, and Shane."

"Tell me a bit about Shane."

"He was in my pack when I was younger, and he's the one who works in your treasury. He was trying to stop Whelan from issuing the challenge when Whelan injured him. I'm glad Enora could heal him. I thought...." He swallowed hard. "I didn't want to think about how I would deliver that news to Kyna. It's bad enough she's now dealing with the loss of her oldest."

Lachlan clenched his jaw. He sat down next to Branan and picked up his hand, staring down at it. "I'd like to say that I regretted killing him, but I know for a fact that if you put me in that scenario again, I would do the same thing a hundred times over, and for that, I'm not sorry."

Branan ran a finger across Lachlan's jaw, titling his head up. "Whelan made his choices, and his choices alone lead to his death. You may have helped him get there, but I gave him plenty of opportunities to not start the challenge and then to yield. There's nothing to apologize for. I'm grateful for what you did. Thank you for saving me." He leaned forward and claimed Lachlan's mouth until a knock at the door separated them.

Enora stepped in with her pouch, Maddock trailing behind her. Lachlan stood so she could have better access to her patient. Maddock narrowed his eyes at Branan. *I'm not sure I like the idea of you being in her head.*

Branan smiled. *You will if she's ever in trouble.*

You're right, this could be a benefit for us. "It's good to have you back in the land of the living," Maddock declared.

Branan leaned forward as Enora unwound the bandage from his chest. He glanced down at the neatly stitched wound, which was now a thin, dark pink line any surgeon would be proud of. "I love how quickly shifters mend," Enora noted before she got out her scissors and tweezers to remove the stitches.

Another knock at the door, and Torin stepped inside. "Oh! Lovely to see you up, Branan," he said. "I see our new healer has already earned her keep ten times over."

Lachlan smiled. "Best investment I ever made."

Enora blushed.

"I'll make sure Callie knows he's awake since she's been hounding Evin and I every five minutes on his status. I know she's been worried, but I fear for my son's sanity," Torin joked.

Branan closed his eyes and found Callie's thread. *Callie, you can stop worrying. I'm fine, and you can come see for yourself soon.* Just like Enora, he felt her surprise at his words through the bond and then her excitement. He could almost picture her bouncing up and down on her heels downstairs. When he opened them, Enora pulled the last remaining piece of the stitch out, inspecting her work before rubbing some salve on top of the now healed wound.

"I don't even think you'll scar."

"Thanks to you, of course."

Enora smiled. "I can't take all the credit. There was a very nice blonde wolf who provided you with a blood transfusion to help flush out the poison."

Branan's heart warmed. He had no idea Shane had done that and sent him a thank you down the bond.

"Now, if we're all done here, I'd like to spend some time with my mate now that he's awake." Lachlan grinned widely.

Maddock coughed to cover a laugh while Enora added, "No strenuous exercise for forty-eight hours, and you'll need to shift first to make sure." She giggled as Maddock hurried her out the door.

"Actually, sire, there was a purpose for my visit," Torin stated, and Lachlan groaned.

"Shane is here, accompanied by a woman who looks to be his mother. She's requesting to speak with you and

Branan."

"Kyna and Shane are here?" Branan asked.

"Most likely about the other brother who's currently in our dungeon. I was going to wait a bit to mention that, but we'll have to figure out what his punishment should be for attacking you with the poisoned blade during the challenge."

Lachlan frowned. He shared the memory over the bond of Callie and Shane questioning Malcom after the battle.

Branan sighed. "Allow us a few minutes for me to get dressed and we'll meet with them." Torin dipped his head in acknowledgement and left the room, closing the door behind him.

"Are you sure you're up to it?" Concern laced Lachlan's voice. Branan nodded.

"No decisions have to be made today. We can just listen to them," Lachlan added.

"I know. I'm sure it won't be as bad as whatever you're thinking. Kyna cares about me, too." Branan scooted toward the edge of the bed, swaying slightly when he stood. Lachlan was there in an instant, offering him his body for support. He tried to bend over and winced when the muscles where the stitches had been protested. "I think I'll leave these pants on for now." He couldn't imagine trying to pull on his leather pants right now. "But I will need a shirt."

Lachlan went into his closet and pulled out one of his own for Branan. "I have shirts in my room, you know."

"And at the moment, they're too far away, so you're stuck with mine." Lachlan arched an eyebrow, almost begged him to continue the argument.

He lifted the white tunic to his nose before he slid it over his head, secretly pleased to be covered in Lachlan's scent all day. Judging by Lachlan's smirk when he finished, his thoughts may not have been so subtle. Either that or he was just as pleased by the thought.

"Alright, we take all of this at your pace. You say the word and we can have them come back later if you're not feeling up to it."

"I'm fine," Branan grumbled.

Lachlan kept his sigh to himself. He had come too close to losing Branan, so he would not apologize for being overprotective now, not when Branan was still healing. The bruises on his body had been tough to look at, not to mention the wound that had almost killed him. And what he told Branan earlier was the truth. He had absolutely no regrets about killing the bastard who almost took Branan away from him. The other one, the one in his dungeon though, he still didn't know what to do about him. At the very least, he no longer held a place in the guard. As for the rest, he would like Branan's opinion on it before he decided.

Branan did well getting around. He was slower on the stairs, and Lachlan could tell by the end of their journey he had tired quite a bit. Lachlan led him into the throne room and sat him on the other throne right next to his, the one that had sat empty since his mother had passed.

The woman in front of them looked surprised, but the

blonde wolf just grinned widely, along with Torin. When he sat and nodded at the pair, Shane spoke.

"Thank you for agreeing to see us. Ma needed to see for herself that Branan was okay. Is it alright with you if she approaches him?" he asked formally.

Lachlan agreed and the woman rushed up to the throne, throwing her arms around Branan.

"I was so worried about you, Bran. I'm so, so sorry. Shane told me everything that happened, and while my heart breaks at the loss of my eldest son, I have a feeling I lost him long before the challenge. He never was the same after Shaw died. I just never imagined he'd want to hurt you so badly."

Lachlan's heart warmed when he saw Branan relax Kyna's arms. He must have been worried she would blame him for her son's death. Which would have been misplaced since Lachlan was the one who'd killed him, not Branan.

The woman stepped back, wiping her tears off her face before cupping Branan's. "Raymun would be so proud," she whispered, before stepping back to her son.

Then Shane approached. He put a hand on Branan's shoulder and squeezed. "It's good to see you walking around."

"I hear I owe you for the blood transfusion," Branan said, but Shane shook his head, his brown eyes serious as he inclined his head.

"Anything for my alpha."

Branan ruffled Shane's hair and both of them smiled.

"Now, I assume you're also here to speak on your other son's behalf," Lachlan said toward the woman, bringing them back to the matter at hand.

"Yes, sire, my name is Kyna. First, I wanted to apologize for Whelan's and Malcom's actions. They have disgraced our family and their position in your guard, one that my husband served with pride."

Lachlan's heart softened, remembering both wolves from Branan's pack and been members of the elite guard.

"I ask that you show Malcom some mercy for his actions last night. I already lost one son, and while I am not condoning what he did, I would ask for you to spare his life."

He turned and looked at Branan, who frowned.

What do you think?

Malcom was always a follower, letting his brother make decisions for him. I don't want to see him dead, Branan replied.

Lachlan turned back to the pair. "And what say you, Shane?"

"I would also ask for his life to be spared. I believe he was led astray by my older brother, but he can be redeemed."

"Shane, since you came to our aid last night and offered your own blood to save my mate, I grant you this request." Lachlan felt Branan's warm pleasure through the bond. Kyna exhaled loudly, almost tipping forward, but Shane caught her.

"Thank you, your majesty. You're incredibly kind," she bubbled.

"He'll still face consequences for his actions, the least of which will be expulsion from the guard, but I haven't yet decided on what else those consequences will entail. He'll face judgement in two days' time now that Branan is on the mend."

Exile? Branan asked.

I'd like your opinion on that. We could exile him from Seelie lands for a century or to the human realm for a shorter period of time.

Hmmmm, Branan replied, clearly weighing both options.

We still have time to decide, he added before pulling his attention back to the pair in front of them.

"We'll be back here then," Shane said as he and Kyna bowed before turning to go.

"Oh, and Shane," Lachlan called. "I could use someone like you to fill Lord Aedan's position on the council if you'd be interested."

Shane's eyes widened. "I'd be honored, your majesty." He bowed lower this time before turning to leave.

"Council member, huh?" Branan sat with his arms crossed, eyebrows arched.

"He was very level-headed last night in the face of tragedy and chaos. His questioning of his own brother was very logical and sincere. Plus, I checked with the exchequer this morning and he's never made an error in his calculations during his time in the treasury. I think he could provide unique insight."

Torin snorted behind them. "Wonder where you got that idea," he mumbled.

"It's past time we made some changes around here. When I took the crown, I'd been so worried about maintaining the status quo that I hadn't really given much thought about what I wanted to do with it."

Branan reached over and grabbed Lachlan's hand. "I

think that's a wonderful idea."

Torin guffawed and turned, leaving the throne room, and Lachlan laughed.

"I can't totally claim the idea, but Torin made some excellent points when he'd presented it."

Branan chuckled. "I'm sure he did.

As they exited the throne room, Callie and Evin found them. Callie threw her arms around Branan, hugging him tightly. "I'm so glad you're okay." Then she released him and smacked him across the arm lightly. "That's for making me worry." Then she smacked him lightly in the other direction. "And that's for talking in my head. That's like, uber creepy. You need to warn a girl first."

Evin laughed, pulling Callie's smacking hand into his own. "Maybe we shouldn't be hitting the King's mate," he offered pointedly.

Her eyes widened slightly, flicking between Branan and Lachlan before narrowing. "Nope, that's not how that works. He was my friend first. I get a pass," she declared.

Lachlan laughed. "Do you mind if I steal her for a moment?" He asked Evin, who shook his head.

Lachlan held an arm out for Callie, who linked it with his before walking a little way down the hall.

"Should I be worried?" Evin asked.

"Not in the least. I'm pretty sure he's asking her to be a part of the council," Branan surmised before the pair stopped.

"Wait, like what would that all involve? Because I am *not* dropping out of college," she exclaimed just within earshot.

Torin walked up behind them. "What are we looking at?" he asked, peering around their heads until his gaze landed on Lachlan talking to Callie. He smiled.

Lachlan said something too low for them to catch, but judging by the way Callie grinned and the excited twinkle in her eye, it must have been good.

She stuck out a hand, and the king shook it, then she bounced back toward them. "Bow down bitches, you're looking at the newest member of the council."

Torin laughed. "Guess I'll start talking to the ones who wanted to retire." He shouldered past them. "Congratulations, dear. I knew you'd be a good fit." He hugged her, and Callie looked like she might cry with happiness.

"He said he wanted someone highly involved in the human realm with a unique perspective to offer some new suggestions on things and help him think of the bigger picture. For now, I'll be on a consult basis until I finish my degree, and we'll meet when I'm on breaks. I can't wait to tell Ianthe!" She spoke so rapidly it was a struggle to keep up, but Branan was happy for her.

Lachlan rejoined them, tugging on Branan's hand, "Now, if you don't mind us, I'm going to put him back to bed to get more rest so he can fully heal."

"Of course. Go! Heal! Oh, wait. When will you be leaving, Branan?"

Branan rubbed an invisible itch beneath his nose. They hadn't really talked about it, but his plans remained the same. He just hoped Lachlan agreed. "In a few days, when

Enora has given her blessing, but I'll be back."

"Promise?" she asked, putting on her best puppy dog eyes.

"Callie," Evin admonished. "You know I told you that you can't go around saying that anymore. Promises are something different for Fae."

"Oh right. Sorry, Bran."

"I'll be back before you leave for the human realm," he reassured her.

She did a little dance before pulling Evin down the corridor talking on and all about all the things she planned to change when she attended her first council meeting.

Branan chuckled. "You're going to have your hands full with that one."

Lachlan smiled. "I think she'll bring energy to reinvigorate the place. That and she'll be an asset to help me convince Enora to accept a position."

"A defected Unseelie on your council?" He whistled lowly. "I can see some of your citizens taking issue with that."

"She has earned my trust, and that should be enough. I'm tired of playing by everyone else's rules. It's time to create my own, starting with you." He stopped and faced Branan. He went down on one knee right there in the middle of the hallway. Branan's heart stopped. Was he about to….

"Will you move in with me?" he asked dramatically, and Branan laughed, smacking Lachlan's shoulder as Callie had hit his own shoulder earlier.

"Yes. I'll still need to return to my shop at the goblin market and tie up loose ends there, but I've been thinking that I could open up a shop here in town."

"Really?" Lachlan's face lit up like a human child's on Christmas morning.

"Yes, but only if…." he paused for dramatic effect. He took Lachlan's left hand and raised it to his lips, pressing a kiss against his knuckles.

Lachlan narrowed his eyes slightly. "If what?"

He slipped his fingers into his pocket, retrieving the ring and sliding it onto Lachlan's finger. "If you'll agree to be mine." His heart thudded in his chest while he waited for Lachlan to answer.

Lachlan's mouth fell open as he looked down at the ring. "I'm already yours. I've always been." Warmth and love radiated through both of them as Lachlan reached for Branan, pulling him into his arms before kissing him senseless.

Ours, Branan's wolf rumbled in agreement.

ACKNOWLEDGMENTS

As always, my husband, Hassan, deserves a huge thank you for being my biggest cheerleader, for understanding all the days I ditched you to go write or edit. I hope you see pieces of yourself in all the male love interest I write, because they're a reflection of you and how you've shown me what is possible.

Thank you to my beta readers: Callie Vestal and Hassan. Your feedback is invaluable to me. I'm so glad you're willing to give me your honest opinions and catch my inconsistencies.

Thank you, Chelsea Mueller. We need to do more writing retreats. Your advice and willingness to help me out with anything (especially fight scenes and the curse that is blurbs) means the world to me. I love you, bestie!

Thank you, Kristann Monaghan, my one and only seester. I love our writing dates together and how you're always there to help me bounce ideas around. I'm so lucky that I can consider my sister one of my best friends. I love you, Sissy!

A huge thanks to my friends who artistically added to this book in some way:

My cover designer, Murphy Rae—your work continues to amaze me. It's like you pluck an image out of my mind and bring it to life.

My editor, Amanda Bonilla—my story wouldn't be as complete without you. Your comments are always spot on and polish my story in ways I didn't know were possible. I appreciate you and all that you do and how you've helped me grow as a writer.

Alyssa at Uplifting Designs—thank you for making the interior of my book as beautiful as the exterior and understanding my crazy requests to include different fonts for letters or notes and designs.

Thank you, Stacy Garcia, for the beautiful teasers you've created to help promote my series as well as the stickers and bookmarks for signing events. Your work is greatly appreciated.

Thank you to all my family and friends who continue to support and encourage me in my author journey including my parents & stepmom, my father-in-law, my mother-in-law, my brother & sister, Peggy Durbin, Haley Wolf, Callie Vestal, Cassie Graham, Anna Pertsovsky, Vanessa Burke, Tonya Shaw, Cynthia Valera, and so many more!

Finally, my readers, thank you for standing by me through this journey and loving my characters as much as I do!

About the Author

Cathlin Shahriary lives in North Texas with her husband and fur babies. By day she is a language acquisition specialist, supporting teachers and multilingual learners. By night (weekends and school breaks), she is an avid reader, cat fosterer, and writer. You can usually find her fangirling over books, authors, K-pop and K-dramas. She still believes in the existence of magic and the power of love.

Visit her website: www.cathlinshahriary.com

Follow Cathlin on:

Facebook
www.facebook.com/authorcshahriary

Instagram
@cshahriary

TikTok
@readloveteach

X
@cshahriary

FAE REALM SERIES

(In order)

Fate
Exile
Sacrifice
Peril
Bound (short story in the *One More Step* anthology by
The Bookworm Box)
Elusion
Oath

Made in the USA
Columbia, SC
05 August 2024

39476944R00236